THE GENTLE INFIDEL

THE GENTLE INFIDEL

BY

LAWRENCE SCHOONOVER

NEW YORK

THE MACMILLAN COMPANY

TO MY WIFE

Under, above, and about, are the motions of the elements; but the motion of virtue is none of those motions, but is somewhat more excellent and divine. Whose way (to speed and prosper in it) must be through a way that is not easily comprehended.

AURELIUS CAESAR, Book VI

ACKNOWLEDGMENT

To the Turkish lady, the priest, and the rabbi whose counsels have aided me in representing, as faithfully as my ability permits, the religious convictions of several of the principal characters in this book, my sincere appreciation:

Miss Selma Ekrem, author of *Unveiled: The Autobiography of a Turkish Girl,* and *Turkey, Old and New.*

Rabbi Hillel A. Fine, M.H.L., Graduate Fellow, Hebrew Union College, Cincinnati, Ohio.

The Reverend Grieg Taber, D.D., Rector, Church of Saint Mary the Virgin, New York.

For his kindness in affording me access to his precious library of Orientalia, my deep gratitude to:

I. C. Gordon Campbell, F.S.A.Scot., F.R.A.I., M.A., F.R.N.S., Secretary, St. Andrew's Branch, The League of Prehistorians; and for many years Assistant Headmaster of the English High School for Boys, Istanbul, Turkey.

And to:

Gordon A. Atwater, U.S.N.R., Chairman and Curator of the Hayden Planetarium in New York, my thanks and boundless admiration for fixing the date of the terrifying eclipse of the moon which dismayed the Christian defenders of Constantinople on Tuesday, May 22, 1453. This eclipse contributed significantly to the fall of the city, and has bemused historians of the siege from Edward Gibbon to this day.

THE GENTLE INFIDEL

THERE is a season in autumn, called *Mehltem* by the Turks, when a steady, cold wind from the northeast begins to blow. Rising over the barren steppes of Krim Tartary, it sweeps across the Black Sea, driving a tide of hissing billows before it, piling them up in a thunderous surf upon the rock-strewn sinuosities of the Anatolian shore. At such a time the Current of Satan surges through the Bosphorus, whipping the strait into a mile-wide channel of whitecaps that race to destroy themselves against the Devil's Isles in the Sea of Marmara.

This current has always been dangerous to small craft. Often, when the Russian wind blew, the ferry to Scutari could not cross from Constantinople to the Asiatic shore.

That is why, late in the autumn of 1444, Joseph of Adrianople, called in Turkey Yousuf the Prudent, had had to wait two days on the Christian side before he could pass over to Scutari in the empire of Murad. In Turkey a Jew always knew where he stood. In Turkey, Joseph had prospered.

It was not fitting for Joseph to ride a horse. Like the Christians, he was forbidden the use of horses. By imperial law he must ride his mule unarmed. By imperial law also, his shoes and his house in Adrianople were somber black; but he carried in the velvet purse attached to the belt that cinctured his lean waist an imperial safeguard bearing the seal of the sultan's vizier. The Christian Greeks in Constantinople honored it on sight. So did the Turks of Scutari.

The guards who constantly stopped and questioned the traveler could not read; but they all knew the vizier's seal, floridly ornate with exquisite Turkish squiggles and curlicues. Christians nodded respectfully. Turks touched their hearts and their foreheads with the parchment before handing it back to Joseph.

He directed his beast through the crowded market, out beyond the walls of the town into a pleasant countryside, along a path that began to rise abruptly as the land sloped upward toward the foothills of Bulgarlhu Dagh, the Mountain of Wheat Meal.

The mountain took its name from the fertile grain fields spread out around its ample base. They were yellow now. Among them, here and there, lemon and orange groves lay in rectangular patches of dark green, spangled with ripening fruit. Terraced vineyards, laden with purpling clusters, rose above them in neat crescent strips on the mountain's rounded flanks before they lost themselves in the darker foliage of cypress, olive, and plane trees that covered the crown.

Joseph drew the cowl of his mantle over his head. The cold wind whipped the skirts of his black Eastern tunic around his legs and tangled the strands of his uncropped graying beard against his chest. The upturned cowl and the patriarchal length of his beard made him look very like a Greek monk, an effect which was heightened by the silver-clad leather of the mule's rich caparison.

Houses, gaily painted in all the colors of the rainbow, clustered near the walls of Scutari and dotted the fields for a little distance beyond them, and then thinned out as the land rose away from the city and the sea.

Halting his mule to breathe it a bit after reaching the plateau atop one of the foothills of Bulgarlhu Dagh, Joseph beheld spread out below him a vista of incomparable majesty, the mightiest citadel of the medieval world: the triple-walled city of Constantinople, capital of the Roman Empire of the East. The golden domes of its thousand churches blazed in the light of the setting sun from the fortress of the Seven Towers to the estuary of the Golden Horn. Here, with this eastermost city of Europe, Christendom ended.

Joseph stood on a Turkish hill a league away and watched the narrow channel of the Bosphorus between Europe and Asia slowly darken from blue-white to blue-black as the sun went down. The hilltop was the end of Joseph's tedious journey from Adrianople.

A squat stone mansion, solid as a castle, stood close by. It was built of marble quarried from an island to the west, in the Sea of Marmara. The colors of the stone were said by the older inhabitants of Scutari to be wonderfully matched and artfully chosen. But no one knew for sure any more, because a Christian had owned the house for many years, and it was, accordingly, painted a drab shade of gray, like all Christian houses. And yet the same imperial law that forced its owner to daub gray paint over the splendid marble of his house also taxed him so lightly that Nicolo da Montelupo, the Venetian merchant, chose to live on the Turkish side of the strait rather than among his fellow Christians in Constantinople.

He was not expecting Joseph. There was no light in the house, and Joseph was not immediately certain whether the merchant was at home. It seemed unlikely that the Lord of Montelupo should have returned to Venice so early in the year, before the fruit was picked, before the grapes were in, and, above all, before the last of his fleet of trading ships had arrived. A caravel, patently Italian, probably Venetian, was tugging at her lines in the Propontis below.

Actually, Nicolo da Montelupo sat in the house, in the gathering dusk, watching the ship, praying that the lines would hold, when Joseph knocked at his door. Joseph began to pound, muttering impatiently, "Peace be to this house and all who dwell therein," for he shared with the Turks the conviction that it is proper to bless a habitation into which one wishes admission. (If there is no one within to return your salutation, the angels will answer.) Nicolo sent his steward to the door.

No angel, the steward, a superannuated seaman with a bad temper, grumbled, "Now what do you want, you old buzzard?"

"Buzzards? Ravens? Ravens did a great thing once, in the Holy Land," Joseph answered smiling. "Remember Elijah. Go tell your master that Joseph of Adrianople is at the gate."

"Master Joseph! I beg your pardon. Splendor of God! I should have known you." He kissed the visitor's hand. "It is my eyes, good Master Joseph. I thought you were one of those Greek priests, always saying "Peace" and asking for money. The master refuses them, you know, though I always give something to the dervishes. Do not betray my insolence, I beg you. Do you know of anything that will help my eyes? I'll tell the master of your arrival at once."

The kissed hand held a small gold coin. Joseph could afford to be generous. The habit of giving alms to the poor and extravagant gifts to the rich was strong in the East.

The steward muttered, "Bless your worship! I could not believe the gold was for me. Heaven will recompense you."

"Through the agency of ministering buzzards, perhaps. There appears to be nothing wrong with your eyes." The servant went in to announce him.

Nicolo da Montelupo bore a name that was ancient and honorable in the great Venetian Republic. A venerable register of old patrician families, called the Book of Gold, listed one ancestor who had sat in the great council of 1171. Another had crushed the tumultuous Quirini in the sedition of 1310. Nicolo himself had fought with honor in the war that won Friuli from Sigismund the Austrian. Had Nicolo chosen to remain in Italy, he might have expected a seat in the doge's council, or in the Council of Ten at the very least. Since Friuli, however, Da Montelupo had devoted himself to trade, which, after the Church, was the highest, most lucrative calling in Italy.

It was a praiseworthy thing for a Venetian to make money. Nicolo made it honestly. For his services at Friuli, and on payment of a somewhat higher rental for the state-owned ships that comprised his fleet, Nicolo da Montelupo enjoyed a monopoly on all the shipping from Scutari. He spent most of the year in the East, returning to Venice only during the coldest months, when trade was at a virtual standstill.

When Nicolo da Montelupo had rebuilt the marble house that he bought on the Turkish side of the Bosphorus to avoid the ruinous Byzantine taxes, the local workmen had been astonished at the dimensions of the fireplace he had erected in the great hall. Except for the one in the old castle that had stood in the town since the Greeks lost Scutari a hundred years before, there was not another fireplace on the Turkish side. It was commonly held that such central heating apparatus enervated the body and poisoned the air. And the dervishes considered fireplaces immoral, since their presence indicated an impious refusal to accept such weather as Allah chose to send upon the earth.

He stood warming himself before the great fireplace that had caused such consternation among the workmen. His black hair reached to a little below the ears, in the fashion of the period. On

4

hearing that his guest was not a Turk, he had thrown aside the long gray mantle which custom and the law required him to wear in the presence of the faithful.

Thus when he greeted Joseph he was dressed almost as he might have been in his own home in Venice, in a European doublet of dark-green Flanders wool and sober purple hose. His heavy gold senatorial chain of office hung around his shoulders. His Christian shoes were gray, almost as dark as Joseph's own.

"Be welcome, old friend," he said. "Did my impudent servitor greet you decently? He usually growls at the sight of a beard."

"He was the soul of politeness, my lord Nicolo. Stabled my charger"—Joseph smiled at the "charger"—"kissed my hand, and called me the name of a beautiful bird. Before I knocked at your door, I stood for some time watching a flock of birds flying over the strait. I have never seen them so thick."

Nicolo nodded. Local legend had it that these great, silent, black birds carried in their crops the souls of the damned—especially from the other side of the Bosphorus. They flew all day long from the Black Sea to the Sea of Marmara and back again. They never appeared to flap their wings, and were never seen to alight. It was true that in the last two weeks their number had visibly increased.

"I know it's nonsense," Nicolo said, "but they give me the shivers sometimes. I, too, have never seen them so thick. Pray, sit, friend Joseph, and tell me how I can be of service to you."

The steward drew up a chair to the table for his master, and then slipped another under Joseph.

"Surely the friend of Khalil Pasha does not need money," Nicolo suggested. "And yet, if you do, I shall be willing to advance you a certain amount. Even a substantial amount in a month or two. At the moment I confess that my funds are low. I lost a number of ships at Varna."

"You lost *ships* at Varna?"

"Lost, literally lost. No ships were sunk, as I understand it, but some of mine have disappeared. If the Hungarians stole them, I shall never see them again. If the Turks temporarily sequestered them after their victory, perhaps I may. I do not own the ships, of course. I simply rent them. And now I am under heavy bond to the republic in the full amount of their value."

5

The steward brought two silver goblets full of wine and set them before Nicolo and his guest.

Joseph sighed: "You appear to be well informed about the events at Varna. You lost some ships, perhaps; but the king of Hungary lost his head. Did you know that?"

Nicolo sighed. "Yes, I knew."

"The sultan had it fixed to a pike and paraded among the remnants of the Christian army, with a crier running before it shouting: 'Look upon your king! This is what happens to those who break faith with Murad!'"

"That I did not know, though I knew the Christians had broken faith. The truce was to have been for ten years. It lasted nineteen days."

"I think your ships will be returned," said Joseph, who seemed to be even better informed than his host about the battle of Varna. "In the meantime, put your mind to rest about the object of my journey here. I have come, not to beg, but to buy."

"To buy what, Joseph? Grain for the sultan's troops? You can see for yourself it isn't ready. Surely not my fruit. Fruit is cheaper on the other side of the strait. Not so good, of course. And you cannot want my wine. Not for the sultan, who never drinks anything but coffee."

"One of His Majesty's errors," Joseph murmured appreciatively into his goblet.

"Chain mail, perhaps? The last Persian caravan brought hundreds of suits of it, exquisitely wrought and proof against an arrow at twenty paces. Michael tested one on a dummy."

"So?"

"He's going to be a fine shot before long. . . . Or do you want velvet and silk and pretty spangles for the Kislar Agassi's Abode of Felicity? I've a few bales left, I suppose, though I think one of my ships put in tonight and will probably take the whole warehouseful back to Venice in a day or two. I plan to return soon myself."

"You are close, Signore Nicolo. As for His Black Excellency, shall I really inform him that you have materials and ornaments of quality suitable for the sultan's imperial harem? I am not commissioned to buy such things. The Kislar Agassi is a shrewd trader, you know."

"You shall yourself be the judge of the quality if you honor my house with your presence tonight and look at the stuffs tomorrow. Of course, I had planned to ship it all back to Venice. It will fetch a higher price there."

"I don't know. Perhaps it wouldn't. I'll look at it in the morning, though I repeat I am commissioned to buy no such merchandise."

Nicolo finished his goblet of wine and motioned to the steward to fill it again. He was smiling. It appeared to him that the trading was at an end, at least until morning.

"I am grateful for your hospitality," Joseph said, and then he suddenly added, "Nicolo, I came to buy unset jewels."

Da Montelupo scowled. "I don't sell unset jewels, Joseph."

"But you have them."

"How do you know?"

"I know."

"Who told you?"

"Who could tell me?"

Nicolo pondered. "Not the merchants who sell them to me. They're all in Persia and China and Arabia. They don't even know each other. Michael wouldn't have mentioned it. The steward knows, of course, but he wouldn't talk. Only those two, and Filippo Bernardi, my oldest business associate, know of my harmless passion for unset jewels. If you tell me that your informant was one of them, my son, my steward, or my old friend, I shall question you no further."

Joseph did not answer directly, but he said: "If those three people know, then four people know, and I am the fourth, and no one else in the whole wide world, as God is my witness."

Nicolo was satisfied.

"Oh, I don't actually care who knows. After all, it's an innocent hobby. Jewels are a safe though unproductive investment. I'd rather trade in merchandise that moves a little faster."

"Of course you would. Who wouldn't?"

"But I do have some rather unusual stones in my collection. Would you like to see them? Tell me first, though, why you happen to be in the market for unset jewels."

"They will not be unset long, Nicolo. The vizier plans to present His Majesty the Sultan with a magnificent scimitar in a scabbard covered with gems. It is to commemorate the victory of Varna, and the vizier has weighty reasons for making such a gift. It is a graceful gesture. It will prove to His Majesty that Khalil Pasha is not, as he is commonly called, 'The Foster Brother of the Infidel.' It will demonstrate that he feels a commendable happiness at the great victory over you perfidious Christians. Your pardon, friend. I am merely quoting the grand vizier. And, most important of all, Khalil Pasha probably feels—though I am no longer quoting him—that such a splendid military gift may serve to deter His Majesty from again abdicating the throne and going back to live in that convent of dervishes in Magnesia. For if the sultan should actually abdicate now, Khalil Pasha might no longer be vizier. He might lose his commanding position in the government. He might even lose his head, like the unfortunate king of Hungary."

Da Montelupo looked gravely at his guest. "It will be a bad day for Christendom, the day that Khalil Pasha loses his head. He is our best friend."

Outside, the cold wind from Russia blew the sound of bells across the strait from Europe. The thousand churches of Constantinople were ringing the hour of vespers. Their music sounded far away, curiously soft and sweet, rising and falling like a tide, riding the wind. Nicolo crossed himself reverently. Joseph bowed his head slightly, out of politeness, and waited for the sound that he knew would instantly follow.

Very close, from a Christian church below on the Turkish side, three harsh, tuneless, unbeautiful notes burst over the fields in the twilight and echoed among the foothills of Bulgarlhu Dagh. *Boom!* for the Father; *Boom!* for the son; and *Boom!* for the Holy Ghost, and that was all that was permitted in Turkey. Christian noises must not disturb the faithful who, at sunset, were also at their prayers. Christian churches must be only one story high: no Gavour steeples must look down upon a mosque. And the Koran forbade religious bells. The three notes came from a large, half-inch-thick slab of cast iron, called by the Greeks the *hagiosidere*. It was slung by ropes from the roof of the modest little church. The Christian priest beat it with a long-handled leather mallet, and thanked God that even so much was allowed.

Nicolo scowled and grumbled. "We live a dreary, confining life here, Joseph. In Venice this hour is glorious."

"Is it, Nicolo?" He chuckled. "Not for me, my friend."

"That's different."

"Here the Turks allow you people a church. Imagine a synagogue in Italy!"

8

"I can't."

"Neither can I. A few more generations in Turkey will teach you how to accept trivial restrictions. My people are used to them."

"There won't be any more generations in Turkey. I seriously plan to give up my residence here. Michael is growing up. He has begun to talk Turkish like an Imam and Greek like a Byzantine; but his Italian sometimes astonishes me, all lisping and soft."

"Why don't you just go over to Constantinople?"

"You know it's on account of business. Bernardi is a good friend, but he'd never share the Byzantine shipping with me. Actually, I have done very well here in Scutari. If I should retire from business tomorrow, Michael would not starve."

"I believe you, signore. You remind me how unnecessary it is for you to sell your jewels."

The change in the trader was instant. "Not at all," he said quickly. He rose and went over to the fireplace and touched a little recess in the masonry. One of the stones swung lightly out of place on silent iron hinges. Nicolo stuck his arm into the black hole and drew out a leather bag about as big as his clenched fist. "Not at all," he repeated. "I am perfectly willing to sell part of my collection, unless your terms are too harsh. Since you come from Khalil Pasha himself, perhaps they will be fair."

"Even generous, Nicolo, if the gems are good. I have already told you the vast political implications of the vizier's gift. Perhaps I shouldn't have. Probably the price of your jewels has already gone out of reach."

"I understand you perfectly," said the Venetian, looking at the Jew. "You are threatening not to buy. You imply that the sultan will then abdicate, the grand vizier will lose his head, Christians will lose their few privileges, and I shall lose my position here. It is possible. Ah, but my friend"—here he swept a handful of diamonds, rubies, garnets, turquoises, opals, sapphires, and pearls over the polished surface of the table in the candlelight in front of Joseph almost into his beard—"what price is too high for such jewels as these?"

For a moment Joseph was taken aback. The table blazed as if Nicolo had conjured the stars out of the sky and set them to shining in a smaller, more accessible firmament. It is a wonderful thing to handle a star.

Jewelers of the period habitually distinguish cut diamonds of three sorts: table cut, for flat, thin stones; facet cut, for stones of somewhat greater substance; and point cut. Only gems of the finest color, flawless and deep-bodied, could be cut to a point. When they were, the incomparable brilliance of their internal fire made them the most precious in the world. Half of the gems on the table were point-cut diamonds.

Joseph recovered quickly from the momentary shock of so much concentrated wealth.

"It would take hours to examine every stone. I am persuaded, however, that you know each one well."

"Like my own hand. It is a hobby, as I said. I know every sharp ridge, every clean facet of every gem. Will you accept my estimate of their value?"

"I think so."

"Would you pay a hundred ducats a caret for such diamonds as these?"

"Gladly."

"There are a thousand carets on the table."

"A hundred thousand ducats is a large sum. And the opals, rubies, pearls, and such?"

"They are included."

"You are generous for an Italian."

"To Khalil Pasha's friend it would be folly to be otherwise. Also, I am thinking how these stones will be used. And anyway, at a hundred thousand ducats, I shall not actually lose money."

"I did not, of course, carry a hundred thousand ducats on me, in coin, all the way from Adrianople."

"Naturally not."

"There ought to be another stone, however," Joseph mused. "A larger diamond than any of these. Near the hilt of the sword the designer has indicated an enameled crescent and a star. It struck me when I saw the drawing that a very large diamond might look well in the center of the star. Do you happen to have such a stone?" Joseph smiled. "Is there another secret door in your remarkable fireplace, signore?"

"No," the Venetian replied shortly. "The rest of the fireplace is as solid as it looks. Would you build two such caches into one fireplace?"

"I confess I should not."

"If thieves discovered one, they would pull the whole structure to pieces looking for the other. Nor do I have a diamond such as you describe. Would not a green stone be more suitable? Green is a holier color here."

"So it is, so it is," Joseph mused: "the turbans of the pilgrims from Mecca, the turbans of the descendants of the Prophet, the holy standard of the Prophet himself. Green. All green. What do you have in mind, signore?"

Joseph was mentally revolving the momentous realization that there is only one stone more precious than a diamond, a green one, and that the color was distinctly more suitable for the star in the crescent of the sultan's sword. Da Montelupo's generous inclusion of the opals, rubies, and pearls might prove less generous than he had imagined. His respect for the Venetian's trading powers, always high, soared.

Nicolo called: "Michael! Come here a moment. Come here, my son."

There was a clattering of shoes on the stairway, as if a dozen people were answering the summons, and the boy called Michael bounded into the room, sliding the last three feet and coming to a dizzy stop before his father's chair. Having reestablished his equilibrium, he bowed respectfully to his father, and when Nicolo said, "Joseph, this is my son," he bowed to Joseph also, not quite so deeply.

"Is that the way I have taught you to enter a room?" Nicolo asked sternly.

"He's grown to be a big lad," Joseph observed.

"No, Father," Michael answered shamefacedly.

"Go back and walk down again like a gentleman, Michael. And bring the emerald with you."

"The emerald, signore?"

Both Nicolo and Joseph smiled.

"The emerald wrapped in chamois skin and hidden in the little drawer in the commode beside your bed. It's all right, Michael. Joseph is my friend."

"Oh. Yes, signore."

"And walk softly. You're not a child any more. Mind your manners, son."

Michael disappeared as quickly as he had entered, but more quietly.

"He certainly isn't," said Joseph. "Wild oxen and towropes would not have dragged an acknowledgement of the emerald out of him. How old is your tall, handsome son, signore?"

"Twelve," Nicolo answered proudly. "He knew all about the emerald, of course. I always keep it there. He has forgotten your face and the last time you were here."

"He could not even talk, then. He could hardly walk. The Signora da Montelupo was just teaching him." There was a delicate question in Joseph's voice. Nicolo answered him frankly and at once.

"Friend, my wife is dead. Last year, at home, in Italy. I am a widower now. This boy is all I have left in the world."

Joseph impulsively reached out his hand to give the merchant's arm a consoling pat, but withdrew it again, remembering how long Nicolo had lived in the East and the fastidious Eastern aversion to physical contact. Had Nicolo been a Jew, Joseph would have rent a small ceremonial slit in his own garment and embraced him.

Michael returned with something in a soft yellow chamois. With great delicacy he handed it, not to his father, whose face began to shine in approval, but to Joseph.

"I had forgotten it, sir," he said.

With his hand Joseph gently cleared aside some of the jewels on the table in front of him and set the chamois down in the bare space.

"Observe," Nicolo said, teaching his son, "that our friend knows how to handle fine jewels. If an emerald is accidentally dropped among diamonds, the diamonds will scratch it because an emerald is the softer stone. The polish might be permanently ruined, the value lost."

Joseph unwrapped the emerald. It was about as deep as his thumb. Placed over his thumb it would something more than have covered the nail. It was perfectly circular, and cut, like the diamonds, to a point. Joseph had seen bigger emeralds, but none ever so clear and flawless, nor so brilliant. The whitish patches, which can be either slips along the planes of the crystalline structure or the intrusion of foreign material, were lacking. Joseph held it close to his eye, incredulously. Nicolo smiled. Joseph laid it down on the chamois again.

"It is genuine, of course, since it is yours, Signore da Montelupo.

If it belonged to anyone else, I should question its authenticity. The pebbles and striae that are common tests of real emeralds are not there. This jewel is clear as a diamond. And the fire—I have never seen anything like it. It is genuine. It must be."

"Of course it is. Do glass emeralds flash yellow and red and blue fire as well as green? It came from India, with a silly history of idols' eyes and murdered Buddhist priests."

Joseph touched it lightly with his finger, tilting it back and forth, watching the play of fire in its heart.

"I do not share your Western skepticism. I can well believe a story of robbery and murder in connection with this jewel. Dare I ask you how you came by it?"

"Honestly enough. I bought it from a beggar who had deserted a caravan. How he got it I did not inquire. He was garroted later, for some petty thievery or other."

"Are you telling me that nobody knows that you own this jewel?"

"Precisely. I've had it seven years, and it has never caused me any trouble. There is no bad luck in it. It is merely a singularly perfect, flawless emerald, the finest gem in my collection, as you can see for yourself."

"What is the least offer I can make for it that will not insult you, friend Nicolo?"

"Wouldn't you say that a stone of that water and fire was worth, say, half of the very reasonable estimate I have made on these others?" He indicated the diamonds on the table, pointedly including the opals, rubies, pearls, and such.

Joseph of Adrianople sighed. Apparently he was not to have such a fabulous bargain after all.

"Undoubtedly," he answered in a firm voice. "Fifty thousand is a fair price."

Before Joseph rode off toward Adrianople next morning, he engrossed for Nicolo in the Italian language an instrument of credit, a money order called a *polizza,* or check, drawn on the Bank of San Vitale in the Republic and city of Venice. Nicolo had requested a form of payment that would not be subject to a 40 per cent discount in Constantinople. Joseph, flattered that his credit should be good so far away, was delighted to comply.

"If it assures you against a usurious Greek discount," he said, "it also helps me, since I shall have the use of 150,000 ducats, which really belong to the imperial treasury, during the month or six weeks that the check will take to clear through the San Vitale." He forgot about the velvets and silks in the warehouse. Nicolo, satisfied with his trading, did not remind him.

When Michael and his father said goodbye, Joseph took occasion to point casually to the flock of black birds wheeling over the Bosphorus between the two seas.

"If I were a superstitious man, gentlemen," he said, including young Michael, who flushed with pleasure, "I think I should be tempted to attribute the increase in that flock of birds to the slaughter at Varna. How few of the slain must have been pure, how many damned! On both sides. The sultan will surely need replacements for his army. I am not superstitious, of course, yet if the ship in the strait is yours, Nicolo, why not sail her back to Venice at once? You and Michael."

"It is my ship," Nicolo said. "I had rather planned to go back on her in a few weeks. But you mean something. What do you mean?"

Yousuf the Prudent chose only to answer: "At once, my friend. Even today."

CHAPTER
2

WHAT Nicolo da Montelupo had said about his ready funds was true. The merchandise in his warehouse, brought by the last caravan from Asia, had had to be paid for in gold. And gold was what the Byzantine bankers across the strait had demanded for his bond on the ships still missing at Varna. Although he had in his possession an enormous money order from the Jew, there was virtually no cash in his till.

It was always unwise for a Gavour not to have money on hand for unexpected contingencies; and to run up bills in the town for the very considerable day-to-day expenses of his household was unthinkable.

In this minor emergency Nicolo had recourse to his old friend Filippo Bernardi, who lived in Galata on the other side of the Bosphorus.

There were actually two cities lying across the strait from Scutari: Constantinople, which occupied the larger portion of the triangular European isthmus, and the suburb of Galata, separated from Constantinople by the deep estuary of the Golden Horn. Greeks lived in Constantinople, for the Roman Empire of the East was Greek, not Roman; and in Galata lived many rich Italian traders.

Like Nicolo, Filippo Bernardi was a Venetian. His commercial position in Galata corresponded roughly to that of Da Montelupo in Scutari. Between them they controlled all the Venetian shipping on both sides of the Bosphorus.

15

Most of the houses in Galata were wooden; but Bernardi shared with his fellow Venetian a preference for solid stone, like the palaces that lined the canals of their native city. He had built a mansion with a high, cool porch on the side toward the harbor so that he could sit in comfort and watch the ships in the Golden Horn. He appeared to be watching them with more than his usual interest when his major-domo announced Nicolo and Michael da Montelupo.

His daughter Angelica, whose young eyes were keener than his, helped him to look. The aspect of the Golden Horn did not seem to please him. He turned an anxious face toward his guests "from Turkey," as his major-domo pompously and distastefully announced.

Many people considered Da Montelupo's residence among the infidels eccentric, but not his friend. He took off his glasses and saluted Nicolo warmly and affectionately. Angelica and Michael kissed on the mouth, like the children they were, or Angelica at least, who had to stand on tiptoe.

"Welcome, dear friend, to my house," he said cordially. "Enrico! Bring wine for his lordship." He added pointedly, "his *Venetian* lordship," looking sternly at the servant, "and for Michael, also, if his father will allow him."

But Michael and Angelica had disappeared into the garden, where the grapes, she had whispered, were practically edible if one looked sharp for the purple ones. They had known each other all their young lives and were still too young to be self-conscious in each other's presence. Nicolo had half heard the whisper.

He answered his colleague: "I thank you for your welcome. It is good to be welcomed in a house where one can see the stones. I always feel as if I were on a holiday when I come to see you. Sometimes my painted house depresses me."

"I should think it would," Bernardi replied, "though I never saw a more handsome interior. You cannot help what they make you do to the outside. Sometimes I envy you over there." He was about to refer to Nicolo's light taxes and the commercial freedom he enjoyed among the Turks, but Enrico returned with the wine and he did not mention Turkey for fear the major-domo would gossip. "Myself," he said casually, "I do not feel like a holiday. Did you ever see the harbor so deserted?"

"It does look empty today."

"And yesterday, and the day before. And probably tomorrow."

Nicolo thought he knew what was in his friend's mind.

"It has been very windy," he suggested. "One of my ships could not make the strait last night."

"Perhaps you were lucky to see her at all. But surely you did not come to talk about the Russian wind, Nicolo."

Da Montelupo said frankly: "No, I did not, signore. I have recently invested heavily in some particularly fine Asiatic goods; and because of the troubled times, I have had to pay for them in gold. You know my cautious methods and my belief in ample reserves, so you will not think me boasting when I tell you that I was easily able to pay, though prices are high now."

"Very, very high," Bernardi said.

Nicolo continued. "Quite suddenly, two weeks ago, I was called upon to furnish bond for three of my ships, which unfortunately were at Varna when the battle occurred. The ships have not been heard from. Perhaps they are lost. The bonds were very costly. I have hoped that you might be willing to help me out of my temporarily straightened circumstances."

"Have I ever refused you?"

"Never."

"Have you," Bernardi smiled ruefully, "ever refused me, and I think I have applied to you more often than you have to me?"

"I do not remember refusing you."

"Because you never did! And we flattered ourselves that at least two Italians existed who never took interest from each other, didn't we? Ah, my friend, I don't know whether to laugh or cry!" He took a deep draught of the wine in his cup.

"Nicolo," he went on, "I am intensely embarrassed. When I saw you, I said to myself: 'Perhaps no ship, but at least Nicolo has come to Galata!' I, too, lost ships at Varna, and I have no hope that they will be returned." He drained his cup and began to laugh mirthlessly. "I'm a silly old fool to keep looking at the harbor, but I go on hoping. They carried contraband, Nicolo—swords, mail, spears, arbalests, and Greek fire. I have had definite word by courier that the Turks seized the cargoes and confiscated the ships. I took a risk, I thought, in a good cause."

"It was a good cause," Nocolo said.

"But it was illegal. The authorities in Constantinople look down their snub noses and quote their laws, in bad Italian. There is no recourse. It will take me months to recover from the blow. I was bonded, too, you know; and now my bonds are forfeit."

"Abomination!" Nicolo gasped. He would have eaten wheat meal, like the Turks, rather than have asked for a loan if he had known the circumstances. "I have a large money order, Filippo. Do you want it?"

"On Constantinople?"

"No. On the San Vitale at home."

"Heavens, no. You'd lose almost half. It isn't so bad as that. I didn't lose all my ships at Varna. But I tell you that unless you are very badly off, I cannot help you at the moment."

"I should never have mentioned it. I'm not actually too badly off. My bonds were high, but at least they are not forfeit—not yet, anyway."

"Who was your broker?" Bernardi asked.

"A Turkish businessman. Turkish bonds are cheaper than Christian ones, and just as safe."

"That is true. Was it a *noble* Turkish businessman by any chance? A prince, perhaps?"

"Well, yes; it was Machmut, called the Beglerbey of Roum. Who was yours?"

Bernardi looked sheepish: "The Beglerbey of Roum. Did you make a good bargain?"

"Not too bad."

Bernardi said: "I did very badly. Machmut must have a sliding scale when it comes to the rate on his bonds. Where are the children, Nicolo?"

"I think they went into the garden." Then Da Montelupo added, "I didn't know Prince Machmut operated on the Christian side of the strait."

Bernardi snorted: "He'd *swim* the strait for a scudo! Rich as he is, he's ambitious and grasping. He'd like to control some, even a very little, of the shipping here. He's a blabbermouth, too. He told me once you were a Turk."

"You know I am a Christian."

"I think he has always been jealous of you. Would it not be the part of wisdom to go home for a while, just to remind him that you are not really a resident of Turkey, not a subject of the sultan?"

Nicolo da Montelupo rubbed his clean-shaven chin reflectively.

18

"Curious," he mused. "You are the second good friend in the space of a day to hint that I am no longer welcome in Turkey."

"Oh, I dare say you're welcome enough, with a son like Michael. He'd be a wonderful asset to Murad's janissaries, after the losses at Varna."

"Nonsense! Everyone knows I pay my *karatch*. I'm a European, a Venetian. Michael isn't taxable."

In Europe this singular statement would have required considerable elucidation. Everyone knew that Christians in Turkey paid a small *karatch,* or poll tax, which assured their civil liberty, their commercial freedom, and a remarkably tolerant exercise of their religion. It was far less burdensome than a very similar sort of extortion that Jews, Turks, and other infidels were subjected to, legally or illegally, in western Christendom.

The Holy Koran, the law of all Islam, dealt in three summary ways with non-Moslems who chose, like Da Montelupo, or were forced, like some of the conquered Balkan peoples, to live in the Mohammedan world. They might embrace Islam and be admitted at once, without prejudice, into full citizenship, a prudent expedient widely adopted. Or they might retain their religion and customs on payment of the *karatch*. Or they might refuse to do either, and then they were strangled.

For two hundred years the Ottoman Empire, under a succession of brave and able princes, had been expanding, particularly at the expense of the venerable, decrepit Roman Empire of the East.

What was to be done with the fatherless, motherless children of a hundred conquered Christian cities? The law of Islam provided a generous answer. No book in the world preaches charity to orphans so consistently, so unequivocally as the Koran, revealed through the mouth of Mohammed, himself an orphan.

The pious result was the establishment of state-owned orphanages, where the little Gavours were brought up to be good Mohammedans.

Their mature careers were frequently so brilliant that the Turks had come to look among their former Christian protégés for men to fill positions of trust in the state, and, more especially, in the army, where they had proven uncommonly good fighters.

About a hundred years before Nicolo da Montelupo made the remark, "Michael is not taxable," a special corps of the Turkish army had been organized. In the reign of the first Murad and the viziership of Kara Khalil Chendereli, a thousands youths of Christian birth were admitted to its arduous, select discipline. It was a high honor which no native-born Turk was permitted to share.

The vizier drew them up in parade before Murad himself, who was so pleased with their promising aspect that he called on a very important personage to give them a propitious name.

The venerable Hadji Bektash, founder of the Bektashi Dervishes, whose purity of life gained him sainthood in Islam, drew the sleeve of his mantle over the nearest boy: "They are janissaries," he said, *"yenicheri"* (Your Majesty's New Troops), and blessed the corps.

In the hundred years since its founding, the janissary corps had grown to twelve times its original number of a thousand. The ranks were always full, not only because so many youngsters were captured in war, but also because many poor Christian subjects of the sultan were ambitious of having their sons numbered among these favored citizens of the state. For if the boys grew up to be pashas and governors, the parents shared in their glory. Even the office of grand vizier was open to a janissary who displayed a statesmanlike turn of mind.

Yet there was a somber aspect to the janissary organization. For sometimes, after sanguinary battles like the recent carnage at Varna, the ranks of the janissaries were not full. And then the law of Islam reminded the faithful that the Prophet had said: Know that whenever ye gain any spoils, a fifth part thereof belongeth to God.

Therefore, every fifth boy among the sultan's Christian subjects was taken from his home and forcibly enrolled in the janissary corps. As a rule the children were seven or eight years old, so that the shock of separation would not be too severe. In times of great stress they might be older, so as to be the sooner of fighting age.

Nicolo murmured again: "Michael is not taxable. I am a citizen, a senator of the Republic of Venice."

"I know, I know," Bernardi answered. "I am apprehensive and out of sorts today. The world looks gloomy. Perhaps you are right to stay in Scutari. While you do, you can at least prevent acquisitive Turkish noblemen from interesting themselves in your shipping. Where are those children of ours, did you say?"

"In the garden, I think. Thank you for your friendly warning, Filippo, but I feel secure. The Beglerbey of Roum has always been friendly. I shall not sail for Venice until Christmas, and I plan to return to Turkey by the first ship in the spring, as usual. Michael and I shall leave you now, before we weary your hospitality. I have some tedious necessary affairs to attend to in the warehouse."

There was nothing for Nicolo to do in the warehouse, but he thought it wise not to prolong the grape eating in the garden. He persuaded himself that the fruit might be green and indigestible. However, he had a shrewd Italian notion that more than the grapes might be ripening in the garden. He had detected certain signs in his son, and Angelica made him sigh for his own puberty.

On the way home Da Montelupo inquired casually, "Where is your dagger, son?" He cocked a quizzical eye at the empty little scabbard at Michael's waist.

It was customary for a well bred boy to carry a small dagger, counterpart of the costume of his elders, when he reached a certain period of his adolescence. In much the same way boys of a more advanced and bloodier age were to play with toy guns. The daggers were never very functional. The edges were dull, the points blunt; but a boy's first dagger was his proudest possession, and it marked the advent of his manhood.

Michael covered the empty scabbard with his hand, as if to hide it from his father's searching glance, and kicked industriously at some pebbles in the road. Greatly embarrassed, he said, "I think I must have lost it in Signore Bernardi's garden."

"A man does not lose his weapons," Nicolo said severely. "Do not tell a falsehood, Michael. What happened to it?"

Michael kicked at the pebbles furiously.

"We-ell—what actually happened—that girl, Angelica, she admired the little crosses on the hilt—"

"And so you gave it to her!"

"You know how girls are, Father."

"Hm," said his father, repressing a smile.

"Always liking something shining and pretty. They're funny."

"A momentous discovery, my son."

Michael said: "Yes, I gave it to her; I confess that I did. I didn't want it any more. I hoped you wouldn't mind."

Nicolo smiled broadly. "It doesn't matter, Michael. You're nearly old enough for a sharper one, anyway."

CHAPTER
3

ONLY three men in the feudal world claimed and were universally acknowledged the right to possess the lofty title of "Majesty": the Emperor of the Roman Empire of the East, a Greek; the Holy Roman Emperor in the west, an Austrian; and Murad II, Emperor of Turkey. The lesser kings of Europe contented themselves with My Lord, Your Grace, Your Excellency, or Your Highness.

Murad, whose empire lay partly in the West and partly in the East, bore also some fanciful Asiatic titles, among them Lord of the Three Seas, Brother of the Sun, Shadow of the Universe, and Commander of the Faithful. God had a thousand names. To Islam, Murad was His Apostle, Vicar of the Prophet on earth. It was fitting that a prince in whose person merged the civil, military, and ecclesiastical dignities of the founder of Islam be distinguished by sonorous titles. Eugenius, the Pope, occupied a somewhat analogous position in Christendom. Thus, some of Murad's titles were holy, some administrative, and some, of course, mere flattery. But they were legion.

Inevitably the fashion spread downward among his servants, from the grand vizier to the humblest mayor of a village. Among the lesser civil employees of the sultan was a functionary called the Tournaji Bashi, whose title meant Head Keeper of the Cranes, or Game Warden. In the raw, uncivilized days of the empire, such an official did actually tend the cranes at which the earlier sultans delighted to fly their hawks. But that was long ago, at a time when the French grand master of the horse was only one step above a stableboy, and the Eng-

lish lord chamberlain personally tidied up the bedroom for his pow-
erless king in a foggy isle in the far-away, cold North Sea. Traditional
titles change slowly. Empires reach maturity and power still calling
their chief ministers by names that originated in the scullery, the
stable, and the bedroom.

By Murad's time no one remembered that a Head Keeper of the
Cranes ever tended the sultan's game, and the title Tournaji Bashi
had come to mean only a hard-working official of some small, occa-
sional military importance.

The day after Nicolo returned from his fruitless trip to Galata,
he received a visit from the Tournaji Bashi of Scutari. The man was
dressed in a white turban and yellow shoes, like a janissary. A spot-
less, new military tunic, distinguished by a narrow border of marten,
reached to a little below the knees. He was not ordinarily entitled to
the dignity of a sword-bearer. Nicolo, who knew him slightly as one
of the town's most affable and respected citizens, was astonished to
see a selictar solemnly marching before him, bearing his sword as if
the provincial little Tournaji Bashi were the vizier himself.

Perhaps he had risen in the world. Nicolo greeted him, calling
him Excellency out of sheer caution.

The official protested mildly. "Nonsense, Nicolo. I'm no more Excellency than I ever was. I merely bought a new tunic because it will
be a little warmer—where I'm going." He ran his hand proudly over
the fur. "And I hired the sword-bearer so I wouldn't alarm the boys."

Nicolo went white. The Tournaji Bashi frowned slightly.

"Naturally, I don't want to alarm you people either. I think I
appear friendlier unarmed."

"Your Excellency has always been friendly, and you do not alarm
me in the least."

"Thank God for that." This time he did not protest at the title.
"It is my first commission of this sort, you know, and this is my first
call. I was told that you rayahs would welcome me; but somehow I
couldn't believe it." He drew in a deep breath and let it out as if an
unpleasant load had been lifted from his shoulders.

"I am not a rayah, Excellency."

A rayah was a Christian subject of the sultan.

"Come, Nicolo. You are. Everybody knows it. At least your name
is on my list. I am specifically commissioned to recruit Michael, son

23

of Nicolo da Montelupo, into the Corps of His Majesty's Janissaries. It is a great honor. Congratulations."

"I do not want that honor."

The Tournaji Bashi frowned again. Something of the original suspicion that his commission might be unpleasant returned.

"I am not a rayah." Nicolo continued as calmly as he was able. "I am a European, a Venetian. My sovereign is not the sultan, but the Doge of Venice. I live here only part of the time. My son is not taxable."

The Tournaji Bashi shook his head.

"My information is that you live here all the time. The lists are always correct, checked by the very highest authorities. You are a good rayah, and as a rule you pay your tax."

"I always pay my tax. I am not a rayah, but I always pay my tax."

"Again, sir, my information is that you did not do so this year. But then," he shrugged, "all the taxes were late this year."

"I do not see how that can be. The *karatch* was collected months ago."

"Even if you'd paid your tax, I dare say we'd have to recruit extra boys this year. The losses at Varna were heavy. Nobody knows how heavy, except a few of us in the government." The little Tournaji Bashi puffed up like a pigeon. "Come now, Nicolo. Do not waste time. I've a number of calls to make today. Where is that fine son of yours? Oh—hm."

Michael had heard some of the conversation. He stood in the shadow of the door a little behind his father.

"I see you, Michael!" the visitor called cheerily. "Come out in the sun, lad. Your father and I want to talk to you."

Michael stepped out of his father's shadow and looked up at the official, who ruffled his hair in a friendly way. "About as big as my own boy," he commented. "But my boy can't ever have such an honor. That's what it costs him to be a Turk. When my temporary commission expires, even I shan't be permitted to wear a janissary's white turban and these yellow shoes. Don't you feel lucky, Michael?"

"I don't know, sir."

For a moment Nicolo would have traded every drop of his pure Venetian blood for pure Turkish blood.

"There is some dreadful error," Nicolo said. Michael had never before heard his father speak in just that hollow, threatening tone.

"It is true that I live most of the year here in Scutari, but I always spend sufficient time at my legal home in Venice to establish my residence there. My margin of safety, you might call it, is slim. My affairs here require a great deal of time. But never, never have I lived continuously in Scutari. I cannot possibly be classed as a subject of His Majesty the Sultan."

The Tournaji Bashi said, not unkindly: "Your name is on my list, signore. Michael must come with me whether you like it or not. You are certainly upsetting the boy, and I think it's unkind of you."

Michael had begun to understand, but only an imperceptible trembling of his chin betrayed his anxiety. Nicolo instantly shifted his tactics.

His voice under control again, he said: "I have been unpardonably discourteous to His Majesty's emissary. Pray, come into my house, you and your selictar. Perhaps you will take a cup of wine. It is not intoxicating."

The Tournaji Bashi looked interested, but he glanced at his sword-bearer, remembered himself, and said regretfully, "Certainly *not*. Wine is forbidden."

"Or at least a cup of coffee," Nicolo persisted.

"Well, yes; I might do that." He instructed his sword-bearer to wait outside. "I want you to trust me, Nicolo. To show that I trust you, I come unarmed into your house. I shall even show you your name on my confidential list."

It was a cold day. Nicolo's hearth was blazing brightly. The Tournaji Bashi grew mellow in its warmth. Sipping his coffee, he confided to Nicolo: "I'd have taken a bit of your wine, my Christian friend, since you say it isn't intoxicating, but I was afraid the selictar would smell my breath."

Michael appeared about to leave the older men so that they could talk alone over their coffee, but the official said: "Stay here, Michael. We're going to be great friends."

Nicolo's heart said, "Stay, son, stay, stay forever," but aloud he remarked: "Perhaps he'd better not stay. Michael, let me talk to the Tournaji Bashi alone for a moment."

"Eh?" the official grunted. "Oh, very well. But don't start running away, Michael, or I'll never let you be a janissary."

Nicolo thought, There is nowhere to run, and aloud he said, "Just go to your room for a while, Michael."

The Tournaji Bashi dug in the purse at his sword belt. There was no sword attached to it now. Nicolo thought how easily he could kill him. Then he thought how impossible it would be for him to hide the murder. A Christian who killed a Turk inevitably suffered a most painful death. Even if he and Michael should escape to Constantinople, it was quite likely that the timorous Greek authorities would hand them both back to the Turks on the slightest hint from the sultan's ambassador. What was one Italian trader more or less to the sly, shaky old Roman Empire of the East?

"Here it is," grumbled the guest. "Here is the list and here is my commission, sealed by the sultan himself." He looked very pompous. "I do hope you are not going to cause any trouble, sir. This isn't a job to my liking, but maybe the poorer rayahs won't take it so hard as you rich ones."

Nicolo scanned the Turkish script on the parchment sheets. There indeed was his name, among a dozen others. And the Tournaji Bashi's commission indubitably bore the sultan's great seal.

"Oh, I did not doubt your word, Excellency. Perhaps a few poor rayahs won't mind losing their sons. But I beg to remind you that I am not a rayah, even though my name appears on your list. And, as you say, I am rich. Richer than anyone dreams."

"I am glad for you, sir."

"Perhaps you should be glad for yourself, Excellency. It struck me a moment ago, when you pulled these imperial documents out of your purse, that your purse was a lean one for a man of your consequence."

"It is true that I am poor. It is no disgrace to be poor. I understand you. I cannot possibly do what you are thinking. It is a wicked thing to take a bribe, and anyway," he sighed heavily, "I couldn't get away with it."

Nicolo protested that no such thought had crossed his mind. "I had only hoped to make you a small gift," he suggested. "Not to deter you from taxing Michael, which of course you must do since your commission demands it. I thought merely that you might give me a day or two to see the authorities; I am convinced that there is an error in your list. I cannot imagine how my name came to be placed there."

"In a day or two Michael will be in camp. I would not dare wait that long. He and the other boys are leaving tonight."

26

"Where is the camp?"

"I am not permitted to say. You will be informed in due time. Fathers always are."

Nicolo knew that it took months for fathers to be informed of their sons' whereabouts. He quickly shifted his tactics again.

"I understand. I know that the wisdom of the authorities teaches them that rayah fathers—not that I am a rayah—sometimes want to visit their sons in camp. It is most wise not to let them. It would upset the splendid discipline. My only thought was that you might be willing to accept a gift of a few hundred aspers and put my name down at the end of your list instead of at the beginning. Come back again this evening. This afternoon even. Perhaps by that time I can have seen the governor of Scutari. He knows me well. This error can easily be rectified."

Nicolo's ship was at the dock. How simple to go aboard within two hours, within the hour even, and sail her away from Turkey forever!

"We all know you, sir. But Bismillah! You said you were rich! For a moment I thought to myself: I could, perhaps, reverse the order of the list. I could make the calls in the city first. I could come back in the afternoon. But now you insult my integrity with a few hundred aspers!"

Nicolo groaned.

"Believe me, I am rich. But it just happens that I have only a few hundred aspers in coin in the house. That can happen to a merchant." Suddenly he rose and went over to the fireplace. He swung aside the hidden door and drew out a little bag like the one he had showed Joseph of Adrianople. "Look," he said. "Do you believe me now?" The bag was full of very large diamonds.

The Tournaji Bashi drew in his breath. His eyes began to glitter like the gems. Nicolo whispered, his tone intense: "One of them. All of them, Excellency. They are yours. Go away, in God's name, if only for an hour. I want to talk to my son. I want to tell him that it is an honor, yes, indeed it is, but also it is a mistake. I think you believe that it is a mistake. I think you know that he will be home again in a week."

The Tournaji Bashi's breath came out again in a great sigh. "I have heard the imams read in the temple, 'The provision of this life is but small.' How true is the Holy Koran! In a Christian's house I

27

learn how true it is. Why should I continue to be a poor man when an infidel possesses such jewels? But you are trying to trap me. You know that I would be arrested if I attempted to sell even the smallest of these stones."

It was true. Nicolo bit his lip and restrained an almost overpowering impulse to hurl the diamonds into his visitor's placid face. He changed his tactics yet again. Letting the jewels lie on the table beside the porcelain coffee cup that the Tournaji Bashi had already drained, he produced the money order which Joseph of Adrianople had given him.

"This is a piece of paper," he said desperately, smoothly. "It is worth a great deal of money, though I have so little in the house at the moment. It is all in this paper. It is worth not so much as these diamonds, but it is worth as much as any three of them, even the largest. Take it to any bank in Constantinople. They will give you 90,000 Venetian ducats for it. Or if you wait till it clears the San Vitale, you will get 150,000." Nicolo was speaking precisely the truth, but the Tournaji Bashi had never heard of the San Vitale Bank. He turned the paper over and over.

"How do I know this is worth money?"

"It says so. Read it, man!"

But the Tournaji Bashi could not read Italian. He could hardly read Turkish.

"I dare not take it. I'm afraid of you. Come, come, Nicolo. No more of this. Call your boy. I must get on with my work."

Nicolo was not immediately able to call Michael. "At least," he said huskily, "do not let him think it is forever. Tell him it's only for a week or two. By then I shall be able to straighten out this mistake."

The official thought a moment. There was just the possibility that a mistake might have been made. The Christian was influential.

"Very well," he said soberly, "I'll tell Michael it's for, say, three weeks. We'll both tell him that. A fine holiday, eh?"

Nicolo nodded his head. The Tournaji Bashi looked at him compassionately.

"Drink a cup of your wicked Christian wine, my friend. Find your tongue and call your boy and tell him it's a holiday. I promise I shan't tell him anything different, all the way to camp."

"He likes to shoot," Nicolo said in a low voice.

"Good! That's the first thing they teach the boys!"

"You tell him. I can't. Say that he'll get a beautiful Turkish bow, all sinew and horn. I've always meant to buy him one."

"That's the truth. That's just what he'll get. I'll tell him."

The Tournaji Bashi did. But Michael was puzzled.

"Is it true, Father? Is it all right for me to go?"

"It is all right."

"Will it be for long?"

"Only a couple of weeks, son."

Nicolo needed desperately to believe what he was saying. How could it be otherwise? He was *not* a rayah. His tone was firm and reassuring, to himself no less than to Michael.

Thus Michael was not entirely unhappy when he left his father. He and some other Christian boys were merely taking a short holiday among the janissaries with the pleasant Tournaji Bashi.

MICHAEL was not permitted to take with him anything but the clothes on his back, and Nicolo knew that even these would soon be changed.

He threw his own heavy cloak over the boy's shoulders. Michael obediently wore it a little way, but it reached to his ankles and embarrassed him. As soon as he thought his father was not looking any more, he took off the cloak and carried it over his arm.

Nicolo was watching, however, from a window. "I hope he doesn't throw it away. It will keep him warm tonight."

The selictar marched before the Tournaji Bashi's horse, carrying the sword. Michael walked close to the Tournaji Bashi's knees, looking up into his face, talking in an excited fashion. About the beautiful Turkish bow, Nicolo supposed. Then the picture through the window dissolved into formless flashes of light, like sun shining through water. The tears Nicolo had feared to shed in front of his son, lest they betray the fiction of the holiday, now ran heedlessly down his cheeks.

He shouted to his steward to harness a traveling chest to a pack mule and to bridle two others for riding. They were going to Scutari.

The steward said, "Yes, my lord Nicolo; instantly, signore." He was shaken himself, but he dared to observe, "It is only half a league to Scutari." Perhaps his master was momentarily possessed. Nicolo's stricken face was perfectly motionless. Only the tears moved.

But if demons possessed Nicolo's mind, they made it function with wonderful precision and extraordinary speed. He shook the tears out of his eyes. "It will be a week!" he cried angrily. "We'll be riding for a week!"

The steward muttered, "A week to ride?" He went out to prepare the mules, sadly shaking his head.

Nicolo's thoughts had outraced his tongue. He knew they must be prepared to ride beyond Scutari. There would be need for speed. "Oh, why cannot a Christian keep horses in Turkey?"

Nicolo's hands flew among his papers, swift and unerring as cormorants diving for fish. Some of the documents he selected as precious—the dates were right. They bore indisputable evidence of his having spent three months in Venice in the year 1441, three months, one week, and two days in 1442, and almost four months in 1443. That was last year. These, with all his Turkish tax receipts, he carefully wrapped in a heavy sheet of glazed parchment, sealing it with wax so that it was perfectly waterproof, tied it up with a tape, and hung it round his neck under his tunic.

There were other papers which yesterday he had valued: title deeds, warehouse inventories, ship manifests, a copy of his hereditary patent to the Scutari shipping rights. These he carelessly thrust into a sack. He opened the cache in the fireplace and took out all the little bags that contained his jewel collection. He hurled them into the sack among the papers, cursing them frightfully. But on second thought he selected a bag of small ones and emptied them into the purse at his belt.

Then he spent an hour penning a complicated document. As soon as it was finished, Nicolo and the steward rode down into Scutari to see the governor.

To gain access to an important official in Turkey quickly, it was necessary to be either wretchedly poor or extremely wealthy. Beggars were admitted at once, out of charitable motives. Indeed, many hard-working, middle-class citizens envied them. And the wealthy, of course, by the lavish exercise of the universal custom of giving costly gifts, seldom cooled their heels long in official antechambers.

The governor of Scutari was one of the most important civil and military men in the empire, the natural result of Scutari's strategic position. He was a pasha of the highest grade. His standard was distinguished by three horsetails. Only two men in the empire were entitled to more: the grand vizier to five, and Murad the sultan to seven. The horsetail was a coveted symbol of rank. It was the ambition of every pasha to add them one by one to his standard, just as nobles in Europe were ambitious of adding regal insignia to the armorial charges on their shields. Few knew where the custom originated, and even the scholars held different opinions. Many believed that it was anciently the tail not of the horse but of the Siberian yak. For it was on the backs of these stately Asiatic animals that the rude and hardy Mongolian ancestors of the Turks had first learned the art of war. They were of Tartar blood, it was believed, kin to the Russian Huns, pagan and uncivilized before they learned religion and good manners from Mohammed the Arabian. Such, at least, was the opinion of one leading school of antiquarians. Most people simply saluted the horsetail standards and thought no more about the matter.

The pashalik of the governor of Scutari extended beyond the confines of the city from the Sea of Marmara to the Black Sea and far to the south of Bulgarlhu Dagh. The district was populous and wealthy. The governor-pasha was a busy man and required a considerable staff of subordinate officials to assist him.

The governor's major-domo, who fixed the hours for all his appointments, was an elderly eunuch named Piali. In the governor's infancy Piali had shared the child's early care with the women of the harem. Later, when he reached adolescence, the age at which it was proper to transfer a Turkish boy, step by step, cushioning the shock, from women's care to the care of men, Piali had overseen the governor's education. As the governor grew older and rose in the world, he remembered his faithful tutor and rewarded him with marks of favor and posts of distinction, the most lucrative of which Piali now occupied. He had grown rich as the governor's major-domo. But even his enemies had to admit that he was honest, industrious, capable of infinite detail, and willing to reciprocate the favors he constantly received if he could honorably do so.

The governor-pasha had as his residence the old Greek castle in the town, a somber stone pile that was chilly even in summertime. Piali's apartments adjoined the great hall, which served as the governor's audience chamber. They were cramped and ill lighted, wholly at variance with Turkish love of sunshine and fresh air; but both Piali and his master had to live in the castle because it would

32

have been unseemly in Murad's well regulated empire to have lived anywhere else. However the sons of the galloping Tartars might long for the open sky, the ranking military representative of the sultan must live in the strongest, most dignified edifice in town. That was the old Greek castle.

Piali had had his dark rooms hung with costly lamps which burned an oil that was perfumed with cedar and musk. No glass enclosed them, because even Piali could not afford glass, but their flames were not quite naked: the shades were of thin brass, hammered into delicate floral designs and pierced, whenever a leaf was depicted, to let the light through. The brown stone walls were draped with green damask. There were Persian carpets on the stone floor; and in a corner, close to where Piali sat on an ample, cushioned sofa, glowed a bronze Arabian brazier. One of Piali's house servants worked a small pair of bellows from time to time to keep it burning briskly. There were reed pens in a silver vase on the ebony table within easy reach of the eunuch. He took great pride in his calligraphy and had a passion for writing things down. It was one of the reasons he was such an efficient major-domo to the governor-pasha.

A black castle guard brought Nicolo into Piali's little room.

It was not customary for a Gavour to enter the presence of the faithful and immediately begin to talk. The major-domo did not look up from his writing as Nicolo made a deep obeisance and then stood, his arms crossed, palms against his breast, his fingertips almost touching his shoulders. It was merely the formal posture of respect that good manners required, though it looked (and had once been) an attitude of abject submission, especially when one also bowed his head. But Nicolo's chin was up at anything but a submissive angle.

Good manners also required Piali to acknowledge his visitor's existence; and if Piali had not been so intent on completing the ornamental tail of a particularly difficult character, he would have done so. But the pen was heavy with ink. The word would mean something else if a drop should accidentally splatter. Piali heard the European heels and glimpsed the gray shoes. The Christian would have to wait.

The word completed, Piali glanced up, greeted the merchant cordially, and smiled.

"I rather expected you, Signore da Montelupo, though perhaps not quite so soon. I take it that the Tournaji Bashi has already visited you."

"He has, Piali Effendi. That is why I came to see you. It is my hope"—Nicolo's trembling fingers found in his purse a stone about the size of a pea that he knew to be particularly clear and fine—"that Your Excellency will condescend to accept a token of the great esteem I have always had for you. I find myself short of the gold pieces that you have sometimes honored me by accepting. Perhaps you will take this diamond."

Piali saw the gem and began to beam complacently. "When Heaven is short of virgins and Hell is short of devils, Nicolo da Montelupo will be short of gold. You cannot expect me to believe you, signore. This is a delicate gesture. I deserve it, of course, but I thank you just the same. I did not realize that you were aware of my admiration for fine jewels." He took the diamond. "This stone is beautiful. Your gratitude is gracefully demonstrated."

Nicolo said, "Effendi, I do not understand your reference to gratitude."

Dazzled by the fire of the diamond, Piali did not hear him.

"It is my happy fate to acquire diamonds these days!" he said. "A noble friend of yours gave me another just a week ago, larger than this, but not so alive, I think. His request prompted me to do what I did for your son, and his gift was the same as yours. It is just. It is poetic. Of course, I had to overlook one detail. I told him that I knew that your legal residence was Venice. At first I didn't see how I could help you." Still looking at the diamond as if he were hypnotized, the eunuch lowered his voice to a confidential tone. "But he intimated that you might soon profess the true faith. He reminded me that you spend so little time in Italy that many people consider you a rayah. Deigning to explain, when he might have commanded, he made me a gift and mentioned our thousands of soldiers lost at Varna. So I stretched a point and placed Michael's name on the list, the first of them all!" He looked smilingly up from the jewel that still flashed in his palm. Then he saw Nicolo's face clearly for the first time. It was fury. Piali almost dropped the diamond in astonishment.

Nicolo shouted, "Who was the perjured friend who tricked you into stealing my son?"

Thirty years of observing the unpredictable reactions of passionate men had taught the eunuch tact. He did not always understand them, but he had learned how to quiet them. It dawned upon him that Nicolo had not wanted his son taxed.

"Do not raise your voice in this place, you Christian pig," he said placidly, not unkindly. The epithet, formalized and common-place, was not insulting. "I thought I was doing you a favor. It would not have been the first time that an ambitious parent had asked me to do such a thing."

Nicolo's hands shook. "I will murder the man who suggested this."

"Softly, softly, signore. Do not talk about murder. Your own heathen law says you ought not to kill. I conceive that there would be blood on my own hands if I should divulge the identity of your friend. Especially since there is no impediment in the way of Michael's quick dismissal from the corps."

Piali's fingers closed on the jewel again. He slipped it into the velvet purse at his ample girdle. Out of the corner of his sharp little eyes he stole several quick glances at Nicolo's face, noting with satisfaction that the taut mask of hopeless rage had relaxed. Nicolo flushed and began to tremble in spite of a great effort to regain his composure.

The eunuch thought: Their blood turns to ice when they despair; it thaws when they hope again. How odd. I must remember in the future that some fathers love their sons. The way I like my pretty cats, perhaps. Or even, Bismillah! perhaps the way I adore His Excellency the Governor! Good heavens! My stupid error may involve His Excellency as well as myself.

It was now Piali's face that became a mask, a smiling one, but his piercing eyes began to shift about in an anxious manner. His voice, always high and clear, rose a bit higher as he repeated em-phatically: "No impediment at all, signore. The laws that regulate the inestimable privilege of entering the sultan's janissary corps have never been so stringently executed as in the reign of His present, pious Majesty, Murad, whom God bless, immeasurably."

"Whom God bless," repeated Nicolo, as was customary when-ever the sultan's name was mentioned.

"But you must bring yourself to understand, Signore da Monte-lupo, that it will take some small effort on your part to achieve the release of your son." He waved his pudgy white hands. Every finger on both hands was decorated with spectacular jeweled rings. "You cannot expect me to admit publicly that my great consideration for you prompted me to overlook your status as a foreigner and put your son's name on the Tournaji Bashi's list. The boys are chosen by lot: every fifth one. If a single error is admitted, the entire list is suspect. It will be said that I have interfered with the workings of fate. I shall be accused of thwarting the will of Allah. I shall be besieged by irate parents claiming that the lottery was tampered with, all insisting that their sons be admitted. It might even be necessary to put all the names back into the box and have the imam draw out an entire new quota of names. There would be a scandal. The whole pashalik would be dishonored. In the present troubled times no such situation will be permitted to arise. Rather than risk such a catastrophe, powerful interests will intervene, and you will find yourself instantly and irrevocably registered as a rayah. And as for Michael, he will simply remain a janissary."

Da Montelupo retreated quickly. "Do not threaten me, Excellency. I want no scandal. All I want is my son. Perhaps you will allow me to see the governor. A word from him will release Michael."

"I know it would; but it would cause precisely the scandal I have mentioned. The governor-pasha is so just a man that he would forget the loss of prestige. He would upset the orderly routine of the whole district simply to right what he considered to be one little injustice. Michael would be restored to you in a day." The eunuch's eyes narrowed. "But can you imagine how uncomfortable I could make it in Turkey for you after that?"

Nicolo could imagine, but he said, "I am not interested in my comfort."

"Or in your health, signore?"

"My health has already suffered."

"Or in Michael's health, signore?"

That was different.

"What am I to do, Piali Effendi? I do not want to cause a scandal."

The eunuch's eyes stopped shifting and fixed intently on Nicolo's own. "It is a short, pleasant journey to Adrianople," he said blandly. "Go to the sultan's court. Present your petition in person. I am sure it will be granted. You have friends in the capital. Your son will be returned to you in a month at the most. In the meantime he is perfectly safe."

Nicolo could not deny that. No one in the Turkish Empire was subjected to quite such solicitous care and supervision as a fledgling janissary.

Piali concluded positively, "I really cannot permit you to upset the whole local government in order to get your boy back in a day instead of a month."

Nicolo had expected something of the sort. He made a last valiant effort, however, to obtain some tangible help from Piali. He suggested, "Perhaps a letter from the governor-pasha, or from Your Excellency, might serve to piece out the evidence that I can already present to prove I am a foreigner."

Piali shook his head.

"Merely a note addressing me as a Venetian, a Christian swine, for example? I will go to Adrianople. But if Your Excellency could only see your way clear to write me a short note, about the crops, about my ships, about anything, so long as you refer to me, not as a rayah, but as a European? I beg you!"

"Quite impossible, signore. Go to the sultan and win your suit alone. You must not expect me to involve all the pashas and beys of Scutari in your miserable little affair. But perhaps I can do something." He thought a moment. Actually, he was almost as anxious as Nicolo to have Michael released. He had prudently neglected to mention that of all the officials in Scutari he himself would be the first to suffer in the event of an imperial investigation. "What I will do for you, since you seem to be in such undignified haste about this matter, is to give you a special safe conduct that will smooth your way and speed your journey. I shall affix the governor-pasha's own seal."

So much, but no more, the major-domo was willing to do. Nicolo was given the passport and dismissed.

"I told you we would ride for a week," Nicolo observed to his steward on the ferry to Galata. "Now we must go on to Adrianople. I feared I should not see the governor. I suppose I ought to be happy that I accomplished so much as I did."

"It is a long journey," the steward replied. "I trust that your lordship will not attempt it too rapidly. It has seemed to me lately that your lordship has looked a bit puffy about the ankles."

Nicolo said, "You're an impertinent old rogue. That's just my unhealthy fat, like Piali's." But Nicolo was not fat. The steward knew he had not let out his sword belt a notch in twenty years.

"I am glad you got the passport, master."

Nicolo nodded his head. "Even the Greeks will be frightened when they look at it. And when we pass through the Eastern Empire and enter Turkey again, it will be of immense value. I didn't do too badly."

Da MONTELUPO spent the night with Bernardi in Galata, who was amazed and a little apprehensive when his friend returned so soon. Perhaps Nicolo's need was greater than he cared to admit, he thought, and mentally calculated how much he could spare. The Galatan was reluctantly preparing to embarrass himself if necessary.

Nicolo's steward thought at first that his master had heeded his advice to travel by easy stages, to sleep heavily and long in the house of his friend before they set out next day on the arduous journey to Adrianople.

But Nicolo and Bernardi ate a gloomy, silent supper and retired immediately afterward to Bernardi's study, a close little room, with walls so thick that not a sound could penetrate them. It did not appear to the steward that his master would get a good night's rest after all.

Many of Bernardi's most successful commercial enterprises had been initiated in this quiet, private seclusion. It was here that he interviewed his ship captains, who always brought him political as well as commercial news from Europe, and his couriers, who carried his confidential orders out to his agents scattered all over the Eastern Empire. The couriers were paid, not only to carry messages back and forth, but also to keep their eyes open on the way. Bernardi would have rejected any suggestion that he was a commercial soothsayer, but there has never been a time when commerce could not profit by shrewd guesses concerning the direction of the political wind. The commerce of the Venetian Renaissance, frankly monopolistic, was inextricably tangled with politics. A special kind of commercial statesmanship was required to succeed in it.

"What little success I have had here in Galata," Bernardi observed to his guest, "I attribute to my life-long habit of keeping well informed. Your sad news distresses me, Nicolo, and I reproach myself that I did not more forcibly warn you of the danger to Michael. The Greeks here chatter all day long about the Turkish losses at Varna. You'd think Christendom had won a great victory instead of suffering an overwhelming defeat. I should have emphasized my warning."

"You did your best, signore. I blindly refused to listen to you. I have been assured, however, that I have only to present my petition to the sultan and the error will instantly be rectified. Piali admits it's a mistake, but he's so confoundedly touchy about his master's good name that I must go all the way to Adrianople and beg for what I have a legal right to demand. It's exasperating but," he shrugged, "it might be worse. I'm sure to get my son back."

"Piali's good name is involved, too, Nicolo."

"I know that. But Piali rises and falls with his master; I think he's perfectly selfless in this."

"There is no doubt, I suppose, that Michael will be returned?"

Nicolo said: "I genuinely believe there is none at all, though naturally I am terribly anxious. Piali convinced me that he thought he was doing me a favor."

Bernardi shook his head thoughtfully. "You have lived too long among a people who speak with honey on their lips. You forget how suddenly the Turks can act. Sternly. Cruelly, Nicolo."

Nicolo said heavily: "No, I do not forget. This has made me begin to fear them, though they have treated me kindly for years. Europeans brawl. Greeks talk. But the Turks act. Their actions are swift and inexorable. I tell you, Filippo, I tremble for Christendom! Once my boy is returned to me, I will give up all my holdings in Scutari and return permanently to Venice."

Bernardi raised his eyebrows in some surprise. "Oh, come, it's not so bad as that. Everyone knows that Murad is too busy in Albania to attack Constantinople. Besides, he tried that once and failed. I don't like the Greeks any more than you do, but they would fight for this city. It will never fall. It is protected by impregnable walls, and also," he added with perfect conviction, "by Our Lady Herself, who, in a blue robe, walked upon them during the last siege."

Nicolo, who had blessed the sultan out of politeness earlier in the day, now crossed himself, as did Bernardi, reverently. The Virgin had been observed by both armies; and the Turks (Islam also revered Her) were thought to have been considerably disturbed by the miracle, especially the pious Murad, whose favorite wife was a Christian.

"Your experience has overwrought you, my friend," Bernardi continued. "Upon my word, you are gloomier than I was yesterday. If Piali assures you that Michael will be released, I'm inclined to agree with you that you have nothing to worry about as far as your son is concerned. Whatever I may think of the Turks, their word is good. And as for the city, believe me, the cross will never come down from the dome of Santa Sophia. But tell me, why do you suppose Piali thought he was doing you a favor? Unless he mistook you for a rayah?"

"He admitted that he knew I was not a rayah. He said a friend of mine had requested the favor. I gave Piali one of my diamonds as the usual present—you know how little ready money I happen to have—and Piali became quite rhapsodic about the coincidence. He said he had got another only a week ago from someone who told him I wanted Michael taxed into the janissary corps. Before Michael and I leave the East, I shall deal with that man, whoever he is."

Bernardi nodded quietly. "You could honorably take your revenge in your own home. It was the sanctity of your home that he violated. Possibly a slow poison, administered at your own table. Or perhaps finely crushed diamond dust, to puncture his bowels in the usual painful manner, since diamonds have figured so largely in this affair. I'd be the last to blame you. Though he'd have to be drunk to take the diamond dust: it grates on the teeth. Who is your enemy, my friend?"

Nicolo shook his head, thinking carefully. "I cannot be sure. Piali is cautious and clever, and he dropped only the vaguest hints. He intimated the man was a powerful Turk. And at the very beginning of the audience, before he saw how angry I was, he said that the man had given him a diamond as a gift for putting Michael's name on the list."

Bernardi said quickly, "Did you see the eunuch's diamond? Was it cracked?"

"No, I didn't. He said it was a big one, but rather dull. It might have been cracked."

"I wish you'd seen it."

"Why?"

"Because I know a Turk who is jealous of you, and it has come to my ears that he has been buying some big, badly flawed diamonds lately. There may be some connection."

Nicolo's eyes widened in anger. "I don't think there's any doubt about the connection! Who is the man?"

Bernardi lowered his voice even in the soundproof room. "He is wicked, powerful, and passionately ambitious, a dangerous man to have for an enemy. If my guess is correct, he hopes to frighten you back to Venice, you and Michael. Then, exerting his enormous influence on both sides of the Bosphorus, he can secure expropriation of the Scutari shipping and take the monopoly for himself. Turkish nationalism is rising. He could make it seem a patriotic gesture to oust a Venetian and put the Scutari shipping into the hands of a noble Turk."

Nicolo's pale face contorted. "He has chosen a cruel and effective means of ousting me. You have intimated whom you suspect. Is it Machmut, the Beglerbey of Roum?"

Bernardi nodded sternly. "It is."

"Then," Nicolo said, "when I return from Adrianople, I shall have the pleasure of murdering him. Why are you so sure it is Machmut?"

"Because if I were in his position, I couldn't think of a better scheme myself."

Nicolo smiled. "That is very convincing, my friend. Only a priest, probably, knows so much wickedness and lives so blamelessly as Filippo Bernardi!"

Bernardi acknowledged the compliment with a quiet smile and said, "Do, pray, let me know if I can be of assistance when you come to exterminate our exalted Turkish broker. I have a score to settle with him myself, in the matter of my forfeited bonds. When I think what he charged me for them! Have you planned the details of the murder, Nicolo? It must be cautiously wrought."

Nicolo was worn out. He rested his head in his hand. "I'll think of something," he said slowly and distastefully. "I don't know what's come over me lately. Thinking never used to be an effort. Retaliation for an injury never used to revolt me. Now I feel myself grown soft, and my thoughts come slowly, all dreamy and confused, like my own dear sire's in his last days. But he was eighty, and I am little more than half of that. My breath is short; I tire easily, like a baby or an old, old man, and I long for quiet. Sometimes I think we merchants lead too sedentary a life, Filippo. Perhaps the long ride to Adrianople will do me good. The cold winds will blow the cobwebs out of my brain. Then I can plan to deal with Machmut. Though perhaps we are both mistaken. Just because he bought cracked diamonds does not necessarily mean that he bribed Piali with one and thought up the scheme of getting Michael taxed."

Bernardi shrugged. "It would be evidence enough for me. You are too charitable, my friend, or maybe the Greeks have taught me to be too suspicious. I must say that I have never noticed any confusion in your thoughts. You are, as I say, merely overwrought. I have kept you up too long. If you still plan to ride out so early in the morning, you surely should go to bed now."

Nicolo said soberly, "Before I go to bed, I must ask you to do something for me."

Bernardi answered frankly, "Is it money, Nicolo? Under the circumstances, of course! Any amount I can lay my hands on."

"No," Nicolo said. "I have plenty for the journey, and whatever gifts are required at court I can make out of my jewels. I have them all with me."

Bernardi smiled at that. "One would think that you planned to bribe the Sultan himself, and you probably could if you're taking your whole collection with you."

Nicolo answered: "They say that Murad isn't interested in wealth. He spends half his time in a *tekkyeh* of dervishes, almost like a monk."

"An unusual occupation for the Grand Turk," Bernardi observed. "And I still have to meet the human being who can withstand the temptation of a fat bribe."

"I need no money, Filippo, but I do need assurance that Prince Machmut in my absence will not suddenly show up at my warehouse armed with a formidable Turkish document and attempt to take over my establishment. Such an illegality would certainly bring a

43

Venetian protest, but we are a long way from Venice. Machmut could cause me a great deal of embarrassment."

Bernardi said: "Now it's you who are too suspicious. Machmut would never dare! But pray talk no more about your senile intellect. You reason with the subtlety of a Greek, which is to say that what you propose might just possibly happen, preposterous as it seems. How do you plan to defend yourself against such an unlikely event during the few weeks that you will be away?"

Nicolo said very seriously: "I plan to make over to you, signore, everything I possess in the world, if you will burden yourself with that responsibility temporarily. You, here, on the spot, with your influence in Galata and Constantinople, can act unrestrictedly in my name if anything should happen."

The effect on Bernardi was tremendous. He grasped his friend's hand. He did not attempt to conceal the tears that started from his eyes and made two wet streaks down his cheeks.

"I have been called many hard names in my time," he said in a low, slow voice: "skinflint, miser, usurer; a driver of hard bargains; a commercial spy—all the jealous names that a merchant can be called, just because God has seen fit to allow me a greater measure of success than falls to most people. And I have been called many false, flattering things, by people who wanted favors from me. But no one ever called me so good a friend as you have by this act of faith! But it isn't necessary, Nicolo! I'll look after your interests while you are away. It will be a pleasure to cross over to Turkey. I'll go every day. And I'll make money for you, too. But you don't need to sign over—good heavens, man! What a drastic step! I cannot allow such a thing."

"I must insist that you do, signore. I'd feel better that way."

"I am not even sure it would be permitted legally. You cannot just write a simple note and say, 'Everything that I own now belongs to Filippo Bernardi.' Take my word for it, dear friend. I shall look after your interests while you are gone. And if His Excellency the Beglerbey turns up, I'll find a way to deal with him, too. Don't trouble yourself about him. Have a pleasant journey to Adrianople on your mule. Leave Machmut to me."

"I shall not write a simple note, Filippo. Though I could, of course, and you know it. It might require a little clarification by the courts if anything should happen to me——"

Bernardi had sedulously avoided mention of this possibility. Does any man know when he will die? Nicolo's note would then become a will.

"Do not suggest such a thing!"

"I only say that even a simple note can convey power of attorney if the person who writes it is in his right mind. Is it not a proof of right-mindedness to fear an enemy and trust a friend?"

"I concede your sanity, Nicolo, and I am your friend."

Nicolo drew out of his purse the document he had spent an hour engrossing that morning.

"When I went to see Piali, I feared that I might not obtain an audience with the governor. I felt sure that I should have to apply to a higher quarter for help. I took the liberty of presuming on your friendship, my friend, and this morning, even before I saw Piali, I made over to you my entire estate, enumerating all my possessions, even down to the names of my ships. I took considerable care," and he handed the document to Bernardi, "as you can see. I have even presumed to give you a little advice—not that you need advice—such as: 'Enter not into long-term contracts' and 'Keep fluid as much of my funds as you conveniently can, the times being disturbed,' and also, 'Purchase jewels if the profits on ordinary merchandise rise over 600 per cent net,' beyond which I have always considered profit hazardous. This is not a simple note, Filippo. It is a competent power of attorney that needs only to be witnessed. It is already signed. We can have it witnessed in the morning. Will you do this thing for me?"

Bernardi thought he would make some jest about the wildly unorthodox methods of certain businessmen, and then he thought he ought to protest again. But he read the solemn document, and ended by saying simply:

"I will do it, Nicolo."

IT TOOK some time next morning and a monumental bribe, which Bernardi paid, unknown to Nicolo, to find two reputable witnesses who could be trusted not to gossip about the extraordinary action of the merchant of Scutari.

To keep the witnesses silent, Bernardi engaged himself to pay them their bribes in weekly installments, graduated upward, so that the last installment, due about the time Nicolo would return and reclaim his property, was worth as much as all the others. After that it would not matter how much they talked. In fact, Bernardi reflected that any subsequent gossip could only redound to his credit, for he was aware that his reputation, however high from a commercial point of view, had sometimes suffered with regard to his humanity. It was true that he had often been called a stickler for the letter of a contract, a merciless driver of hard bargains. Would it be his fault if the witnesses prattled and, for once, spread a story about his generosity? Moreover, it was something for Bernardi, rich as he was, to have held absolute sway for a month over the wealth of the Lord of Montelupo.

Nicolo and his steward left Galata in the middle of the morning, immediately after the witnesses had signed their names to the power of attorney. Bernardi felt a little foolish holding in his hand all the worldly goods of his friend, who rode off on a mule, so out of keeping with his station in life, almost as if Bernardi had robbed him. But the Eastern Empire was so shrunken, Nicolo and his servant would so soon pass through it and be in Turkey again on the northern side, that there was no point in relinquishing their good mules now and riding horses to the border, only to be forced to relinquish them and ride on problematical Turkish mules the long, long rest of the way.

The road to Adrianople was a hundred and fifty miles long and a thousand years old. It was three feet thick, and it had been built when the whole civilized world spoke Latin. Greek was now the legal speech in the remnant of that nation which still called itself the Roman Empire of the East, though its frontier now stood but a few leagues beyond the walls of Constantinople, the ancient capital. In the vast area to the north, the conquerors spoke a mellifluent tongue that no true Roman had ever heard or had reason to fear; the musical idiom of the Osmanli Turks.

Neither Greeks nor Turks had ever repaired the old Roman road. On ridges in some places it stood like an aqueduct, the soil having eroded away from the sides. In a few low valleys the ancient stones could no longer be seen, because the mud of centuries had washed over them and solidified, forming a subsoil where trees had sprouted and grown to be centuries old, their roots striking deep among the huge old stones, slowly completing the ruin of the road. The surface was everywhere worn, pitted, and rough. A Roman legionnaire would have considered it a military menace. But it was the best road there was. The genius of the Greeks was theology. The genius of the Turks was administration. It was to remain for another people in a newer world to recapture the genius for building roads.

Now the gait of a mule is two and three-quarters miles per hour. Try as he would, Nicolo found that he could not spend more than ten hours a day on the back of his beast. More made his head swim. Nicolo supposed it was merely fatigue, the long hours, and the unaccustomed exercise. He reproached his servant who, unable to restrain his concern for his master, had suggested that they stop before sunset at one of the Turkish inns.

So, at noon on the seventh day they entered Adrianople, the sultan's capital, just as the muezzins were calling the faithful to prayer from the minarets of a score of mosques. Prudence as well as good manners required that a Gavour make himself as inconspicuous as possible at such a time.

They dismounted and stood motionless in the shadow of a building until the prayers were concluded. Then they remounted,

47

and Nicolo respectfully asked a beggar whether the gentleman could direct him to the house of the Jew, Yousuf the Prudent, and the beggar did so, very courteously.

Everyone knew Joseph. His house was unmistakable, very big, very black, and in an undesirable part of town.

Joseph greeted Nicolo with great friendliness and some concern, blessing him in Hebrew, wishing him peace, thinking perhaps he needed it. The rich, round words of the ancient tongue, so nearly identical with the Turkish *salaam aleikem,* yet curiously softer and more sonorous, rang with unfeigned sincerity.

The long ride and the dusty wind had spread a flush of pink suffused with a hint of blue over Nicolo's ordinarily pale countenance. It was a transparent color, wholly unlike the resplendent leathery tan on the steward's face. Nicolo could have commanded a hundred couriers to carry a message anywhere. That he had elected to ride personally into the heart of the Turkish Empire, at some cost, it was apparent, to his health, seemed a very suspicious circumstance to Yousuf the Prudent.

"Come into my house, signore," he said, "It shall shelter you as long as you care to remain. What brings you to Adrianople? Did you kill a man? He was a wicked one, to have died at the hand of my gentlest of all friends; and a great one, or Your Lordship would never have had to flee. You will be safe in my black house, unless—" The friendly concern on Joseph's face turned into fear. "Unless the rascal was a Turk. Say it was not a Turk, signore."

Nicolo smiled at him oddly. "Your Oriental imagination is running away with you, Joseph. I have killed no one. Yet." He told him what had happened. "Be assured that your hospitality is spent on neither a murderer nor a fugitive."

Joseph compressed his lips and said quietly, "In such a circumstance you were welcome were you both."

Nicolo answered: "My friend, I think I might have been. I am grateful."

"But I confess that I feel more at ease learning that the occasion of your visit is so simple a matter." He swung wide the polished ebony doors of his splendid house. They were massive and richly carved in deep floral relief. The ornamentation was orthodox to Islam and Israel alike, since it depicted neither man nor beast; the

48

material was socially proper, since it was black. The effect was magnificent.

"I shall be happy if the matter is a simple one. Piali said it would be simple, but I am afraid it will take a long time."

Joseph brushed the suggestion aside with both expressive hands. He said: "Even alone you could win your petition in a week. With a little help from me, you will win it tomorrow at the morning audience of His Majesty. Meanwhile, rest, my friend. Your journey must have wearied you. Refresh yourself." He laughed and said with suppressed pride, "I have recently had constructed in the cellar one of those Turkish baths that I have always enjoyed. Since I cannot go to the public ones, I have built my own. The vizier gave me specific permission on condition that I allow the paupers and mendicants that crowd the court on audience days to be washed in it before they are dressed to enter the Presence. Khalil Pasha knew, of course, that the beggars would be too proud to set foot in a black house. So I have the bath all to myself. There you shall be refreshed, signore. And then you shall dine in the apartments that are already being prepared for you. It will not be necessary for you to go up and down stairs at all today. You have already sufficiently exerted yourself. You shall not move a muscle except to eat and drink until we go to court tomorrow. Meanwhile we shall talk, and I shall tell you how simple the matter really is."

The mention of the bath was tempting. Nicolo, who was excluded from the public ones no less than Joseph, could have used the hot steam and the cold water; but he said: "I am still too troubled to relax. For a week I have thought of nothing but my petition. Even at night, exhausted as I always was, I would lie awake thinking about it. If the matter is simple, tell me at once why it is simple; and then perhaps tonight I can sleep."

"Well, then, friend, listen to me." Unbidden, a silent servant brought them sweet Greek wine in a crystal decanter, which Nicolo instantly recognized as some of the newest work of the artisans of his own city. It was worth a thousand ducats if it was worth a scudo. He wondered how Joseph dared live so luxuriously in Turkey. Joseph followed his glance and remarked parenthetically, "Few Turks ever come here; even fewer ever take a cup of wine. Be assured that the faithful, when they do, see only my silver. Glass is exquisite, isn't it, signore? Like youth, its fragility and impermanence lend it value. Perhaps when you return to Scutari you will allow me to present you with the decanter and the goblets, though I am aware how trifling a thing it is to give glass to a Venetian." He had thought Nicolo stared too long at the decanter.

"God forbid!" Nicolo said vehemently. "I've never had the new-fangled stuff around. My sailor servants would smash it. And now I've a superstitious fear of it. Do you know what the Turks call a janissary pasha? The kind that strut about the streets with selictars and horsetails? 'Statues of Glass' they call them, because they can be broken so easily. It is natural for a man in my situation to be apprehensive of anything reminiscent of the janissaries."

"Forgive me, signore. I should have remembered. I am growing old and careless. I have lived too secure too long. I am already in your debt because of the diamonds. Now I am doubly in your debt because you arrive in my house and remind me that I am Yousuf the Prudent. A mistake of this kind can ruin a man in Turkey."

"You paid me for the diamonds."

"But the vizier had reason to be delighted with them. There were quite a few left over when the lapidaries selected enough for the sultan's sword. Naturally Khalil Pasha kept them—for fear some of the others might fall out of their settings. I never said a word."

Nicolo said: "Did he also return a few to you? You were entitled to a commission, I should think."

"Well, no. Khalil Pasha never, ever, parted with anything once he got his hands on it. But he thanked me and promised to continue to show me favor. I was satisfied. Sometime, I knew, I would need his favor. Now I have decided that he himself shall sponsor your petition."

If such a remark had come to the ears of the sultan, the grand vizier would instantly have lost his place, Nicolo would have been thrown out of Turkey, and Joseph might very well have found his neck in a bowstring. *Sponsor a petition?* Since when did a petition to the Commander of the Faithful, Vice Regent of the Apostle of God, require a sponsor?

It had been a long time, though the pious Murad was unaware of it. In the early days of the empire it had been the custom for the sultan to sit at a rude, turbulent audience every morning, where anyone who desired a favor or had suffered a wrong might appeal personally to him for help. Since the reign of Osman it had been the boast of the Turkish emperor that no subject was so exalted as

50

to rise above the restraint of his justice, no beggar so lowly as to sink below its protection. Suits were brought with great speed and informality and settled, on the whole, with wisdom and good sense.

But the Turkish Empire now spread over two continents, a complex, active organism, intensely alive and still expanding. Only the outward form of the government preserved any resemblance to its primitive simplicity. Murad knew, of course, that his audiences were better behaved than those of his ancestors. But that every petition was phrased with meticulous care, after exhaustive consideration of its effect on his own temperament, he did not know. Nor did he know that the beggars were washed beforehand so as not to offend his sensitive nostrils, and clothed to appear less bedraggled. Murad was a good man, and set great store by his public audiences, but he was not and could not be as close to his people as he thought he was.

Nicolo said, "I had thought perhaps you yourself would sponsor my petition." The servant had taken away his empty crystal goblet and replaced it with one of gold. The glass decanter had disappeared.

Joseph shook his head. "It would never do, signore. His Majesty has often honored me in court by consulting me with regard to commercial matters. I owe the enmity of many men to his imperial condescension. But I cannot sponsor you. In Turkey a Jew cannot sponsor a Christian's cause without incurring a curious, reversed kind of suspicion. Everyone would think I was advancing some cause of my own in a roundabout manner. It will be more effective if Khalil Pasha himself sponsors you. You are seldom naïve, signore, but for a man who has lived so long in Scutari you are singularly guileless."

"I don't care who sponsors my petition so long as it is granted. As for living in Scutari, I am prepared to prove that I have never lived there, legally, at all."

"Good. That will please the vizier and make it easier for him. His wife is a Christian, you know; and it will look like the most likely thing in the world that he should sponsor you. What sort of proof?"

"Documentary proof; dated tax receipts, passports. Incontrovertible proof."

"That was wise of you. I shall show the papers to the vizier. Now let us get your petition written. You will hold it up when it is your turn to speak. The audiences are supposed to be spontaneous, but actually they are superbly regulated: a request for preferment usually follows a denial of outrage; financial matters always alternate with local administrative injustices, and so on. Your own plea will undoubtedly be considered a local administrative injustice, and I dare say it can be worked in directly after the request of the Pasha of Salonika, who is asking for funds to sink a new conduit into the hot springs of the neighborhood and build a big public bath. It is a foolish request. Murad would rather build mosques. I am confident it will be refused. The sultan, having refused a foolish request, will be in a mood to grant a just one."

"What must I do?"

"Say first: 'I am not so fortunate as to be a rayah of the Commander of the Faithful.' His Majesty fancies his ecclesiastical title. He affects disgust, and may feel it, that he has had to spend so many years of his reign fighting. He quotes constantly a verse of the Koran which says, 'Invite men by wisdom and mild exhortation; dispute gently with them,' or words to that effect, and complains that he has accomplished his prodigies over you Christians by a lifetime of battle rather than by the wisdom and mild exhortation his scriptures prescribe.

"Say next," Joseph counseled, " 'My son, Michael, is lost to me.' His Majesty will assume, of course, that Michael is dead, like Ala-ud-din, his own first-born, at whose death he once abdicated and retired among the dervishes of Magnesia. The sultan understands affliction. He will think you have come perhaps to beg permission to bury Michael. Say then, 'I desire my son returned to me.' Who would not? So does His Majesty desire Ala-ud-din. Then spring the surprise; say then, 'He has been illegally taxed into Your Majesty's janissary corps.' Make the usual obeisance and stop talking. Do you follow me?"

"Perfectly."

"Undoubtedly the sultan will simply ask the grand vizier whether you are a rayah. The grand vizier will have an answer. I shall arrange for Khalil Pasha to reply, 'No, Commander of the Faithful, he admits that he is a foreign Christian dog.' "

Joseph carefully explained, "You understand, signore, that 'Christian dog' is simply a form of speech, like 'Unspeakable Turk' and 'big fat Jew.' Some words just naturally follow each other by reason of long, long misuse. My own people have some very expressive

52

ones. We also apply them rather heedlessly. No offense should be taken."

"I know, I know. It isn't important."

"Then, I fancy, His Majesty will say: 'Lala'—that is what he calls Khalil Pasha when he is in a good mood, and his mood is wonderful these days—'Lala,' he will probably say, 'Varna has taught us that the word of a Christian swine is suspect. But let us remember that our own is inviolable. Restore the boy to his father, and may the mercy of Allah rest upon the father and the son and incline them soon to the true faith,' or some such pious remark. It will all be over. You will have won your suit. Your petition will have been granted. The order for Michael's release can be prepared beforehand. I tell you, Signore da Montelupo, this is exactly the sort of petition that Murad loves to grant; this is exactly the kind of wrong he loves to right.

"It is even possible," Joseph concluded enthusiastically, "that the Commander of the Faithful will send you back to Christendom on a horse!"

NICOLO spent an hour in Joseph's Turkish bath. It was faced with Persian tiles from floor to ceiling, cerulean blue at the base, rising course after course of lighter and lighter shades, spreading over the barrel vault of the roof in a smooth, cream-colored expanse like a warm, near, personal horizon. In a porphyry basin sunk in the center of the floor, a fountain of boiling water bubbled and seethed and threw out a cloud of wet white vapor, perfumed, Nicolo thought, with the odor of forest pine. It was a clean, invigorating scent. He forgot the dust that had stung his nostrils for seven days. Never had he breathed so easily. Never had his limbs felt so light and alive. He would have liked to linger in the cleansing, penetrating atmosphere, but an attendant appeared and said it was time for the cold room.

The man spoke respectfully. He was dressed in a togalike sheet and he had a towel wrapped round his head like any other bath attendant. His tone, however, was not quite that of a servant's.

"Madonna! Lord Nicolo," he said in excellent Italian, "Your Lordship will dissolve into a jelly and drain out into the gutters if you don't come out of the hot room!"

"And who are you, pray?" Nicolo asked. He was a little annoyed at the man who, to judge by his profanity, must be a Christian, for neither Jews nor Turks ever swore by the Virgin.

"Rodolfo," the attendant replied, "of Treviso," and from the way the fellow spoke Nicolo could not be quite certain whether he was announcing the Italian city as his birthplace or claiming it as his patrimony. Nicolo smiled, however, for it was good to meet an Italian in the heart of Turkey, regardless of his position. Rodolfo hastened to make his position clear. "Rodolfo of Treviso," he repeated, "to serve God and Your Lordship. Joseph, my master, has sent me to attend you. I am his personal physician. But come into the cold room, signore. Your feet are beginning to swell in this heat."

"Your master honors me," Nicolo said politely but rather absently, much as he might have spoken to his own steward. The craft of medicine was held in low esteem by the gentry of every civilized country, Moorish Spain only excepted, and there the Arab physicians had preserved for humanity some of the skill and much of the writing of pagan medical antiquity. "And do not worry about my feet, Messer Rodolfo. They are always that way. I'm just getting lazy and fat, that's all."

The air of the cold room was chilled by thin metal pipes full of running water from a deep natural spring. Nicolo felt as if he had suddenly entered a cave, and his teeth chattered at the change in temperature. Rodolfo doused him with a pailful of icy water and rubbed him till his skin shone pink.

"Your Lordship is in wonderful health," Rodolfo pronounced professionally, and indeed Nicolo thought he had never felt better or hungrier. The physician swathed his glowing body in a big thick towel and hustled him out of the cold room. "Except for Your Lordship's legs, which remained white too long after I struck them during the massage—and one still bears the imprint of my hand— Your Lordship might still be in his twenties."

Nicolo thanked the doctor, who then shaved him, combed his hair, and helped him dress. Nicolo ate a heavy supper.

That night, when he said his prayers, he thanked God for the good friend in Turkey who assured him so confidently that his petition would be granted. He slept deeply and contentedly, and the bad dreams that had plagued him all the way from Scutari were far from him. He did not dream at all.

At dawn he heard the muezzins calling the faithful to prayer: "Awake! Awake! Prayer is better than sleep!" and the ancient exhortation, "La illah il Allah, Mohammed roszul Allah!" The call came singing from every direction, chanted from all the mosques in Adrianople. At home the cry of the muezzins was far away, indistinct, half submerged by the sweet ringing of Constantinople's bells. Here in the Turkish capital, close, clear, and full of the feeling of power, the voices overwhelmed and menaced him. Still only half awake, he began to sweat in a sudden panic: his mission must have failed! He heard, or thought he heard, the *boom! boom! boom!* of the *hagiosidere* on the little Christian church. He was back in his gray house on the foothill of Bulgarlhu Dagh. But it was his own heart thumping in his ears. Nicolo raised his head from the pillow and saw where he was.

"Gesù!" he murmured and crossed himself. "I must have been dreaming again." He was dizzy for a moment and a little nauseated. He thought perhaps he had eaten too much supper.

Over the breakfast table Joseph said soothingly: "It is natural to be nervous at a time like this; but your apprehensions are groundless. I have good news. I saw Khalil Pasha last night while you were sleeping. Your steward is a faithful man, Nicolo. He slept across your doorsill, as if my house were full of murderers, and he told me you didn't stir all night. Do try to eat something. It may be a long morning. Everything is arranged. The order for Michael's release is already signed!"

"I thank God!"

Joseph nodded his head and said gravely: "Amen! We can also thank Khalil Pasha. He classes your petition as a local administrative injustice, as I thought he would; and you are to speak directly after the Pasha of Salonika is refused."

"He is certain to be refused?"

"Absolutely. Unless a miracle happens to Murad. The sultan sometimes signifies his refusal merely by shaking his head; but in the case of the Pasha of Salonika, both Khalil Pasha and I suspect that he may make a speech. It is enormously important that you do nothing unseemly. The beggars in the audience would tear you to pieces if, for example, you should interrupt His Majesty."

"I wouldn't do that even if he were just an ordinary man."

"I know you wouldn't. But you might make a slip. Murad sometimes hesitates, or meditates—at any rate he pauses. You may think he has finished. Also, there is considerable ceremony and etiquette at the court here. You may not be familiar with all of it. You must speak at precisely the right moment. Now, Khalil Pasha has a habit of stroking his beard. He does it very gravely, and it makes him

56

appear enormously wise; but this morning he will stroke his beard only once, after the case of the Pasha of Salonika is decided and he knows the sultan has finished speaking. Watch the grand vizier closely. When he touches his beard, that is the signal for you to raise your petition and call attention to yourself. Khalil Pasha will notice you, nod to you, and you will begin to speak. It is all arranged, all very simple. Just do not move or talk until you see the signal. Now won't you eat?"

But Nicolo could not eat. The ghost of the note of the *hagiosidere* still thumped in his ears. He would have traded an extra year in purgatory, and he was a shrewd trader, for a draught of brandy or even a cup of wine. But it was not proper to go to the court of the Brother of the Sun with liquor on one's breath. So Nicolo drank several cups of coffee; but the strong stimulant only made the *hagiosidere* boom louder in his head. He began to sweat again as they entered the outer court of the palace.

Visitors of rank were met at the gate by high officials and domestics of the palace and conducted into the throne room with every mark of respect and, if they were important enough, with very elaborate ceremonial.

But on audience days when, as Murad thought, anyone could see the sultan, the gates were thrown wide open. The proud lines of janissaries sheathed their scimitars and held their white-turbaned heads a little lower than usual, looking with well simulated meekness at the heterogeneous throng of petitioners who had come to seek justice or favors from the sultan.

Today Murad himself, as he often did, watched them as they passed into the inner court. He sat behind a black gossamer veil that hung from one of the arches of the palace balcony. Through it he could see the people, but they could not see him.

Black was not always the color of degradation in Turkey. Applied to the sultan, it had a holy significance. Black had been the color of the garments of the incredibly sacrosanct caliphs of Baghdad, whose successor Murad was acknowledged to be. Black, too, were the heron tops on his turban, signifying to Islam the three empires of the world, different ones than the Christians recognized: Babylon, Trebizond, Constantinople. Only the plumes of the herons of Candia were black enough, perfect enough, lustrous enough for the sultan's turban. A jeweled clasp of gold wrought into the shape of a crescent held them in place.

The sultan saw the Pasha of Salonika, a standard-bearer proudly holding erect the painted spear from which the pasha's three horse-tails proclaimed his high rank. Adrianople was a long way from Salonika. Murad wondered what had brought the testy old fighter so far. Murad also saw one of his Jewish advisers, a wizard at finance, a faithful rayah, Yousuf, whom he himself had named The Prudent. The Prudent One had a gray-clad Christian with him, with wild black eyes and a mottled countenance. The sultan thought of Mara, his Christian wife. For the first time in the history of the Ottoman dynasty, one of his line had allowed a Christian chapel to be built in the palace. Mara never gave up her religion.

The sultana one day had attempted to explain to her husband the mystery of the Christian sacraments, and had likened them to his turban: "They are composed, my dear lord, of an outward, visible part, like the white folds of my lord's very distinguished headdress; and an inward, invisible part, like the red felt conical cap around which the scarf is wound."

"And the heron tops, my treasure of a woman?"

Mara had looked at the three magnificent plumes, and diplomatically repressed a reference to the Holy Trinity.

"My lord, I do not know."

Murad had chuckled. "You speak with a woman's contempt for detail, or perhaps with Christian equivocation; for you seem to forget that the fez protrudes a hand's breadth above the folds of the scarf. It is not invisible. Leave me my turban, pearl in my breast, and I'll leave you your sacraments. There is absolutely no resemblance."

"There is not, my dear lord," Mara had slyly replied.

Murad had looked at her sharply.

"Allahim," he prayed, "make me strong, my Allah, to preserve my integrity, that I swerve not from righteousness for the love that I bear the sultana and her son."

Most of the petitioners, of course, Murad did not recognize; but it seemed to him that the beggars looked less ragged than usual.

Machmut, the Beglerbey of Roum, whose title meant Prince of the Princes of Turkey-in-Europe, one of the sultan's attendants that day, was standing directly behind him.

58

"The beggars look happier today," Murad observed.

Machmut, who had the concession for their clothing, instantly answered: "They dwell in the warmth of Your Majesty's smile, they can never be cold; and the prosperity Your Majesty brings to his empire reaches down even to these mendicants."

"How are you so sure they're so warm?" Murad looked accusingly at his exalted servant.

The sultan was actually reproving Machmut only for an overflowery remark; but Machmut's conscience was heavy with the guilty thought of how he stripped the clothes from the beggars' backs after each audience and sold them again to a new batch of petitioners every audience day.

"Inshalla, if it please God, they are warm, Your Majesty—because so many clothes are now available from the infidels slain at Varna."

One could never be sure how much Murad knew. Machmut's left eye, afflicted with a slight congenital droop, almost closed. He was nervously making a mental note that the next beggars to appear before the sultan should look somewhat less prosperous.

"I shall go down now," Murad said.

His throne was not a throne as thrones were known in Europe, but rather a raised dais backed by a low rail, about four feet wide, that he could lean against. The dais was covered, according to the needs of the occasion, by one of eight sets of draperies. For the ambassadors of Constantinople it was black velvet embroidered with huge pearls of incomparable luster, some round, some oval, some button shaped. For the ambassadors of the Republic of Venice it was white, ablaze with rubies and emeralds set in bezels so as to display them to advantage and keep them from falling out. Some coverings, of course, were merely velvets of different colors embroidered with gold. And one was a simple gold brocade with no embroidery at all, reserved for weak and little known nations like England and the Khanate of Lesser Tartary; for the sultan knew how to level his own magnificence gracefully to that of the princes he would honor.

No diplomatic receptions were scheduled on audience days. The throng of petitioners who clustered around Murad's throne were all Turks or rayahs, or at least persons living in his empire and subject to his laws. It was characteristic of Murad's paternal care for his subjects that, for such a gathering, the throne was draped in its most gorgeous covering, the black one with the pearls, not out of vanity, but in the conviction that nothing was too good for his own people.

There was a balcony round the throne room, and in each arch stood a tall, silent janissary in a long military tunic of deep blue. These were Murad's bodyguards. They stood with one hand on their bows in identical postures, motionless as statues. Their position was so easy that they appeared to be resting, one hand behind their backs. Murad knew he was guarded, but he had no idea how well. There were thirty-one arches in the balcony, thirty-one janissaries, and the floor of the throne room below was divided into thirty-one imaginary squares. Each apparently casual guard had his own little square assigned to him, and he watched it like a hovering eagle searching the ground below for a mouse. In less than a second any guard could have shot an arrow into the eye of any man in the room. For the hand behind each janissary held a ready arrow.

An almost imperceptible stiffening of the janissary guards on the balcony signified to the waiting audience that the emperor was about to enter the room. A hush fell over the people. The great silver doors swung open and the Capi-Aga, Grand Master of Ceremonies, in a tunic of blue embroidered with silver, carrying his ebony staff, stepped into the audience chamber. There followed five officials, whose Turkish titles and imperial offices tangled the tongues and bemused the brains of visiting emissaries from Western nations whenever they attempted to fathom the intricacies of Turkish protocol.

They were: the Kizlar Agassi, Grand Master of the Virgins, a black eunuch in charge of the imperial harem; the Chokadar-Aga, Grand Porter of the Royal Robe, a white eunuch; the Hazada-Bashi, Imperial Grand Chamberlain; the Rikabdar, Stirrup Holder to the Sultan; and the Selictar-Aga, the Imperial Sword-Bearer, who today proudly carried the new sword that Khalil Pasha had given the sultan. It was sheathed because the empire was at peace. The jewels in the scabbard blazed like a constellation in the Selictar-Aga's hands.

Then followed Murad himself, in full court dress of black velvet consciously reminiscent of the sober, holy costume of the ancient Arabian caliphs of Baghdad: the ample sleeves, the long skirts of the tunic. But the overmantle was stiff with embroidery, and so covered with ermine and pearls as to appear white. The heron tops on his turban nodded as he walked. His face was calm, contemplative, and a

60

trifle thin. He was known to make the Great Fast severely. Under the voluminous robes of state the body of the sultan was slight.

After Murad came the Aga of the Janissaries, the only man in the empire not required to cross his arms on his breast in the Oriental posture of submission when speaking to his sovereign. And beside him walked Khalil Pasha, the Grand Vizier. He wore the most spectacular costume in the whole imperial procession. It was a long robe of white satin, heavy with flashing embroidery stitched out in thread-of-silver and trimmed with Siberian sables. His turban was twenty-five inches high, composed, not of cloth, but of white felt, shaped like a cone cut off at the top, and distinguished by a four inch band of gold running diagonally down from right to left.

Khalil Pasha was the most powerful official in the empire, but no one ever envied a grand vizier. An inquisitive Greek, after studying the life expectancy of all the grand viziers since the reign of the first Osman, had come to the interesting mathematical conclusion that their tenure of office amounted to an average of three and a half years. It was notorious that they were usually assassinated by enemies or strangled by their imperial masters.

Immediately on the entrance of Murad into the room, the people prostrated themselves, touching their foreheads to the floor. They rose again and crossed their arms against their breasts when he sat down, cross-legged, upon his throne. The officials grouped themselves behind him, except for the grand vizier and the master of ceremonies, who stood close at his right and left hand respectively, so as to be available if the sultan wished advice on any of the petitions, as he usually did.

Then, for three hours, with great decorum and speed, the people presented their troubles, their injustices, and their requests for money or preferment to the personal adjudication of their sovereign. Murad treated them all, rich and poor, beys and beggars, with equal gravity.

Joseph, having placed Nicolo in a position at the edge of the crowd under one of the arches where he could see the face of the grand vizier, prudently left his friend standing alone, in order that their drab, infidel clothing might not be too conspicuous.

Nicolo had not anticipated that simply standing on his feet with his arms crossed would fatigue him so. In an hour he began to be envious of one of the crippled petitioners who by reason of his infirmity not only did not have to stand but was given a cushion to sit upon by one of the court functionaries at the express order of Murad. Moreover, although scores of cases had been decided, no one was allowed to leave the room before the sultan. The air became stifling. Nicolo was tired. His head ached painfully, and his eyes smarted from staring too fixedly at the grand vizier's hand. Nicolo was afraid to blink lest the grand vizier stroke his beard in the fraction of a second while his lids were closed. He thought: We shall not sleep, but we shall all be changed, in a moment, in the twinkling of an eye . . . in the twinkling of an eye we shall be changed. . . . Now why did I think of that? Nicolo could hear the *hagiosidere* in his ears again, booming louder and thumping, as if the church were marching over the plains of Turkey, coming to Adrianople.

Murad noticed the Christian at the edge of the crowd and recognized him as the companion of Yousuf the Prudent, whom he had observed through the black veil. It was not unusual for foreigners, unaccustomed to Turkish etiquette, to grow faint during the long audiences. For an instant Murad thought of speaking directly to the rayah who stood so rigidly, like a dervish in a trance.

But the newly appointed governor of Varna had begun to present a complicated request that had to do with the disposition of some foreign ships confiscated after the battle. The sultan forgot about Nicolo, decreeing that only such ships as had carried contraband were to be retained. The others, of all nations, were to be returned to their rightful owners.

The *hagiosidere* was very close now, booming and throbbing in Nicolo's ears. He could hear nothing else. He was not aware that his ships had just been returned to him. They must have a new priest, Nicolo thought confusedly. The old fellow could never strike so hard.

At length the Pasha of Salonika made his request for the new conduits and the big new public bath. During the siege of Salonika fourteen years before, he had suffered a wound in his shoulder, and it still ached most of the time. Murad knew about the wound. He was sorry for the old soldier, and grateful for his military services in the past. But he also knew, though the pasha did not know it, that Salonika's governor had a favorite Greek physician who prescribed large quantities of a strong potion that was nine-tenths wine and one-tenth physic, and that the pasha got roaring drunk three times a week on this pleasant infidel regimen.

Murad chose not to reprove the governor. I shall be forced to remove him if he gets too obnoxious, he thought, but while I leave him in power I must protect his reputation.

He refused the request for the new bath. Murad had a shrewd notion that the pasha wanted it to use as a personal little meeting place for himself and some of his cronies. Under the guise of treating his old wound in the privacy of the *hamam,* they could drink the Greek physician's medicine to their hearts' content. The Greeks were insidious. Long after you conquered them, you had to be on your guard lest the vices that had ruined them ruin you, too. The sultan condescended, however, to give as a reason the much greater need of the city for an adequate supply of pure drinking water and the urgent necessity for strengthening the walls in several places.

Instead of being ashamed at his sovereign's refusal, the truculent old pasha dared to remonstrate, raising his voice and quoting the Prophet, "God loveth the clean!"

Murad was intensely irritated at such impudence, particularly the torturing of the sacred scripture, out of context, to prove a selfish point.

He called for the Koran.

This holy book not only provided spiritual guidance for all good Moslems, but also set forth the civil law by which they lived. Many old laws, of course, were obsolete. The injunction against killing one's girl children, for example, was no longer necessary. By the same token many new laws had had to be devised since the Prophet's time to regulate situations that the Prophet could never have envisaged, since men advance and times change. But no law contrary to the precepts of the Koran could be enacted, nor would it have been obeyed. The Koran was the constitution of Islam. The book was always on hand in every court of law. There was a splendid imperial copy at Murad's assemblies.

The master of ceremonies presented it to the sultan on a large green cushion with green and gold tassels at each of the four corners.

Murad, looking directly at the Pasha of Salonika, said gravely, "It is not right to pronounce a phrase or two of the Holy Apostle's words and apply them to one's proposition without taking into consideration what went before and what comes after."

Khalil Pasha, his face profoundly inscrutable, glanced quickly at Joseph the Prudent, whose face was equally expressionless. Joseph lifted his left eyebrow ever so slightly. The grand vizier allowed his shoulders to rise and settle again an eighth of an inch, shadow of a ghost of a still-born shrug. "Here comes the speech," they were saying to each other.

The sultan continued: "God loveth the clean, indeed, but there are also certain injunctions in the chapter entitled 'The Night Journey' which nullify the interpretation you have placed upon the holy words. To cleanse yourself it is not necessary to build a huge public building in Salonika."

And to prove it, and not quote a verse out of context, the Sultan read the entire seventeenth chapter of the Koran. It concerned the journey of Mohammed through the seven heavens to the presence of God and back again to Mecca the same night. When the sultan came to the words "Thou canst not cleave the earth," he paused, looking sternly at the Pasha of Salonika. It was evident to everyone in the room that the scriptures forbade the governor to sink the conduits, since to have done so would have required some cleavage of the earth. But Murad continued on through the nine miracles of Moses to the end of the chapter. Then he kissed the book and returned it to the Capi-Aga.

Inwardly the Pasha of Salonika seethed. He prayed five times a day like everybody else! He went to the mosque every Friday, never missing a day! Why was he subjected to this?

It was after eleven o'clock when the sultan concluded his salutary, penitential recital of Holy Writ. He would have to hurry if all the petitioners were to be satisfied before noonday prayers; but his throat was dry, his voice was hoarse, and he called for a drink of water.

In Osman's time when the sultan was thirsty, a page turned his back on his sovereign, sprinted out of the room, and brought him a drink of water.

But for Murad II to slake his thirst he had to tell the Master of Ceremonies, who told a page, who told two more pages. One of them walked off to collect fifty aspers from the Treasurer of the Petty Enjoyments, while the other notified the Imperial Cup Bearer (one of the white eunuchs), who thereupon filled a huge golden cup with water, collected his traditional fee, publicly signed a receipt for it, and bore the chalice before his face into the Presence, calling softly

"Su! Su!" (Water! Water!) Two additional pages, one at either side, supported his arms, for the imperial chalice was very heavy. They also served to guide him through the crowd, since he held the cup so high that it was difficult for him to see where he was going. Then the sultan could drink.

The ceremony was colorful and impressive. The crowd loved it. But it was time consuming. Khalil Pasha began to wonder whether there would be an opportunity for the presentation of the Venetian merchant's petition, which Yousuf the Prudent had mentioned to him the night before.

After drinking the water, the sultan looked away from the Pasha of Salonika. The grand vizier decided that that incident was at an end.

Khalil Pasha stroked his beard.

Nothing happened.

He stroked it again, searching at the edge of the crowd where Nicolo had stood so long and rigidly. The gray figure was no longer there.

Suddenly there was a shout from the spot where the Christian had been standing. He was discovered sprawled on the floor in an ungainly attitude, half hidden by one of the pillars that supported the balcony. His mouth was twisted to one side, his eyes were open, and his breathing had stopped. Long before the court physician arrived, every one in the room knew that a Gavour had had the impertinence to die in the presence of the Commander of the Faithful. Joseph, who hurried at once to Nicolo's side, assumed that the pageantry of the eunuch with the golden cup had so absorbed the people's attention that no one had seen Nicolo fall. With far less ceremony than had been occasioned by the sultan's drink of water, Nicolo's body was carried out of the throne room. Death profaned the sultan's palace almost as seriously as it did a mosque. The spot on the pavement where Nicolo died was instantly purified with rose water.

Joseph asked for the body of his friend. It was not practicable to send it back to Christendom even if Joseph had known who could receive it. Nicolo was a widower. Michael was his only relative as far as Joseph knew, and Michael's whereabouts was a mystery. So Joseph obtained permission to bury Nicolo in the churchyard of Virgin Saint Mary, a little spot of obscure, consecrated ground on the bank of the river Tunja, far outside the walls, where no one could see the crosses.

Yousuf the Prudent prepared a manifest of everything Nicolo had brought with him, down to the smallest article of clothing, down to the common ropes that had been used to hobble the mules at night. He gave the sorrowing steward a gift that made him independent for life and dispatched him with Nicolo's baggage back to Bernardi in Galata with a heavy guard whose wages he paid out of his own purse.

Then he rent his garments with the vehemence of a biblical patriarch, far deeper than the little ceremonial slit which the custom of his religion prescribed, remembering the deathless hope of his people, chanted in a hundred nations, solemnly down the ages:

Go thou thy way till the end: for thou shall rest, and stand in thy lot at the end of the days.

The Lord hath given; the Lord hath taken away; blessed be the name of the Lord.

66

CHAPTER
8

EVEN if Nicolo and his son had been able to escape to their ship in the Propontis, it is not likely that Michael would have grown to manhood in his father's house in Venice. Western boys everywhere left their homes at Michael's age or thereabouts.

If their fathers were artisans, they were apprenticed into the shops of other artisans to learn a trade in another town. If their fathers were noble, they went as pages into distant castles of friends or relatives to learn manners and the use of arms, eventually to become squires and knights. The plausible conviction that nothing is too good for a son but that he learns more quickly under stricter discipline than a father is likely to enforce was fundamental to the medieval mind, and, in the magnificent public schools of the English, persisted for centuries after feudalism was to disappear.

As yet, however, the strange new restlessness which would one day sweep into history the immemorial usages of chivalry, stigmatize the period by the name of the Dark Ages, and itself become known as the Renaissance had scarcely touched Italy. Elsewhere in Europe it had not been felt at all.

Therefore a relative, it Michael had had any, would have been less grieved by his absence from home, which had to be expected shortly anyway, than by a certain aspect of his education. It was the great age of Christian faith. It would have been a hard thing for a relative to know that Michael had become a Moslem. But since

Michael was left an orphan by his father's death, there was no relative to fret himself over the lad's new religion.

Few Europeans knew very much about janissaries except that they were intrepid fighters; they were seldom taken alive in battle, and they were deadly accurate shots with their quick-firing long-range bows. Eastern Europeans, closer to the perpetually expanding frontiers of the Ottoman Empire, knew them better, and reluctantly admired them, so far as an enemy could be admired. The Byzantine Greeks especially were at a loss to explain the janissaries' high code of personal honor, their invulnerability to corruption, and their contented acceptance of celibacy. These Byzantines, who knew them best, despairingly attributed such devastating virtues to some secret, unholy wisdom bestowed by the Devil himself and imparted by the Turkish teachers.

Actually the education of a janissary was diabolical only in its efficiency. The teachers were the ablest men in Murad's empire. Their intelligent, concentrated discipline had been particularly fruitful in forming Michael's character.

At least, so thought Hassan of Ulubad, his closest friend, a giant of a man, who had once been utterly contemptuous of the awkward, homesick, Italian rayah boy who had turned up in the train of the Tournaji Bashi of Scutari five years before.

Hassan recalled distinctly that Michael had hardly been able to ride a horse—not that a Christian could be expected to ride anything but a mule—but now Michael could throw his turban to the ground, gallop past it, and catch it on the point of his spear so deftly that he didn't even puncture the cloth. This was a trick Hassan had taught him. By a reversal of the technique involved—and this, of course, was the value of the exercise—you could penetrate the hard steel armor into which the Gavour knights foolishly locked themselves.

Janissaries were traditionally infantrymen, and in battle they fought on foot. But in the year 1449 the cleavage between the janissary foot and the spahi horse was not complete. It was Murad's boast, in the later years of his reign, that both his favorite army corps were skilled in each other's weapons.

Michael's memory of his first day in camp was fuzzy and confused, but Hassan remembered it clearly. Michael, along with some other recruits, had been assigned to his barrack. It was customary to sep-

68

arate boys from the same town so that cliques would not form. Michael had been very ill behaved, he remembered, protesting angrily that he was no rayah boy and that this was not his idea of a holiday. It took some weeks for Hassan to find out what he meant by its being a holiday. Then he learned from the captain-bashi that Michael's father had worked a silly ruse on the boy, telling him he was just going for an outing so he wouldn't be frightened. Why hadn't the father told Michael the truth? After all, it was an honor.

The captain-bashi himself condescended to explain the deception to Michael. It was not an unusual circumstance, and he had a stock answer, planned, like all the other indoctrination that Michael had been subjected to for the past five years, to appeal to his manhood.

"Your good father didn't realize what a brave man you are." (The captain-bashi had with calculation said "man.") "He thought you'd be afraid to leave home." (That was for Michael's pride.) "We don't take everyone, you know. Only one in five. We want only the best men," he looked pleasantly at Michael, "like you. Your father is a rayah" (and the captain-bashi thought he was telling the truth), "and he's glad you're here, for his own sake as well as yours. I'm glad, too. I'm told you like to shoot. Well, Michael, you're going to have your choice, now, of hundreds of Turkish bows, the finest, most powerful in the world!" That was Michael's first taste of the glittering promises that were systematically held out to a janissary to fire his ambition.

Since a part of what the captain-bashi said was true, Michael reasoned rather foggily that it might all be true; but when he lay down that night in Hassan's barrack, he was homesick, confused, and extremely perplexed that his father had not been absolutely honest with him.

Because he never heard from his father, the conviction grew on him, as months passed, that he actually was a rayah like all the other new recruits. It would have pained Nicolo to have witnessed how quickly his place in his son's affections was taken, first by his wrestling master, a eunuch named Korkud, who switched him smartly whenever he failed to throw the boy he had been paired off with that day, and gave him a sweetmeat when he won. There was always a sweetmeat for the winner and a switching for the loser. The switch, a slender wand of willow painted white, was the badge of

69

the eunuch's authority. It hurt, but not so much as losing the contest or the sweetmeat, which was precisely the intention.

After he ceased to idolize Korkud, Michael's hero became the captain-bashi himself, tall, bronzed, gray in the mustache, his tunic formal, long, and trimmed with fur like those of the visiting pashas who sometimes inspected the camp. Michael nursed the hope that some day, when he grew older, he too would be a captain-bashi, and once, in Hassan's hearing, he voiced such an ambition to another boy. It was perhaps a year after he had first come to camp.

Now Hassan was neither particularly friendly nor antagonistic toward him at the time. He had noticed that Michael was doing as well as anyone, running, jumping, wrestling, riding, shooting his arrows accurately and growing very rapidly. But he knew the remark was important. He was well trained. He had handled recruits for a long time. He instantly reported to the captain-bashi.

"Michael, the boy from Scutari, is ambitous, Effendi," he said, and painstakingly repeated Michael's remark, word for word. "Perhaps if the captain-bashi could see his way clear to notice him—"

"Mashallah! That is good, Hassan. Thank you for telling me."

That night Michael sat among the others on the ground in the chilly air close to the roaring fire over which their supper cooked in a huge bronze caldron. These caldrons were precious and close to the hearts of the janissaries. They carried them in parades. An honorable significance attached to them. They stood outside the door of the barracks in camp and outside the commander's tent in the field. Michael sat cross-legged—he had forgotten how to sit in a chair—eating a ragout of mutton and rice when the captain-bashi walked into the firelight. All the young men set down their wooden bowls and jumped to their feet. They stood respectfully with their hands at their sides, lowering their eyes, not as far as the captain-bashi's yellow-shod feet, as they would have done for a pasha of three horsetails, but to about the level of his splendid silken girdle, from which his scimitar swung and swayed as he walked.

He went straight to Michael. "Is the ragout good?" he asked pleasantly.

Michael had never known him to speak so informally to one of the men. He quickly crossed his arms over his chest, swallowed a mouthful of mutton, forgot the captain-bashi's title and stammered, "Excellency, it is excellent!"

70

The captain-bashi smiled, nodded, and walked slowly out of the firelight, which colored his white turban first yellow, then orange, then red, the diminishing illumination running down through the spectrum as he disappeared majestically into the darkness.

Most of the awed youths congratulated Michael on his good fortune. None of them had ever been singled out to be spoken to. One little Greek boy, somewhat older than Michael, but not so tall, muttered: "You're just currying favor. Go get cut!" (You're not a man; you ought to be a eunuch.) "The captain-bashi is 'Effendi,' not 'Excellency,' and you know it!" Michael was too overwhelmed to heed the criticism; but he had made an enemy who might have caused him trouble if he had remained that winter in the Brusa camp.

The captain-bashi noticed the "Excellency," too. "Michael is a little *too* ambitious," he observed to Hassan of Ulubad. "I think it is time for his country training."

After the captain-bashi, the man who most nearly took the place of a father in Michael's affection was the venerable hodja who taught him the Koran. And after all these emotional transferences, Michael had only a vague, tender memory locked up in his heart of a father who had forsaken him. Many of the young men had similar memories, but they were never encouraged by their preceptors to speak of their former lives, as if somehow they had not been quite honorable; and after a time they did not mention the subject even among themselves. They were becoming statues of glass, more completely than the man who had made the epigram had realized. Glass that could, indeed, be broken at a blow by the power which favored them and raised them to their eminence; but glass also by reason of a certain brittleness in their hearts. Hard as glass.

The hodja was a scholarly old man with a double right to wear the green turban. First, he had made the pilgrimage to Mecca; second, he was an Arab whose genealogy indisputably traced directly back to the energetic Apostle of God, like that of so many of his countrymen. In Arabia he might have begged a profitable living on the streets. All good Moslems must support the descendants of the Prophet, no matter how lazy or disreputable they might be. The injunction was ancient and the custom was religiously observed. But Abdullah the hodja was neither lazy nor disreputable.

He had been chosen as preceptor to the sultan's new recruits, not only for his fluency in their many European tongues and for his

71

theological attainments (which were considerable), but also because he had a large family of his own by his four wedded wives and the several slaves of his household. Despite his own advanced years, he was a man who knew and admired youth.

He would sit on a clean mat of plaited rushes, the Koran open on a low wooden stand before his crossed legs. The young janissaries sat respectfully and attentively before him, repeating after him the difficult, explosive Arabic syllables, while the hodja beat time with his long extended forefinger to emphasize the poetic rhythm of the words. Then he would translate the verse into Turkish, which they all already spoke with varying degrees of excellence, so that while they were learning Arabic and religion they were also perfecting themselves in the speech that they would have to use all the rest of their lives. Sometimes he would speak Greek to them. Greek was the native language of about half of them.

"It is wise to know the language of the enemy," he would murmur.

And from time to time he would teach them Persian, that other important branch of the Turkish humanities, "because," he would say, "you are gentlemen, and Persian is an elegant tongue, much spoken at the court of the Commander of the Faithful, whom God bless and preserve."

They would make the response, "Whom God bless and preserve." Everyone knew how frail the sultan's health was.

"A governor-pasha of three horsetails, or a grand vizier, who has five, must speak Persian as a matter of course," the hodja might remind them if they were lax in their studies. None of the instructors, from Hassan of Ulubad to Abdullah the hodja, ever missed an opportunity to remind his charges that any man in the empire, save only the sultan himself, might one day stand humbly before a janissary with arms crossed in the posture of obedience. Exposed to such potent appeals to their pride and ambition, it is no wonder that a period of country training was necessary.

Michael had little difficulty with the languages, since, having lived so long in Scutari, he already knew Turkish and Greek. But the hodja detected in his dark, intelligent eyes more than the usual confusion which the students always displayed after the first few readings from the Koran.

The earlier lectures came from portions of the scriptures that any

72

Christian might read with easy faith and conviction; for they merely praised God, affirming His goodness, mercy, and forgiveness with matchless eloquence. Later came the lessons that stressed the unity of God, and that, too, was nothing to shock a Christian. Then came the praises of the Virgin, Her immaculate conception, Her chastity, Her faith, Her devotion, Her obedience; and it began to appear to the students as if Islam and Christianity were, after all, very much alike.

Ultimately, of course, came the Moslem doctrine touching Her Son, which, while it placed Him on a par with all the Old Testament prophets, specifically contradicted everything else that Michael had ever learned about the Lord. It was then that the alert hodja thought he observed resentment and incredulity in Michael's eyes.

He was far too able a pedagogue to make an issue of Michael's inarticulate rebellion. He simply shifted a little the order of his lectures:

"Tomorrow," he said gravely, closing the book and wrapping it carefully in its scarf of blazing ciclatoun, "tomorrow I shall teach you how a regrettable error in the reading of a single letter in a single word has blinded the Christian nations to a prophecy of the Prophet Jesus, who foretold *by name* the coming of Mohammed, the Apostle of God."

And the next day he did, to everyone's satisfaction, even Michael's who was excited that day because he had been given a bow for his own. Not merely a bow in the arms room, assigned to him to practice with and care for. A bow in his own right, his own property, the only property he possessed in the world.

The Turkish bow was a beautiful object, exquisitely shaped like the upper lip of a girl. It was formed of horn, wood, and sinew, in that order from front to rear. Michael's weighed seventy pounds, which is to say that a pull of seventy pounds was required to draw the string to the shoulders. He would draw a hundred-pound bow, like Hassan of Ulubad, by the time he and Hassan were friends. Contemporary English longbows, wreaking such havoc in France, could just shoot three hundred yards. Michael's sinuous Oriental bow could kill a man at that distance. It bent forward when it was unstrung. Strung, it was in a state of stress even before the arrow was drawn. Michael learned to draw the bow using the ancient Mongolian "loose" which the Turks had brought with them out of the

73

depths of Asia. It was a method of drawing with the thumb, a technique typical and characteristic of the East. To protect his thumb, which otherwise would have become chafed, Michael had whittled himself a wooden thumb ring. Some of the older men had very elaborate and decorative thumb rings.

The purpose of the country training, to which every young janissary was subjected as soon as he displayed any spirit, was to teach humility. For nearly a third of his life, Michael had lived in a camp composed half of rapidly developing boys, half of seasoned fighters; but the personnel of the latter was constantly shifting, and with them the boys had little contact. For nearly a third of his life, since he first learned to make up his turban under the critical, perfectionist eye of the barber-eunuch, he had been daily reminded that he was a man set apart from the ordinary run of the sultan's subjects. His mission in life was special, honorable, predestined. The training for it had been severe. Even his sleep at night was noisy, for a functionary clattered all night long over the alleyway in the barrack on noisy wooden clogs, to train the boys to sleep without the luxury of quiet. To prevent their becoming conditioned to the rattle of the clogs, the noises were constantly varied: a loud monologue, a cacophonous jangling of kitchen utensils, interminable singing, and every so often the clash of swords, which brought every boy instantly out of his roll of blankets, wide awake and alert, ready for action.

And periodically the hodja would remind them that they were gentlemen. Throughout a boy's rigorous training he was educated in the elaborate Eastern punctilio of courtesy to his comrades and to his masters. Rome, old and new, was the ideal, the mentor, and the adversary of the Ottoman Empire. If it takes centuries to build an imperial city, reasoned the Turks, it may legitimately take years to build an imperial soldier, which they set about to do with Oriental finesse and imprejudice. The result was the education of a janissary.

It would have been unnatural if such solicitude did not develop unweaning pride or inordinate selfish ambition, and the country training was designed to offset both these undesirable characteristics as soon as they appeared. In Michael's case it was a little too much ambition, which the captain-bashi thought he detected in the too grand title, the fumbling remark, "Excellency, it is excellent."

Therefore, instead of going to a rich country estate for his period of servanthood, Michael was sent for a year as a hired hand on the

74

rocky farm of a poor Anatolian peasant. This man had only one wife. His temper was soured because in twenty years of industrious married life his wife had produced but a single child, and that child was a girl.

The joy of the peasant at the prospect of a free laborer was tempered by his knowledge that at any time a sergeant from the Brusa camp might pay an unexpected call to check up on the condition of the sultan's janissary. He shuddered at the thought of what would happen to him if, for example, the discipline he was permitted to exercise over the young man should result in a broken bone.

"Whipping will be adequate if he needs punishment," the sergeant had said when he brought Michael to the farm. "Whipping will not injure the limbs, which are engaged only temporarily in removing the rocks from your desolate fields. After that they will do nobler things."

The farmer observed that his fields held only such rocks as Allah had chosen to create there, and that perhaps rocks were written on his forehead, where every man's fate is written.

"Maim him not," the sergeant cautioned. "Actually, I don't think you'll have to punish him often. Usually he's a good lad."

The farmer would have preferred a stockier one. He said rather peevishly: "His Imperial Majesty honors me with a young soldier-servant who is skinnier than a dervish after the fast. These tall thin ones have terrible appetites. If he doesn't gain weight, he'll be too weak to work. If I build him up so he does gain weight, there'll be nothing left for me and my family to eat. The Merciful One has not blessed either my land or my wife with productiveness."

It revolted the polished janissary officer to hear the farmer, in defiance of all good manners, mention a woman of his household.

The sergeant said shortly: "His diet is your affair. I'll drop around once in a while to see him."

"How well I know that, Effendi. How well I know! And if there's so much as a bruise on his little finger, I know you'll strangle me with your girdle!"

"With a bowstring," the sergeant corrected pleasantly. Only people of some consequence were strangled with the girdle. "Not, however, if Michael has been disobedient."

"I shall do my poor best to deserve the honor that God and the

75

sultan have seen fit to bless me with," the farmer said with no enthusiasm.

The sergeant gave him a purse, the gift that always accompanied the honor. And the farmer gave the sergeant a cool cup of sherbet. The sergeant sipped it, politely averting his eyes from the peasant's daughter, who ought properly to have stayed in the house at such a time, even though there could obviously be no adequate harem quarters set aside in the small, dilapidated structure. Veiled, of course, but still unnecessarily bold, she made several trips to the spring, as if she expected it to go dry at any moment and were intent on building up a reserve of water in the house.

"Michael has seen very little of women," the sergeant stated, looking idly up at the topmost branch of a fig tree. "Once only, as far as I know, he sneaked out of the barrack at night and went into the town, as they sometimes do when they reach his age."

The peasant took instant offense. "I keep a proper house, Sergeant Effendi. Only the unexpectedness of your arrival prevented me from warning my family to remain indoors. Be assured that so lax a breach of manners will not occur again. Your young man is not unattractive to women, perhaps, now that I take a closer look at him."

The sergeant mentally shrugged his shoulders. He remembered the occasion of Michael's disappearance from the barrack, and the punishment that had followed the next day: sixteen blows on the soles of the feet from the whistling willow wand of Korkud the wrestling master. Not for what Michael might have done in the town, which nobody actually wondered about, but because Michael's marksmanship had suffered next day on the range. As far as the peasant and his household were concerned, the sergeant was merely discharging his duty by tactfully calling attention to the fact that a young janissary's country training was not expected to end in marriage. Celibacy was the janissary code.

Letting his eye wander momentarily from the fig tree to the girl at the well, the sergeant decided to call often at this little Anatolian farm, where the discipline was so lax and the daughter so slender and tall—to watch after Michael's welfare, of course. Celibacy was indeed the janissary code, but it was broadly interpreted, and included continence only in theory.

Throughout the conversation Michael stood looking straight in front of him, as close to them as they were to each other, without any sherbet. They spoke as if he were not expected to hear what they said, and he betrayed no indication that he did. But he understood that he was being given instructions that were to guide him during the next year of his life.

He tended sheep and learned to slaughter them. He plowed the land with a wooden plow and came to abhor the massive, docile ox that pulled it. From time to time the sergeant visited the farm, hardly speaking to Michael, never bringing him news of his friends or the camp. The sergeant's duty was to oversee Michael's physical welfare, not to coddle him or interfere with the arduous labor of the country training. Unexpectedness was always a factor in the sergeant's visits. Once he showed up for three days in succession.

Michael tried at first to clear all the rocks from the fields, but there were so many of them that after a while he came to believe with his master that Allah had created them with some special purpose in mind and wanted them to remain there. There would certainly never have been so many if the Merciful had wished them removed.

He planted the grain, and when it was ripe he helped harvest it. In his quiet bunk in an outbuilding that had once been a stable, he sometimes dreamed of broader fields on the foothills of Bulgarlhu Dagh, an eternity away in time. But when morning came, he scrubbed his face clean and shining (lest the devils enter those sensory doors, the eyes, the ears, the mouth) and then said his prayers, facing west where Arabia lay, and the Holy City of Mecca. As he prayed, he forgot the grainfields that once, perhaps still, looked down on the distant Bosphorus. They were Gavour, infidel, out of his heathen past.

Michael's appetite proved alarming to the peasant at first. But on trying to bend his bow one night when Michael was asleep, the farmer decided that such an animal was worth feeding. In the year that Michael worked for him, much of the adolescent angularity left the youth's frame. The bones that had grown too fast took on a sturdier sheathing of muscle, and Michael began to look like a man.

And the first to detect it was Leyla, the peasant's daughter, who had thought from the first that the coming of the janissary-servant to their little farm was something almost as miraculous as the triple blast of the angel's trumpet that would one day end the world.

His Turkish came from the city. The elegant Persian words that slipped into his speech made it sound to her like the speech of a pasha of three horsetails direct from the sultan's court.

Her father grudgingly acknowledged that Michael had caught on to the farm work as well as a city man with a military training could be expected to. If only he wouldn't practice with that bow of his on the grapes, picking them individually off the clusters; but he killed so many of the birds that appeared every autumn to eat them that the farmer had to admit that he saved more than he ruined.

There was a small vineyard planted to the south on the side of a gentle hill, not for wine, but for raisins that were sent to the city for sale in the streets. They had to be picked at just the right time. Near the end of Michael's dull, dusty country training, a prolonged, unseasonable period of hot weather brought the grapes to sudden ripeness, and it was necessary to pick them all at once. If Michael and the farmer had had to pick them all alone, many would have rotted on the vine.

The farmer struggled with his conscience.

A wife of the Prophet had ridden alone with a man through the space of a whole night and suffered no loss of reputation thereby. Would it be reprehensible if his own wife and daughter (heavily veiled, of course) helped gather in the grapes? Would he not be in a better position to give alms to the poor, poor as he was himself, if a little relaxing of good manners permitted him to make a profit on his vineyard? Wasn't it better than turning beggar, as he persuaded himself he might do if the grapes were left to go bad?

So the four of them worked until dark for three days, picking the grapes, piling them carefully on reed mats in the shed that was part of the same building where Michael had his quarters. And when the light failed, they hung the purple clusters by their stems from the rafters with twine raveled out of the rope of old harnesses, working in the light of a flickering oil lamp that burned the lard of swine. Swine's flesh was inedible, of course, but the hides were valuable as leather.

The long hours, the unaccustomed labor, her considerable fat, and her suffocating veil (which she had worn very seldom before Michael came) fatigued the farmer's wife, who fainted one night before the grapes were tied up to the rafters. The farmer flapped his wife's veil up and down to give her air, without, however, quite removing it. Leyla bent over her mother solicitously. Michael ran and fetched a pail of water from the stables, and the farmer sprinkled a little of it on his wife's forehead. She opened her eyes, moaned slightly, and closed them again.

"Perhaps I ought to take another look at the moon," Michael suggested. "It rose foggy and red an hour ago. If it's still red, we'll have rain. There are a few grapes in the fields. They will surely go bad, unless God wills it otherwise."

It would never do for him to remain in the room while a woman's face was on the very point of being stripped stark naked.

The farmer growled, "Oh, plague your fancy speeches!" It had suddenly occurred to him, Mashallah! that the fainting fit might betoken another pregnancy! It had happend to Abraham! "Help me carry the Great Lady into the house! And gently, or I'll break every bone in your exalted body!"

Great Lady was the title of respect given the first wife of the harem. It distinguished her from the Second Lady; also from the third, or Middle Lady; and from the fourth and last wife allowed at one time by Moslem law, who was called the Little Lady.

The farmer had only one wife, but he always used the title, sometimes out of affection, sometimes to impress a person who might not be aware how few wives he possessed, and sometimes in the hope that someday, somehow, he might acquire more.

Michael hesitated whether to pick up the body of his master's wife by the legs, which would surely have exposed her ankles, or by the waist and shoulders, which struck him as even more intimate. But the farmer resolved the doubt in his mind by passing his arms under the woman's recumbent figure.

"Take hold of my arms," he ordered.

Michael did. The woman lay in a cradle formed of the men's arms, and they carried her up to the house and deposited her on the farmer's bed. Her bulky weight gave Michael the wry notion that here was a Great Lady indeed. He doubted if she were really very sick. Her breathing was strong; her color was good. He suspected that the farmer had simply driven her a little too hard, as he sometimes did his work animals.

The farmer was elated with his own theory of the Great Lady's fainting fit. Yet he was also anxious at the fate of the grapes which would squash of their own weight and rot if they were not hung up at once. He ordered not only Michael, but his daughter as well, back throught the moonlight to the barn to salvage the fruit of his vine-yard, while he knelt at the side of his unconscious spouse murmur-ing: "Malkatoun, Malkatoun, thou treasure of a woman, speak to me! Praise God and whisper that the babe hath leapt in thy womb!"

Michael, on the way back to the barn, overheard the entreaty. For all he knew, the farmer might be right. Under her voluminous garments the body of the Great Lady betrayed its generous ab-dominal proportions. Leyla knew better, but for some reason she chose to encourage her father's folly. Pausing before she obeyed his command to help Michael with the grapes, she said, "It could hap-pen, if God please. Treat her gently, my father, and waken her not too brusquely from the swoon, lest shock and the Devil set a spasm to twitching her bowels and rudely dislodge what the Lord may have hidden there. Like that cow that aborted last spring when she ate the black wheat." Then she hurried out of the house, furtively loosen-ing her veil, laughing a little under her breath. Leyla was lustily, boldly alive, good-natured and unprejudiced. She was sympathetic, understanding, and even enthusiastic when she watched the farm animals do what they did to the other farm animals.

She had left the only lamp they possessed by her mother's side. Her father, mentally in the first, at least, of the seven heavens, was murmuring: "Thou treasure, rest gently for a while. Stir not too suddenly, Malkatoun."

Michael's heart gave a thump in his breast when Leyla appeared at the door of the barn. He had never before been alone in such an intimate situation with a woman who made any claim at all to re-spectability.

"Father himself sent me to help you," she said. "Aren't you glad?"

Michael gulped. "I certainly am."

But she was dismayed at the pile of grapes. There were hundreds of them.

Michael remarked, "It will take a long time to hang them all up." He flattered himself that he was calculating with diabolical finesse. "We must be careful not to bruise them when we string them up to the rafters. It will probably take a long time." And she'll be here a long time, he was thinking to himself.

Leyla said, "They'll dry just as well under the hay. Lots of farmers make raisins that way. Just so the air gets to them. I'm too tired to work any more tonight."

Michael replied very politely, in his best Brusa manner, "If Leyla Hanoum is fatigued, then that is surely the thing to do," and they began to hide the grapes under the hay. Michael worked hastily, in great excitement. Dust rose up out of the dry old hay when they moved it. They both began to sneeze.

"Perhaps a cloud of dust has got caught under your veil," Michael suggested. "It would not be immodest to remove it here in the dark. That will give the dust a chance to escape. Dust is very bad for the lungs."

"I know it is," said the girl, "but that would be terribly bold. I'm afraid you'd look. I ought not to in all this moonlight."

Michael wasn't sure what would happen, how far he could persuade her, what she would allow. "I've lain awake nights imagining I would one day catch a glimpse of the beauty hidden under your veil!"

"That was an impure thought." The voice was prim, but not accusing.

"Any man would feel that way about you, Leyla. I promise I shan't look. Anyway, I can't see a thing in this light. I suppose my eyesight is a little dim."

Leyla had observed Michael's accuracy with the bow, to the detriment of her father's vineyards, and she knew that his eyesight was unerringly accurate. She wished she had painted that little black mole on her chin with henna. She wished he had shot all the grapes off the vines. Such a pile of them on the floor!

"Well, be sure you don't look!" The tide of battle was turning in his favor, Michael thought. She began to cough as if the cloud of hay dust were still under her veil. "I suppose I really ought to remove it, for the sake of my health."

She removed the veil. The moon through the barn door shone full on her naked face. Blue lights glinted in her long black hair.

The effect on Michael was precisely the same as if a Western woman, alone with an excited man, had suddenly stripped off her bodice.

"God's name!" gasped Michael, "You're beautiful!"

Leyla knew that her mother would not swoon forever. In part of her generous heart she hoped that the Great Lady would waken soon, despite the unpleasant realization that that would shorten her time with Michael.

"I am terribly tired after these three days of so much work," she said languidly. "I think I'll rest for a moment." She lay down on the soft hay in the moonlight. Michael resolved to do the same, with a quick look toward the farmhouse, where the lamp still burned in the bedroom. But he felt he had to excuse the action: "You will be chilly down there. Let me put my tunic over you."

In a little while she suggested that her father ought not to find hay in her garments, and forthrightly removed them.

An unexpected, fire-new, all-embracing experience, like a wound in battle, or like a body, close, unknown, and conquered in a spasm of ecstasy, can compress a long lapse of time into the twinkling of an eye, or stretch an instant into an hour.

Two of the little strings that they had used to tie up the grapes lay in the sharp rectangular patch of silver moonlight on the floor. The strings were so close together that Leyla could not have placed a little finger between them without touching them both. One of them happened to lie, like a point of reference on a sundial, exactly where the shadow of the lintel threw a dark straight line across the floor. The shadow had not crept to the other—a phenomenon which the spinning earth would effect in about ten minutes—when suddenly, out of eternity, Michael heard the crunch of shoes on the gravel coming from the house. Glancing up, he saw his master, with the lamp, walking toward the barn.

"Gesù!" he swore, astonished and frightened half out of his wits. He had not used the Christian oath for years. He was much too startled to wonder how he came to remember it. It must have been hours, he thought, since he had persuaded Leyla, with such cleverness, to remove her veil.

"What does 'Gesù' mean?" Leyla asked quietly, contentedly. She was a little in awe of Michael now. How could so smooth-skinned a youngster be so strong?

"It's your father!" he gasped, jumping up, resuming his tunic and frantically beginning to tie up grapes three at a time.

" 'Gesù' my father? Is that Persian?"

"In God's name make yourself presentable. Your father is walking down from the house! He'll kill us both!"

Leyla had a shrewd notion in the back of her practical head that her father might raise an awful fuss under the circumstances. But murder his only daughter? Slay the janissary? She didn't think it likely. There were other solutions. But she prudently took no chances, and in an astonishingly short time she was properly attired again, hanging up the grapes along with Michael, rather more stolidly, one at a time, her veil precisely in place and securely tied.

The farmer was in one of the worst of his frequent bad tempers. "Go up to the house at once," he ordered. "It is a shameful thing to be alone with a man." Then he saw how industriously they were working. They had reduced the huge pile of grapes on the floor to a handful. Nothing too serious could have happened with so much work obviously disposed of. "Your mother needs you," he explained, relenting somewhat. "It is the flow of blood," he added miserably.

"Poor mother!" Leyla said sympathetically. "I'll hurry." The farmer followed her heavily up to the house.

Michael spent most of the rest of the night searching in the hay, retrieving the grapes and hanging them up to the rafters. At length he lay down in his roll of blankets, confident that he would not rest that night, of all nights. But in the chill of the early dawn a few drops of rain splattered down on the roof, then fell by the million in a gentle soaking shower that lulled him to sleep in spite of himself.

The farmer, slogging in bare feet out to the stables next morning, beheld his rafters purple with clusters of grapes, saved from the rain in the fields, saved from the damp of the barn floor, hanging plump, rich, and fragrant, like an arbor in the bountiful paradise of God.

Michael was up. He had washed and said his prayers and was cooking his breakfast. The morning was half spent already. He knew he had overslept, but he was not aware how late it actually was because of the dark, cloudy weather.

"You certainly take your time in rising," the farmer rasped. The disappointment he had sustained during the night still soured his temper.

"I was very busy last night, sir," Michael said, glancing up at the grapes.

Following his glance, the farmer nodded his head. "I shan't punish you. I grant that you did a good job."

Michael thanked him, grinning slightly.

The farmer sighed. "Anyway, this is your last day here. Your country training is over. I trust that when you return you will see fit to report to your commander that you have been fairly treated, seldom punished, and properly trained."

"I can say that in all honesty, sir."

"Perhaps they will send me another janissary," the farmer suggested.

Michael replied, "I have enjoyed learning what I have learned on your estate, Effendi." The "Effendi" raised the farmer several notches in the social scale.

"Now that's a good lad," said the man who had been his master for a year.

The sergeant brought Michael a brand-new tunic, cut to an ampler measure than the one he had been wearing and long since outgrown. Care was taken that the young janissaries returning to the Brusa camp carried none of the rusticities of country labor back with them.

"Did you have a hard time of it down on the farm?" the sergeant asked familiarly as they rode away.

Before they had gone many miles, Michael, because he was still so young, launched into a vainglorious recital of the grapes, Leyla, and the moonlight.

The sergeant glanced slyly at him out of the corner of his eye. Then he remarked in a wonderfully bland voice:

"Do you know, I always considered her beauty marred by that little mole on her chin."

The sergeant pulled sagely at a corner of his mustache and cocked a knowing eyebrow in Michael's direction.

Michael's jaw dropped. All in a rush he remembered the sergeant's frequent visits. He had flattered himself that his own welfare was their sole object. He bit his lip.

The sergeant said sternly: "You'd better learn not to talk so big, young man. Especially about women. You can get into a lot of trouble that way."

So much for Michael's final lesson in humility!

84

CHAPTER
9

THE city of Brusa, where Michael spent the year that followed his country training, had once been the capital of Turkey. The first six Ottoman sultans established their capitals not in the most secure but in the most dangerous parts of the empire so that their residence might always be close to the enemy.

But time and the Turkish wars had pacified Asia Minor. Northward, across the strait, on the continent of Europe, Adrianople was now the capital. And Adrianople itself fell farther and farther behind the border each year as the empire's frontier marched deeper and deeper into Christendom.

The former capital still retained its cultural and economic pre-eminence, however. There were great mercantile establishments in Brusa, important military headquarters, busy administrative bureaus, mosques, colleges, hospitals, orphanages. The population compressed within its walls was variegated and cosmopolitan: artists, poets, soldiers of fortune from many lands, holy men from Bokhara, merchants, civil and military pensioners, pashas, beys, and beggars.

In teeming, busy Brusa there was quiet only for the dead. The sultan Orchan and Suleinan his son lay entombed in a stately mausoleum that once had been the venerable Church of Elijah in the days when the city was Greek. And the body of Osman, *Ghazi*, the Victorious, reposed under a splendid dome of pure and shining silver. For once, the puritanical austerity that everywhere else restrained the architecture of Islam was relaxed to glorify the founder of the Turkish Empire.

Outside the crowded city walls lay the permanent camp of the janissaries, and south of the camp loomed the dark, majestic bulk of Kechish Dagh, where the Mysian Greeks had hunted game and which they had called Mount Olympus.

For six years the Brusa camp had been Michael's home. It was difficult for Michael, the man, to remember his life as Michael, the boy, in the gray house at the foot of that other mountain, Bulgarlhu Dagh, that looked across the Bosphorus to Constantinople.

Training and discipline had strengthened his body and taught him self-control. He drew a hundred-pound bow now. If his black eyes ever grew soft, no one saw it. Once an archery master had set up a corpse in full armor such as Christian knights wore, for target practice on the range. The eye that aimed the arrow glinted obsidian-cold. The string snapped out of his powerful right thumb, which years of practice had so developed that it was larger than his left. The arrow penetrated the armor and the body of the dead man. As they took their turn at this realistic target, all the other men shot with equal calm and lack of emotion. This was the training that won wars. Later, all the arrows were snapped off flush with the mail, the corpse was carefully removed from its casing of armor, and a precise Arabian surgeon dissected it, lecturing learnedly and at length, teaching the janissaries: it is established, gentlemen, that an arrow through the eye kills quickly, an arrow through the bowels kills surely but slowly, slowly; whereas an arrow through the limbs does not kill. One does not, therefore, waste arrows on the limbs.

Michael had no name. That is, he and the other men of his age were still called by the names they had had as Christians and would be forced to retain until they won new names by distinguishing themselves in war.

In the last years of Murad's gentle reign, there were no wars in which to win distinction. Promotion in the armies was slow, but Michael's marksmanship was impossible to overlook. In the spring of the year 1450, for reasons of state unannounced to the people, the quota of recruits was suddenly doubled; and presently the Brusa camp began to bulge with the raw, new levies. They were told that they would be fortunate if they were assigned to Michael for instruction in archery. To Commander Michael. It was a wonderful thing to hang one's scimitar to the red girdle that marked a commander.

Promotion had been rapid also for Hassan of Ulubad, who had seen war. Hassan had been raised to second in command after the commandant, a pasha of one horsetail entitled to be called Excellency. It was generally believed that Hassan would take the pasha's place when the old gentleman retired on his pension.

In the strictly masculine society of the janissaries, Hassan of Ulubad was held in awe and affection. His honorable career, his imposing stature—he towered head and shoulders over every other man in camp—and his fanatical attachment to the corps won him loyalty and respect. The young men leaned on him and drew strength from him, and he in turn fashioned the young men, in accordance with tradition that was centuries old and rendered the janissaries self-perpetuating.

Hassan stood beside the range one day while Michael was supervising the archery of some of the new boys. Inevitably one of them missed badly. Hassan walked up and examined the target. It was not a disc with painted circles such as the sultan shot at to amuse himself in the gardens at Adrianople. This target was a straw man.

Hassan shook his head. The clasp in his turban that distinguished his rank flashed in the sun.

"They'll never get to be good shots practicing on a scarecrow all day," he commented, a hint of disappointment in his voice. "No life. No blood." Some of the boys wondered what the redoubtable veteran of Ulubad was going to suggest. Then Hassan said: "Let's take them hunting, Michael. Olympus is full of game."

The newest, rawest boy began to cheer. Michael quickly silenced him. Hassan ignored the undisciplined exuberance. The others tried unsuccessfully to hide their expressions of pleasure at the prospect of a holiday. Behind his composure Michael was almost as delighted as the youngster who had cheered.

"Hassan Effendi is right," he said to his young charges. "A live target is much better to shoot at. It's harder to hit, but there's more glory when you score."

Next morning they went up into the forest on the flanks of the mountain. There was game of all sorts in the woods of Olympus: bittern, geese, partridge, pheasant, wild sheep, rabbits, leopards, red and roe deer, as well as some inoffensive brown bears that ate honey or berries or ants and ran away at the sight of a man. Sometimes, if the man stood still and threw them a sweetmeat, they would come up to him and be captured, and dance for the rest of their lives in the bazaars to entertain children for pennies.

There was also a family of Himalayan black bears in a cave that spring, two cubs and a mother with a white horseshoe mark on her chest. This species ate meat.

One of the minor privileges permitted a commander was separate living quarters and an orderly to prepare his meals. Michael also found room for a pet. It was a Persian lynx, midway in size between a leopard and a wild cat. When it stood on its hind paws and leaned against Michael to be petted, its forepaws reached just a little higher than the red girdle. Michael had bought him young, mangy, bedraggled and half starved in the Brusa bazaar. He had wanted a hunting companion, he said, ashamed to admit that he felt sorry for the beast.

The lynx had flourished with care. It was an elegant creature now, chestnut above, whitish underneath. Its fur was sleek, like a wet otter's. The ears were pointed, erect, and topped with tufts of bristly black hair at the tips. It had a savage temper for strangers, and even at Michael it growled and hissed and spit when it was hungry. Michael had taught it to stalk cranes, kites, and the smaller birds.

The men who were left behind saw and envied the little group who departed in the early morning light just after breakfast in charge of the most popular officer in the camp and the best archery master, with the red leather leash on his wrist and the beautiful pet that looked and acted exactly like a leopard.

The hunting party pitched their camp in a level clearing on the bank of the brook that flowed down the mountain into the city of Brusa, where it was dammed and formed part of the water supply. The reservoir there was planted with yellow aquatic flowers and shone so placidly blue under the blue Anatolian sky that it was called the Guek Su—the Azure Water. But here on the mountain where the rocks were profuse and the gradient steep, the frothy stream was called the White Water.

The black Himalayan bear had had her cubs early in the spring, just as the snow melted off the mountain. They were more than half weaned now and beginning to waddle awkwardly about the woods by themselves, poking their noses into anthills, getting bitten for their pains, trying their sharp young claws on the fragrant bark of the ilex trees, and going home again to the cave when they were exhausted and hungry. The mother was still thin from the winter sleep, and fretful because the milk in her drying dugs flowed painfully just as her cubs grew most demanding. Instinct drove her to the brook, where speckled trout swam in the White Water and rested lazily in a rocky, shallow pool that a tall broad willow kept always in the shade. There she would plunge her head into the water up to the ears. With precision and speed astonishing in so bulky an animal, she would snap at a fish and catch it in her teeth. Then she would carry it back to the cave, the head and the tail still flapping on either side of her mouth, and the cubs would eat it.

Michael and his boys were shooting at partridges, which the lynx, hunting not with its nose but with its eyes, flushed out of the bush by the score in a wide area around the camp. To have eyes like a lynx was a compliment in any language that had a name for the animal.

The boys spread out in all directions, laughing and shouting to each other whenever they scored. Michael snapped the leash onto the collar of his pet and knotted the other end to a sapling at the edge of the camp. He did not want the lynx, which was not a retriever, to mangle any of the game. Then he hastened to make a round of the young hunters, partly to give them an encouraging word on their marksmanship but also to caution them that hunting should be a quiet business.

Suddenly from the direction of the brook one of the boys screamed. The cry was followed instantly by the hiss of an arrow in the air, then the angry snarling of a wounded animal.

One of the bear cubs had been sniffing at an anthill. It knew the insects were delicious, but it had acquired no skill in eating them. They were stinging his nose. His head was down, his eyes were rolling. His tongue slavered out, trying to lick the ants off his nose. The boy had seen him, very close, rapidly waddling closer. The cub in its plight looked ferocious.

The terrified boy shouted and shot at him, but his aim was bad. The cub took the arrow in a leg, turned tail, and ran squealing and snorting into the clearing where the lynx was tied.

The back of the lynx went up in fright and he strained at the leash, trying to escape, screeching. The snarling cub was dangerous now. Maddened by the stinging ants in its tender nose and the pain of the arrow through its leg, it charged the tethered lynx.

Hassan heard the cry of the boy and the screech of Michael's pet and ran into the clearing, to find the lynx in the grip of the wounded cub. Hassan instantly dispatched the little bear with his dagger. He wondered for a moment what to do with the cub. The skin would be valuable. It was black with a blaze of white on the chest and would fetch more than the common brown ones, but it was not the sort of pelt that could be used to trim a tunic: the fur was too shaggy.

Michael was some distance away when he heard the boy's frightened cry and the desperate noises of the animals. He began to run back to the camp.

Another pair of ears also heard the little bear's snarling, and recognized agony in it. The mother dropped a fish out of her mouth. She scrambled up the rocks and began to lumber through the bush, hunching her huge ungainly body into a black ball and extending it again in giant strides. She covered the ground with amazing speed. She smelled men and the blood of her cub.

Still looking at the cub, Hassan heard a tremendous crashing and snapping in the woods behind him. He spun round, instantly alert, to meet whatever was coming, the bloody dagger still in his hand. Seeing her cub on the ground, the infuriated bear reared up and received the man into her monstrous forelimbs like a lover.

Michael sprinted to the edge of the clearing. He saw the head of the giant bear towering over the head of the giant man. Sunshine glinted off the bared white teeth in the cavernous open mouth, glinted off the polished horn of the claws. The bear was lowering her head.

Michael had once seen the body of a man who had met a bear in the woods. There was no face left. And the animal had hooked its claws under the shoulder blades and torn them out.

Michael plucked an arrow from his girdle and let fly. And then another. Both arrows stuck, one in the mouth, the other in the neck. But a bear is not built like a man, and neither arrow killed it.

Hassan was pinioned against the beast and could not use his

dagger, a situation to which he probably owed his life, for if he had been able to inflict wounds elsewhere on the bear she would not have been conscious exclusively of the pain caused by Michael's two arrows.

The first one she bit off at the shaft, tossing her head up and down, attempting to dislodge the other half that stuck out through the back of her neck. Suddenly she released Hassan, who fell away from her as she struck frantically with her paws at her neck, trying to brush the arrow away.

This bared her chest, against which she had been crushing Hassan the instant before.

Hearing the commotion, some of the boys rushed back to the camp; and the first ones emerged from the trees just in time to see Michael draw his sword, leap over the body of Hassan, and plunge the sharp curved blade into the heart of the bear. She died quickly, opening her jaws full of sharp, blood-stained teeth in an effort to breathe. She floundered heavily for a few moments, twitched spasmodically, and then lay still.

The boys gathered round the body of the big black bear, awed, curious, and shaken at the sight of their captain.

"Do not go too close," Michael cautioned; "the soul of the beast has departed, but the body may still have some life in it." Like every other well instructed Moslem, Michael knew that animals have souls. They would waken again at the last day, like the souls of men. "She might still kill a boy," he said, and they drew back again from the beast while Michael saw to Hassan.

The suffocating hug against the matted hair of the great beast's chest had stopped Hassan's breath, turned his face purple, and rendered him unconscious. When he came to his senses, he vomited into the brook, and a devil with a red-hot hook, he thought, was ripping open the skin of his back. There was a searing sting in his scalp, and he was dizzy.

Michael had carried him to the White Water and was washing the lacerations made by the bear's teeth and claws.

Hassan sat up groggily. "God's name!" he shouted. "Leave me alone!" Then his angry blazing eyes came into focus on Michael's face. He remembered what had happened, the dizziness left him, and he spat contemptuously into the brook. "Ugh, that creature stank! She'd been eating fish and foul meat."

Michael said, "Lie down again, Hassan Effendi. There is dirt in the cuts on your back and in the gash in your scalp."

"Scratches, Michael, scratches. I've suffered worse." He tried to get up. But Michael let him raise himself only a little, slipping his own turban under Hassan's cheek as a pillow to elevate the head as much as possible, and then firmly pushed him belly-down again on the turf beside the brook.

"One little moment, sir, till I stop the bleeding. The boys are preparing an astringent."

Hassan grumbled and complied. "Oh, all right, all right; but I'm old enough to know when I'm hurt. I haven't lost any blood yet. What do the boys know about astringents?"

"You've lost enough. And I told the boys to cut ilex and oak bark and mash some sumac leaves in the cooking pot: what you yourself would have told them."

"You're a cool one, Michael. Oh, very well, it's good to have them learn something about wounds, I suppose. Go ahead."

Presently the youths ran up with the cooking pot half full of bark that they had shredded with their daggers and sumac leaves that they had reduced to a pulp with stones. At the bottom of the pot there was half an inch or so of greenish-brown liquor that they had leached out of the vegetable matter.

Michael tore a clean strip from the inner folds of his girdle and swabbed the brown liquid into the wounds in Hassan's back and the gash in his scalp. Hassan's jaw set as the painful, powerful astringent penetrated into his torn flesh; but the bleeding stopped.

Michael bound up the wounds and Hassan got up on his feet, refusing help, and walked back to the tent where they made him as comfortable as possible on a chair improvised from a log set against the trunk of a tree. When one of the boys took off his tunic and stuffed it with grass to make a cushion for his lacerated back, Hassan protested only slightly and leaned wearily against it. He reflected that he had shed no violent blood since Ulubad. He was a little ashamed that the boys had seen how gray about the temples his hair had become.

"You should have put on my turban quicker and bound it more

tightly," he observed, frowning slightly at Michael. "I think the cut in the scalp should have been treated first."

Michael answered, "The cut in the scalp bled profusely at first, Hassan Effendi, then stopped of its own accord."

Hassan said, "Of course. That always happens. I had forgotten. You were right."

"And I thought it no harm," Michael added grinning, "for the boys to see their captain's red hair, red like the Prophet's, sir."

The thought of his blood-red hair amused Hassan and he laughed softly. "A *very* cool one! You think of everything, Michael. That was a delicacy worthy of a pasha. I confess that I am a little sensitive about my graying hair—it's premature, of course."

"Naturally," Michael nodded.

Hassan added: "The Prophet dyed his hair with henna and his beard too, or so they say; henna is certainly preferable to this method. I suppose I'll have to sleep in my turban for a week and then soak it off. Oh, well. Do you know, Michael, I'm hungry."

"The boys are washing the pot. I told them the herbs are poison. A couple of them are drawing the partridges."

"Good, good. Wheat meal and beans and stew we can get in camp. They'll deserve some roast partridges: they've shot well enough today." Hassan paused awkwardly. "So did you shoot well, and strike well too, my friend. I thank you for what you did."

Later in the evening, Hassan, comfortable, full of supper, and a little careless of what he said, observed in a low voice: "Sometimes I think there's a little of the infidel left in you, Michael. It was generous, but impractical, not to let the bear kill me. Nobody would have blamed you if you had, well, let us say 'stumbled' when you came running to help me. You are aware, of course, that the commandant will shortly retire, and I'll probably get his place. Do you not also know that if that happens you will get mine?"

Michael looked up, astonished. "I did not know, Hassan Effendi. How could I have known?"

"Oh, the decision might just conceivably have leaked out. Since you didn't know about your appointment, I'm glad I told you. After what you did for me today, the least I can do is to let you know what is in store for you."

"It is a wonderful honor for one who has never won a name in war," Michael said.

Hassan replied: "It's no more than you deserve, but it is also a sign of the times. Some of the visiting pasha inspectors from the court have admired how well you train the new men. Haven't there been a lot of recruits lately, by the way? I can't remember so many since Varna, when you joined; but that was after a battle. We haven't had a good war in years. These increased levies are puzzling. Some people say the Heir Apparent is teaching his pious old father the value of us janissaries. Young Mohammed, Allah bless him, thinks more of the armies and less about those confounded dervishes that his father dotes on. I wonder if I'll get religious when I get old."

Michael said, "Did you think I would stumble on purpose and let you get killed when it pleased God to allow me to prevent it?" Michael colored slightly. "That was a base suspicion, my friend. It wasn't even very polite."

"Bismillah! I'm never polite! Actually, you're too young to be a pasha even if I should die. It takes experience. Just the same," Hassan shrugged, "many men would have stumbled."

Michael smiled. "Maybe there's a little of the sentimental infidel left in you yourself, Hassan. Otherwise you'd never have told me an important secret like this."

Hassan exploded with laughter. "Me an infidel! Me a Gavour!" The laughter was infectious. At a respectful distance, whispering among themselves, the boys joined in it. "A Gavour, me, Hassan of Ulubad! Maybe I'm just being shrewd, my friend, binding you closer to your future commandant. That would be clever strategy on my part." And the grateful janissary was telling the truth, in part at least.

Yet in a long-forgotten corner of Hassan's heart, the gentle Christian Gavour slept spellbound and unsuspected, as it did in more of the sultan's elite troops than the sultan was ever to know.

Hassan possessed a magnificent bow ring, valuable alike for its materials and the consummate artistry that had gone into making it. It was green Chinese jade, wrought by the cunning Oriental craftsman into a thin, broad circlet to fit the thumb. The delicate, precious stone was set in a strengthening base of pure gold. The inner surface was functional, with a groove to hold the bowstring till the action of the thumb released it and sped the arrow to its mark. The outer surface was exquisitely carved into the beautiful Turkish characters that formed Hassan's name.

Before he left the campfire that night, Hassan gave it to Michael as a gift.

CHAPTER
10

At Adrianople in February of the following year, while his son was in Magnesia, Murad II died.

The death of an emperor was always a critical moment in the precarious career of a grand vizier, who usually went out of office to make way for a favorite of the successor.

Khalil Pasha, however, was determined to attract favorable attention to himself. He knew the temper of the young man who would mount the throne. Dispensing with all formality, he dispatched a hardy courier on the fleetest horse in the imperial stables, bidding him carry the news with all speed, promising him an enormous gift if he could make in three days the five-day gallop into Asia Minor. Khalil Pasha later presented the gift with a lavish hand and a happy heart, for the intelligent courier not only covered the distance in the allotted time but also tactfully reported that his speed was due to the loyal solicitude of Khalil Pasha, *Sadr-Azam*, the grand vizier, who had lived only to serve the late Majesty of Turkey, and now lived only to serve the new. Khalil Pasha secured his place for several years by this diplomatic burst of speed.

Mohammed was inordinately anxious to reign. He had never had any patience with his father's gentle, tolerant policies. Mohammed rode promptly up to Adrianople to be invested with the dignities of his new, imperial station.

Meanwhile a long train of unhappy subjects, noble and common, one in their mourning, solemnly bore the body of the great dead sultan into Anatolia. They buried him in Brusa in a tomb prepared in strict accordance with his explicit directions. It was utterly formal, without even the simplest ornamentation, far less a silver dome. He lay in a grave of earth edged with pure white marble. In the rock dome above, the reluctant masons had been forced to leave a small circular hole open to the sky; for Murad had insisted that his grave be exposed to the rain like those of the poorest of his subjects, saying: "It is fitting for a Prince, whom God hath exalted in life, to be humble before Him in death." Mohammed privately considered this an excess of piety, but he prudently kept his own counsel and publicly praised the virtues of his imperial father.

Mohammed II began to reign the instant his father died, but the formalities that marked his coronation had to wait until the distant parts of the world could be notified.

By springtime Adrianople teemed with Moslem and Christian ambassadors, all eager to tender their sovereigns' respects and to observe, if they could, what the new sultan was like.

That he was comely and young everyone could see. He was cultured, he spoke several languages, he appeared to be affable. Beyond that, little was known of him, though it was proven at once that his justice could be swift and terrible.

In the last year of his father's reign, one of the old sultan's wives had given him a handsome baby boy. It was, except for Mohammed, Murad's only male child. It had been named Achmet. Within a week of Murad's death, Mohammed let it be known that a clumsy female nurse, who had been entrusted with the care of the imperial infant, had somehow allowed it to drown in the bath. The unfortunate woman was publicly stripped of her veil, her hair was shaven from her head by a barber, and she was strangled in a noose of wire, which two condemned thieves, one at either end, slowly tightened between them. The body was thrown from the battlements and left to the scavenger dogs outside the walls.

Some of the more cynical among the visiting diplomats whispered privately among themselves that the death of his little brother might not be an unmitigated sorrow to the new sultan since it eliminated a possible future aspirant to the throne. No such rumor ever reached the streets of the city, of course, which was becoming more crowded and cosmopolitan every day.

Adrianople gradually acquired a military aspect also. The janissaries were everywhere, quiet, decorous, disciplined, restrained; but they were there, hundreds of them, for all the ambassadors of Christendom to see. As the coronation drew nearer, a holiday spirit pervaded the city. It was inevitable that a janissary would sometimes meet some honest Western man-at-arms in the narrow streets, often steadying himself with his pike because the infidel beverage to which they all seemed addicted had temporarily tangled his legs under him. Then the janissary would cross his arms mockingly on his chest in the posture of submission, murmur "Mashallah! What God can accomplish!" and give the Gavour room to stumble in. But just as often a janissary would meet a European knight, cold sober, clad in his jacket and skintight Western hose, walking about, enjoying the sights of the Turkish capital. Then they would each give way a little, turning aside just far enough so as not to touch when they passed, and take level stock of each other, coldly and gravely.

The captain-bashi of the Brusa camp had retired during the year, taken one wife, and begun belatedly but energetically to raise a family. Hassan of Ulubad had taken his place, and Michael had been raised to second in command, just as Hassan had foretold on the day when they killed the bears on Mount Olympus. Both men were at Adrianople on a military mission—not a dangerous one, since only a madman would attempt to murder a sultan in his own throne room, but certainly not dull either, especially for Michael, who had never been to court. It had fallen to the commandant of the most famous janissary camp in the empire to guard the sultan during his coronation.

The janissary tunics were formal, long, court fashion, fur trimmed and cerulean blue. Their boots were red leather, an astonishing thing in the eyes of the Greek emissaries, to whom red was an imperial color which only an emperor might wear.

Hassan stood under the arch at the end of the throne room facing the sultan, Michael under a similar one at the other end of the room; and between the two officers stood a tall, silent janissary under each arch of the balcony, one hand on his bow, one behind his back, grasping a ready arrow, looking down at imaginary squares on the floor below.

One of the elderly Jewish financial advisers of the late sultan quietly moved away from an inconspicuous position at the edge of the glittering assembly. He had suddenly become uncomfortably aware that some years before a dear friend of his had died behind that very pillar. Michael's quick eye caught the movement of the black figure. For an instant he imagined he had seen the grave, kindly face somewhere before. Fantastically, he saw it in candlelight, with diamonds and emeralds in the beard. But of course that was absurd. In any case, Michael's attention was immediately recaptured by the historic scene being enacted below. Joseph was forgotten, dismissed as an obviously harmless old court official.

Michael surveyed some of the Christians who had come to see the emperor crowned:

. . . . Knights from the Island of Rhodes, an enormously powerful fortress of rock only ten miles off the Turkish coast. These men were tall and bore themselves proudly, as if they knew how to fight. They had crosses embroidered on their tunics, but apparently the sultan was going to overlook this detail since no orders were given to shoot them.

. . . . A delegation of influential traders from the rich Italian colony in Galata. These men looked prosperous and peaceful.

. . . . The bushy-faced representatives of Vasily Temny, the blind Grand Duke of Moskow. They wore long, barbarous mantles, extravagantly embroidered, and they held in their hands tall headpieces of fur. Michael sensed that the Russians were angry at having to stand bareheaded.

. . . . The imperial ambassador of the Empire of Trebizond, surrounded by his suite of wily men. It was Basil, the Great Logothete, who had instructions to suggest that if Mara, Murad's widow, should care to share another imperial bed, John of Trebizond would offer his.

. . . . Princes of the Peloponnesus, Thomas and Demetrius Palaeologoi, governors of Lesbos, Chios, and extensive provinces in the Morea, brothers of Constantine, the Byzantine emperor. Little men, Michael thought.

. . . . The suite of the Doge of Venice, their golden Phrygian caps in their hands, their mantles one solid mass of gold brocade. Everyone knew how rich the proud Italian republic was.

. . . . The Hungarian emissaries of John Hunyadi, wild, poor, and unkempt, but sent by so brave a prince that Michael had to admire them. Hunyadi had troubled the northern frontier for years.

Michael looked in vain for the Albanians. Scanderbeg sent no delegates. Scanderbeg, the apostate who had torn off his turban and deserted the janissary corps, had been informed that his representatives, if he dared to send any, would have turbans forced onto their heads and firmly nailed there.

The hereditary enemy to the north was represented by George Phranza, the imperial Chancellor of Constantinople, a grave, learned, capable man, surrounded by his ambassadorial staff. They had had the foresight to come bareheaded so they would not have to hold their hats in their hands. Phranza was empowered to tell the new sultan, should the sultan look bellicose, that Constantine would consider a somewhat smaller annual subsidy for keeping Orchan, the sultan's elderly uncle and aspirant to the Turkish throne, safely in prison. (Even the tolerant Murad had thought it wise to keep Orchan out of Turkey.) The silk tunics of the Greeks looked soft, like a woman's, Michael thought.

There were European plenipotentiaries of many nations that Michael had heard of but never seen: France, Burgundy, England, the Spains, the Netherlands. They were tall and blond, with their mantles belted and their limbs sheathed in tight hose that made them look spindly and must have been uncomfortable.

Michael saw Hassan's eye run critically over the line of guards. Not a man moved.

There were also the more familiar turbaned figures of the pashas and beys of the sultan's own domains: Thrace, Macedonia, Bulgaria, Thessaly, Anatolia; and of the neighboring Islamic nations: Seljukian Syria, Egypt of the Mamelukes, the khanates of Greater and Lesser Tartary, and the kingdoms of the Black Ram and the White Ram in Mesopotamia.

The officiating minister at the coronation of the sultan was the Sheik-ul-Islam, the chief ecclesiastic of the Mohammedan Church. In Turkey he crowned the sultan just as, in Christendom, the Pope crowned the Holy Roman Emperor. The prestige of the Sheik-ul-Islam was enormous. Imperial proclamations carried his seal as well as the seal of the sultan. He was the only man in the world who could relieve the sultan of an oath. He wore the black garb that had never changed since its adoption by the Abbasid caliphs seven centuries before.

Before the assembly that represented all the nations of the world, he cast over Mohammed's shoulders a black mantle and placed in his hand the staff of the Apostle of God. He held over Mohammed's head a crown signifying his reign over the East, and another signifying his reign over the West. At his hand the sultan was girt first with the imperial sword of state, blazing with jewels; and then with the somber sword of Osman, the ancient, heavy blade that his great-great-great-great grandfather had worn in battle. Mohammed II was the seventh of his dynasty to wear it.

The Sheik-ul-Islam then raised his voice and cried: "La illah il Allah! Mohammed roszul Allah!" (There is no God but God! Mohammed is the Apostle of God!) It was the cry of the muezzins, the call to prayer, the affirmation of Islam, particularly apt for a sultan bearing the same name as the Prophet.

At this point tradition required that every man in the room touch his forehead to the floor, and they all did, except, of course, the watchful janissary guards. Michael was awed by the spectacle of the world's great, prostrate at the feet of his emperor. Strangely, he felt a sudden stab of loneliness. Moslems, Christians, and Jews could revere the emperor, but he and Hassan and the other men under the arches— what were they? The thought lasted only an instant. A herald began to shout the titles of the new emperor. Mohammed II was now sultan in theory as well as fact, by reason of his solemn coronation and investiture. The assembly rose.

But the janissaries stood guard several hours longer while the sultan received the congratulations and gifts of the ambassadors— living things: costly slaves, rare wild animals, curious birds, and an idiot jester; precious things: work of the goldsmiths and silversmiths of foreign lands, incense from Persia and jewels from India. The Genoese contingent presented a remarkable little silver handgun, which they said would shoot a stone farther than a bow could shoot an arrow. They explained that one filled it with a black powder and ignited it with a flame.

The sultan thanked them absently. He gave the impression of being fatigued and disinterested.

"I have heard of the silly new toys," he said.

Most of the men in the room were ignorant of the terrible potentialities of gunpowder. The Byzantines, who should have worried most, had no inkling of its danger. What could ever supplant their unquenchable Greek fire? Michael and some of the other janissary officers were better instructed; they concluded that the youthful sultan was either marvelously discreet or monstrously ill advised when he called the murderous little thing a toy.

Mohammed's first official act was to extend for three years the uneasy truce with Hungary. His second was to advise the Byzantine delegates that he would continue to pay the annual stipend of 300,000 aspers so long as his uncle continued to accept the hospitality of Constantinople. The Byzantine ambassador, George Phranza, bowed profoundly and answered that he felt sure that would be a long time.

The sultan then rose, promised peace to the whole world, gracefully invited everyone to enjoy his gardens, and retired to another part of the palace.

The garden was called Paradise. The elegant Persian word was used in its original sense and meant "a pleasure ground." The ancient gardens of Persia had been so exquisitely lovely that neither the fathers of the Christian Church nor the later theologians of Islam could think of a better word for their several heavens. It was full of flowering trees, shaded walks, drinking fountains, and beasts of the chase.

But many of the foreign dignitaries were elderly or corpulent or had fallen arches or suffered from the gout. Standing so many hours had exhausted them. They preferred to go to their apartments and refresh themselves and ponder the significance of what they had seen and heard.

Most of the younger foreigners took one look at the garden and found it uninviting. Lions and leopards and tigers wandered unchained among its pleasant vistas. The visiting young diplomats sought more familiar adventures in the town, which was adequately prepared to receive them.

As a result, only a few of the Greeks and other Easterners who knew the secret of the sultan's gardens chose to walk there; but many Turks and some of the janissaries accepted the public invitation. Michael had heard of the deep ditches that confined the animals. They were artfully concealed behind hedgerows, outcroppings of rock, and little rises in the terrain. An artist and an engineer had merged their talents to give the illusion of quantities of wild animals in a natural surrounding without iron cages or tethering chains.

Some Turkish women elected to walk there, too, among them the fourth wife of Machmut, the Beglerbey of Roum. There was nothing socially inadmissible in this, since she was properly escorted by two very black, very expensive eunuchs.

The reason black eunuchs cost so much more than white ones and were always honored by responsibilities in the harem was that the operation which created them was performed more drastically than that visited on their white colleagues, depriving them not only of the organs which might stimulate a passion calculated to make a husband jealous, but also of the organ which would have rendered its consummation possible.

Slave dealers had repeatedly calculated with great statistical accuracy that the major operation ended fatally six times as often as the minor one; and as a consequence, the Ethiopians who survived it were six times as rare, six times as costly, six times as proud of themselves, and six times as harmless in the eyes of a husband like Machmut.

The clinical history of the operation was said to date from the penetrating acuity of one of the early sultans, a savagely jealous man, who, on a hunting trip, had seen a horse that he knew to be a gelding behaving in a manner that he had thought the exclusive prerogative of a stallion. On his return to the palace, all his unfortunate black eunuchs had been forced to submit to a second operation.

The two who escorted Machmut's fourth wife into the Paradise of Mohammed II were so tall that she looked like a child walking between them. Their height was accentuated by the turbans they wore, which were not the conservative ones dictated by Turkish fashion, all of a color and soberly styled, but huge, round as melons, and formed of bright, parti-colored silk scarves, wonderfully interwound. A decorative clasp of flashing gems clipped to the front leant an air of distinction to the rainbow-hued headgear and kept them from unwinding in the wind; but the costly jewelry had never tempted a thief. Long, heavy scimitars slung from the girdles of Usamah and Umarah belied their rotundity and bespoke enormous strength in their big, black, roly-poly bodies. Their names would have indicated that they were Egyptian if their turbans had not.

The slippery, degenerate sultanate of the Burji Mamelukes on the Delta had little but Islam in common with the Ottoman Empire. Islam itself was corrupt in Egypt, at least in the eyes of the orthodox Turks. For there dwelt in a palace in Cairo a man who claimed to be the caliph of the whole Mohammedan world, an area of planetary scope. He was an impotent figure, entirely dependent on the Egyptian monarchs for the liberal pension that supported his lavish ecclesiastical court. His claim was in direct opposition to the powerful Turkish emperor's, and nobody paid very much attention to it except the Egyptians, who tolerated and even revered him because he gave their kings a certain dignity despite the fact that they were often common men and overthrew each other in rapid succession, very like the Caesars of old Rome in the last days of the empire.

In Turkey recently, the rumor of Egyptian corruption had received new impetus when the emissaries of the Beglerbey of Roum had interviewed the caliph in his palace on a matrimonial mission. Murad had deemed it politic to flatter his shadowy rival by commanding one of his most exalted subjects to marry a daughter of one of the caliph's concubines. The girl had arrived in Turkey with an imposing train of slaves, a large personal fortune, and an immense dowry.

Her name was Aeshia, the name of the Prophet's own wife, a fitting name for a daughter of the Prophet's self-styled Apostle. She was possessed of a beauty that would have been gratuitous under the circumstances, except that it warmed and excited Machmut so thoroughly that he clutched his beard and muttered Mashallah! when he saw her.

The Turkish emissaries who initiated the interesting rumors reported that the walls of the palace of His Egyptian Holiness were not only painted, but that they were painted with figures, in defiance of all good manners. Nor was this the end of it. The figures were human, even female. And the females, alas, were unveiled, unclothed, stark naked, and rapturously dancing. Yet not all the figures were female. The palmy breezes that play over the fecund delta of the Nile blow different thoughts into men's minds than the cold Russian wind that sweeps out of the Asian steppes into Turkey.

On her mother's side, Aeshia could claim Tamerlane as a grandfather, that dreadful all-conquering scourge. In the memory of men still living, this macabre genius, half Mongol, half Hun, had struck down all the Eastern nations from Samarkand to Hindustan, piling the skulls of his enemies into huge, memorial pyramids in front of the battered gates of their ruined cities. But if he killed more humans than anyone ever before him, he also begat an enormous number, as if Nature or the demon that cursed him with lust for destruction had planted in him a compelling, compensatory passion. Up to the age of seventy, out of his loins sprang a multitudinous progeny, from Hindustan to Samarkand.

Aeshia, *Kutchuk Hanoum,* fourth wife, the "Little Lady" of Machmut, walking in Paradise with Usamah and Umarah her slaves, was not aware of the extent to which the immiscible blood of her ancestors ran hot and cold in her veins, making her craftily calculating one moment, impetuously ardent the next. She was vividly aware, however, that she hated the body of Machmut and greedily loved the position that his wealth and princely status accorded her.

She would guard her tongue in the future and keep her eyes down, with Allah's help she would, when she passed a handsome man, and never, never let it be seen how she hennaed the palms of her hands—though everyone did that in Egypt. Please God, weren't hands created to be warm on the body of my lord? How could they look warm without henna? But, of course, this frigid Turk could not see in the dark, and he never set foot in the harem in daylight. Turkey was not Egypt. Her husband made money all day. Usamah and Umarah said he even stooped to extort money somehow from beggar petitioners at the sultan's court. There was nothing wrong with money, of course, but couldn't it be made in a more dignified manner? Selling an extra horsetail to an ambitious pasha, for example?

When she suggested that, Machmut was so angry that he divorced her. "I do all those things!" he roared. "It is not a woman's business to advise her husband." He had remarried her immediately afterward.

Another time she had twitted him about his failing powers, likening him injudiciously to Usamah and Umarah. This sent him into a paroxysm of jealousy, suspicion, and shame, restored all his powers momentarily, and put Usamah and Umarah in dire peril of their lives. Machmut had them searchingly examined. They were discovered to be utterly harmless. Machmut, in a rage, divorced the Little Lady for the second time.

The third time it would count.

The Prophet had sagely ordained that a woman thrice divorced cannot remarry the same man—or at least not until some other man has married and himself divorced her. This wise and understanding statute had contributed to the domestic happiness of Moslems for centuries.

Aeshia did not want to lose her position as a princess for the third and last time. The hot blood of Tamerlane whispered in her heart, "He'll never give up his pretty little barbarian"; but the crafty blood of forty caliphs counseled: "Aeshia, your prince is old; he'll be glad to be rid of you. Don't take a chance." So Aeshia was conscious only of confusion. She thought: I will not, no, I will not look at those two janissaries here in the garden, especially the handsome young one with the green thumb ring on his strong right hand.

"Machmut's hands are hairy," she said aloud.

Usamah and Umarah instantly bent their colorful heads to listen. "Did the Little Lady address her slaves?"

"I did not," she said. "I am going to get a drink."

"The Little Lady did not speak," Usamah and Umarah assured each other, nodding and grinning with a sparkling display of extraordinarily white teeth. They were well acquainted with Machmut's hand: they had often felt the whip in it. They were not much troubled with hair themselves, and they thoroughly disliked the Beglerbey of Roum. The Little Lady walked over to one of the fountains under a pink-flowering almond tree.

There was a dry, dusty breeze in the sultan's garden, ruffling the manes of the drowsy lions, which were always fed at sundown so that they would be quiet during the evening prayer. Michael and Hassan were thirsty, too, and a little cramped in the legs after standing motionless on the balcony all afternoon. They walked briskly to loosen their muscles. The water in the fountain shone like gold in the light still lingering in the west, and some almond flowers floated on its surface.

Out of politeness Usamah and Umarah stopped a few paces short of the fountain while Aeshia knelt and cupped a hand in the water. She heard two men, very close, rapidly walking closer over the gravel path. She smiled, because a convincing thought had suddenly leaped into her mind: I can always say I thought it was my eunuchs!

She drew aside her veil, exposing her whole face, and drank the water from her palm with her lips as if she were kissing it. Out of the corner of her eye she caught a glimpse of the red dress boots and the blue court tunics of the janissaries; but she pretended not to see and looked up, still smiling, full into Michael's face.

Neither Hassan nor Michael knew who she was. Hassan eyed her disapprovingly and said formally: "We hope that the honorable lady will pardon our indiscreet advance upon the fountain."

She should instantly have dropped her veil and ignored their existence; but she was very slow about it. She did not answer Hassan directly.

"I thought you were my slaves," she said, still looking at Michael, the smile still on her moist lips.

Michael had a queer, instantaneous sensation of giddiness, as on that humid day when he and some other soldiers had gone through maneuvers on a cloudy, precipitous mountain trail. He had wanted to step off into the soft, caressing unreality of the fog. He took a step toward the girl; her face was close. It was a face to give a man dreams and make him curse the morning.

"I am your slave," he said in a voice pitched instinctively, cautiously low, but so intense that it carried dangerously. Hassan heard it; so did the eunuchs, who had begun to walk toward the Little Lady, their hands on their swords.

And, as it happened, so did Machmut, the Beglerbey of Roum; but he did not hear it very distinctly because he was out of breath and the loudest noise in his ears was his own thumping heart. He had been walking all over Paradise, skulking behind the hedgerows, narrowly missing the ditches, annoying the animals, trying to spy on his fourth and most disturbing wife.

Hassan saw him, and the big janissary's face changed a little. Not to fear, but to the alert look of a seasoned soldier in a tight place when a powerful enemy advances. Hassan instantly knelt at the fountain and quickly took a drink with one hand. With the other he grabbed Michael's wrist and pulled him down to his knees.

"Drink," he ordered, as if Michael were a horse.

Aeshia followed Hassan's glance, saw her husband, and instantly adjusted her veil. The eunuchs crossed their arms over their enormous chests and bowed to Machmut.

When the twilit scene came into focus for Machmut's weak eyes, he saw two janissary officers drinking at the fountain, and his Little Lady, properly veiled, walking toward him with her two faithful eunuchs, who were perfectly expressionless as always in his presence. He scanned them all suspiciously.

"It is late to be walking," he said, scowling at his wife. "Go home at once."

"I was just going, my lord."

"Who are these men?"

Hassan and Michael rose to their feet, momentarily crossed their arms, which the janissaries did for very few people, bowed slightly, and stood respectfully still.

"What men, my dear lord?" Aeshia asked in a silky voice.

Hassan said, "I am Hassan of Ulubad, Excellency, and this is Michael, my first officer."

It was never wise for even a prince to be impolite to the sultan's military favorites; but Hassan saw murder in Machmut's shifty little eyes. As for Michael, he was sure they could discern on his face the emotion he struggled to conceal.

"It is a beautiful evening," Machmut said sourly. "There is poetry in the air. I could swear that I heard somebody say he was somebody's slave."

"I said that," said Usamah and Umarah in unison, and then looked at each other confusedly.

"If you did, then your voices are changing. I'll have the matter looked into."

Aeshia said: "I had asked them to walk close to me, my lord. The gardens are full of wild animals."

"Aren't they!" Machmut snarled. He glared at Michael and spun on his heel without a word and hustled his wife off toward his apartments in the palace.

Michael stood a long time looking at the spot where the lissom figure of the Little Lady had disappeared into the trees. The moon had risen over the walls, and its silver light set the animals to prowling uneasily along the confining ditches.

"I've got to see her again," Michael said.

Hassan replied impatiently: "I can't think offhand of a quicker way of getting yourself strangled. You're in trouble enough already. Do you know who that was?"

"A rose from the gardens of Nishapor! The most beautiful creature in Islam!"

"Hm-m. Personally, I don't think you're far wrong; but she's the Kutchuk Hanoum of the Beglerbey of Roum. My friend, you are playing with fire."

But Michael said, "I am not playing."

CHAPTER

11

Mohammed II promised peace to the whole world, and most
of the foreigners who witnessed his solemn coronation and investiture believed him.

It was noted that he would continue to pay an enormous annual
sum of money to Constantinople. That looked almost as if he
accepted a tributary status. He apparently did not care to fight the
Greeks. Also, he had extended the truce with the troublesome
Hungarians. Apparently he did not want to fight them, either. And
it was thought particularly significant that he continued Khalil Pasha
in power . . . Khalil Pasha, his gentle father's grand vizier, "Foster
Brother to the Infidel" because he, like the dead emperor, had married a Christian. Apparently this handsome, young, inexperienced
sultan was not going to fight anyone.

Or so thought the Western ambassadors, talking among themselves, sipping their sweet infidel wines, which they imported to
Adrianople on the backs of mules, since neither camels nor horses
were permitted to transport intoxicants. They congratulated themselves that they could now go home to Europe and continue their
own absorbing wars.

But the Byzantine Greeks were closer at hand. Having already
lost most of their empire to the Turks, they were not so complacent.
No sultan since Osman failed to take something away from them.
George Phranza approached half the ambassadors of the Western
nations and politely inquired what their governments' attitudes

would be if the new sultan proved more warlike than he looked. The ambassadors told the elegant chancellor of the Roman Empire of the East that they would have to consult their sovereigns.

Eastern and Western Christendom were irreconcilably separated, physically, economically, and religiously. The old animosities dated back to the Fourth Crusade. Phranza got not one word of encouragement, and some of them broadly suggested that no one but a cowardly Greek would be alarmed by the affable young Majesty of Turkey.

But if Europe would not treat with Constantinople it would trade with her. Since Murad's death certain farsighted, patriotic merchants had secretly begun to place enormous orders in Europe for arms and armor, especially in Italy, where the sharpest, toughest steel in the world was made. This trade was illegal, because it was contrary to an old treaty between John Palaeologus, the late emperor of Constantinople, and Murad II, the late sultan of Turkey.

Now the new sultan heard of the rearmament and determined to stop it. Mohammed II had plans of his own for the Eastern Roman Empire.

The very evening of his coronation, when Mohammed retired, as everyone thought, to his harem, he was neither so fatigued nor so disinterested in state affairs as he pretended to be. With rose water he purified his face, his hands, and his arms to the elbows, as the law required the faithful to do after conversation with the Gavours. He summoned, not his wives, but Khalil Pasha, his grand vizier, to his presence. Khalil Pasha summoned the Aga, commander in chief of the janissaries. The Aga summoned Hassan of Ulubad. And Hassan, after this rapid succession of interviews, summoned Michael privately into his quarters.

Hassan sat cross-legged before a little writing table on the floor, bent over a piece of parchment. It looked bigger and more important than the military correspondence with which he usually dealt. Michael stood respectful and silent while his captain accepted a cup of sherbet from an orderly. Hassan ordered another lamp, and then he sent the orderly from the room and sat for a full minute tugging at his mustache. Michael could not read the veteran commander's impassive face. He did not know whether he was to be reprimanded for the incident in the garden or whether Hassan had called him at this late hour on some piece of military business. He could not politely stare at the parchment, of course, but even at a respectful distance he could see that it bore the great silver seal of the grand vizier.

At length Hassan asked, "Can you still speak Italian, Commander?" The question was totally unexpected.

"I confess that I can, Captain Effendi."

"Fluently?"

"I am afraid so, sir."

"How do you know?"

Michael looked ashamed. "I still dream in Italian."

Hassan smiled slightly. "You dream too much," he said. "Oh, well, that's another matter. As for your heathen tongue, don't fret about it. Perhaps it's going to be of service to you. Would you hand me that pen, Michael?"

Michael reached over and picked up one of the reed pens which the captain's orderly kept cut to a point, ready for instant use. Hassan dipped it in the inkwell, rapidly inscribed a word in a blank place in the script on the parchment, and handed the pen back to Michael.

"There," he said, blowing on the ink to dry it. "That relieves my mind considerably. You are going to Galata."

Michael flushed hotly. He strongly suspected that the parchment document was an order of some kind lacking only a name, and that Hassan had just written in his own. He thought he knew why.

"I no longer need a nurse, Captain Effendi," he said angrily. "If the grand vizier wants you to send someone to Christendom on a mission, do not pick on me because you want to get me out of danger from Machmut. Or," he added in a lower tone, "from his Little Lady."

Hassan raised his eyebrows, grinning broadly.

"From way across the room! Such eyesight! How did you know it was an order from Khalil Pasha?"

"His seal is as big as the full moon."

"You are just the man to send. I knew you were."

"I can take care of myself here."

"Now that, Michael, is flattering yourself. Such self-confidence is one of the privileges and limitations of youth. It is not my purpose to get philosophical, however. I know very well by now that you can take care of yourself anywhere. Actually, I'm afraid I'm sending you into greater danger than you'd ever be exposed to from Machmut.

When I said that I was relieved that you were going to Galata, it was not that I wanted to interfere with a foolish flirtation. That is none of my business. I was simply relieved that I happened to be telling the truth when I told the commander in chief that you spoke Italian better than any other of my men."

Hassan tapped the parchment.

"This is merely a passport," he said, "but the verbal orders that go with it are very important. I think perhaps they originate with His Majesty himself."

Michael noticed that Hassan instinctively called the new sultan Majesty, whereas everyone had always referred to Murad as the Commander of the Faithful. In the space of a few hours since his coronation, the young monarch's temperament was already reflected in the choice of titles that his subjects applied to him. Mohammed II gave military orders the first night of his reign, while his father slept in a peaceful grave that was open to the sky.

"News has come to me from the Aga," Hassan said, "that a Christian merchant in Galata, in defiance of the Gavours' plighted word, is running arms into Constantinople. The corps is highly honored that His Majesty has chosen, not a diplomat or a spy, but a janissary to look into the matter. I have it from the Aga himself that the sultan wishes to send a military man, frankly and openly, to warn the smuggler. Naturally, it is a great honor for the soldier who is chosen."

Michael's face began to shine. Such a mission could well be the making of a man. He forgot everything else.

"You, Michael, are to go to Galata and investigate this Christian merchant. Find out if he is the smuggler we think he is. Obtain a confession if you can. Do not look offended. In some respects you will be a spy, but your mission does not end with the mere gathering of evidence. Once you discover that the merchant is actually trafficking in illicit arms, you are empowered to deliver a verbal message from the grand vizier. You are to say that if he does not immediately stop his unfriendly political activities, you will report him to the Byzantine authorities. They would hand him over to us for trial at once, as you know. You can tell him that we will execute him and that his head will be stuffed with hay and sent back to Constantinople, there to be nailed to a wall in the hippodrome with a placard under it recording his crime."

"Where does the merchant live in Galata?"

"On the Golden Horn."

"What is his name?"

"Filippo Bernardi. He is a powerful figure on the Bosphorus, controlling the Venetian shipping on both sides. He already has a bad name with us because it is known that he smuggled arms once before, years ago, at the fall of Varna. Why do you look so, Michael?"

Michael was frowning, thinking hard. He was dimly aware of a succession of confused images: a little girl, some delicious grapes, and a pair of Gavour spectacles. But these fragments out of his heathen past were nothing that he was honor bound to reveal to Hassan.

Hassan said: "If I have inadvertently touched on anything to offend you, I am sorry. On the other hand, if you happen to remember anything than can advance your mission, you must relate it, no matter how long ago it may have occurred." This was to inform Michael that his Christian childhood might be mentioned without reproach.

"I can truthfully say that I remember nothing of value to this mission, sir."

Hassan gave him the passport with the great silver seal. Michael crossed his arms and bowed deeply to his commander. "May Allah bless you with long life and happy days," he said gratefully. "Your friendship distinguishes me with an honorable mission."

There was a ghost of a smile on Hassan's face. "It wasn't just friendship: I simply couldn't think of a better man to send to Galata tomorrow."

Thus on the second day of Mohammed II's reign, an officer of his janissaries, with a guard of honor, galloped out of Adrianople, bearing a grave warning to the Christians. Hassan heard the horses, arose from his breakfast, and took the salute of their flashing scimitars as they thundered past his quarters.

"That takes care of Machmut's Little Lady for a while," he sighed to himself. "Lucky for me the lad could still speak Italian."

THE quartering of soldiers on civilians has never been popular in any age in any country. It is always a nuisance to have self-assured young men with enormous appetites invade one's home, disrupt one's domestic routine and, in Christian countries, make temporary love to one's unsecluded daughters.

In Turkey there was a venerable institution called *Gazaldic,* the hospitality tax. Military or civilian officials might suddenly appear at the door, especially the door of a Gavour, either Christian or Jew, and honor the householder for three days with their unwelcome, expensive presence. The traditional three-day limit was often stretched to a week, to the greater honor of the host, and, of course, to his greater expense. It was a custom born of a sly sense of humor, common to the Orient. In India it was carried to a degree that became proverbial when reigning potentates took to bestowing gifts of white elephants on their exasperated subjects.

The silver seal that the vizier had set on Michael's passport opened the gates and silenced the guards, Christian and Moslem alike, all the long way from Adrianople to Galata. Michael and his men took the old Roman road, the same route followed in such feverish haste by Nicolo da Montelupo so many years before; but fast Arabian horses now bore Nicolo's son and his escort at a speed which would have been unthinkable for the ailing, anxious father on the mule. Nicolo would have found the pits in the road not visibly deeper. The trees were not noticeably larger. The janissaries passed easily from the Turkish capital to the Byzantine capital in four days, arriving at Bernardi's house on the Golden Horn after what they considered an exhilarating and not especially arduous ride.

Bernardi was soundly built, like the honest old Roman road, and except for a slight thickening both at the waistline and in his curious Gavour spectacles, he too had changed very little. Michael had cudgeled his memory, striving to obliterate in four days the cumulate mental habits of all his mature life. Childhood memories grow vague and inaccurate even when a life flows as evenly as an uninterrupted stream from infancy to manhood. Michael's childhood lay locked behind the monstrous dam that marked his entry into the janissary corps, and he had disciplined himself for years to consider that childhood shameful.

Now, however, he was free to search in his past, as Hassan had ordered, for any scrap of memory that might advance his mission. There was almost nothing. He could not bring himself to think of his father at all. Michael could remember nothing about Bernardi when Bernardi met him except: I met this man once. I was not alone. This Gavour is probably not all bad. It was not the sort of thing Hassan, who knew that Michael had come originally from Scutari, had expected him to remember about the Galatan smuggler.

On the unannounced arrival of a dozen mounted janissaries at his gate, Bernardi came out personally to admit them. In the last days of the Roman Empire of the East, all the Christians were extraordinarily polite to the Turks. The Emperor Constantine had just named a corps of his own Greek guards "Imperial Janissaries" as a politic gesture to his majestic colleague in Adrianople. Vigorous Europe laughed at the heathen name and called it another example of the slippery Eastern hypocrisy that had usually been successful in the past and would probably be again. Europe was far away, and laughter was easy.

Bernardi was familiar with the Turkish hospitality tax. It could not be imposed in Christendom, of course; but Bernardi felt that if someone in Turkey chose to designate his house as a likely source of hospitality, he would be the last to dispel the impression. Not that his conscience hurt him: on the contrary, he considered his motives pure, patriotic, Christian. Yet at that moment Bernardi was making more money than ever before in his long, prosperous life.

He stood on the ground at the gate and bowed profoundly to

Michael on horseback, carrying his hand to his heart. It was a compromise between the Eastern posture of submission and a European salutation.

"Be welcome," he said gravely, "in God's name. I and all my house shall be honored to serve the close and friendly imperial soldiers if you choose to stop here. Though I must say, there are greater men and greater houses in Constantinople, across the bay, where you would be just as welcome."

Michael looked at him oddly. Then to the astonishment of his guards he got off his horse.

"Our mission ends here, signore," he said in Italian. Bernardi betrayed no surprise at hearing his own Venetian tongue. One never knew where the janissaries came from. One of the youngest guards whispered, "The commander is careless of his dignity." An older companion shot him a warning glance and answered, barely moving his lips: "Quiet, you fool! He dismounted to be diplomatic." Michael continued: "We are going no farther, signore. Khalil Pasha suggested that your house was commodious, your temper hospitable, and," he could not help adding, "the grapes in your garden extraordinarily good."

He drew his passport from his girdle, touched it to his forehead, and presented it to Bernardi, who started slightly when he saw the seal. Why had so exalted a personage sent a company of mounted soldiers to snoop into his highly irregular business? Who had talked? He made a quick motion with the passport toward his heart and handed it back to Michael as if it were burning his fingers. The janissaries had witnessed many reactions to the vizier's seal, all of them rooted in fear. They were not therefore surprised when Bernardi bowed again, even lower than before, and, repeating his welcome, himself led Michael's horse over the exquisitely kept lawn of his garden. After the sudden, momentary shock, Filippo Bernardi had his wits about him again.

"Your august minister is well informed as to my hospitality," he said smoothly—too smoothly, Michael thought. "I am honored to be well thought of so far away; but the grand vizier is unhappily ill informed about my little vineyard. You can see for yourself that nothing is ripe for picking here."

The windows were full of the scowling faces of frightened servants, who hated to see their master acting like his own groom.

Michael's quick eye also caught a glimpse of the naked face of a pretty girl. A day in Christendom had not accustomed Michael to such nudity. Bernardi's major-domo stabled Michael's horse, and all the servants moved out of their comfortable rooms. The alert Enrico warned them that since the master himself had unaccountably elected to play stable boy to the Turkish leader, they would all undoubtedly have to sleep in the kitchen to make room for the Turkish retainers.

"He is not a coward," Michael decided, "not a coward, but obviously guilty." Michael took no pleasure in the thought.

Enrico, the major-domo, succeeded in finding rooms for all the men. They tried the chairs, wondering at the stiffness of European men, whose legs Allah had obviously created without joints. They felt as if they were still perched atop their high horses. And they bounced up and down on the soft beds. Their own beds were blankets stretched over a hard wooden floor; they could not remember anything softer. These springy beds vastly appealed to their young, ardent, celibate imaginations, and were designed, they decided after a long and agreeable discussion, to give motion and speed to the love life of the lazy Gavours. With such a device, they concluded delightedly, a lusty Turk could bounce to the ceiling.

If Bernardi heard the beds bouncing and the Turks laughing in his servants' quarters, he gave no indication of it. Michael's face was serious. Studying it, the merchant decided not to offer him wine, though he had known Turks who would accept it. He ordered some for himself, however. Enrico brought it in a handsome glass decanter. The goblet was glass too, clear as rock crystal, with a design carved into its substance in a cunning manner. There was a long stem at the bottom; it could be grasped without the heat of the hand taking the chill off the liquid. From where they were sitting on the porch overlooking the Golden Horn, Michael could see the cross on the dome of Santa Sophia, the Church of the Holy Wisdom, across the bay.

If Michael had been a Christian youth, Bernardi would have liked him. There was a chance angularity about his jaw line which something Bernardi had forgotten caused him to associate with rectitude. Since Michael was obviously a spy, and a military one at that— something of a new departure in Turkish technique—Bernardi was naturally wary and resentful. But he knew the strict code of the janissaries. He was aware that his daughter was beautiful. It would be safe to expose her, and her presence might conceivably help him out of a difficult position if, as he assumed, he was in one.

"I shall not insult you with an offer of a forbidden drink," he said pleasantly. "This is wine, of course; quite intoxicating when abused, but delightful when drunk in moderation." He patted his comfortable belly. Michael saw the flash of a spectacular diamond ring that extended from Bernardi's knuckle to the middle joint of his forefinger and equaled the finger in width. It was so brilliant that it appeared self-luminous in the twilight, and it sparkled with all the colors of the spectrum, though the twilight was as golden as the glistening, distant dome of Santa Sophia. The wealth of these Christians! Something akin to the ambition that consumed the heart of the sultan leaped in Michael's heart when he considered how easily these soft fat people could be overwhelmed and their treasures appropriated.

The Christian continued to speak: "Aids the digestion!" he pronounced affably, "as you can see." Michael evinced no interest in the merchant's digestion and refused to smile. Bernardi's eyes narrowed slightly: whatever this man had come to do, he might do fast! Without a pause the merchant continued: "Yet you will surely not refuse a goblet of sherbet after the long ride that has ended so fortuitously at my house today. I cannot entrust the making of sherbet to my careless old Enrico." Enrico was the best major-domo in Galata. "Only my daughter can bruise the violets, crush the citrons, and measure the honey that will make an acceptable drink for a man whose face—you must pardon my European directness—proclaims his good taste and betrays his resolution." He sent Enrico with a message for his daughter.

This speech presented something af a linguistic problem for Michael, who had learned no Italian since he was twelve years old. He understood it, but he could not possibly answer it properly.

"I'd be delighted, signore," he said, and when he spoke again he spoke Greek, in which he was better instructed. Bernardi sensed the reason for the change of language, changed himself, and made no comment. Michael had begun to talk politics.

"You have welcomed me and my men with wondrous courtesy," he said. "Having met you, it is hard for me to believe that not all Christian merchants are so honest and straightforward. I must tell you that I am commissioned to dissuade a Christian trader from illegal commerce in arms in defiance of a treaty between our two friendly empires. Perhaps you will tell me you find it hard to believe such a thing?"

Not believe it? Bernardi could believe anything, especially from a mysterious Greek-speaking janissary with infant Italian also on his lips.

"Incredible," he murmured absently, looking hard at Michael's jaw line. It exasperated him not to be able to place it. He thought perhaps the janissary's name might give him a clue; and he determined to try a trick to discover it. He waited impatiently the arrival of his daughter, calculating shrewdly that the presence of an unveiled, respectable young woman of unusual attractiveness would momentarily upset the janissary's poise. And when she came with Michael's dewy glass of sherbet, Bernardi, noting Michael's appreciative eyes, said five rude, astonishing words:

"What was your Christian name?"

"Michael," said Michael, but he did not say it alone, for Angelica also cried, "Michael!"

Bernardi half rose from his chair, gasped and fell back again, suddenly very pale.

"Da Montelupo! Oh, Blessed Lord Jesus!"

Michael blushed crimson. The insult was double. His past was violated and he had admitted that he had no name. It enraged him suddenly to be on the defensive.

"It's no more Christian than Moslem. Or Jewish either, for that matter."

Angelica impulsively burst out, "It's the name of an angel!"

Bernardi, suddenly taken aback, found himself in unutterable confusion. The young man was now standing, shaking with rage. His hand was on his sword, and for an instant it looked as if he might slice off the merchant's head with his scimitar. Angelica drew back with a startled gasp, wide-eyed and frightened by his height and his menacing attitude. Bernardi's eyes dropped to the janissary's yellow shoes. He saw the costume of the Turkish soldier. Its import struck him. A hesitant smile of welcome withered on his face. Dear God, he thought, my friend never came back and neither did his son. This body may once have been the son's but the soul is changed, like the clothes.

"I was sent here by the grand vizier to order you to stop smuggling," Michael said sternly, controlling his anger and using the strongest words he knew.

Bernardi quickly collected his wits: "Softly, softly, sir, I beg you. Do, please, take that sherbet from my daughter before she drops it. You're frightening her half to death. Sit down, Angelica."

"If you knew anything at all," Michael said, "you'd know enough not to ask a janissary his name. At least a janissary who still carries his shameful Gavour name. I don't know how I happened to tell you." He glared at Angelica, who did not drop her eyes like a modest Turkish woman but stared at him, brazenly, he thought. "I was ordered here, I tell you. I assure you I didn't want to come." He thought of the Kutchuk Hanoum of the Beglerbey of Roum. "I had no desire to see either my father, who forgot me years ago, or his infidel friend."

He was no longer on the defensive. He accepted the sherbet, coldly appraised Angelica's hair as yellow, her mouth red, full, glistening as if she had just sampled his sherbet, and he observed with some irritation that she wore a gown immodestly snug, like all the bold Christian women, instead of the graceful, flowing garments of decent people. Then he sat down, perfectly composed, thoroughly convinced that Bernardi's head would look well on a wall, stuffed with hay, a placard beneath it in elegant Arabic script: *smuggler*.

If Michael had been a Greek, Bernardi might have made some display of his fabulously expensive ring, observing perhaps that it didn't fit very well any more and wouldn't Michael like to try it on. Michael would have gone away perfectly happy, the ring on his finger, without further mention of the little matter of smuggling.

But janissaries and priests were always hard for the practical merchant to fathom, since they appeared to cleave to a special set of values. Bernardi feared no immediate personal danger, for he knew well enough that if the Turks had wanted him they could simply have arrested him on his wharves in Scutari. Or if he happened not to be in Scutari, a suggestion from the Turkish ambassador in Constantinople would have delivered him trussed and gagged across the Bosphorus in a matter of hours. Khalil Pasha had always been friendly. This insolent delegation traveling under his great seal confirmed all Bernardi's suspicions about the new sultan. The diamond would be wasted on this janissary officer, who appeared to Bernardi a particularly ominous example of the extraordinary Turkish system that was threatening the Greek Empire and perhaps all of Christendom.

While the merchant was puzzling how he might treat with his unwelcome guest, the angry blood drained out of Michael's face. He had begun to sip his sherbet.

Angelica said softly, "Your father did not forget you, Michael."

Bernardi hastily interrupted, "Don't call the commander Michael!" and he looked reprovingly at his daughter. Inwardly, however, he addressed a quick prayer to St. Mark, the heavenly patron of Venice, who had blessed him with a daughter who always said the right thing. Now he knew what he should say. Then smoothly to Michael:

"It may cause you some pain, sir, that your father has never expressed any pleasure at your admirable career in the sultan's distinguished corps. Yet I think I feel somewhat the way he might if he were sitting here now. Surely he would have been proud of your progress in a company where, as everyone knows, advancement comes only through merit. Unfortunately the Lord of Montelupo died seven days after you left for camp." Bernardi spoke without a trace of compassion.

Angelica saw the janissary's hand tighten and grow white at the knuckles. The slender stem of the glass snapped in his fingers. Oddly, he was unaware of it. The delicate foot of the goblet fell and shattered on the tessellated pavement of the porch, yet he continued to hold the cup. Not a drop of sherbet spilled, but a little cut from the broken glass dripped red on the sharp crystal shards. Michael did not feel the cut, and in the dusk none of them saw the blood.

"I did not know Father was dead," Michael said tonelessly, slipping unconsciously into Italian. But Bernardi continued in Greek. He was taking no chances, well aware that the death of a father whom one has not seen for years would not change a janissary back into a Christian.

"Thus he could not feel the pride which I, his friend, do in your obvious progress. In fact, he told me that he was convinced that a mistake had been made when your name appeared on the list of Christian boys to be honored. He rode all the way to Adrianople to have the mistake rectified, and in Adrianople he died, before his well meant interference could ruin your career."

Bernardi's revelation had been sudden and sharp and unexpected. Michael turned his face away lest the quick pain be observed. Through the window he saw the gloomy, dark mountain of Bulgarlhu Dagh looming over the city of Scutari across the Bosphorus. This was the closest he had come to his former home since the day in his youth when the Tournaji Bashi arrived with the selictar to take some Christian boys on a holiday. There were lights on the flanks of the mountain. One of them came from the church with the *hagiosidere*. One probably came from the old gray house he had lived in with his father.

"How do I know my father is dead?" Michael asked heavily.

Bernardi sighed and said: "I wish I could not answer that. Unfortunately there is no doubt about the matter. One moment, Commander." He stepped into his study and returned with a paper in his hand. Bernardi gave Michael the paper, saying with a note of anxiety in his voice: "In the tolerant reign of the late, revered sultan, the Gavours enjoyed many privileges, as this paper attests. I do not know how it will be now. Your father lies in a Turkish grave, yet it is consecrated to the faith he loved."

Michael read the Turkish script. It was a formal permission for burial, phrased in almost, but not quite, the usual manner:

> *To the priest of the Church of Virgin Saint Mary in Adrianople: This is to certify that the body of Nicolo da Montelupo, damned yesterday, may be concealed underground.*

To Michael the harsh word "damned" meant only that his father had died a Christian, beyond the redemption of Islam.

In the light of the lamp, Angelica noticed his bleeding hand.

"You have cut your finger, Commander," she said softly. "Let me tie it up."

Michael looked blankly at the little gash, wondering how it had happened. Then he saw the broken goblet.

He said: "I broke your glass. I'm sorry." Bernardi smiled wryly. Michael wondered whether this civil, sophisticated merchant had ever heard about the Statues of Glass and how easily they were broken.

Bernardi said: "It wasn't really mine. It belonged to an old friend of mine. I was just keeping it for him. I doubt that he'd mind if he knew my guest had accidentally broken it." Angelica offered to bandage the cut with a tiny silk handkerchief, but Michael would not let her touch him.

He said wearily, "I would like to retire now." His gaze rested, dark and inscrutable, on his host for a moment. Then, without a word, he followed the major-domo to the room that had been prepared for him.

Bernardi rose and bowed profoundly when his guest withdrew. His eyes glinted behind their thick spectacles at the foolish, touching appearance of the intensely proud young man walking off to bed with a broken cup of sherbet in one hand, the mournful scrap of paper in the other.

Bernardi mused aloud. "Perhaps he is still half human, though I doubt it. I doubt also whether he'll have pleasant dreams tonight."

"Poor Michael!" Angelica whispered in reply. "Why didn't you tell him everything, Father? Why didn't you save him, instead of asking me to make that sherbet? I'd have refused you, Father, if I had known whom it was for."

"Save him? How can I save him? Far better to save ourselves, daughter. The sherbet won't hurt him."

"But Father, you must tell him who he *is!*"

But Bernardi shook his head. "Why should I? Money means nothing to these changelings. He'd probably think I was bribing him. Maybe he'd slit both our throats, or get me into trouble with the authorities. This infidel means nothing to me or to you." Angelica's expression altered and set with a stubbornness her father had seldom observed in her before. Bernardi repeated sternly: "I forbid him to mean anything to you. Let me think, daughter, let me think."

The major-domo politely remained in Michael's room for an instant. Was everything to the commander's liking? Did the commander wish the windows opened? Would the commander require another light? Michael sent him for a basin of water. Then he looked at his hands and saw that he was still idiotically holding the mutilated goblet and the burial certificate. He slipped the paper into his girdle and eyed the glass uneasily for a moment, debating whether he ought to treat it very carefully and take it back to Turkey and have it repaired. The broken glass could not be restored, of course, but maybe one of the silversmiths could fashion a new foot. Then the goblet would look as if it had been made that way intentionally. Michael considered the thought only for an instant. Then he laughed shortly, scowled, drained the cup at a gulp, and angrily crushed it to pieces under his heel. "God's name! These Christians are putting a spell on me! I'll be fearing the jinn and the afrits next. Myths! Myths!"

Bernardi and Angelica, tiptoeing past his door to their own rooms, heard water splashing.

"At least he's clean," Bernardi observed wryly. He shook his head, anxious and puzzled.

Michael was ceremonially purifying his mouth and his hands to the elbows after conversation with the Gavours, prior to kneeling to Mecca to say his prayers. After his ablutions Michael examined the death certificate. It was signed by an obscure civilian official and was properly witnessed by someone who had been at great pains to sign his name twice, once in Turkish script, Yousuf the Prudent, and once in the Latin, Joseph of Adrianople. Michael suddenly remembered the old man. He had given Joseph the emerald years ago in his father's house, and now he realized that he had seen this same Jew at the sultan's coronation. Apparently the man was still in favor. So highly placed a person might be of use to a military man. He could also undoubtedly ruin a career if he happened to be unfriendly.

But the curious thing about the death certificate was the restrained language in which it was couched. It referred to "the body" of his father, not, as was usual, "the impure, stinking corpse." It said "concealed underground," not "buried," almost as if some day someone might come to claim it and take it away. Burial certificates of the sultan's Christian subjects were usually worded with extraordinary severity and disgust, for however tolerant Islam might be of the living, it was unrestrainedly contemptuous of the dead who had died unconverted. Since the document was phrased so politely, Michael began to regard it as a possible indication that his father might not actually have been a rayah at all, but a foreigner who owed the sultan no allegiance. If so, he knew that the merchant might well have spoken the truth when he said his father considered Michael's admission into the corps an unfortunate mistake. Bismillah! The document was dangerous! Next this slippery host of his would be telling him he wasn't a janissary at all.

He held the paper up to the lamp and burned it.

Outside the door, Enrico, the major-domo, peeking through a crack, watched him and hurried off to inform his master.

"My lord, the terrible Turk has stamped on the goblet and destroyed my lord's document in the flames!"

Bernardi said: "He's a fool. I declare that I am sorry, but I am not surprised. Now I know what I shall do."

Michael then said his prayers. In a Christian house in this soft Christian land he could have found it in his heart to pray for the soul of his dead Christian father. Yet he recalled how the Prophet himself had burst into tears at the sepulcher of his mother at Al Âbwa, saying: "I asked leave of God to visit my mother's tomb, and He granted it; but when I asked Him leave to pray for her, He forbade me." So Michael could not pray for his father.

He lay down to sleep, and at first he dreamed pleasantly that Aeshia was there with him in the great, soft infidel bed; but a chilly wind blew in through the open windows. The sleeping man moved restlessly. All Aeshia's raven-swart hair changed into yellow, she grew taller, more slender, and all at once she was Angelica, under a dome of glass. The dome filled with green liquid, the liquid froze, and the dome became immense, a mountain of solid ice with the girl frozen in its heart. Even in the nightmare Michael knew that he did not love Angelica. If she were imprisoned in a block of ice, so much the worse for her; but an irresistible compulsion drove him to attack the mountain. He tore at it frantically with his bare hands, cutting them to ribbons, stricken with panic, because if the mountain were not destroyed he himself would be destroyed in some frightful, unknown manner.

While Michael slept, sweating and hagridden on the big soft bed, two servants stole silently, expertly out of the house and down to the waterfront, as if they were used to walking in the dark. There was an enormous amount of subdued activity in the warehouses till nearly dawn. And one of Bernardi's ships, low in the water, still heavy with the cargo she had brought from Europe, quietly loosed her lines and slipped out of the Golden Horn, not a light showing.

When Michael awoke, the sun was hot and high, and he wondered what he had eaten or drunk here in Christendom to make his mouth feel so dry. His bed was drenched with sweat. Never, he thought, had he slept so late before. For an instant the thought of poison crossed his mind, but he had obviously not been poisoned because he was still alive, very hungry and extremely thirsty. He blamed the big bed.

126

No one had thought to warn Michael that the pharmacopoeia of the Greeks was practical and diversified. One of their learned aids to nature could make a young man senile to dementia. Another could make an old man youthful to priapism. And one was a harmless, delectable sherbet that could put any man soundly to sleep.

No one disturbed him, though as he awoke he had an uncomfortable feeling that he was being watched. And indeed, the moment he stirred, the major-domo appeared with exactly what he wanted most, having apparently read his mind. Enrico had a silver tray with a Chinese porcelain cup of steaming coffee and a goblet—it was silver this time, not glass—full of cool fruit juice. He knelt at Michael's bed, holding the tray perfectly steady within convenient reach, and politely averted his eyes, since Michael was not wearing his turban and probably felt uncomfortable.

"The commander need not exert himself. None of my clumsy staff must wait upon the commander. I myself am to make the commander comfortable. Would he care first to drink the juice? It is a very hot day. Then perhaps the commander will wish to take coffee."

If this steady-handed, polite man was the household official whom Bernardi had called careless, it seemed to Michael that the domestic service of the merchant must be most enviable. He knew he was being skillfully handled; it enraged him to like it. He downed the fruit juice and muttered gratefully, "Mashallah! I wanted that!" Then he drank the coffee. It was excellent. He felt like the sultan. A janissary had to acquire some horsetails before he could command such service; Hassan of Ulubad was not nearly so well served.

Then Enrico, still not looking at him but again reading his thoughts, ventured to suggest: "If the commander should wish someone to make up his turban, one of my staff is very skillful at it."

"God's name! Do you dare employ the faithful as servants?"

"He is only a Persian, Your Excellency."

"Oh."

Michael held the sturdy Turkish view that the gay, unorthodox Persians would do anything, for pleasure or for money.

"He will also shave you, sir, if you permit it. Or I should be honored to do so myself."

The janissaries had been clean shaven ever since some resourceful Bulgarians once in a disastrous battle had hit upon the stratagem of immobilizing them by holding on to their beards. Michael declined the proffered service, since there was little to choose between a Shiite and a Christian razor, and asked for one of his own orderlies to make up his turban and shave him.

Michael was at some pains to make himself presentable, as befitted the dignity of his mission. The young orderly brushed his tunic till his own began to wrinkle and wilt from the effects of the strenuous exercise. Michael was angry because he had to admit to himself that he was conscious not only of Bernardi's scrutiny, but also of Angelica's. He wondered whether she had got out of her block of ice. He strode stiffly down the stairs, scowling at the thought that she would probably be there at the breakfast table, her yellow hair streaming down her back, her face naked, her infidel gown too tight. Christian men squeezed themselves into suffocating armor. Perhaps it was only consistent that their daughters squeezed themselves into dresses that fit in places like another skin.

As he walked down the stairs, he was struck by so preposterous a thought that he burst out laughing at himself for the first time in his life. Angelica was not actually ill favored, he decided. She would look bewitching in a veil! The absurdity of his own notion, all twisted and hindside before, amused him so that he took the last three steps at a bound.

Bernardi and Angelica had already had one breakfast and were waiting to have another with their gloomy Turkish spy. Bernardi had expected him to be sleepy. When he saw Michael laughing, leaping down the stairs, he whispered:

"What in the world did you put into his drink?"

"Only what you told me to."

"It must have been the wrong bottle!" and then to Michael, "It is a pleasure to see you so high-spirited this morning, Commander. I plan a little inspection tour of some of my properties today. I hope you will see fit to honor me with your company. Meanwhile we have dared to presume that you would breakfast with us." There was no ice on Angelica; she was smiling, frankly, hospitably; and Michael could see for himself that she looked well even without a veil. If only the Christians were as honest as they appeared.

"Father says I may come, too. If it won't shock you, Commander. I love the ships and the smell of spices and silk."

Michael's exuberance left him. He had not expected his mission to be difficult, but how easily one might learn to enjoy being corrupted by these carefree, luxurious people. After only one night, and a restless night, in Bernardi's house he found unattractive the mental picture of his host's head nailed to a wall in the hippodrome. He sat down and ate with them.

"I was going to suggest just such a tour," he said. "I had not expected your daughter to go with us, though that will be pleasant. Of course, I shall not believe anything I see. It is incredible that you should show me anything that will incriminate yourself."

With a great show of candor Bernardi replied: "Our conversation on the subject was interrupted last night by a painful personal matter. Let me explain at once, Commander, that I have nothing at all to hide. I am smuggling no arms. I am a Venetian, not a Greek. Venetians do not usually like Greeks. Remember, too, that this is Galata, not Constantinople. Here, as you know, we enjoy complete political autonomy and friendlier relations with your great empire than Constantinople itself. I have lived here for many years. Long ago I made all the money I or my daughter shall ever need. If you believe nothing else, believe me when I say that I have no personal interest in adding to my treasure. Smuggling arms would perhaps be very profitable just at this time, since some of the Greeks are worried about the political future; but why should I jeopardize the security I already possess for myself and my only child by engaging in the monstrously hazardous project of smuggling arms?"

"That, sir, I cannot imagine. But you did it before."

"Father! You didn't!"

Bernardi shrugged. "Yes, child, I did. The Turks always know everything. I thought there was some hope for Varna; but if war ever comes, which God forbid, I'm afraid there is none for Constantinople."

Michael was not enjoying his breakfast.

"I wish you were a Greek, sir. You talk like one, plausibly and, as I know, falsely. You have lived here too long. I wish also that you had not known my father, or that I had known him better. You must be aware that such an avowal is difficult for a man in my position."

Bernardi nodded his head. "I know. Believe me, I know, Commander."

"We were prepared to have you deny your guilty, illegal actions. After listening to your unassailably logical argument against yourself, I cannot imagine why you persist in them. I think I do not want to inspect your ships or your warehouses after all. I am perfectly convinced that there isn't so much as a dull little dagger visible anywhere on your premises. You've sent all the arms off to sea again, or they're hidden under the corn of a granary, or you've moved them all into a confederate's warehouse. Why should I inspect your property?"

"Commander, for a military man you astonish me! I assure you that I'm not a smuggler, but if I were I'd have had difficulty thinking of all those ruses!" Bernardi smiled a little. That last device, with a few modifications, might prove particularly effective.

Michael did not smile. He said: "All I want is to go home; but before I go, since you continue to deny your guilt, I must tell you something. Khalil Pasha has ordered me to warn you that unless you stop running these arms into Constantinople you will be killed. Not assassinated. We don't do things that way. You will be fairly tried; but you are guilty, and so you will be executed." Michael opened his mouth to say what would happen to Bernardi's head. But Angelica looked so frightened and her father's face appeared so grave that Michael considered the rest of the threat superfluous. He repeated in a low voice, "You have lived here too long."

Bernardi said wearily: "I know, I know. Perhaps you are right. Angelica hasn't been in Europe since she was a little girl. Commander, you recall me to my duty. Seeing you a man, a prominent man in your adopted country with a glorious future, reminds me that I am old. My future is short. It should be peaceful. I wish the whole world were peaceful. You cannot imagine how an old man longs for peace. Your visit has given me more pleasure than you think, sir. Believe me when I say that I plan to retire from business shortly; as soon as I can put my affairs in order. In some respects I have been retiring for several years now. Much as I long for peace, the air of the East is heavy with the scent of war. I feel the coming storm in my bones."

So the smuggler would go home to Venice! That delighted Michael. He had frightened the old gentleman back to Europe! The merchant might be lying, of course, but his words had a ring of complete sincerity, and his logic was certainly realistic.

"It would be extremely hazardous for you not to retire from a certain kind of business," Michael said. "It is no part of my mission to tell you that your execution would cause me a certain amount of pain."

Bernardi reflected that it would cause *him* a great deal more, but he affected to take the remark at its face value. "It was kind of you to say that, Commander. Let me tell you something just as frankly; it will enhance the value of the report you make to your superiors. Tell them that I admitted to a very slight complicity in one small smuggling transaction. Say that you got me drunk, Commander. Say that I rolled on the floor and confessed!"

Angelica looked horrified. "Father!"

"But my dear, it's only fair. Think of the service this friendly young man has rendered me. He's too intelligent to look for evidence; he knows there isn't any. He reminds me of my duty, of my age. He gives me, shall we say, a chance to escape."

"I can't say you were drunk," Michael protested. "You weren't drunk, and nobody would believe me. Sir, I think Khalil Pasha ought to have sent a diplomat to deal with you. What possible motive could I ascribe to your making such a confession?"

"Greed, Michael, pure greed."

"Father, you mustn't call the commander Michael!"

Michael nodded, smiling gravely. If the elderly, talkative merchant forgot himself and called him Michael just once, it didn't matter. His mission was already accomplished, all in a day. Now I can go home, he thought, with a white face. For a Turk to have "a white face" was to have honor; just as to have "a black heart" meant dishonor in a European.

His young guard would have liked to spend one more night on the European beds. Their dreams had all been uncommonly pleasant; but Michael paraded them out on the street under Bernardi's balcony. Not once did he glance toward Scutari and the mountain of Bulgarlhu Dagh. He ordered a salute from the swords of his men to the merchant and his daughter. As they wheeled to depart, just at noontime, the air over the twin Christian cities filled with a mighty, cacophonous clanging from uncountable thousands of church bells. Michael and the janissaries passed over to Constantinople and galloped out through the triple walls of Byzantium, Constantine, and Theodosius unchallenged. He had only to wave his passport. It could have been an old shoe, however, since the Greeks were glad to see the Turks depart. The gates flew open before them. Michael was back in Turkey again before sunset, so shrunken was the Roman Empire of the East.

Bernardi and Angelica had waved to their thirteen departing guests from the balcony. The instant the tail of the last horse disappeared, Enrico was astonished to behold his dignified master embrace Angelica and give her a resounding kiss on the cheek, so heartily that he knocked off his glasses.

"Father, you're behaving so queerly today. And you've broken your glasses!"

"Everybody's breaking glasses. But I've plenty more. So has Michael, but he doesn't know it. Oh, that foolish young man! Enrico!" he shouted. "Glasses!"

"Glasses to drink from, signore?" The major-domo could well believe it.

"Ten thousand devils, *no!* Glasses to look through, you old idiot! I can't see a thing. Oh, Angelica, my dear, what a merchant that man would have made! He gave me the most beautiful, profitable, satisfying scheme I have ever had in my life. Angelica, your father is going to build a warehouse!"

"You've always had plenty of warehouses."

"Yes, child, but not like *this* warehouse! It will be very secluded, very safe, and under another name. It was Michael's idea. Oh, Nicolo, wherever you are, guard that precious son of yours!"

"You're impious, Father."

"I know it, Angelica. You say the prayer for me. Enrico! My glasses! Even without them, my dear, I can see that you will say it."

MICHAEL rode back to Adrianople so fast that his guard would have grumbled had they dared. They all knew that their sudden, daring descent into the heart of the Christian empire had frightened the wily old merchant half out of his wits. Hadn't the commander himself told them that this Gavour had agreed to stop his illegal trade in arms and to retire permanently into Europe? Wasn't their mission successfully concluded, all in a day? Were they not all returning with honor, with faces white? Was this burst of speed necessary?

Or if the commander was merely making the most of an opportunity to harden them to a long, fast ride (which seemed reasonable enough), why had he not at least taken advantage of the minimum hospitality tax and stayed three days, as custom and good manners required? As they rode, they remembered the pleasant beds, the naked, exciting faces of the unsecluded serving girls.

And was the commander totally blind to the beauty of the merchant's daughter, whom Michael's orderly had observed closely? "Her face is like the moon!" he confided to the other young men. "Like a cypress she is tall. Ripe cherries are not so red as her lips, and her cheek is white, like an ostrich egg!" The young men sighed.

A European would have had difficulty recognizing blond, slender Angelica, with her blue eyes and delicate, expressive features, in the alien Oriental imagery. But to Michael's orderly and to every other youthful, literate Turk, there was no skin so delicate as a skin like the shell of an ostrich egg, and no face like a moonface.

At that moment Michael was blind indeed to every woman except the Little Lady of Machmut, the Beglerbey of Roum; and if he remembered his dream of Angelica he blamed it on the Christian afrits, or the jinn.

In Adrianople, Hassan greeted him without enthusiasm.

"You certainly lost no time, Commander. Why are you back so soon?"

Michael shrugged. "There was no reason to stay longer. The merchant protested that he was innocent, and then confessed that he was guilty. He solemnly swore that he was not a smuggler, and then promised to stop smuggling. He said that he was extremely rich, which is not unlikely—he lives like a pasha. He said he had no ambition for further riches, but then he said he was greedy for even greater wealth. And finally he stated that he had made up his mind to retire from business and return to Venice, because he could smell, as he said, war in the air. His speech was perplexing and contradictory, like a Greek's; but I am persuaded that he will leave Constantinople, if only for the sake of his daughter."

"I had expected you to stay a little longer and enjoy yourself. Constantinople is said to be hospitable these days. In your place I think I should have stayed." Hassan smiled. "Or was the daughter intolerably ugly?"

Michael said casually, "Oh, the girl was attractive enough. At least I heard my orderly telling the men behind my back that she was tall and fair."

"You yourself did not notice, of course."

"Frankly, I do not remember. I was anxious to come home. I did not enjoy myself in Christendom."

"You ought to be stricter with the men, Commander. You know they're not supposed to talk on a march. Oh, well. You kept them in the saddle night and day. It was all right for you to relax the rule about talking a bit. Since you're back so soon, I want you to take plenty of time with your report. Write it clear and big on the official parchment. Highly placed persons will read it. This merchant's activities are being watched more closely than you imagine, by higher authorities than you think. So let the appearance as well as the substance of your report reflect credit upon the corps. I might add," Hassan continued reflectively, "that I'd rather have you in camp for a day or two, out of sight, working on this important report, than sneaking around the town at night like a recruit, looking for—whatever you might be looking for. In fact, I command you to stay in camp."

Michael crossed his arms in the posture of submission, as if the interview were at an end, looking levelly and angrily at his friend. Hassan tugged at his mustache.

"Oh, don't be so infernally proper, Michael. I have not dismissed you. I suppose I may as well tell you, as have you hear it from someone else, that the Beglerbey of Roum has divorced his Kutchuk Hanoum again."

Michael could hardly control his face.

"It's the third time!"

"Don't sound so delighted. I know it is. So does everybody else in town. The scandal is frightful. Every miserable beggar and kitchen slave in Adrianople is laughing at the irascible old prince. And mark you this: they are also making very pointed allusions to the janissary commander who meets her every night in the sultan's garden."

"Meets her every night! Shameless, lying tongues! You know I never saw her before. The poor little girl!"

"Softly, Commander. The poor little girl has retired to her own house, one of the best in the capital, apparently on her own Egyptian fortune. And Machmut is behaving himself in an exemplary manner, consoling himself with his other good wives. Or somehow. In any case, I think the encounter at the fountain in Paradise will soon be forgotten; you're probably a very lucky man. Just stay in camp and write your report. I must confess," he said looking away, "I do not want to have the guards find you strangled in a gutter some morning. It would set a bad example," he explained to a corner of the room. "Now you are dismissed, Commander."

But Michael did not linger or labor over his report, nor did he write it in courtly language, though Hassan had warned him that highly placed persons would read it. He used none of the pious Arabic words that would have pleased the stately entourage of the late sultan, who had made religion fashionable even among the unreligious. Nor did he employ any of the affected Persian words that would have pleased so elegant a person as, say, Khalil Pasha, the old grand vizier. He used straightforward Osmanli words, realistic, factual, the report of a busy, alert soldier truthfully telling what he had seen and heard.

135

Hassan shook his head when an orderly handed him the report early next morning. Clear, undoubtedly clear; but how could so unadorned a recital reflect honor on the diplomacy of his command? No compliments. No fashionable foreign words. Might it not be said that his officers lacked manners? Hassan considered rephrasing the report. But then he reflected on the urgency of his orders, and he could not in conscience delay the document simply to make it more flowery. Dubiously he sent it to the Aga, and the Aga sent it to Khalil Pasha. What Khalil Pasha did with it would have astonished even Hassan, who had expected highly placed personages to see it.

For Khalil Pasha, working at a speed unknown in Murad's reign, overburdened with details he had once considered beneath his dignity, swiftly and obediently brought it under the quick, discerning eye of the sultan himself.

Nothing was beneath the dignity of the busy, able new sultan of Turkey. He scanned Michael's report, observed that another source of illegal arms to the Byzantines bade fair to be dried up, absently thanked Allah, and paused to inquire: "Who is this janissary with no name who writes dispatches like a man and does not waste Our precious time with old-fashioned rhetoric?"

Khalil Pasha gravely replied, "Had Your Majesty's janissary known that Majesty itself would condescend to look upon his words, he would doubtless have written his report less informally. The investigation and warning in the case of Filippo Bernardi, this Christian smuggler, have been carried out vigorously and openly for all the world to see, as Your Majesty commanded. The janissary commander and his guard rode uniformed and armed into the Christian capital. Yet I deemed it prudent, if Your Majesty forgive me, to execute the operation on a low level, lest Your Majesty's glorious name be involved, signing his passport only with my own poor seal."

"Naturally," said the sultan.

"Michael, the janissary, is nameless, as Your Majesty has so penetratingly observed, perchance because he is still too young to have seen war. He has won what authority he now enjoys purely as a result of a certain excellence in archery, which makes him, after Your Majesty, the deadliest marksman in Islam. Who Michael is, Sire, I have never inquired. Shall I do so?"

"No," said the sultan, "I know I keep you busy enough. It is not important. Sometimes you are not a numskull," the sultan continued, and the grand vizier reddened with pleasure. "Perhaps you are wise to counsel prudence at the beginning of great events. This Michael, whoever he is, will have plenty of opportunity to win himself a name. So will all my other nameless young janissaries. Let it please Allah to send the war quickly."

"By all means, Your Majesty; but not too quickly. Not until Your Majesty has put down Thomas and Demetrius Palaeologoi, the princes of the Peloponnesus, who might otherwise aid their brother in Byzantium." Soon the sultan and his vizier had forgotten Michael and passed on to consider whether a military expedition into the Morea or trans-Aegean bribery on a colossal scale would be preferable as a means of insuring that the Eastern Roman Emperor got no help from his imperial brothers in the tremendous war that Constantine did not know was coming. Either means was sure to succeed. It was merely a question which was cheaper and quicker.

As the two most powerful men in Islam fashioned the dire pattern of history, Michael quietly stole out of the janissary camp to present himself, not to Aeshia, Machmut's former fourth wife, but to an obliging old lady whose reputation as an entrepreneuse was well known.

In Christian Europe a young officer without kinsfolk in a similar situation would have engaged a troubadour to sing in the great hall of a castle, after the ladies had retired, out of sight but not out of hearing, from the table where the men continued to sit, to gossip, and to drink. As the men grew duller and sleepier from the effects of the local beer, brandy, or wine, the troubadour's ballads would switch cautiously and imperceptibly from battles to love. And when the men's eyes glazed, or their heads fell into their plates, the troubadour's song might contain certain specific allusions to a knight under the grating in the south rampart, or a squire standing at the moat under the rose window of the chapel. And then some lady would prick up her ears behind the arras and signal, if no one was looking, that the message was understood.

But in Turkey there were no troubadours because there were no love songs; and there were no love songs because the practical, patriarchal Turks considered it a foolish waste of time and an unproductive expenditure of energy to obscure under a flood of poetic words an acknowledged urge which legally or illegally, honorably or shamefully, one way or another, always spent itself in the same

137

manner. But there were men in Turkey and women in Turkey; and despite the seclusion of the one and restrictions on the social deportment of the other, it was by no means impossible for a man to see a woman privately.

Just as nothing like the gay, wandering troubadour ever existed in Turkey, so nothing in sturdy, outspoken, feudal Europe ever existed like the Turkish marriage broker. This discreet and indispensable functionary had been honored and respected since remotest antiquity in all the great Eastern nations.

Theoretically, a young Turk when he claimed his bride knew nothing about her appearance. In actual practice he was likely to be very well informed, either by a female relative or, if he had none, by a marriage broker.

Marriage brokers were all women, since only women and a few eunuch slave attendants of no social standing had access to the women's public baths. And only in the public baths could the cloistered women of Turkey cast aside the veils that concealed their faces up to the eyes and discard the graceful, long garments that made all their figures look exactly alike.

When marriages were arranged by relatives, neither of the contracting parties had any choice in the matter. They did as they were told, as they did in Europe and everywhere else in the world where parents traditionally chose spouses for their children. But janissaries had no relatives and when, occasionally, they married, they went to the marriage brokers.

It is a commonplace of history that Europe forgot how to bathe after the Romans and learned again only after the Crusades, which, along with an alien taste for sugar and spice, reintroduced, from the East, the custom of bathing.

In Turkey bathing was physically an art, socially an institution, and, from a practical point of view, an incalculable aid to nature. If a lady were too plump, there was always a tireless eunuch to knead again into shape the spots which offended. If a lady were too slender, she might spend several hours in the *halvet,* clean, comfortable, warm, never moving a muscle, eating quantities of a sweet confection that was part curd, part honey, and very nourishing. Eastern peoples have always been scantily supplied with beards and body hair. Some Oriental races always classified mankind not according to skin color, but according to whether the person is smooth, like a Mongol, or hairy, like an ape. In Turkey the passion for clean, smooth, hairless bodies evoked the world's first and most extensive use of depilatory in an age when, in Europe, the beards of kings and the tresses of queens crawled with vermin. Depilation was available in the baths, till the body shone as naked and clean as Praxitelean marble, a few of the particularly fastidious carrying the art to an astonishingly intimate degree.

If a lady were just right, of course, she sipped cool sherbet and gossiped with her friends.

In a country where beauty was an art, polygamy the law, and celibacy a reproach, an unmarried woman was proud to claim a marriage broker among her best friends. No effort was made to conceal from their cool, appraising, penetrating eyes her most secret physical charms, her most persuasive personal accomplishments. If a girl were lavishly endowed, the exact amount was whispered into the marriage broker's ear. Thus a successful marriage broker carried in her practical head a neat catalogue of all the available girls in town, their family, their prospects, their secret lives, their social status, their financial standing, and their mental, moral, and physical characteristics.

Even happily married women never quite dared to neglect them. For one never knew when Allah, in His wisdom, might send the dread angel Azrail to separate the soul from the body of my lord. And who wanted to be a widow for the rest of her life if—the wisdom of Allah is inscrutable—so lamentable an accident should occur?

Having brought the principals together, the broker collected a fee if a marriage took place as a result of her efforts. Sometimes, however, no marriage took place. The woman might not please the man, or the man might not please the woman; and women exercised a larger choice in the matter than was generally admitted. For a man does not lightly introduce into the closed circle of his wives and concubines a disturbing personality who might upset the peace of his household, or one who has pronounced him repugnant to her. But even in such a case the marriage broker had not necessarily wasted her time. She could always count on a gratuity from the man for having preserved his domestic tranquillity, and often from the woman as well, who might incautiously have risked her reputation by consenting to a secret, private interview in the house of the entrepreneuse.

The fashionable, elderly lady whom Michael visited lived in considerable luxury in the best part of town. Her fees were high, her clientele distinguished by wealth and position. Some of the pashas and beys who engaged her services dated back two reigns to the days of the Sultan Mohammed Chelebi, "the Gentleman," grandfather of the present monarch; and to these solid, influential, uxorious noblemen Safiyé Hanoum owed much of her wealth and most of the liberty that she enjoyed in the practice of her profession. The laws against pandering were very strict, but the line dividing an honorable clandestine meeting from an immoral clandestine meeting was fine. The distinction was scrupulous. One must know one's principals. One must keep everything on a high plane.

Safiyé Hanoum was thought to be a Persian, because sometimes she lapsed into Persian profanity with an ease and colloquial accent impossible to a gently reared Turkish lady. Yet the name by which she was known was Greek, or a Turkized version of Greek, recently imported from the hereditary enemy, Byzantium. It meant Madame Wisdom.

If few of her clients were young, they were by no means all superannuated either. Safiyé Hanoum was known to be partial to middle-aged, retiring janissaries, in whose interests she bestirred herself as energetically as if their modest fees—all they could afford on their retirement pensions—were precious to her.

"I have my reasons," she would say. And perhaps she did. No one was ever impolite enough to enquire.

At the gate a jovial black eunuch, his daggers and scimitar flashing in the half-light that filtered out of the window casements, noting the white turban and red girdle that marked a commander, called him Excellency and, with notable tact, did not ask his name.

"Undoubtedly His Excellency has an appointment," the guard said; and a white eunuch, with less obvious armament, answered, "Undoubtedly," and conducted him to the door.

"Or did you, Commander?" he inquired, pausing. "It is a trifle late in the evening. Madame Wisdom is about to retire." Michael understood.

"Perhaps you can persuade Madame Wisdom to see me," he

suggested. The guard slipped the coin into his sleeve, smiling amiably: "For that, Commander, or even for less from a janissary, of course!"

Michael waited a few moments, and then the white eunuch, with every mark of respect, conducted him into an inner chamber. It was very small, without a window, bare of furniture except for lamps, some cushions to sit on, and a little table in front of Madame Wisdom. A Greek slave girl, too young to appeal to any except the oldest, most lecherous clients, fanned away some annoying insects from the regal head of the entrepreneuse, who sat modestly cross-legged on a cushion of cut velvet. The ample folds of her damask gown were spread about her like an idol's or a sultana's.

Her eyes, a remarkable shade of green, looked calmly and fixedly at Michael, the lids lightly shaded with Egyptian Kohl. Only the languid lids, void of a wrinkle but drooping and fatigued, gave any hint of her great age or betrayed the secret of a beauty long lost, of a woman who had seen everything, known everyone, and done too much. Her veil was embroidered with yellow caterpillars and green and gold butterflies, stitched with incomparable artistry by Persian craftsmen, who did not mind depicting living things. They lent a lightness to the heavy substance of the obscuring veil and signified, perhaps, to her elderly clients that life is eternal and what is dead shall rise again.

"Sit down," she commanded, "you foolish, nameless, impetuous young man."

Michael flushed angrily, but he sat down. Then he flushed redder than ever, ashamed because he had so quickly obeyed the curt, unceremonious order. He could not know that pashas of three horsetails had obeyed the rich, authoritative voice just as readily, startled by the hissing Persian accent, overcome by the green, compelling eyes.

How can a woman have a voice like an angel and eyes like a snake? Michael asked himself, but aloud he said, "If it amuses you to insult me five times before I state the purpose of my visit, I have no recourse against a woman—"

"Though you'd strangle a *man* who insulted you. I know, I know, Commander."

"That is true," Michael said, more than ever annoyed because she had taken the words out of his mouth.

"If I have insulted you five times," Safiyé Hanoum said severely, "it is because I dislike having towering young men look contemptuously down at me; me, Madame Wisdom, who has been honored by nobles of—well, a *great* many horsetails! Foolish I called you, and foolish you are to expect me to arrange an assignation. As if I would stoop to assignations, who have brought about some of the most notable marriages in the empire, all honest, all religious, all respectable. Young you certainly are: look in the mirror some time. Or look at the face of this creature who has forgotten to fan me. Zoë! Can't you see there are flies buzzing horribly about my ears? Watch me, not the commander! And impetuous you are also, for you wear the red girdle of authority, yet you desert your duties in the middle of the night. If I have insulted you, grant that you yourself are to blame, for I have said nothing untruthful. As for being nameless, everybody's nameless nowadays. When was there a war? It was different in the old days."

The slave had begun to fan again because she saw her mistress's brow begin to glow with the heat of her outburst.

Michael said, "If ever you had a heart, and ever lost it—"

But Safiyé Hanoum interrupted: "Do not try to play on my sympathies. I'm far too old."

Michael bit his lip and looked unhappily at her. "I merely wanted to say that I don't give the paltry skin in the slit of a smallish fig whether I wear the red girdle of a commander or gird myself with the dirty clout of a beggar. And I have not come for an assignation. Perhaps I am not the most worldly-wise of men, but I'd know where to go if I wanted an evening's entertainment. It would not be to Madame Wisdom. But God's name! The woman I love is so fair and far that a pasha would speak her name with reverence. It was my hope that perhaps you knew her, or had access to her, or could speak to her of me. If you cannot, then no one can."

The slave girl paused. Safiyé Hanoum's eyes narrowed. "Zoë, you wretch, fan me. No, fan the commander! Commander, I do not carry lovesick messages to ladies!"

"Madame, if I did not tell you at once that I wish to marry the lady, believe me it is because I was ashamed; she is highly placed, of noble, even sacred foreign blood—and great ladies do not marry janissary commanders."

142

Madame Wisdom looked away from the intense, unhappy man. She was far too clever to allow a client to observe the emotion that had crept against her will into her proud green eyes and softened them.

"Sometimes they do, Commander. Sometimes they do. I beg your pardon. I had no idea your intentions were serious. So fatally serious, I might say. No, I will not say it. You know that marriage will mean the end of your career. Baricallah! How you must love her! Who is she? No, do not tell me. I might know her. I know almost everybody. Tell me first, Commander, have you considered the consequences of so drastic a renunciation of your career? I know something about the janissaries. She might accept you, you know. Mm-m. Might very well, now that I look at you. Sacred blood or no sacred blood. What am I saying? Did you say *sacred* blood? There is precious little of it in Turkey. Beard of the night-flying Prophet! Of course I know her! Oh, you deluded fool, you are playing with fire!"

It was the second time in a fortnight that Michael had been told he was playing with fire.

He said, "I may be. But if I were I shouldn't care. I've seen other ladies many times, some of them intimately, and they never touched my heart. But in one little glimpse of Aeshia my soul dissolved, my career lost meaning, everything but this girl became unimportant. If the army continues to exist or disbands tomorrow, it is all one to me. Cannot you believe such a thing can happen to a janissary? There is blood in a Statue of Glass! All I can see when I drill the men is Aeshia's red lips, smiling, and her soft eyes slanting at me. How can I think about troops, glory, war, and advancement?"

"I shall tell you something in confidence," said Safiyé Hanoum, not unkindly. "I have heard such words before. Once, anyway, a long time ago. And I am still enough of a woman to feel friendly and warm when a man speaks in a manner that his training should make impossible. But what is this about the smiling red lips? The eyes, of course—that is nothing. Girls use their eyes all the time, sometimes merely to learn how to use them effectively; but the whole face— the lips—that is another and a serious matter. When did you see the unveiled face of the wife of Prince Machmut?"

"When she smiled at me at a fountain in Paradise. I dare to hope that she drew aside her veil for the purpose of smiling."

143

"So you were the man, Commander! Everyone talks about the encounter at the fountain, but nobody knows who the man was. The prince never told. Oh, well, then." Madame Wisdom shrugged and raised her finely penciled eyebrows. "Perhaps your passion is requited. Girls do not habitually draw aside their veils in public for a man to stare at. Now, it is simple enough for me to visit the lady, though I never see her in the public baths. She never goes there, since she has a wonderful one of her own. It was proper, prudent, and wise of you to consult me, Commander."

She eyed him thoughtfully. "But have you considered how poor you will be when you go on the inactive list? Have you asked yourself why Aeshia should bother with an impecunious commander on half-pay? That's all you'll get in the married reserve. I wonder why it is called the 'inactive' list, by the way. In any event, she could marry almost anyone, you know."

Michael smiled, and wondered in a little corner of his mind how Madame Wisdom happened to be so well informed about the retirement pay of the janissaries. Answering her question, he said: "Of course I have considered those things. All of us, by long training, consider everything, coolly and impartially, at least as far as our minds are concerned. That's the result of good discipline, but this passes anything I have ever experienced." He rested his head in his hands, fists clenched against the temples, staring at the floor. "She won't have me. That is what breaks my heart. What have I to offer her?" (Zoë, forgetting again momentarily to fan her mistress, could have told him.) "But I long for her the way a tired man longs for the boards and the blanket roll after a march, or a camel for the oasis in a sandstorm. I long for her as midnight longs for the dawn."

Madame Wisdom thought kindly: The soldier is not only practical, he is also a poet. Perhaps he has Persian blood in him; his eyes are dark enough. Or maybe it's just the boiling of the blood, bubbling up to the surface and bursting into words.

Michael continued: "I should hate to have her think that I was unprepared to sacrifice all I possess to possess her, little as it is. I am ashamed that it is so little."

Madame Wisdom shrugged again. "One cannot sacrifice more than one has," and she added: "In her place I should listen to you sympathetically. But I warn you, do not expect a marriage to be the outcome of my carrying this message. Yes, I will do it for you. And if by some monstrous prank of fate a marriage *should* result, no good will come of it. I repeat, you are playing with fire."

Michael's face lost its look of despair; the tense muscles relaxed, and he began to smile.

"I came prepared, of course, to take care of your fee. At least," he stammered, "if it is not too high."

Safiyé Hanoum retorted: "It is enormous. You couldn't possibly afford it. I shan't ask you to try. Not an asper will I accept. You'll need all your money—if you have any—to get out of the trouble I find myself sentimental enough to help you get into. But no fee. Put it down as one of Madame Wisdom's eccentricities. Indeed, I may not be able to help you at all. I make no promises."

Yet Madame Wisdom had a shrewd notion that if the fire the commander insisted on playing with was as violent as she suspected —and the gossip rife in the capital tended to confirm the suspicion— there was an excellent chance that a fee might be had after all, and not from Michael.

She walked with him as far as the gate in the outer wall, signaling imperceptibly to her attendants to draw the shades around their lanterns so that no one could see her or her visitor.

"Many years ago," she said softly, "it was my lot to be happy for a space, with a noble young man of your corps, a commander, like yourself. To wed me, he, like yourself, was glad to renounce a career. No other wife ever came under our roof; but the end was not as happy as the beginning, for he died, and our children died. But because a measure of good once came from an exceptional and unconventional situation—for Allah works His mercies in ways that are difficult to comprehend—know that Safiyé Hanoum will advance your suit to the limit of her ability, with guile, if need be, to the full extent of her power." The dignified old lady crossed her arms against her breast and bowed unexpectedly to Michael. "And my power is not inconsiderable," she added with a trace of pride.

Michael bowed in return and stealthily retraced his steps to the camp, unobserved.

The popeyed little Greek slave, who had never known her practical, hardheaded mistress to behave in quite this manner, breathed: "Surely my mistress is accepting an unprofitable client and advising

145

the janissary against his own best interests! To give up his career, when any girl would have him without the formality of a marriage!"

"Slut of a wanton Greek, speak when you are spoken to, and do not advise me!" And if Safiyé Hanoum shared the sentiments of her slave, her slave had no way of knowing it. The green eyes were hard again, like a snake's; and the lids were more languid than ever.

F ISCAL matters of high importance now occupied Machmut, the Beglerbey of Roum. Like many men whose domestic establishments have suffered a stunning blow, he sought to forget his troubles by throwing himself violently into some other activity.

The prince had always enjoyed making money. It was widely known that he did not care how he made it, honestly or dishonestly, in an irreproachable real-estate transaction, by selling bonds at flexible rates on either side of the Bosphorus, or by buying up a concession for clothing the beggars at the sultan's court. Into the coffers of Machmut poured pennies from the begging bowls of the street mendicants and crisp new letters of credit on distant foreign banking houses. It was money. It was power. It was all the same to the Beglerbey whether the amounts were big or little so long as the aggregate was enormous.

Heretofore Machmut's transactions, shady though they might have been, had never been actually treasonable; but the hesitant thief, with practice, was learning to be a daring thief. The flirtation in Paradise and the rumors about Aeshia that ran through Adrianople completed the anesthesia of his conscience. Like a brooklet grown into a stream, and a stream swollen into a flood, the prince's capacity enlarged and grew broad on a lower and lower level, until it could comprehend murder and, presently, treason.

It was a crime to assassinate a janissary, and Machmut was a cautious man. The prince, therefore, investigated Michael thoroughly, and at first the matter seemed simple. So simple that action could be delayed for a day, or a week, or a month. For with Aeshia out of the house, he found himself longing for her, conjuring her back in his dreams; and sometimes she did not return alone. The elderly, complex prince, to his own mild amazement, discovered himself experiencing a perverse thrill in the conviction that Aeshia would not always be alone in her closed gardens or behind the elaborately grilled windows of her gaily painted house during the three months that the law of Islam required her to remain single.

For, contrary to the liberal custom of Christian countries, the stern, uncompromising law of Islam, with its tender solicitude for children, forbade remarriage within that period. The Prophet himself, an acknowledged expert in such matters, had wisely revealed to the faithful that no awkward questions of paternity were to be tolerated. The mental picture of what he foresaw in Aeshia's new house both titillated and enraged the beglerbey.

Further investigation of Michael also deterred him from the murder, for he learned of the janissaries' ride into Christendom, and the reason for that ride.

The reason struck him as tremendous: arms, being smuggled through the tight Turkish blockade! When all Turkey knew that it was only a matter of time until the ancient enemy empire across the strait was to be annihilated! What fortunes a daring man might make running arms into Byzantium! Lust for revenge gave way to a stronger lust for money, and Machmut's agents were told to forget Michael and look into the shipping activities of Filippo Bernardi.

At first it appeared that the janissaries' warning had been fruitful. The merchant had ceased smuggling.

And then, through a trusted courier, filtered the whisper that the smuggling had not stopped after all, for fleets of Christian ships arrived as regularly as ever. Some of Machmut's strong Turkish spies, swimming the strait, reported night movements of a suspicious nature in the upper reaches of the Golden Horn. That, however, was so far for even a strong man to swim that they had lacked the strength to linger or observe very much very closely. Then renegade Christian informers corroborated the evidence of the swimmers, until finally it became clear to the prince that Bernardi was still smuggling arms into Christendom, but not, it appeared, from Scutari. Bernardi's real estate on the Turkish side had been searchingly inspected. Not an ounce of contraband had been found, nothing but spices and silks; and the Turks were glad to permit importation of such expensive luxuries into Constantinople. Cinnamon and silk would never win a war.

Instead of reporting his discoveries instantly to the sultan, Machmut suddenly left Adrianople, neglecting to say goodbye to his wives or his concubines, and galloped toward Galata as long as the horse could stand the strain. His conscience was asleep, and a daring plot that was Turkish treason was taking shape in his troubled heart.

Machmut was soberly dressed, having shorn himself of half his princely insignia. He wanted his visit to attract no comment. His attendants were few, slight, and browner than any Turk that ever was born. They were a trusted and very special bodyguard of Indian origin.

He rode up to Bernardi's house, and there, though he had traveled so inconspicuously, he announced himself by his own name, with all his sonorous titles.

Bernardi's major-domo reported to the merchant that there waited at the gate a pasha of three horsetails, Machmut, the Beglerbey of Roum, Prince of the Princes of Turkey-in-Europe. Bernardi remembered Machmut vividly—the stunning loss of those ships of his confiscated years ago after the battle of Varna, the double loss he had incurred when Machmut, discovering the ships to have carried contraband, repudiated the bonds. "Dear God! The rascal that robbed me! And now he's after my precious ships again!" The thought of the half-dozen vessels which that week had quietly disposed of their illegal cargoes sent him into a sudden panic. Perhaps the Turks had found out about his persistent, uninterrupted traffic in arms! Perhaps Machmut had come to take him back to Turkey for punishment, as Michael had threatened might happen. Bernardi knew that so highly placed an official as the beglerbey could arrest almost anyone in Galata, which prided itself on its extreme degree of collaboration with the sultan. Perhaps he was about to be extradited across the Bosphorus into the jurisdiction of the Turkish courts. No doubt Machmut had a whole regiment of janissaries with him.

Bernardi sent Angelica to her room. He fortified himself with a glass of wine before ordering Enrico to admit the visitor with all speed.

"How many soldiers accompany him?" he whispered nervously to the major-domo.

"No more than a handful, signore. And they do not look like soldiers. Very dark. Not Turks."

"How odd."

When Enrico ushered Machmut in, Bernardi beheld the noncommittal garb of his guest and was even more confused. Not a disguise, exactly, he thought, but my exalted visitor obviously does not want to attract attention to himself. Bernardi looked searchingly at the beglerbey.

At first glance everything about the prince appeared comfortable, genial, and large: his pudgy hands and the ornamental rings on his fingers; his ample girth and the folds of his silken sash; and the length of his decorative scimitar. His face was broad; his jowls hung loose and fat under a thick, carefully combed beard. But the mouth was thin behind the mustache, and the eyes, almost hidden by black, shaggy brows, were little and hard. The left eye had a disconcerting droop.

Bernardi bowed. "Your Excellency is welcome to this house."

Machmut did not remember Bernardi or his dealings with his former minor client. Machmut pressed his hand to his heart. His thin lips parted over some broken teeth in what he fondly trusted was a winning smile. Machmut saw exceedingly well at close range and judged people quickly. "Cautious, greedy, and proud," was his satisfied estimate. He bowed profoundly, and for an instant his eyes rested on Bernardi's European hose, deceptively conservative. One would think them inexpensive unless one happened to be an expert in woolen stuffs, like, say, the concessionnaire of the apparel of the petitioners at the court of the sultan. And Bernardi's shoes were embroidered in thread of gold. "He will collaborate," Machmut decided.

"Peace," Machmut said aloud in a greeting, "to this house and its noble master."

Then, having said the proper things and taken stock of each other all in a few seconds, they sat down. Each was so anxious to please the other that Machmut cautiously lowered himself into a European chair, and it looked for a moment as if Bernardi were about to squat cross-legged on his own carpet in the Eastern fashion. But Machmut said, "I am not a provincial, my lord Filippo. I am quite accustomed to your Western ways. Some of them I actually relish."

"The Beglerbey of Roum honors the conventions of Rome," Bernardi replied. "Perhaps Your Excellency will not take it amiss if I offer you a cup of wine. Quite mild, Your Excellency, guaranteed not to heat the blood."

"My dear host!" Machmut ran his tongue over his lips as if the custom were not totally unknown in Islam either. "Even if it did. Even if it *did!*"

But when Enrico brought the wine, Machmut mumbled a cautious prayer before he touched it, calling on his soul to leave his body for a space and not to return until he had drained the cup, thus absolving himself from breaking the law of Islam.

The wine was heavy and sweet. To Machmut, whose body ached wearily after his exhausting ride, it tasted delicious. When the first cup was empty, he banished his soul again and accepted a second; and when that was gone, he banished his soul once more and took a third. After the third cup his weariness magically vanished, and for an evil instant Machmut found himself ruminating on the injustice of the Prophet's prohibition of so friendly, so mystical a liquid. Then he abruptly recalled his soul, repented, made a polite allusion to the clemency of Christian weather, looked his host squarely in the eye and touched lightly on the purpose of his visit.

"Your generous hospitality affects me the more deeply," he said, "because the displeasure of Allah, or perhaps the lamentable political situation, has recently somewhat cooled the warm spirit of understanding among some of the citizens of our two great empires."

That sounded a little threatening. Bernardi looked grave and compressed his lips.

The prince continued, with an ingratiating wave of his hand, "I am grieved when I think that an acute and enlightened merchant like yourself should share these unfounded feelings of distrust and suspicion."

"Believe me, Your Excellency, I suffer from no unfounded suspicions against the Turks."

"Ah, but you do!" Machmut stared into the empty depth of his goblet, which he twisted idly by the stem, round and round, slowly, in his fingers. There was a noncommittal smile lurking on his lips under the black beard, enigmatic as a Buddha's. "It has come to my ears that your wharves and warehouses in Scutari contain nothing but pepper and ivory and silk." The eye droop grew a little more pronounced; the other eye widened ever so slightly: the effect was the look of guilty invitation which Bernardi had sometimes seen on the faces of thieves who came to dispose of stolen goods at enormously attractive prices. "Whereas," the prince resumed after a pause, "I am reliably informed that your ships on the Byzantine side invariably carry not luxuries but, shall we say, *hardware.*"

Bernardi breathed a little faster. He protested: "The water on the Scutari side is shallow, that is all. Naturally I send my lighter ships there. The heavier ones tie up in the Golden Horn."

"Of course, signore. How magnificently you put it! And yet, it is scarcely possible that in the short space of a month or two Allah, in His wisdom, has silted up the sea bottom about Scutari. Until *very* recently, signore, the Scutari water was deep enough to float any of your ships, big or little. No. There is some other reason. Do you know what I think, signore? When I discovered that your warehouses contained only little luxuries, I said to myself, 'The noble Venetian merchant is afraid. He has succumbed to the threat in the political atmosphere. He is ill at ease because he thinks some slight infraction of some old commercial treaty may have alienated all his influential friends in Turkey.' Those were my thoughts, Filippo Effendi. Believe me, you are not friendless."

He continued: "It is unbecoming of me to speak so freely to a Gavour, perhaps. I dare say that your wine has loosened my tongue, in spite of its nonintoxicating properties, just as coffee might have done after my fatiguing journey. But no, surely not this excellent wine!" Machmut arched an eyebrow at his empty cup.

Bernardi exclaimed, "A thousand pardons!" He clapped his hands, and when Enrico appeared he nodded at Machmut's goblet and then at his own.

Machmut protested, "No, really!" But he held the goblet without a tremor as the yellow wine bubbled into it, filling it to the brim. Bernardi's own hand was not quite steady, in spite of the considerable relief he now felt after the Turk's preamble.

"It is always good to hear that one has friends," Bernardi said cautiously, sipping his wine. "Let me ask you, however—perhaps you will pardon the blunt ways of a European merchant—precisely what does Your Excellency propose?"

Machmut gazed into his cup and then at the ceiling, and said in a dreamy voice: "From time to time I, too, have been a merchant of sorts, purely as a distraction from my official duties. I have dealt in clothing and jewelry and horsetails, and sometimes in incautious documents that I happened across—letters that officials wrote and ought to have burned. They had no time to do so, perhaps. So I would burn them myself, and the officials were so happy that they made me gifts for my trouble, quite lavish gifts, in conformity with my dignity. Yes."

Bernardi gasped mentally at this brazen confession of robbery and blackmail. Only an immensely powerful man, a man secure in his position, would have dared to make such an avowal, even to a Christian. The prince glanced away from the ceiling and looked the Venetian straight in the eye:

"I have decided to go into the shipping business!"

"The shipping business?"

"Hardware. From Scutari."

"Your Excellency cannot be serious about wanting to import pots and pans into Scutari."

Machmut's little eyes hardened. "Not import, signore, export. And not pots and pans. The hardware you handle does not fry flesh; it slices flesh. You are repaying my candor with hypocrisy and evasion. You need not pretend to be so stupid. *Arms,* then, since you will have the word: swords, mail, arbalests, pitch, saltpeter and oil for the Greek fire. I know the desperate need of the Christians for arms. Someone is still smuggling this contraband. I am certain it is you. And since I do not know where you hide it, naturally I admire your skill. It will be a pleasure to learn such a business from so skillful a master."

Bernardi suppressed a smile, mentally thanking Michael for that priceless, inadvertent suggestion of a hidden warehouse. The heated beglerbey had just divulged some comforting news: the Turks obviously had no inkling of the commodious, secluded warehouse in the upper reaches of the Golden Horn on the Galata side. Bernardi had rented it under another name and decorated it with some bulky loads of sugar cane for appearances' sake. But he realized that he was still under suspicion. The beglerbey had apparently guessed that he was

153

making enormous profits. Bernardi finally could not help smiling. His profits were huger than any other merchant's in the business.

"All my warehouses are above reproach," he said blandly. "You or anyone else may inspect them, on this side or on the Scutari side. I am running no arms." Bernardi now felt reasonably secure.

Machmut said: "I have seen your Scutari warehouses, signore. The quality of the stuffs is delightful. They are above reproach, as you say. That is why I am so interested in them. If a man in my position should purchase an interest in such immaculate property it would, of course, remain above reproach. Who in Turkey would dare inspect a ship or a warehouse that was protected by the Beglerbey of Roum? And my conscience—I am impelled to mention my good Moslem conscience, signore—would be at rest. My face is white. The little 'hardware' I should make available to you Christians will be of no importance if a great war should break out. On that day the janissaries of the sultan will topple your rotten walls in an hour. Meanwhile, it will be a pious thing for me to make a profit. I am prepared to pay you 100,000 aspers for the property."

Bernardi mused, "You'd do well in the 'hardware' business, very well. The demand is tremendous, as you say. I heard of a man only recently who made 100,000 aspers in a month, net."

Machmut smiled and nodded his head pleasantly. "I congratulate you, my friend."

"The property is really worth more."

"If such profits are to be made, then I could be persuaded to make a higher offer."

Bernardi looked as if he were being tortured. Why shouldn't he sell? What was Michael, the renegade, to him? The acquisitive habits of a lifetime had been sharpened since he controlled the immense resources of Nicolo da Montelupo. Every week Bernardi planned to return to Venice, and every week he delayed, to make just one more deal, to unload just one more ship. And now came this powerful, traitorous Turkish prince, holding out a golden bait that was diabolically alluring, making an offer that represented far more than Bernardi could hope to realize from the shrinking luxury trade at Scutari. Also, Bernardi's religion was involved: this Turk could use the Scutari docks for smuggling arms into Constantinople. Bernardi could not. Christendom would benefit. So Bernardi tried to persuade himself that it would be wise to dispose of all rights to a place which, in the event of war, would become valueless; but no, that wasn't true. Bernardi groaned inwardly. He knew that the Scutari shipping rights would never be valueless, not to Michael, because Michael was now a Turk. If war should come, no matter who won it, Michael's claim would stand firm.

Machmut watched the conflict on Bernardi's face. Then, unhappily, Bernardi said:

"No."

In a coffer where he kept his most precious documents, a miniature of Angelica when she was an infant, and a strand of her hair (odd that it should have been black at first!) clipped from her head on the day she was born and sealed in the heart of a jewel that he had had made hollow for the purpose; in the coffer that he never opened because he was ashamed to appear sentimental even to himself, Bernardi had laid away the last thing that Nicolo da Montelupo had ever written: the temporary power of attorney that had become Nicolo's last will and testament.

"No," Bernardi repeated, "I cannot do what you ask."

Machmut was used to hagglers, but there was something on Bernardi's face unlike any haggler's he had ever seen. It was more like the sultan's in one of his most determined and stubborn moods.

Nevertheless Machmut persisted: "Come, come, my Christian friend, I have already signified my willingness to go higher. Be the merchant. We can come to terms. Name your price as frankly as I have named my offer."

"No."

Machmut raised his voice and shouted angrily, "In the name of the four thousand prophets, *why?*"

"I cannot sell what I do not own."

"Eh?" Machmut stared incredulously. "What did you say?"

Bernardi repeated the words, slowly, with unfeigned regret and utter finality.

"You do not *own* the Scutari shipping rights?"

Bernardi shook his head. "I merely hold them in trust for the son of a friend of mine, a man who years ago trusted me further than anyone ever trusted me before. Two things I will not sell: my daughter and the patrimony of my old friend's son."

Machmut snorted. "God's name! Now you are really stupid, and you are not pretending. How much, do you think, the rights of your precious ward will be worth when war comes? What rights to shipping from a Turkish port will a Christian retain when we win the war, when Constantinople is overthrown, and the Bosphorus becomes a Turkish river?"

Bernardi grinned. "And who said that my ward was a Christian, Your Excellency?"

Machmut stared harder than ever. "What would he be if he isn't a Christian?"

"A Turk."

Machmut thought a moment and said: "You are lying. No Turk needs to be the ward of a Christian. Islam knows how to take care of the waifs of the Osmanli blood."

"I didn't say he was of Osmanli blood. His blood is pure Venetian, but he is a Moslem. He thinks like a Turk and he acts like a Turk, just like all the rest of the unfortunate children that you people have kidnaped and reared in your faith and somehow transmogrified into janissaries. I saw him recently. He is very able, very happy, a commander. If war comes, he will win an honorable name in it. I despair of his ever returning to the land or the faith of his birth. If war comes, even if you win it—particularly if you win it— he shall some day come into his birthright and his fortune. Never while he lives will I sell any part of his patrimony."

Bernardi in his emotion had failed to notice the slow, ominous change in Machmut's expression. He might just as well have mentioned Michael by name, for Machmut knew that Bernardi could have seen one and only one janissary commander recently, the janissary who had ridden from Adrianople with the warning: Michael. When Bernardi again glanced at his guest, he was astonished to see Machmut's face turned claret-rose. The prince was trembling as if he were suddenly taken with an ague, and the veins beat furiously in his forehead. Bernardi fancied he could hear teeth grinding.

It was more than Machmut could bear that one young man, by a walk in a garden and a ride into Christendom, could have robbed him of a wife and now, all in a month, threatened to rob him of a fortune also.

Bernardi was amazed when the beglerbey suddenly left the house. He was more than a little bewildered by the remark of which Machmut delivered himself before he mounted his horse and rode away:

156

"Your fidelity to your ward touches me. I doubt whether you realize what he has cost me. Perhaps this is my fate, everlastingly written on my forehead. Perhaps we shall speak of the shipping business at another time; but if we do not, it is because I am determined never to mention the matter again while your ward lives. He is fortunate in his guardian."

Surly, erect among his men, galloping out of the Christian city, the Beglerbey of Roum knew that Michael was altogether too fortunate. A wife and now a fortune so huge it was worth risking treason to possess! Machmut hissed through his broken teeth into the dark mass of his beard: "Vanish the visions! Michael shall be destroyed."

In a day or so Filippo Bernardi shut up his house in Galata and moved with his daughter across the Golden Horn into Constantinople. He felt that he had attracted too much attention from too highly placed a Turk. He felt, too, the war coming closer. If it should break out unexpectedly, he would feel more secure behind the high walls of a strong city that was sure to be a belligerent than behind the low walls of a weak city that was certain to adopt a policy of cringing neutrality.

Meanwhile, he left Enrico in Galata with minute instructions touching a fast little ship that was to be permanently moored and manned at the secluded warehouse which everyone thought was full of sugar cane.

CHAPTER

15

MACHMUT writhed with frustration, for no occasion for the destruction of Michael immediately presented itself.

While the Beglerbey of Roum was in Galata, Mohammed II was also absent from Adrianople, accompanied by a considerable army, his personal guard, which included Michael and Hassan, some few of his wives, since he expected no more strenuous activity, and the Sanjak-i-sherif, the holy, green standard of the Prophet, in its cylindrical, betasseled, waterproof casing of ciclatoun, like an enormous golden sausage. In the event of a local war, it would be well, the young monarch concluded, to fire his soldiers with holy, patriotic zeal.

He undertook the expedition on the advice of his old grand vizier, Khalil Pasha, who had warned him that it was always wise, when annihilating an enemy, to make sure that the enemy has no allies, no friends.

In the Peloponnesus, which is the ancient peninsula of Greece and is also called the Morea by reason of its resemblance on the map to a maple leaf, dwelt two imperial brothers of Constantine XII, Emperor of the Roman Empire of the East. Their military power was not great, and their personal courage was suspect. There they ruled, as despots, small but potentially troublesome principalities. Their ancient names and imperial blood weighed heavily with other Christian princes. Should they cast their lot with their Byzantine brother, who knew but that other nations also might rally round the double-eagled Byzantine standard?

To pacify them, Mohammed made his sudden incursion into the Morea.

There were some minor skirmishes when sturdy frontier guards, having no other instructions, conceived it their duty to die for their princes in a forlorn attempt to repulse the mighty invading foreign army. From the Turkish point of view there was no encounter of sufficient importance to justify a man winning a name.

Then the emissaries of Mohammed arrived at the courts of the brothers of Constantine with reasonable demands and assurances that the sultan had no territorial ambitions in the Morea so long as Thomas and Demetrius Palaeologoi left him a free hand in Byzantium. The timorous Greek princelings were happy to purchase immunity. The Turkish emissaries were shown every courtesy, treated with cringing respect, and dispatched back to the Brother of the Sun with costly gifts and repetitious assurances of the benevolent neutrality of Thomas and Demetrius Palaeologoi.

And so in time the sultan returned to Adrianople, the Sanjak-i-sherif still in its sheath of cloth of gold and two priceless neutrality treaties in his hand.

In spite of the relatively short distances involved, the several skirmishes, rugged terrain, and especially the interminable diplomatic receptions and fêtes of the Morean Greeks consumed four months of the fall and winter of 1451. At the end of that time, Khalil Pasha could gravely assure his lord: "You have now isolated the Eastern Roman Empire in the little patch of ground that Constantine, this anachronous Caesar, still commands. When a brother will not help you, who will?"

"Surely the war can start now, Friend?" pleaded the impatient sultan.

But the elderly vizier cautioned: "My lord could win against any combination of forces. My lord could defeat a legion of angels or devils, so puissant is my lord. But many souls, unnecessarily wrenched from their bodies, would cross the razor-edge-narrow bridge, arching over the pit of hell, into the Paradise of God, were my lord to begin operations now. It is not my lord's destiny in this world to assure the speediest possible entry of the greatest possible number of souls at the earliest possible moment into the bliss of the life to come."

159

The sultan said, "It is not!"

"Permit me to point out to my lord that a bridgehead on the European side of the Bosphorus is highly desirable."

So Mohammed gave orders to build Roumeli Hissar, the infamous "Castle in Europe," on Christian soil and under the Christian nose of the Emperor Constantine, the minute the weather permitted.

CHAPTER
16

Ｉｎ the gardens of the sultan the winter-fallen leaves drifted languidly over the empty walks and blanketed the broad, dry, dormant lawns. No one disturbed the animals now, and those which Allah had ordained should hibernate, hibernated. Palace guards, with time on their hands, locked the gates against the public and shut off the fountains. There was no one of any importance left in the palace to enjoy them.

Business fell off in the bazaars, and slave dealers who catered to the luxury trade complained of the healthy appetites of their living young merchandise. Bismillah! How could an honest man make a living with all his lusty clientele away on an expedition into the Morea? The somnolent capital anxiously awaited the return of its monarch.

The weather was cold. Aeshia cast one impatient glance at the dreary Turkish sky, another at the desolate Turkish streets, and shut herself up in her splendid house. There, servants worked chamois-leather bellows against the coals of a Chinese brazier and contrived to make warm as Egypt any room that their mistress commanded.

The brazier was shaped like the head of an angry dragon. The coals were in its mouth; when they glowed, the eyes shone red. When it tainted the air, and it always did, Aeshia would wrinkle her slender nostrils delicately and drop into the glowing embers a tear of pearl-white olibanum. The costly incense was instantly consumed in a bright white flame, shooting up like a sharp, momentary tongue out of the dragon mouth; and on the destruction of its tiny substance, the air breathed with a penetrating sweetness that was a stimulant to some, a sedative to others.

Aeshia had behaved herself with more than the exemplary correctitude demanded of a newly divorced lady in Turkey. She had not been seen in public at all, and she was seen in her home only by those of her friends whose reputations were irreproachable. Thus not only the streets, denuded of young men, but even the conversation of her friends was dull, painfully dull.

It therefore pleased Aeshia that Safiyé Hanoum, who was respectable but not dull, should call on her three months to the day after her divorce.

Banishment from the harem of the prince had stripped Aeshia of the honorable title "Little Lady"; and she was now simply "her ladyship," Aeshia Hanoum, to her visitors.

Madame Wisdom arrived with Zoë, her slave, to fan her, for she knew how oppressively warm Aeshia kept her house in wintertime. The comfortable, big eunuchs, Usamah and Umarah, fanned Aeshia also, with yellow fans. Costly in Asia, unknown in Christendom, such feathers formed the temporary mating plumage of a rare and beautiful bird, one day to be called the bird of paradise, that lived on an island far away to the east in the Indian Ocean. During a certain, short impetuous season the plumes turned yellow, like fine gold, and during that season the coolies stripped them and sold them to caravan merchants from Arabia, leaving the birds bewildered and disconsolate in the jungles, to grow another set next year if they could. That limited the bird population and contributed to the value of the aureate feathers.

"Peace to your ladyship," said Safiyé Hanoum in a greeting, "and peace to this house." She drew off her veil and loosened the voluminous folds of her winter mantle, glancing at the brazier. She noted that Aeshia, sitting on a damask cushion between her two towering slaves, was almost as scantily clad as some of the figures adorning the walls of her father's palace in Cairo.

"And peace to you," Aeshia replied. "There is peace and to spare in my lonely house. I could do with somewhat less of it." She smiled ingratiatingly at her visitor. The quick, flashing smile was so enticingly brilliant that Madame Wisdom sighed at the lost, fat fee which she might have made—would surely have made—if her foolish old heart had not tricked her into this sentimental mission for the janissary.

"Can I offer you a sweetmeat? A cup of coffee? I, myself, must drink only a sherbet of grapejuice and honey," Aeshia explained with a little grimace. "My physician prescribes it to balance the humors during these frigid Turkish winters. He says the grapejuice is beneficial because it has foamed into a froth and then lain quiescent three years in a cave." Aeshia shrugged her white shoulders. What one had to put up with to preserve the glow of health!

With Persian alacrity Safiyé Hanoum agreed that that was a wonderful thing, a wise precaution in view of the inclement weather. Further, she observed that she, too, came originally from a land where the winters were warmer, and suggested with a discreet, ladylike cough that she herself was not averse to a cup of the physician's tonic.

Usamah and Umarah gravely decanted from a silver urn two goblets of strong, sweet, fiery wine which instantly heightened the color and presently loosened the tongues of the two ladies.

"It has been like a widowhood," Aeshia confided, "these last three lonely months! Or like the Great Fast, if during the Fast one were forbidden even at night to assuage the pangs of hunger."

"How true," Safiyé Hanoum murmured, emptying her cup, which one of the eunuchs immediately filled again to the brim. "How sad, and how true. I remember how it was with me at first, after the death of my late great lord. Young, lean, your ladyship, with loins like a panther, assiduous in love both day and night, and never another wife in the house. But night and *day*, your ladyship! as only a janissary can be. With regard to this fasting, your ladyship. You have, of course, hm-m, fasted, have you not?"

Aeshia lowered her glance till the long lashes, shining like silk in the ruddy light of the brazier, half hid her eyes for an instant. Yet did not hide them entirely, for a fire gleamed through, about the temperature of the brazier, Safiyé Hanoum said to herself; and she again thought heavily what a fee such a creature could mean if one were a grasping, unscrupulous marriage broker. Then Aeshia looked at her sweetly and answered: "As God is my witness, by the Holy Koran and the blood in my veins of His Prophet, Safiyé Hanoum, I have fasted."

Madame Wisdom sighed. "I'd heard as much. Your discretion is the admiration of the whole town."

"It wasn't easy," Aeshia admitted laughing. "Daytimes, too, did you say? Oh, dear me! My tubby little prince was so busy making money daytimes that even at night he was too exhausted to pay any attention to his Kutchuk Hanoum. If I had had a little princeling, the old prince might have overlooked some of my—well, some of my harmless, incautious glances at some of the tall young Turkish men, though the tallest are probably not of Turkish blood. What do you think, Madame Wisdom?"

Madame Wisdom thought rather ruefully that the conversation was drifting toward someone exactly like Michael with astonishing ease.

But knowing Aeshia's love of wealth, she determined to divert the course of the talk into a more practical direction. And furthermore, although this was the first day that a reputable marriage broker might properly approach Aeshia, it would do no harm to find out, if she could, the scope and magnitude of her competition. There were scores of marriage brokers in Adrianople.

Aeshia stood up from the cushion and walked lightly across the room, as if the spirits of the impalpable air had borne her, to drop a tear of the resinous incense into the brazier. And when the flame leaped up, Madame Wisdom beheld, for a nostalgic, inaccurate instant, a white goddess at the altar of the fire worshipers, a faulty memory of her Persian youth. The wine and the olibanum made Madame Wisdom a little giddy and melted the fine, pure gold of her conscience. For a moment all the sultan's janissaries, dead and alive, irritated her exceedingly. They and their meager pensions! If her late dear lord, with his panther loins and his midday love, had only been rich, she would not have had to work all these years for a living.

"What do I think, Aeshia Hanoum? I think, dear child—and my years in the business should give my opinion a certain weight with a young, inexperienced girl—that you ought to marry again. Some nobleman in His Majesty's court, tolerant, liberal, wealthy, and wise, who will treasure your beauty like a pearl in the shell. But above all, wealthy. Perhaps such a thing has already been suggested to you."

Aeshia replied, "Candidly, yes, Safiyé Hanoum. All day long, and

164

even," she laughed softly, "even for some time past. The last three weeks, to be exact. Though, of course, no formal proposals."

"Well, I should hope not!" Madame Wisdom frowned. "That would be highly improper. What self-respecting broker would dare make a proposal so soon?"

Aeshia ignored the question, saying: "I loathe beards, Safiyé Hanoum. White ones especially, I abhor. Imagine being tickled and scratched half down the length of your body by a long, gray beard, such as, for example, Khalil Pasha's! Tickled, Madame Wisdom, and scratched, when one yearns for—I do not know the Turkish word, but in Arabic it is pleasure-with-pain, till the stars fall and the man is forgotten, and you no longer feel the strong arms that are crushing you, but, oh, you feel! No, no, my friend. No graybeards for me!"

Madame Wisdom gasped a mental gasp. God's name! This she-devil had bewitched the grand vizier himself! and she wrote in the tablet of her mind an imperative reminder to ferret out what slut of a law-scoffing agent handled that venerable old courtier.

"Your ladyship speaks with passionate conviction," Madame Wisdom said softly. "Perhaps I felt that way myself when I was your ladyship's age, and perhaps the memory of my pleasure and pain brought me here tonight with a message which can never put so much as an asper into my slender, widowed purse."

At last, she thought, she had an accurate measure of Aeshia. Patently, no agent was to get a fee. Madame Wisdom's conscience, after its momentary liquefaction, solidified again into pure gold. She asked pardon of the shade of her late loved lord, sniffed the stimulating olibanum, sipped the tonic wine, smiled fondly at the memory of the panther loins, and whispered: "Not an asper will I accept from my client, your ladyship, though he generously offered to pay me a fee. He is shy and undemanding, like a Frank in love. He was once a Frank. But for the mercy of Allah, he would be a Frank still. No, only to carry a message, he offered me a fee."

"And what, Madame Wisdom, can be the intentions of this infidel-begotten creature who offers money simply to have a message delivered? Any dirty beggar for an asper will always find ways to deliver a message. Why does my reputable friend concern herself with this man?"

"Because he loves you, Aeshia Hanoum, and because he is a janissary, and because what little he has he offers you in honorable marriage. I saw love in his black eyes, love in the pain that contorted his noble forehead, and love in the hopeless fear that bowed down his broad, straight shoulders when I told him, of course, that you would not have him."

It was a cultivated accomplishment of Madame Wisdom's to describe her clients to each other, since they were never supposed to have seen each other, and usually never had. To paint a word picture so graphic that the couples would fall in love at a distance was the highly remunerative object of her art.

Aeshia, of course, knew all about the professional rhetoric of a marriage broker. She had listened all day to some accurately attractive inventories of the person and estates of the Imperial Stirrup Holder and the Imperial Sword Bearer, both of whom had sent their agents a little before custom and good manners allowed. But the agents had been forced to acknowledge that both wealthy old noblemen were saggy (the men's baths are full of spies, your ladyship) in the hips, and that, yes, alas, they both had venerable long beards of a most distinguished gray.

Aeshia had given the agents each a little gift and sent them back to their clients, not with a flat refusal, which would have been the grossest breach of manners, but with the humble avowal that Aeshia Hanoum dared not aspire to so high a station and planned shortly to return to her native Egypt anyway. Which conveyed the same meaning without giving offense.

Aeshia had not actually been approached by an agent of Khalil Pasha. That bedeviled old statesman was far too busy trying to please his exacting new master to go about looking for fresh young wives. Aeshia's hint was a bit of misinformation, mischievously dropped to confuse Safiyé Hanoum.

Safiyé Hanoum, because she knew men better than she knew women, pleaded like a man and repeated, "He loves you, child."

There was a dichotomy in the soul of Aeshia, the intimate, unsuspected spiritual cleavage—Tamerlane, cruelest, most lustful of men, at war with the guile of forty Caliphs in the blood of their common descendant, whose heart was half fire, half ice.

So Aeshia had reasons of her own for listening sympathetically to the marriage broker, for hoping the janissary was the commander she thought it might be.

166

"But all young men are poor," Aeshia said; "and the poorer they are, the prouder they are. If I should marry this panther-loined young client of yours, being poor, he could never support my establishment, and, being proud, he would never permit me to spend any money of my own. We should have to live in a hovel outside the walls, and I should die."

Now Madame Wisdom in her heartfelt reminiscence had described her late husband, not Michael, as having loins like a panther. She had not actually examined Michael's too closely. But since the description appeared to excite Aeshia, she made a mental note to use it again sometime, and she said:

"He'll never know, Aeshia Hanoum. Janissaries are almost like those Christian monks we hear about. No domestic experience, devoted to a peculiar ideal, and notoriously unsophisticated in money matters. Take his half-pay, my dear. Say that your steward is a wizard at household finance. He'll never know the difference. Such things have happened before. I realize, however, that financial considerations may perhaps be something of an obstacle to your happiness."

"Oh, I don't know," Aeshia said. "Father provided for me rather well. I wish I could have a look at this young man."

"*Most* irregular!" Madame Wisdom frowned. "*Most* unconventional."

Aeshia lifted her cup of irregular, unconventional wine tantalizingly, raised her eyebrows slightly, and favored her guest again with the incredible brilliance of her smile.

Madame Wisdom took another grateful sip of the cup, smiled, acknowledged defeat in the verbal tilt, and, lowering her voice to a discreet whisper for the benefit of the servants, said: "Beautiful, subtle, dangerous child! I am glad I am not a man. I made a little slip in accepting this wicked drink, which I now perceive is wine—"

"The very best, Madame!"

"And being already deep in one wrong you seek to sink me deeper into yet another by requesting an assignation with my handsome young client! Of course, I never, never do such things. Almost invariably *never!* And yet for the love of my two extraordinary principals, for the impetuous janissary and your cautious ladyship, I, Madame Wisdom, might break my inflexible rule and arrange a confidential meeting. Though I should be secretly present to watch that no shame came of my generosity."

"To watch, naturally," Aeshia nodded. "I shouldn't mind."

"But as a matter of fact," Madame Wisdom continued, wistfully abandoning the thought of observing so interesting an assignation, "no clandestine meeting need be arranged. Your ladyship has already seen Michael, the janissary, in Paradise. And Michael has seen your naked face, when your ladyship drew aside her veil and knelt for a moment to drink at a fountain. Or perhaps your ladyship does not remember."

Something, the glow in the brazier, the medical prescription of the physician, the panther loins in the happy rhetoric of her visitor, or the memory of the janissary in the gardens of the sultan set a balefire burning in Aeshia's fathomless eyes.

"So it is Michael," she said softly. "For a moment I feared it might be Hassan. Yes. I will have Michael."

The guard in the gloom at the street gate pressed into Safiyé Hanoum's hand a small heavy purse with the whispered words: "Her ladyship's thanks to your ladyship. The servants will light your way home."

Zöe, supporting her mistress by the elbow, guided the old lady's somewhat befuddled steps through the street to her house. Before and behind the two veiled women, muffled in their mantles against the winter wind, Aeshia's torchbearers, all eunuchs, and all armed, lighted and guarded their progress.

"I never intended to stay so late," Madame Wisdom whispered apprehensively. "Whatever will people say!"

She weighed the purse, clutched tightly in her hand, under her robe. So substantial! If it was silver, Aeshia was spendthrift. If it was gold, she was mad, or a devil. "Michael, Michael!" the broker sighed under her breath.

"Did my mistress address her slave?"

"No, little pig." Safiyé Hanoum patted Zöe's hand kindly. "You're a good girl. You didn't open your babbling Greek mouth once tonight. Sometimes I think I'll find you a nice, rich old husband."

Observing that the incense or the wine had tangled Madame Wisdom's inestimable feet and perhaps mellowed her stern discipline, the slave presumed to suggest:

"Could my wise and generous mistress find me a nice young one? With panther loins?"

168

"Slut! You were listening all the time! Now guide me carefully over these stones, can't you? No husband, no husband at all for you, Gavour. You're far too good a slave; but she will have him, little Greek. She said so. Those were her words: 'I will have Michael!' "

"So she said," said Zoë unenthusiastically.

"Baricallah! What God can accomplish! Tomorrow I shall give you an asper. Surely some wicked jinn or afrit has made the cobbles twice the size they were this morning. The walking is very difficult."

WITHIN the month a flying outrider, galloping back to Adrianople ahead of the returning army, appeared at the gates and proclaimed to the people that the sultan had vanquished the Greek princes of the Morea and was returning in triumph to his capital. And when the monarch and his army paraded through the streets, kettledrums beating a tuned, rhythmic march, trumpets blaring, and horsetail standards snapping in the stiff winter wind, the people hailed him as *Ghazi*, "the Victorious." It was a name that had sufficed for two of the most illustrious sultans of his imperial dynasty. A few of his suite, however, knew that Mohammed II had already chosen a more glorious name for the chroniclers to call him.

And the chroniclers do.

But that was to commemorate a greater disaster to Christendom than this easy intimidation of the petty princelings, Thomas and Demetrius Palaeologoi.

The tribute of the Greeks had been commensurate with their terror. The pashas returned with fat purses, and even the humblest common soldier had unexpected aspers to tie up in the scrap of an old girdle. The pious father of Mohammed II had laid great stress on the pleasures of Paradise, which one wins if he die in a war for Islam, just as a Christian knight went to Heaven the instant he died on a Crusade. But Murad's more practical son remembered to reward his army for a victory in which they had not had to die.

On the return of the sultan and his army, the quiet city sprang to life. Trade took a sharp turn for the better in the bazaars. Coins tinkled into the beggars' bowls. Slave dealers observed with delight that sales, rentals, and exchanges were far ahead of the normal seasonal upsurge which could always be expected during the cold, invigorating winter months. Some slyly supposed that the Greek fire which had been shot at the army had got into the army's blood. Whatever the reason, they all agreed that the turnover among their wares was unprecedented; and since trade was good and the world was young, no one, least of all hard-headed dealers in slaves and concubines, ever paused to marvel at the mystical foreknowledge of Nature, who, to perpetuate herself, drives into the arms of women more men than are destined to die.

But the happiest salute to the sultan was not the acclaim of the populace. As Mohammed, his guards, and his personal staff approached the gates of the palace, a dreadful noise like a sharp clap of thunder, originating vaguely in the direction of the enclosed gardens, burst on his ears with a force that he felt in his face, and roared and echoed from one wall across the city to another. Horses reared in fright and people threw themselves to the ground, thinking it was an earthquake at the very least, and in all probability the angel's Blast of Consternation that would end the world. Even the disciplined janissaries, who suspected what it was, glanced apprehensively at one another.

The little guns that the janissaries had often seen, but never used in battle, were so light that a man could pick them up and carry them, and so small a bore that the thumb little more than went into their muzzles; and they exploded with a thin *pop,* like Chinese firecrackers.

Mohammed reined in his nervous, spirited steed, and grinned till his mustache tips, which usually pointed down, pointed up; and then scowled so fiercely that Khalil Pasha, riding beside him, trembled.

At that moment a man named Urban Pasha, a Hungarian by birth, dressed in the curly goatskin mantle of his native land, wearing the turban of all true sons of Islam, came running to prostrate himself on the ground dangerously near the prancing hooves of the sultan's horse.

171

Urban, who had nearly starved in Hungary, was a gun founder. His faith in engineering was absolute. His faith in the triune God was nebulous, for his closed scientific mind could never add one plus one plus one without getting three.

His Hungarian colleagues had shown little interest in making their handguns larger; and when Urban had boasted that he could make a cannon so big that a man could crawl into it, they had called him possessed, stopped his pay, and sent him to a priest to confess that such impossible notions came from the Devil.

Urban had promptly gone over to the Turks, who were not mechanically minded and who refused to believe that so useful an instrument, if it could be made at all, could possibly come from the Devil. Mohammed himself had encouraged Urban to continue his experiments and graciously turned over to him a secluded section of Paradise, where, behind high walls, in complete and protected secrecy, Urban could build his furnaces and cast his bronze. The grateful Hungarian, more prosperous and respected than he had ever been in his life, had praised God, submitted to the painful rite of circumcision, and donned the turban of Islam, glad to be in a practical country where one is always one and three always three and no nonsense about it. Moreover, the sultan had created him a pasha of one horsetail before decamping for the Morea.

Now, on the sultan's return, Urban Pasha, hearing the news of the victories and having just finished his largest cannon to date, had shot it off in a wild, exuberant welcome. It was certainly the noisiest and perhaps the first salute by cannon ever given a reigning prince.

Looking up from the gravel of the palace walk into the scowling face of the sultan, Urban Pasha exclaimed: "Allah and His Mother have blessed my bronze, Your Majesty! The cannon is a complete success. Not so big as I will one day make, but big enough for me to put my head into, Your Majesty, if I take off my turban. And it will throw a stone from Paradise into the river Tunja!" For a moment it looked as if he were going to cross himself at the benevolence of God, who had wrought such things.

Murad would have had him flogged, and even the grand vizier looked shocked; but Mohammed chose to overlook the theological confusion which sometimes troubled new converts to Islam.

"God has no mother, Urban Pasha. Do try to master the simple precepts of Islam; but it is probably not your fault. The hodja who instructed you shall be disciplined. Tell me, did the cannon burst?"

"Shadow of God on this sorry earth, my cannon never burst!"

"How do you know it will cast a stone into the river Tunja?"

Urban Pasha beamed. "Yesterday, Majesty, it did so."

It was a good range. Farther by far than a strong man could shoot an arrow. No gun in Christendom had ever shot half so far. Mohammed thought a moment, twisting his mustache.

Then he said: "For the honor you have done me in saluting me with thunder like the thunder of Sinai, my imperial thanks. For the progress you have made in your art, my promise of advancement and preference. Khalil Pasha," he said, turning to the vizier, "if this man can cast thirty such cannon more, give him another horsetail." Then the sultan's face glowered: "And for the inexcusably stupid noise of your demonstration—who knows what spies may be listening in Adrianople?—sixty blows with a willow switch across the soles of your naked feet!"

That would incapacitate a man for days. The sultan glanced significantly at the grand vizier. "But Urban Pasha must walk tomorrow." Which meant that the willow switch would be swathed in swan's-down and wafted like a fan.

Then the sultan entered his palace.

And that evening Michael learned from Safiyé Hanoum that Aeshia, whose naked face had haunted his dreams, would accept him as her husband. She would have him! He felt sanctified. His eager, inordinate desire for advancement in his career took on a tawdry, self-centered aspect. Once-glorious ambitions now seemed vainglorious. To protect the helpless, exciting woman who had been ignominiously cast off by her lord put into shameful shade all other considerations. Michael was experiencing for the first time the complex satisfaction of forgetting self-interest in love and devotion to someone else.

He had wanted her on any level. She had signified through Adrianople's most reputable marriage broker that she would have him on the highest level. He could hardly believe his good fortune.

The broker had stated that Aeshia was willing, had confided that she was pleased, had even whispered that she was enthusiastic! But for the sake of her reputable standing in the community, never, never tell a soul that she, Safiyé Hanoum, Madame Wisdom, had unethically divulged the secret and the passion!

Thus Michael and Aeshia were married.

CHAPTER
18

REJECTING all revelation to the contrary, the Koran nowhere teaches that marriages are made in heaven.

Shortly before midnight, four months after her marriage, Aeshia lay pondering, among other things, the wisdom of the marital law of Islam. She lay very quietly, so as not to disturb Michael, and watched the sand in the hourglass. She had set it where a shaft of moonlight would strike it, and it shone like a great double jewel.

She watched the sharp little mountain of sand in the nether globe grow taller, as what remained in the upper globe dropped lower and lower. The patch of moonlight also moved as time passed and the earth spun, and Aeshia wondered idly whether the glass would still be visible when midnight came and the sand ran out. The upper globe was nearly exhausted, and Aeshia smiled because it really didn't matter any more. It was almost time to waken Michael. Softly.

Her marriage with Michael, after three marriages with the Beglerbey of Roum, had proved something of a physical revelation to Aeshia; and Aeshia had adapted herself to it with ease and happy alacrity. She would have been the last to gainsay Madame Wisdom's considerable estimate of the janissaries. The half of her heart that was fire was confident and proud. It had not been so with Machmut. Aeshia now wondered how that could have bothered her. It shouldn't have. It never would again.

Michael had hung up the white turban and scarlet girdle that distinguished his military rank and put off his yellow janissary shoes. If he had felt a pang at severing himself from his career, he did not show it. Aeshia almost admired him for that, even now.

But only half of her heart was fire, the legacy of Tamerlane; the rest was cool as the wily minds of the forty scheming caliphs, not whose swords but whose cunning had assured their ascendancy through the centuries, from Mecca to Baghdad and from Baghdad to Cairo.

Fortunately for her sanity, Aeshia could not hear the ancestral voices in her blood, but she obeyed them, since they made her what she was. Tamerlane had had his day. And now at midnight came the whisper of forty caliphs in council: Aeshia, Aeshia, it is better to be the Little Lady of a rich old prince than the Great Lady of a soldier on half-pay. Bismillah! What sort of man gives up a career and digs in a garden?

It was perfectly true that Michael, having nothing better to do and starved for a breath of air not tainted with incense, had dug up their garden with one of the servants' spades. Some janissaries of his old command had looked the other way so as not to embarrass him.

Not that there was anything disgraceful in getting married and leaving the janissary corps. The regulations provided for it. A man lost no honor. More than one of the janissaries who saw his handsome house and spacious garden would have changed places with him. If they had seen Aeshia, even more of them might have been willing to make the change; but it was very unusual for young commanders to retire. It looked like a lack of ambition, perhaps even cowardice, especially in times like the present, when everyone knew that advancement, booty, and names might soon be won.

But Michael had never regretted his choice, and only on nights like this, after one of his infrequent quarrels with Aeshia, did he ever think at all about his life as a soldier or the honorable career he had abandoned.

Michael had dropped off to sleep angry and dissatisfied, not quite certain what they had quarreled about. He was sleeping unquietly, dreaming, Aeshia supposed, about chasing a bear, or whatever a soldier dreams about. He had never appeared to notice her house—he who had lived in a barrack!—though her hangings and divans were

176

crimson satin, her doors of rosewood on silver hinges and ebony inlaid with mother-of-pearl.

Why couldn't he lie still, so she could listen for the footsteps in the garden?

Aeshia was now Buyuk Hanoum, Great Lady, a premier wife and an only one. But God's name! The term was relative. The Little Lady of a great man had a far higher place in the society of the capital than the Great Lady of a retired, half-pay commander.

Aeshia, lying perfectly quiet, her ears alert, her eyes bright, open, watching the hourglass, which moved so much slower than her thoughts, smiled also at the thought of her friends. They called as often as ever, but their approach was a bit patronizing nowadays. And they related with relish, spitefully, Aeshia thought, the absorbing court gossip that their husbands brought them, conscious that Aeshia's husband had no gossip at all.

Then she smiled in a way that Michael and no other man had ever seen. The smile curved downward on one side like a warped bow that has to be thrown away. On other lips it would have been a sneer.

For Aeshia was remembering a letter she had written that day to Machmut. If she knew her former husband as well as she thought she did, it would bring him to her house that night; and if she had fathomed his peculiar nature as deeply as she thought she had then what he would see would restore her to her former status, before she had foolishly flirted with a janissary at a fountain in the gardens of the sultan.

Michael in his sleep was not chasing a bear. It was a summer day, and he was marching away, with the Tournaji Bashi, from a gray house on the foothill of Bulgarlhu Dagh. And so subtly was his dream dissociated from reality that, whereas he had actually been happy that day, in his dream it was wrong, all wrong.

Aeshia glanced at him, wondered why his legs twitched, and looked again toward the glass. Machmut had slept much less actively. He snored, of course, but who knew that? And what was a snore when one was the Little Lady of the Beglerbey of Roum, a princess and a rich one, spending never an asper of her own money, gathering garlands of jewels from her lord and never repelling his advances because, at his age, who had to?

Aeshia noted with satisfaction that all but a spoonful of sand had run out. The moonlight was leaving the hourglass; she and Michael were bathed in its silver sheen.

It was time.

She whispered in his ear that she was sorry for the quarrel. Her love and her shame had kept her awake. Would her lord forgive his slave? Did her lord still love her?

Michael lifted his head and saw her beside him in the moonlight, the lithe white body of such infantile smoothness that on his wedding night he had been half reluctant to touch so young a bride, until she told him the secret of her smooth nakedness.

"Do I love you, my life? God's name, but I love you!"

Aeshia smiled up at him full in the face, happily, Michael thought. He had never seen her eyes so bright and expectant. It was Aeshia's considered opinion that, although the coming embrace might suffer as to duration, by reason of her having delayed it till midnight with the quarrel, it was almost certain to benefit as to activity, and might even be spectacular.

She heard the footstep in the garden now. And so that Michael would not hear it, she whispered fiercely in his ear, "I love you!" and took the lobe of his ear between her teeth and pressed.

Then the curtains at the door parted ever so slightly, and she bit till her teeth drew blood.

The letter Aeshia had written to Machmut said only:

GREAT PRINCE!
Some money matters of importance relative to Your Highness's generous provision for his former slave require your personal, immediate attention. My young, new lord is away on a hunting trip. I beg you to come to me to arrange this fatiguing matter of business, which Your Highness, with the fiscal finesse which has always distinguished him, will put right in an instant and to his own profit. For Your Highness may remember, if he remember me at all, how helpless I have always been when it comes to money.

Humph! thought the Prince of the Princes of Turkey-in-Europe, that I do not remember. A shrewder baggage with an asper I never saw. Let her send her lawyer. But the letter went on:

Your Highness had best come alone at midnight, lest the gossips talk or my lord learn of our meeting.

178

And that decided Machmut. For reputable, married Turkish ladies did not make appointments with their former husbands in the middle of the night—unless they were in danger. Poor child! Could Aeshia be in danger? With a houseful of eunuchs and a professional soldier to protect her? Or perhaps—Bismillah! Was it possible that Aeshia had finally come to realize how infinitely preferable to silly young men a mature, grave, wise, and fatherly protector actually is?

He rose and examined his reflection in one of his costly glass mirrors. It was imported from the Republic of Venice, and was probably invested with a perverse sort of Christian magic, inasmuch as Machmut had detected that although it was actually his left eye that suffered from the slight droop (a minor affliction which all his friends said enhanced the contemplative gravity of his distinguished countenance), in the Gavour reflection the eye droop was on the *right!*

He nodded slowly to the mirror, and his inexplicably reversed image nodded back at him. Why didn't it shake its head? Yes, yes, the face was grave and wise. Aeshia might very well have come to appreciate him after experiencing life with a callow youngster! It could easily be. At midnight! The thought of the late hour sent a flush of blood to his cheeks. It was years since he had been invited to meet a lady at midnight. And what a lady! She had been lost to him for half a year, but the white, warm memory of Aeshia had grown sharper rather than more dim.

There was another reason for the flush in Machmut's cheeks, and the other reason was Michael, whose continued existence still stood between the prince and the profitable Scutari venture. Jealousy and greed merged in a fierce hot wind of hate that oppressed Machmut's breathing and dried up his tongue when he allowed himself to think about it. More than once he had quietly plotted Michael's death; but first Michael and the army had gone away to Greece, and then, after his marriage, Michael never went out at night. And one obviously could not conveniently or safely assassinate a man in broad daylight on the well policed streets of Adrianople.

Aeshia had mentioned money, too. Machmut knew from long experience that it is never wise to neglect anything that promised profit. When he came to think of it, some of his best ventures had been negotiated at midnight.

So Machmut carefully combed his beard, put on a fresh turban, and impatiently watched his hourglass till it was time to set out for Aeshia's house. He went armed, and he walked in the middle of the street, away from the shadows cast by the moon under the projecting upper stories of the houses. He had no torchbearer, since he wished to be as inconspicuous as possible, wanting a scandal no more than Aeshia.

But he did not go alone. Machmut walked unattended in the moonlight over the cobbles in the middle of the street; but on both sides of him, in the shadows of the overhanging buildings, the darker shadows of some strong, armed, cat-footed guards kept pace with him.

The balmy March breeze blew in his face and plastered his beard against the red wool of his best, most becoming mantle. The warm spring wind after the cold winter, the brilliant moon, and the excitement of an assignation exhilarated him. Proudly he thought, No youth of forty ever felt livelier than Machmut, the Beglerbey of Roum!

He entered Aeshia's garden and saw in the brilliant moonlight the door opening silently and the well remembered figures of Usamah and Umarah beckoning him into the house. He entered confidently, without fear. What had he to fear from Aeshia? What motive had she, of all people, to harm him, since some of their investments were still so inextricable that if he died her income would suffer. And Machmut knew also that his guards, advancing hidden under the shrubs and hedges of the garden, would soon be all over the house, like invisible guardian angels. They were East Indian men, bought at a fancy price, and they were said to belong to the famous brotherhood of Hindu assassins and robbers called Thugs. Their special art was "thuggee," a silent, efficient variety of unexpected strangulation.

There was no light in the house, but Usamah and Umarah, one at his right elbow and one at his left, conducted him down the long passage to a curtained arch through which shone a brilliant spear of moonlight as if, inside, a silver lamp were burning.

There he paused, stunned for a moment, overwhelmed at the moonlit intimacy of the embrace of the two young people.

The eunuchs gave him a little shove, and Machmut strode into the room.

The vicious bite which caused Aeshia's white, even teeth to meet in the lobe of her husband's ear was not calculated to exhilarate

Michael. Aeshia instinctively knew more than experience had taught her, and instinct told her that, whereas a small nibble might titillate Machmut, a good, strong, painful bite would infuriate Michael.

Michael instantly did what she had known all along he would do. He sputtered a great surprised oath, thrust her from him, and shook her savagely.

Aeshia at once began to flail her arms and legs about, crying repeatedly for help and shouting "Murder!"

To Machmut's myopic vision it did indeed appear that Aeshia (probably the nether of the interlocked naked bodies, the sight of which a moment before had caused him almost to burst a blood vessel) might actually die of the sudden, brutal, astonishing assault.

Aeshia shouted for help, but no one came to help her. Usamah and Umarah, placidly holding aside the curtains through which they had just pushed Machmut, did not make a move. The dark Hindu guards did not make a move either, since they had orders to protect Machmut, not unpredictable Turkish couples who chose to reenact in the moonlight some of the most extraordinary carvings on their ancient Hindu temples.

It was permissible, in the springtime of 1452, to beat a wife anywhere in Islam, or anywhere in Christendom, but murder! That was another matter.

So, since no one else exhibited any intention of rescuing Aeshia, Machmut, lively as a youth of forty, lumbered forward to save his former Little Lady, upsetting the taboret that held the hourglass and fumbling at his girdle for his dagger. The delicate little table of sandalwood splintered. The ornate timekeeper burst into a thousand shards of tinkling glass, and some of the sand that had marked the hour of midnight spilled onto the bed.

Michael heard the noise and now perceived that he and Aeshia were not alone. The figure of a man with a dagger in its hand was coming toward him. He supposed it was some clumsy robber; and in his anger and confusion he did not pause to wonder how a robber had got past Usamah, Umarah, and the other servants.

Since he was unarmed, he threw a pillow at Machmut's face and leaped at him.

Machmut was unable exactly to distinguish what sort of missile came flying at him, but it was coming swiftly and might be dangerous.

The Beglerbey of Roum hacked savagely at it with his dagger. He was instantly enveloped in a swirling cloud of swan's-down.

Then Michael's flying leap brought him into smashing contact, head first, with Machmut's belly, and the prince went down unconscious, flat on his back. Michael looked for the dagger, with every intention of burying it to the hilt in the throat of the robber. But even Michael, who could shoot grapes individually off a cluster of grapes, could not see in that blinding flurry of moonlit feathers. He felt the hands of the supine figure. They were open and empty. So, with a mental shrug, he started to strangle the man.

Meanwhile the loyal Hindu Thugs rushed headlong into the room to protect Machmut; but one of them kicked the ruptured pillow and the swan's-down swirled higher than ever. They, too, were all blinded and in mortal danger of death at one another's hands. After several near accidents they moved more cautiously, and wisely decided to kill no one with clothes on.

Usamah and Umarah, who knew the room, groped their way to Aeshia; and when they found her cowering on the bed, they placed themselves on each side of her and crossed their scimitars over her.

Aeshia clung to them.

"Who are all these foreigners?" she whispered, and one of the eunuchs answered:

"They are the Indian stranglers of the beglerbey, Your Ladyship."

"He was supposed to come alone! This isn't the way I planned it. Don't let them murder me!"

"Never fear that, Mistress! Shall we let them murder Lord Michael?"

It appeared to the eunuchs that the air was a little clearer now, and one of the Thugs seemed to be approaching Michael and Machmut, whose tangled figures on the floor were becoming visible.

At that moment more servants of Aeshia's came into the room, some with swords and some with lights. The armed retainers of Aeshia and Machmut were now so evenly matched that, having no positive instructions to start a private battle, they all prudently confined themselves to their minimum duties.

That resulted in a concerted rush to separate Michael and Machmut. The Thugs surrounded Machmut. Aeshia's servants formed a protective barrier in front of Michael.

Michael had been confused ever since Aeshia wakened him. He was speechless at what she did now. Pausing only to snatch a coverlet off the bed and cast it around her, she ran to Machmut, knelt beside him, and chafed his hand.

"My lord," she breathed, "live and speak to your slave!"

Machmut slowly opened his eyes. For a moment he thought he was in Paradise.

"Kutchuk Hanoum!" he murmured. "Give me air." Then he saw Michael. Angry strength flooded back into his body. He raised himself to his elbow and pointed a stubby, shaking forefinger, heavy with jeweled rings. "Destroy that man!" he roared.

The Thugs looked willing, but Aeshia's servants scowled and placed their hands on their swords. Only Usamah and Umarah preserved a grave neutrality. It was all one to them how many angry, peculiar, passionate men were killed so long as only their beloved mistress came to no harm.

Aeshia had never planned Michael's actual death. To have to be present at his murder before so many witnesses struck her as endlessly complicating, something to be avoided unless it proved absolutely necessary. From the fury on Michael's face she did not think it would be.

She made her delicate, expressive countenance a mask of compassion.

"Spare him, Great Prince, for the sake of my good name. He is my husband, though a brutal one!" She dabbed at the corner of her mouth with an edge of the coverlet so that Machmut would be sure to see the blood that she knew was there. It was Michael's blood, but how was the prince to know that?

"The beast has struck you!" Machmut shouted. "Yet you defend him!"

"Who will protect me if you kill him?" Aeshia sobbed; and this time she dabbed at her eyes, which required a little more of the coverlet and permitted Machmut to observe the exquisite body that any man would be proud to protect.

"When you summoned me," Machmut said fatuously, "I had no idea I should be the means of saving you from brutality tonight. Is your husband always so violent?"

Aeshia shook her head sadly: "Always, Your Excellency. But whisper. Do not shame me in front of the servants." Aeshia did not

183

want too many of the details to be gossiped about in the baths of Adrianople.

"Brave girl! Noble little lady!"

Michael, barred by half a dozen stalwart servitors, began to understand. Agony burst from his lips. "Blessed Lord Jesus!" he swore, unconscious that he had spoken Italian. No one understood him, of course.

Machmut's dignity required that he match Aeshia's magnanimity. And he, too, was aware how inconvenient it might prove to slaughter a former janissary commander in the presence of his lawful wife and so many witnesses.

"Your husband shall not die tonight," he said.

Michael, whose last words to Aeshia had been, "I love you," now said huskily: "Aeshia has no husband. I divorce her. Be it known that I divorce her." And again he repeated, forcefully, "I divorce her!" The triple renunciation, according to custom already taking shape in Islam and later to be ratified by law, carried the weight of stunning finality.

Aeshia's heart leaped. She could hardly keep from dancing. Divorce she had schemed for and anticipated. How else under the law could she ever hope to remarry Machmut and become again the princess she had been? But so conclusive a divorce she had hardly dared expect. She allowed her head and her shoulders to droop and rest against Machmut's scarlet mantle, as if the shame were more than she could bear.

"Now I am helpless and alone," she murmured, her voice soft and choked with emotion, the coverlet more neglected than ever.

"Bismillah!" puffed the Beglerbey of Roum. "You are *not!* Not now, or ever again." He chucked her under the chin. "Aeshia, I want that young soldier to get out of this house. I'll send him somewhere with my Thugs. I promise they shan't harm him. But get him out. I am very fatigued."

"Your Excellency cannot stay here!" Aeshia exclaimed. "Whatever would people say?"

Machmut pouted, "Oh, very well, then."

Aeshia said, "Tomorrow we can discuss the business matter I apprised you of." The voice was prim. It carried to the four corners of the room; but the eyes and the coverlet were eloquent.

"Good!" Machmut whispered, rising to his feet.

"Commander," he pronounced loudly and judiciously, "wherever you may desire to go, I offer you the service of my loyal Thugs, if you wish a guard. If you prefer other attendants you may have any of Aeshia Hanoum's."

Michael said, half choking, "I shall go alone."

Aeshia shrugged.

Usamah and Umarah took out the white turban, the crimson girdle, and the yellow janissary shoes from the storage chest, where they had been laid away in aloes and cedar dust to keep them fresh, and made a bundle of them to give their recent master who decided to wear them. It was not forbidden a married or retired janissary to wear the uniform, though donning it after retirement was usually reserved for parades or for occasions of rejoicing after a great national victory.

The eunuchs nodded and grinned and congratulated each other, the colorful plumes of their gay turbans dancing in the air and shaking out some few little feathers of swan's-down pillow stuffing that had caught there.

"Men! Men!" they sighed. "How manifold are the miseries that Allah in his mercy has seen fit to spare us!"

MICHAEL walked the streets of Adrianople till sunup, and found himself at the Eastern Gate, which faced the river Tunja. This was a slum area, the ghetto of the Christians and Jews, who were permitted to live within the protecting walls, but who, when they died, were buried outside.

Now the step of a janissary is springy and light, the step of youth. Everyone knew that a janissary could march all day and all night, and, if need be, all day again; but Michael walked heavily, slowly, his eyes on the ground, like an old, old man.

At the Eastern Gate an impeccable sergeant in white turban and yellow shoes barred the way with a drawn scimitar, the blade of which he touched, however, in the eloquent Oriental salute, which meant, "Rather my own than thy flesh."

"The commander should not go outside till the dogs are fed," he suggested respectfully.

Michael shrugged, scarcely glancing at the guard. Since he was walking so slowly and might perhaps be ill, the guard said a little more pointedly:

"The commander may remember that there is some small danger outside the walls till after morning prayers and the feeding of the dogs."

Michael turned on him a face full of such lackluster pain and burnt-out anger as the conscientious sergeant had never seen. In Michael the desolation of love gone dead just as it seemed most alive had merged with the shame of a career renounced for that love. The whole was devastatingly greater than the sum of its parts.

"What God wills," Michael said.

God willed, since it was just sunup, that all the muezzins in Adrianople mount their minarets and call the faithful to the first prayer of the day. Since Michael did not pause, even for prayers, the guard at once decided that he was a madman, and let him pass.

But, facing Mecca on his knees, the guard thought he remembered a face that looked like the face of this weary aberrant commander's, and he resolved to report the incident to Hassan. He resolved also that it would be no more than ordinary compassion toward one of God's fools to send a soldier to follow the man, lest in his madness he destroy himself in the river Tunja or perhaps fall prey to the hungry, scavenger dogs already growling at their accustomed places under the walls. There, after prayers, for a tiny wage, the beggars, the street cleaners, and the ragpickers threw to them each morning the refuse of the city: offal from the butchers' shops, animals that had died in the streets, and, from time to time, the body of a criminal that had been executed during the night.

Some of the half-staved brutes came sniffing and whining at Michael's heels, but he smelled neither of fear nor carrion, and they deserted him for their usual breakfast, which presently came tumbling down the walls. In a little while the guard whom the sergeant had thoughtfully set over Michael also deserted him, since Michael had neither fainted nor fallen. The dogs, gorging themselves, were not dangerous now. Michael had turned away from the river Tunja and taken a neglected path that led to a place where no good Moslem would willingly go: the churchyard of Virgin Saint Mary. Such Christians as died in Adrianople were buried there.

During the long, aimless walk in the night, Michael had sometimes half heard the voice of the merchant in Galata: "He rode all the way to Adrianople . . . and in Adrianople he died, before his petition could interfere with your career."

His career!

And the merchant's daughter had said: "Your father did not forget you."

The words had been a sort of comfort in his ears when the throbbing of his heart did not drown them out. And as a result (since no conscious purpose directed them) Michael's feet had instinctively taken the path toward the cypress trees on the little mound above the river Tunja. In his shame and his intense loneliness Michael now sought for a name in alien Roman script on an alien Christian cross, as if his dead father could somehow bestow a consolation impossible from anyone now alive in the whole wide empty world. For Michael was bitterly aware, as if the whips of his old eunuch taskmasters had flogged the emotion into his orphaned heart, how empty the world could be without love, without ambition, and without a friend.

Suddenly Michael heard someone speak, in excessively polite Turkish with a heavy Gavour accent, behind him. He stiffened imperceptibly and turned his head.

"Is His Excellency, the distinguished Commander, looking for something?"

It was an oily, fat little priest, with a hank of long gray hair sticking out from under his black, flat-topped hat. The veil was awry and the front of his habit unkempt and greasy, as if he were careless when he ate.

In such a mood at such a time, Michael could have stomached a Christian miracle; but the sight of this Christian commonplace, this ingratiating, subservient alien, oozing the self-deprecating ethos of too many rayah generations who had lived in Turkey too long, recalled to Michael a bit of his Turkish pride, in spite of his pain of the moment. Out of habit Michael reached into his girdle and took out an asper. Out of habit the priest accepted the coin, stretched his elastic theological conscience, and blessed him glibly in the words not of Christ but of the Prophet, "Unto such of you as believe and bestow alms, shall be given a great reward. But," the priest added, "what is the commander-pasha looking for so early in the morning in this sorry place?"

Michael said: "I am looking for a name. And I am not a pasha, as you very well know."

The priest looked frightened. "Ah, yes, Excellency. A name. All the janissaries are looking for names. You will win one. When the war comes you will win a name, but you cannot do battle here with the dead. It is too bad you are going to fight us again. We always lose, and the taxes always go up." Suddenly he started nervously. "Holy Virgin! Your Excellency came to inquire about taxes! I always keep the receipts on hand! If your Excellency will only step inside the chapel—forgive me! Of course your Excellency will not step inside the chapel. One little moment. I'll fetch the receipts at once."

Michael said: "I know nothing about your filthy receipts. And the name I seek is on a cross."

"Oh."

The word was very short. The tone was very different. The priest eyed him sharply.

"What is the name you seek, sir?"

"Nicolo."

The priest shook his head. "Nicolo is a common Christian name. Many Nicolos sleep here. Is there another name? It is called a family name. It is the birthright of all Christian men."

Michael did not immediately answer.

The priest persisted: "It does not have to be won, and it cannot be taken away. There is another name."

"The name is Da Montelupo," Michael said, glancing aside.

The priest nodded. "A noble name. A proud man could be proud to wear it. Perhaps you will follow me, sir." The oily voice had dropped the "Excellency" and the "Pasha" and now spoke with a certain cautious dignity.

Over the brow of the little rise, facing the blue expanse of the noble Tunja as it swept round the walls of Adrianople toward its confluence with the Maritza, there was a well kept grave with a stone cross that bore the name *Nicolo da Montelupo*. Although it was only March, the grass was already green, and testified to the care with which the priest dug out the weeds lest they choke the turf, as had happened on some of the other graves. The cypresses at the head and foot, planted as seedlings in diplomatic conformity with the ancient Turkish custom, were taller than Michael.

"The Lord of Montelupo went to heaven some years ago," the priest said simply. "I read the service myself. I take particular care of this grave because a pious man in Galata pays me twice a year to do so."

"Who is that?" Michael asked.

But the priest had already said more than he should have and would not tell.

"I think I know," Michael said.

"Perhaps you would care to be alone," the priest murmured. "I think I smell my breakfast burning. I am not permitted a servant, sir. Not even a server to serve at Mass. If you will forgive me now—" and he turned to go. "I might just suggest," he added over his shoulder as an afterthought, "we Christians sometimes say a prayer which goes, 'Our Father, which art in Heaven, hallowed be thy name—' "

"I know," Michael said, "I know. You may go. I do want to be alone."

But when Michael knelt at the grave of his father, all he could remember of the Lord's Prayer was, "Father in Heaven, Father in Heaven."

It was many years since he had learned the prayer. He had known it once, but he could not remember it now. Was there not something in it that said, "forgive us as we forgive others?" Bismillah! A likely prayer! What kind of people pray like that? Realistic Turkish thinking did not permit him to fancy the sort of forgiveness that he would accord, say, Machmut and Aeshia.

Yet in the quiet Christian cemetery, close to the peaceful dust of the loins that had begotten him, it was comforting to repeat, "Father in Heaven." A Moslem, of course, not only kneels but also touches his head to the ground. Michael did not immediately raise his head, as he would have done if he had been facing Mecca in the usual way. He was a little afraid that the fat Christian priest might be spying on him. It would never do to have it said that a janissary commander had been seen to weep, but the tears would not stop. Michael covered his face with both his hands and remained prostrate in the attitude of prayer.

And after a little while something magical happened, for out of the corner of his eye he saw, or thought he saw, his long morning shadow visibly shorten as the sun miraculously gathered speed and leaped up the sky. When he raised his head again after what seemed only a moment, the tears were dry. Far off in the city the muezzins were shouting, not morning prayers, but noon prayers. Michael felt mystically refreshed in a rather frightening way. Where had the morning gone?

"Bismillah!" he said. "This place has put a spell on me. There is no time here." And then he said more softly to the ground, as if he were addressing a person, "Thy Christian magic is strong!"

But he was grateful for it, whatever it was. And for Michael, for that day, that was enough.

THE miracle, or the sleep, that had occurred in the Christian cemetery cleansed Michael of the shame that had oppressed him during the night; but the loneliness remained.

Michael realized, of course, that he had unwittingly been forced into one of those neat little triangular situations which were sometimes staged to circumvent the law of the Prophet.

Sometimes an irascible, passionate man, having divorced a wife the limit of three times, would desire her again. And sometimes an obliging friend would marry and divorce her himself, all in the space of a few hours, so that she would be free, after three months, to remarry her first husband. The device naturally nullified all the wisdom of the law. Decent people frowned upon such collusion; but it was legal, well known, and there was nothing that could be done about it.

Invariably, however, the offenders were men. Michael had never heard of the trick being played by a woman so that she not only achieved the same end but did it without the knowledge of one, perhaps both, husbands. He wondered to what extent Machmut was in on the scheme.

During the night, walking the street, he had been beaten and dazed at the enormity of Aeshia's betrayal. Without a hint of warning, the thing he had taken for love he saw stripped of its sacrificial glory and reduced to a collusive marital device. He was astonished at the cunning with which Aeshia had managed to bring Machmut into the house, and revolted at the indecency of the moment she had chosen to demonstrate his "brutality" and the means she had used to induce it. Love him? She must always have been cynically contemptuous of him; and Michael, who hated contempt like any other man, wondered if it had given her pleasure to spin out her scheming five months from November to March. He realized bitterly that as far as he was concerned she could have managed it in a week.

For a little while he had been ashamed, with the proud, fierce shame of a Turk to whom privacy is sacred, that the scene had been enacted before so many witnesses. But the moments, or the hours, at his father's grave, where the present and the eternal seemed so mystically merged, purged him of the selfish emotion; he now saw more clearly that it is less important who sees a wife lost than to lose her.

He continued to walk, more like a man again, but still without a conscious goal. He moved slowly, lost in thought. Then, looking up, he found himself near the permanent camp of the janissaries. He took a deep, grateful breath. Here, of all places, the air was not tainted with olibanum incense. Here was the comfortable, familiar smell of leather and sweat, and here was Hassan, his oldest, his best friend.

Michael did not recognize the sentry standing guard at the gate, and the sentry did not know who Michael was.

Michael said, "Kindly inform Hassan Effendi that Commander Michael asks to see him."

The sentry answered, "Hassan *Pasha* shall be informed that one calling himself Commander Michael craves audience," and detailed a subordinate to sprint off with the message.

Michael scarcely heard the slur on his identity, though a day or a week before he would have resented the insolence. As if anyone but a janissary or a retired janissary would dare to wear the uniform of a commander! But the hundredth lash is never felt. Michael simply nodded, noting absently that the paint on the gate was extraordinarily fresh. Then he recalled how oddly the sentry had spoken: "Craves audience." That was the formal old language of the great days of the last reign. Mildly interested, Michael glanced again at the man and saw how old he was. All of a sudden it flashed upon him that the stiff old soldier had corrected him. He had said "Hassan Pasha." Thoroughly alive again to what was going on about him,

Michael took a long, appraising look through the gate into the stockade. Hassan's a pasha already? He had got his horsetail in a hurry. Times had changed!

The appearance of the camp had also changed, for tents were pitched in the parade ground, as if the men were on maneuvers, and the doors of the barracks were all shut, as if nobody slept in them. In the midst of the tents there was a brilliant green one with a green horsetail standard planted in front of it to distinguish the commanding pasha's rank. To this the man with the message ran. In a moment he emerged, replaced the door flap, bowed to the horsetail, and ran back to the sentry. He whispered into the sentry's ear, as was proper, for subordinates did not have the privilege of voicing the commands of a pasha. The sentry's face did not change, but he saluted Michael respectfully and said, "Hassan Pasha will see his friend, Commander Michael, at once. Only my duty here at the post prevents my escorting the Commander Effendi to Hassan Pasha myself."

As Michael entered the green tent, Hassan rose to greet him and presented his hand in the gesture of friendliness which, in Eastern countries, meant more than it ever had or ever was to mean in Europe, where people kissed or wept or handled each other in a familiar manner incomprehensible and repugnant to Orientals.

"I was expecting you, friend," Hassan exclaimed. "You caused a lot of comment with your early morning walk among the dogs. I heard you went for a stroll up the hill, too, to take a look at the river."

Michael said, "I don't know how you know that, but since you do you must also know that I visited a Christian cemetery."

Michael wondered what else Hassan knew, and he prepared to tell him what had happened during the night, but Hassan held up his hand. "Don't burden me with confidences, Michael. Maybe I've visited a Christian cemetery, too, in my time; but I never told anybody. I didn't think it would help my career."

"I wasn't going to talk about cemeteries," Michael said. "Permit me to congratulate you on your appointment. It is a wonderful thing to win a horsetail." Michael found himself surprised at some of the old enthusiasm in his voice.

"Oh, that," Hassan said, with obvious pleasure. "Yes, that's a comfort to an old campaigner. Of course, the tent that comes with it is something of a trial. Makes everybody look liverish. Are you feeling liverish today? I can't quite tell in this light."

Michael opened his mouth to speak, but again Hassan held up his hand. "I repeat, do not burden me with confidences. I know all about what you are going to say. That happened last night. It is now after noon. Remember how fast word travels in Adrianople. The whole town is laughing."

Michael set his jaw till the muscles stood out like cords. Then his face relaxed, and he said: "At first I cared what people thought. I don't any longer."

"Bismillah, lad, they're not laughing at *you!* They're laughing at the beglerbey! 'Never was man more valiant,' they say, 'in a pillow fight!' And they say, 'Who ever slew a swan's-down cushion half so nobly as Machmut, the Beglerbey of Roum?'"

"It isn't funny to me."

"Of course not. But look, Michael. The prince now has what he has. Do you envy him?"

"No, God's name, No! I do not."

"Never do. The fire you chose to play with burned you. I knew it would. I don't suppose you'll ever be burned in precisely that way again. I shan't talk about it any more, but I will just say this: it looks to me as if the Egyptian had bewitched you both with a clever scheme of her own in order to get the rich prince back again, him and his money. The word is that she's got him, too. Nobody can understand why Machmut is going to remarry her—"

"I can," Michael said.

"Lust, Michael, lust. But think, man, would you change places with him?"

Michael did not answer.

"Nobody would in his right mind. It's a pity the thing ever happened. I could use you here now, but I suppose you'll stay in retirement on your pension." Hassan eyed him slyly. "You can get a villa in the territory around Lake Van very reasonably, and the local country wenches that take care of the gentry there have a reputation for being very attentive night and day on the wants of their masters."

"There was more to it than that."

"Maybe there was and maybe some day you will discover there wasn't. But I said I wouldn't talk any more about it."

"Well, I don't propose to play stud to country slaves for the rest of my life. I don't know what I'll do. But I don't think I'll stay in retirement at all. I can go to Spain. There's honor, perhaps a name, to be won in the service of the Sultan of Granada."

"Granada!" Hassan spat contemptuously. "Spawn of Al Ahmar! The Zegri! The Beni Serraj! Moors! Africans! Merchants! There is no honor in Granada. It will not last the century. The line is effeminate, decadent, worn out. The Moors of Granada flutter about, compromising like the Greeks of Constantinople. It would be foolish to throw yourself away in the service of a dynasty that is doomed. Allah is storing up glory for Islam, but not in Spain. This is the place, Michael. Turkey is the land. I could use you, Michael. The new men are raw, ignorant. There are now two thousand janissaries in camp."

Hassan's eyes flashed; Michael began to reflect some of his fire. The old pride of the corps surged back again. And it was good to hear that he was needed.

"What's the matter? Can't they shoot?"

Hassan shrugged. "They could hit a very fat enemy, I suppose. We use a target like the sultan's, round, like the full moon. It's so big that a man's extended arms just reach to its edges. Once in a while they hit it."

Michael snorted. "Not even a Greek is so broad in the beam."

"Oh, the Greeks won't always be so broad; but wait, before I say too much. You don't actually plan to remain in retirement, do you? With so much work to be done?" Michael shook his head, listening eagerly now. "Then I can tell you a secret. I say the Greeks will be narrow and lean and hungry when we're through with them. Do not go to Spain. Stay here and teach my men how to shoot." Hassan saw the gathering spark in Michael's eye and continued hurriedly, enthusiastically: "New recruits are arriving at a terrific rate. The tents that we've lived in all winter—they're to harden them fast. Old officers are coming out of retirement, like the sentry at the gate. There's lightning in the air. Promotions are rapid, almost like wartime. Witness my horsetail. I am allowed a chief archery master now. Bismillah! I need one! Where could I find a better? You, Michael, must take the post. It will be added to your old infantry rank. It will be important where we are going."

195

"Where are we going?"

With the question Michael rejoined the corps.

Hassan cried: "Good lad! We are going where marksmanship will be a sure road to honor and a name. Some exalted personages are going to expose themselves to danger in a noble adventure!"

And he told Michael the plans afoot to build Roumeli Hissar.

MOHAMMED II was neither the first nor the last imperial despot to be faced with the infuriating anomaly of a strip of foreign land lying athwart his empire.

For two hundred years the Turks had been changing the shape of the old Roman Empire of the East; and each successive shape enclosed a little less territory than before, like a puddle drying up in the sun, constantly shifting its outlines, but always getting smaller.

There had been a time when a Byzantine ship could sail for months, across five seas, from Sicily in the Mediterranean to Cherson on the Sea of Azov. From Lombardy to Georgia, far in an eastern wilderness that would one day be Russia, every shore was a Byzantine shore and every port a Byzantine port.

But now the Roman Empire of the East comprised only a little corridor of land between the Black Sea and the Sea of Marmara. In a matter of hours a ship could sight it, sail past it, and drop it astern like a small island. Yet geographically it was not an island, since it occupied the narrow peninsula connecting the two vast areas of the Ottoman domains to the north and south of it, just as the narrow but very important neck of glass connects the upper and nether globe of an hourglass.

It never occurred to the sultan that the Greeks had been there first and had a perfect right to their city and the few outlying towns which were all that remained of their ancient sea empire. Or rather, he did not care to remember that his own able and warlike forebears had successively lopped off and digested one mighty limb after another of the venerable colossus until only the old heart remained, a weary anachronism, still alive and imperially beating, though its pulse no longer shook the world.

What Mohammed saw was an impudent city, circled by fourteen miles of reputedly impregnable walls, flourishing in the very center of his empire, denying him a seaport that still controlled half the shipping of the world; and behind the walls he saw a weak and decadent people of fabulous wealth.

More than one Ottoman sultan, including his own father, had sat down before the walls of this city in protracted sieges, only to march away again without honor from the battlements that forty-four generations of Byzantines had reared to ever more formidable heights. And not only the Turks, but thirteen times before them, nation after nation, the Persians, the Slavs and the Bulgars, the Avars and the Arabs, had retired in defeat from the battlements of Constantinople, until at length, with logic which appeared irrefutable, the Greeks came to believe that the Virgin Herself had the walls of their capital under Her special protection.

It was the sea that had made Constantinople rich for a thousand years, and excepting the one intercession of the Virgin, it was the sea that had always protected her. For even with hordes of her enemies under her walls during a siege, her ships sailed unmolested in and out of the Golden Horn, through the Bosphorus to all the nations of Christendom, bringing in food, arms, and the fighting men of her allies.

Constantinople was accessible from the sea only through the Bosphorus, one end of which, at the Straits of Gallipoli, was already in Turkish hands. It was Mohammed's plan to seal off the other end by building a castle on the Christian side at a point where the Bosphorus is only half a mile wide.

"And when you do," the grand vizier counseled, "you will add the old weapon of hunger to the wonderful new weapon of gunpowder; and Your Majesty will do what no Moslem has ever done before.

"And yet, Shadow of the Universe, build quickly! Western Christendom, by the special mercy of Allah, is preoccupied with its own bloody wars. The hour is propitious. But build quickly, lest they forget their quarrels, discover Your Majesty's plan, and send their fleets to the succor of Constantine. Remember the Crusades!"

The sultan replied, "I will build Roumeli Hissar in three months!"

CHAPTER
22

THE military glory of the Turks was indisputably grounded in dry land. Water was a cleansing element, to be used before prayers, or to be drunk. It was not a path to empire, as it had been to the Phoenicians, the Greeks, and the Venetians, and as it was to be for the Dutch and the English. The origin of the Turks was the high, dry Mongolian upland, center of the mightiest land mass of the planet. The national standard was the horseshoe. The symbol of rank was the horsetail. And horses swim reluctantly, no matter how well.

Nevertheless, in the springtime of 1452 the exasperated Sultan of Turkey had to take to the sea to go from one part of his empire to another. For to pass with his army from Adrianople to the spot on the Bosphorus where he would build Roumeli Hissar, Mohammed had to skirt Constantinople. To Mohammed II the city's existence was an outrage on the territorial integrity of Turkey and a reproach to his personal pride. It confirmed his hatred of the Gavours and inflamed his ambition to extinguish once and for all the Roman Empire of the East.

If the sultan had been less well advised, the history of Islam might have taken an entirely different turn; but his fiery enthusiasm was tempered by seasoned counselors, like Khalil Pasha. Mohammed was also happy in his chief military men: Isaac Pasha, commander of his Asiatic divisions; Karaja Pasha, commander of his European divisions; Urban Pasha, the mechanical genius who cast his cannon, and

Zagan Pasha, a rare combination of statesman and general who shared with the grand vizier some of the heavy responsibilities of adviser in chief. Few of these men were Turks. They were Greeks, Albanians, Hungarians. It was always unimportant to the Osmanli dynasty where their talented servants happened to be born as long as they had talent. This tolerant concept, of course, was in direct opposition to the pride of race that had characterized, say, the old patricians of Rome; but it worked out in practice, and it was to annihilate the last of the Roman empires.

Mohammed was not quite so fortunate in his admiral, a Bulgarian named Baltoglu Sulemein Pasha, who had built the sleek fleet that was now transporting him and his army from Gallipoli through the Bosphorus. It required thirty-nine triremes to move the sultan, his staff, his horses, his arms, his engineers, his workmen, and his guards to the spot on the strait where Europe and Asia approached within nine hundred yards of each other. The triremes were not the clumsy craft of antiquity with three banks of oars. They were light, low, speedy, and narrow, and they were called triremes because, although they had but a single bank of oars, there were three men to each oar.

"What they lose in weight they will gain in speed," the admiral had said, and the sultan, to whom speed was a watchword, had approved his design for the ships, making Baltoglu Pasha a generous gift and praising him publicly. Speedy the ships certainly were, by reason of a lightness achieved by buying half-strength, half-size timbers, and the differential in price was a profit that went into the admiral's own purse, though nobody knew about it at the time.

The admiral, shrewdly noting the sultan's love of color and thinking to please him, had suggested painting the triremes a vivid yellow, "to signify the sunlike brilliance of Your Majesty's glorious reign." But the sultan replied that the brilliance of his reign would not be enhanced by painting his warships target-yellow, which would only improve the marksmanship of the Greeks; and the enlightened admiral thereupon painted them gray, like the sea at twilight.

It was twilight when Mohammed gave the order for the ships to move up the Bosphorus. Such a line of craft would be noticed, of course. Mohammed did not delude himself that his navy was invisible. On the other hand, it would be foolish to be any more conspicuous than was necessary; so, with this thought in mind, he ordered no bands, no trumpets, no loud shouting, and the rowers were promised extra rations if they rowed quietly, and were threatened with flogging if they needlessly kicked up the water.

It takes some time for thirty-nine ships to pass a given point, even when they row swiftly. The silence, the somber color, and the gathering dusk exaggerated the menacing aspect of the Turkish flotilla. A shiver went down the spines of the Greeks watching from Constantinople's battlements. Some frightened Greek ministers said to the Greek emperor:

"Imperial Majesty, whatever they do, we must bear with them a little while longer till the city is better prepared." Constantine asked, "Is there no end to your cautious prudence?" but he had to agree.

That is why Mohammed was able to land unopposed on the Christian side at the narrow spot opposite his Castle in Asia and instantly begin to build Roumeli Hissar, his impudent Castle in Europe. Mohammed had boasted he would build it in three months. He was to build it in exactly 92 days, and the structure was to last five hundred years, perhaps forever, a perpetual reminder, perpetually forgotten, of how empires temporize and fall.

That same evening there appeared on the Bosphorus a guilded craft as noisy, ornate, and flamboyant as the sultan's ships were somber, silent, and grim. An imperial Byzantine galley was returning from Georgia after a protracted diplomatic mission of extravagant triviality. The sails were cloth of silver. The awnings, to protect the ambassadors from the direct rays of the sun or the too violent settling of the dew, were cloth of gold. Scented wax candles in painted lanterns illuminated the decks. Bunting and double-eagled standards draped from the rigging. Music of dulcimers and silver flutes, and the curiously unwavering, sweet soprano voices of a court choir of white eunuchs floated over the Bosphorus to the ears of the Turks, who, in all their splendid ceremonies, could never approach the splendor of the Byzantine Greeks.

This was the ship that was bringing home George Phranza, the emperor's great chancellor, and his embassy of diplomats from the distant, half-civilized principality of Georgia on the easternmost rim of the Black Sea. Constantine, twelfth of the Palaeologoi to wear the imperial purple, had used the time and skill of his ablest statesmen in a search for a bride for himself, while the Turks prepared for war.

In happier days an Eastern emperor might have had his choice of all the most beautiful princesses of Western and Eastern Christendom. In these last days the Eastern emperor, failing all attempts for a more glorious alliance, had offered his hand to a princess that even a European would have considered half savage. Her dazzled father had eagerly accepted, and the Greek delegates, holding their elegant noses, brought back with them some odoriferous betrothal gifts of woolly mutton hides baled helter-skelter with exquisite sable and ermine pelts. They were all of a value to the Georgians, whose hardy mountain climate had taught them only the desirability of keeping warm in winter. There was also a respectable present of gold bullion, from the same Iberian mountains, and this, having no odor, did not offend the sensibilities of the Greeks. And there was a hearty, happy communication from the Georgian king stating that his daughter was healthy, obedient, strong as an ox, and eagerly anticipating an early consummation of the union whenever the Majesty of Constantinople cared to send another ship for her.

Exercising their immemorial gift for elaborating the simple and making out things to be what they are not, the Greek diplomats were celebrating. The music of the flutes wafted over the water as the imperial galley swept majestically into the Golden Horn. The voices of the choir rhapsodized eloquently, if dispassionately, on the beauty of the Georgian princess, and chanted praises of a kingdom as ancient as Byzantium itself. And so Georgia was, but only because nobody had ever particularly bothered with it.

Meanwhile, the Turkish ships slid up the Bosphorus between the hills of Europe and Asia, approaching the constriction in the strait which was so narrow that it had a Turkish name meaning "the strangled throat."

By a trivial linguistic coincidence, the spot on the Bosphorus known to the Turks as "the strangled throat" was called by the Greeks the beautiful name of Asomaton, a term signifying "that which cannot be touched."

Yet a few days after the arrival of the Turkish fleet, Constantine beheld the place swarming with Turkish invaders.

The promontory of the Asomaton was too steep to be farmed, but some industrious Greek peasants had terraced it and planted vineyards there. One day, going to work, they had been turned back by a line of janissaries. Behind the janissaries they saw the vineyards uprooted and trampled under the feet of thousands of humans and animals, thick as ants in a hill, and just as active and purposeful.

Greased wooden ramps extended to the shore. Windlasses worked by mule teams turned round and round, and up from the sultan's triremes in the Bosphorus slid huge blocks of stone, ready cut, ready measured, quarried in Anatolia, finished beforehand to fit neatly into the foundations of Roumeli Hissar. Day after day the work went forward, and every night fresh crews of masons and builders took over and labored by torchlight till dawn. The walls of the castle rose visibly, almost like magic, before the affronted, incredulous eyes of the Greeks.

This blatant violation of Christian soil and the enormous military significance of the castle roused Constantine from all thought of his marriage. He forgot the Georgian princess, and, rising to a stature unequaled by any of his counselors, immediately resolved upon war.

"The intent of the sultan is obvious," he declared. "If we allow the completion of this structure, Mohammed can close both ends of the Bosphorus and we shall find ourselves blockaded, not only by land, but by sea as well, a thing that has never happened before. Let us fight while we still can, before we are helpless, and demonstrate by our courage that we are not unworthy of friends and allies."

But the counselors advised diplomacy. They pointed out the woeful shortage of arms and fighting men, and insisted on a sharply worded protest to the sultan instead of a declaration of war. And since an emperor cannot make war alone, Constantine was obliged to agree.

Mohammed, perfectly willing to gain a little time, replied with charm and courtesy. He disclaimed all territorial ambition in Europe. He represented the promontory of the Asomaton as disputably Asiatic, since it extended so close to Asia (a point which he suggested be settled by arbitration at a later date) ; and in any event, he insisted, the new little castle had no military value. It was only a lighthouse, he said; it would never be garrisoned; it was only to guide the ships of all nations round a treacherous bend in the Straits.

On which Mohammed doubled his guards.

The Greeks replied with the weapon they had taught the world to wield, a weapon that had never failed them: words. Westward to all the princes of Christendom, to the Pope, to Scanderbeg in Albania, to Hunyadi in Hungary, and eastward to Trebizond and Georgia, wherever a Christian prince reigned over Christian subjects anywhere in the world, Constantine dispatched his pitiful pleas for help. While Moslem torches lighted the work of Moslem engineers five miles from his capital during the fateful spring nights, the last weary, industrious Roman Emperor of the East burned a scented taper to melt the golden wax for the seals of his letters, into which he pressed the triple vermilion cross of his imperial signet. When he prayed for weapons stronger than words, some of his ghostly advisers obliquely reproved him for lack of faith. Had not St. John said, *In the beginning was the Word?* But every morning the walls of Roumeli Hissar were a little higher.

It was during the month of May, with its lengthening days and shortening nights, when the Greek farmers were habitually most active with plowing and planting, that the advisers of Constantine hit upon a strategy which they considered monstrously clever, since it put the sultan on his honor.

"While we summon the world to our help," they said to Constantine, "let us beg the Turkish sultan to set some of his guards over the farms of our peasants. They are restless, Your Majesty; they do not understand great affairs, and they complain that the foraging horses of the Turkish militia are ruining their fields. Our own soldiers are needed on the walls, of course."

The suggestion had considerable merit. It would confine the Turks to the promontory of the Asomaton. Without hazarding the life of a single Greek soldier, it would protect the Greek farms from further encroachment. It would force Mohammed to feed all his men and animals by sea. Since there were three thousand builders and more than a thousand guards engaged on the project, much valuable cargo space would now be required for animal fodder and rations for the men. Less would remain for building materials, and the erection of Roumeli Hissar would certainly be retarded.

The advisers reminded the emperor: "While the Turkish guard maintains discipline among our ignorant peasants, who are threatening them with violence, perchance the nations of Europe will come to our aid. The Turks always keep their word. God will forgive us if we break ours. We must bide our time until we are stronger, and then we will fall on them suddenly."

The sultan's honor was engaged. The humanitarian fiction of the lighthouse had trapped him. He reluctantly complied. The absolute emperors exchanged friendly notes, called each other cousin, protested their admiration and affection. Neither deceived the other, but each hoped to gain a little more time.

And as a result, Hassan Pasha of Ulubad found himself saddled with a difficult assignment that made him long for more seasoned troops, because his orders were self-contradictory and required not only obedience but discrimination and restraint: kill no one unless it is absolutely necessary, and then only after direct attack; let no one pass in either direction; above all be courteous to everyone, no matter how mean; until further notice act like the guests of the Emperor Constantine.

It fell to Michael as a sharpshooter, and some older men whose judgment could be trusted, to patrol an area in the ring of encircling guards that sliced squarely through an extensive field of well tended vines.

At this point in his life Michael da Montelupo, hereditary licensee to the Scutari shipping, became the intense but covert object of attention for Machmut, the Beglerbey of Roum.

It was not too difficult for Machmut to find out where Michael had been stationed. The prince reasoned that, outwardly at least, and at least until Roumeli Hissar was completed some weeks, perhaps months away, relations between the two empires would continue friendly. There was still time, as the Greeks became more and more desperate, to go into the shipping business. It set his blood to pounding excitedly in his throat to think how easily the stubborn Christian merchant's scruples could be overcome. From a personal point of view, how pleasant to overcome them! What more devastating proof that Bernardi's integrity was vindicated, that he could at length part with the franchise to an understanding Moslem whose patronage and connivance would aid the Christian cause, than Michael's handsome severed head in a basket, done up like a melon, a gift from the Beglerbey of Roum!

Yes. And before the messenger departed with it to Christendom he would watch Aeshia's face when she looked at it. Aeshia had turned exasperatingly docile since her remarriage, calm, cool, and unexciting, like all his other wives and concubines. "Bismillah!" he cackled, delighted, as he always was at a doubly profitable idea. "I'll hide it under her pillow before I send it to Bernardi. Maybe that will make her expression change a little!"

CHAPTER
24

IN the dull amber light of an old moon, which clears the horizon some hours before the morning sun, all colors look very much alike.

The green of a turban that marks an important personage who has made the Great Pilgrimage to Mecca is distinguished with difficulty from the white turban of a janissary—especially one who has stood guard all night in a windy, grimy area where thousands of men and beasts are engaged in the dusty work of erecting the walls of a castle.

The Beglerbey of Roum had planned well the hour and the method of Michael's murder. Creeping slowly toward the spot in the line of guards where his inquiries had disclosed Michael to be stationed, Machmut ruminated irritably that if Aeshia had not become so uninterested and uninteresting he would not now be belly-down in a Greek vineyard in the middle of the night. He would be at home in bed, with a prettier companion than one of his Thugs.

The dark little man hissed into his ear: "You must accompany me no farther, Excellency. Your Excellency has feet like the wheels of Juggernaut. Not even I can protect you if you make so much noise. Stay here; do not speak, do not cough, do not breathe, and in a few moments I shall fetch you back the head."

Machmut whispered excitedly: "Good, good, good! Contrive but to retain some blood in the head, so the cheeks remain ruddy and lifelike, and Bismillah! You shall have your freedom!"

The Thug answered softly, like a lisp: "Be silent. The blood belongs to Kali Mai." And he slithered away like a snake.

The Thug was grinning a set, fanatical grin, but the dull moon reflected no light from his jet-black teeth, which were filed into fanglike points. He was naked except for a black clout about his loins. He had greased his body and powdered it with dust and dirt of the area so as to be indistinguishable from the earth. He had no weapons except a dagger and a curious rope wound round his waist. The rope had a pear-shaped, leaden weight at the end. It was the mark of the order of Thugs.

The confraternity of Thugs was an Indian brotherhood bound together in worship of Kali Mai, the Dark Mother, and consecrated to an ideal which they called the Good Work which had for its goal the extermination of the human race. Kali Mai was a black deity. She had four arms. Her eyes and the palms of her hands were red. Her tongue, her face, and her breasts were bloodstained. Her teeth were black and pointed like fangs. She wore as adornment a necklace of skulls, corpses for earrings, and a girdle of snakes.

In her honor her devotees filed their teeth to points and stained them black, so as to look less like the teeth of a pig, an animal repugnant to them. In their murders the Thugs experienced a sort of sacrificial ecstasy, because each murder, they believed, intoxicated the Dark Mother with blood; and to the perpetrator of each murder she promised another eternity of pleasure in Paradise. The Good Work would come to an end only when man ceased to exist upon earth.

Indian Thugs made extraordinarily effective bodyguards when they could be procured as slaves, but they were seldom captured alive and only a very rich man could afford them.

Machmut had planned to accompany the Thug only as far as the skiff which would transport the assassin across the Bosphorus, but the eerie beauty of the night and the excitement of the chase exhilarated him. He had crossed the strait and scrambled up the slope with the Indian a little beyond the line of the Turkish guards in the vineyards of the Greek farmers. Then the monstrous idea had struck him that it would be pleasant to receive the head of his quarry while it was still warm; and, against the advice of his more experienced

Thug, he had crawled with him dangerously close to the Turkish outposts.

Lying now motionless, concealed under a growth of vine, Machmut controlled his excited breathing as well as he could and peered out at the dark, vague shapes in front of his myopic eyes. He remembered the scene of his last meeting with Michael, and, though he did not notice it in the absorption of his vivid recollection, his nose began to bleed a little.

A passionate longing to witness the actual murder overwhelmed him. The thought of the strangulation and decapitation of his enemy enveloped him with a compulsion like hunger or love, and, forgetting his slave's advice and his own fears, Machmut crept forward again, panting heavily, forgetting to swallow, his beard wet with saliva, his blood dripping unheeded from his nostrils.

At that moment Michael, leaning on his bow and searching alertly for anything unusual in the patrol area immediately in front of him, saw something move. It moved too clumsily for an animal, though it was obviously crawling on all fours. Michael supposed it was one of the annoying Greek farmers. He instantly covered his hands, face, and turban with his cloak, those light-colored parts of a man that any good scout always knew appeared to shine in the half-light of a dark night. He retired some paces behind the line of guard and concealed himself behind a bush. He could easily have shot the intruder, but he was mindful of his instructions to kill no one except after direct attack. It would be better to capture whoever was approaching after the intruder had crossed the line into Turkish territory. Then the authorities would intern the man, or whatever they did with pestiferous Greeks who violated the friendly agreement between the two emperors.

The creeping Beglerbey of Roum had seen a tall man with a sheaf of arrows at his back, and he had paused for an instant to watch what was sure to happen; but the figure suddenly retreated into the gloom, its outlines changed, and then it dissolved like a genie into nothingness. Machmut thought perhaps his eyes were deceiving him. He raised his head a bit higher and then stood erect, squinting out into the obscurity. He was almost on the spot Michael had occupied a few moments before. Machmut's turban appeared like a telltale sphere of luminosity above the sea of vines.

Suddenly, like the call of a night bird, there was a soft, whistling note in the air, caused by the Thug's rapidly whirling, slender cord with the weight at the end. The note grew deeper as the Thug let the taut cord slide through his fingers. The rope became an ever lengthening radius of an ever expanding circle described by the whirling lead. The longer strings of a lyre beat a deeper, more ominous tone. The soft whistle became a low, hypnotic moan, like far-away wind in a forest of cypress trees.

This was not a sound that Michael or any of the other janissaries had ever heard before. There was an evil unreality about it, and for an instant it froze them in their places, full of the fear of the unknown. Then abruptly it stopped, and Michael, searching anxiously into his patrol area, could no longer discern the figure of the intruder. He fitted an arrow to his bowstring and advanced to reconnoiter the place.

Meanwhile the Thug had discovered his regrettable error. Skillfully he disentangled the triple coil that the whining rope had wound round his master's neck, and, throwing the heavy body of Machmut over his back, crawled rapidly away from the Turkish line and did not stop until, as he thought, he was deep in the safety of the Greek vineyard. There he began to chafe the puffy neck of Machmut in an effort to coax life back into the prince. He could feel the heart beating in the neck veins. His master was not dead.

"Your forgiveness, dear Little Dark Mother," he prayed, "for not substituting the blood of my incautious master for the blood of the janissary. But it is better for the prince to live, who will, by a long life of devotion to the Good Work, contribute more blood to your altars than ever I could drain out of the body of one young man."

His preliminary reconnoitering having disclosed nothing, Michael called a soldier with a lantern, and together they went over the ground minutely. But there was nothing beneath any of the vines as far into Greek territory as, under their orders, they felt free to patrol. Michael returned to his post, bewildered and uneasy.

But the janissaries, Machmut, and the Thug were not the only ones awake in the vineyard that night. Some nervous Greek farmers had observed with apprehension and dismay the unusual activity among the customarily silent janissaries. Perhaps there would be an attack. Perhaps the Turks were advancing their line. There had been an unearthly moan, like a rush of wind, and one of the armed little group of gathering men said that he had seen the cause of it: a monstrous bird—perhaps the fabulous roc was real!—flying through the air with a block of stone for the castle in its claws. Perhaps now the infidels had summoned the aid of their devils to build the walls more quickly! And, of course, they had all actually observed the flickering of Michael's lantern far beyond the line where the Turks were supposed to be.

They stealthily examined their vineyard, and presently they came upon the Thug trying to revive Machmut.

The Greeks raised their silent, powerful crossbows and shot both men dead.

Closer examination revealed the enormity of their crime. Thin streaks of gray, early morning light disclosed the brilliance of the Turk's jewels and the magnificence of his apparel, marking him as an important man. The Thug, obviously a slave, did not matter. The frightened Greeks were thrown into a panic at the thought of all the consequences. In the present state of diplomatic tension, it was quite likely that they would be handed over to the Turks for punishment.

Then one of the farmers, the imaginative one who had beheld the flying roc, was seized with a profoundly Greek inspiration, remarkably akin to the slippery genius of the counselors who had persuaded Constantine to ask for a Turkish guard.

"We can best demonstrate our innocence by appearing boldly at dawn on this very spot," he suggested; and then he asked, "Where does a wise man hide a pebble?" Answering his own question, he replied, "On a beach, in a shoal of pebbles. Let us bury them here, and hide the grave as a wise man would hide a pebble."

It was done; and in the morning the Turks saw the farmers busily piling manure from a cart into many centrally located heaps. From each heap the farmers loaded their hand baskets and distributed the fertilizer over the roots of all their vines. Soon there were so many manure heaps that the Greeks had to think twice before they could be absolutely certain under which one Machmut and the Thug lay buried.

TWO immediate effects resulted from the disappearance of so prominent a person as Machmut, the Beglerbey of Roum. One effect was temporary and unimportant: a great public scandal.

The prince, in his multifarious and secret business dealings, had often dropped out of sight for a day or a week at a time, turning up later, noncommittal and self-satisfied, with no explanation for his absence. Only his bankers, who always received substantial deposits, which might be in beggars' coins or enormous letters of credit on Gavour trading houses, ever had any inkling where he might have been or what he might have been doing; and bankers do not habitually gossip about the eccentricities of profitable clients. This time, of course, Machmut never returned.

In a few weeks the town began to buzz with conjecture and excitement, but before the gossip reached proportions that would have elicited official inquiry, a tremendous rush of more important events made everybody except the priests and his wives forget the beglerbey. In due time the priests pronounced him legally dead, and the wives came into their inheritances, according to the law of Islam. One of them went home to Cairo to the arms of her father the caliph, and, before she died, to the arms of others also, much to their edification, if little to their peace of mind.

The other result that immediately stemmed from Machmut's disappearance had far-reaching historical consequences, affecting distant peoples who never had heard and never were to hear the exotic title of beglerbey. It hastened the war.

Hassan Pasha doubled and then redoubled the janissary guard around Roumeli Hissar, which was now approaching completion. Only the towers and battlements remained to be sheathed in lead. Mohammed felt, with some justification, that the castle was a triumph of Turkish engineering. Not only would Turks first introduce into warfare cannon of significant caliber; simultaneously they would invent a wonderful defense against cannon balls. And they would install the defense before introducing the new weapon.

One of the most dangerous effects of cannon shot was the widespread and deadly splintering of stone that occurred when a battlement was struck. Imagination and experimentation taught the Turks that a rain of death mushroomed out over a large area when a ball hit a wall, killing or maiming any defenders who might be near the spot. So they invented armor plate: thick sheet lead, to cushion the shock and confine the flying stone fragments.

Quadrupling the guard proved something of a drain on the manpower that Hassan had under his command. Even the older men, like the sentry who had stopped Michael at the gate after his sojourn in the cemetery, had to stand guard. Michael, as an officer whose position increased in importance simultaneously with the improvement in the men's marksmanship, found himself relieved of a set hour of guard duty; but his hours actually lengthened because of an assignment to supervise all that portion of the line which ran through the field where the disturbance had occurred.

That had been a month before. It was now Tuesday, the 20th of June, the penultimate hour of the uneasy peace. Something was now to happen that would convince even the Greeks that peace, at no matter what price of compromise, could no longer be maintained.

The janissaries, with a strong castle now rising to their rear, became less scrupulous in confining themselves strictly to their line of guard. In two months on the line they had pretty well trodden all the immediate vines into the ground. The destruction was shocking to the Greek farmers, who, grown familiar and contemptuous in the presence of their well disciplined invaders, threatened and insulted them at every opportunity. Sometimes the Greeks came armed into the field.

Reinforcement of the guards completed the destruction of the

214

vines and eliminated every vestige of cover along the sentry line, so that the Turks now stood exposed in an open strip that had been flattened by their feet into what looked like a hard-packed road running through the vineyard. It was unthinkable to retreat for cover toward the castle. It was equally unthinkable for a well trained sentry in a hostile country to stand guard like a target without cover of any kind. So the men, acting on their own initiative but encouraged by the older, more seasoned soldiers, took cover among the nearest vines on the Greek side, and these, in turn, were gradually trampled into the ground.

Thus the road widened. And as it widened, Charilaos, the unfortunate Greek proprietor of the field, grew more and more desperate. The grapes were his sole means of livelihood. He dreamed, as Constantine dreamed, that an inexorable tide of infidels was inundating his land, threatening to engulf it little by little, until nothing at all remained. The imperial nightmare of Constantine and the humble nightmare of Charilaos were precisely alike, just as big circles are precisely like little circles except for their size: each man stood to lose everything he possessed in the world.

Early on the evening of June 20, less cautious by far than Machmut and the Thug, Charilaos, exasperated beyond all endurance, concealed himself clumsily at a point near one of his most precious, most productive vines. He had nursed them every one, as he had his own children, which were almost as numerous as the vines and added no little to his anxiety about the fall crop. There had been footprints around the vine that morning. There would be more tomorrow. Before long he would behold the bruised clusters of immature fruit, the yellowing leaves, and the ultimate death of the entire plant.

Not the fanaticism of the Thug nor the complex, murderous urge of Machmut, but a desperate, weary resentfulness and a sick desire for revenge despite all consequences smoldered in Charilaos's eyes as he peered out from behind his cover. He held in his worn hands a new crossbow, which he manipulated less expertly than his hoes and his spades. He crouched, waiting for the stiff, arrogant Turk who had trampled his precious vine.

In the simplicity of his faith and the extremity of his hatred, he prayed the Great Mother of Mercy Herself to glance at his crossbow and direct the flight of its bolt into the heart of the enemy, who, he repeated again and again, did not believe in Her Divine Son, as if that assurance would add weight to his supplication. Furthermore, Charilaos was more than a little confused by the weapon, which was a new model. It discharged at a feather-light touch of the trigger and shot, not an arrow, with which he was familiar, but an evil-looking, stubby little cylinder of iron, pointed at one end and fitted with a leather tail at the other.

When the guard changed that evening, Charilaos saw walking toward his ambush the erect and, as he now observed, somewhat elderly janissary who had shown so little regard for his grapevine. With him was a younger man in the girdle of a commander and a turban decorated with the insignia of an archery master. Charilaos, taking a deep breath, muttered to himself, "The two shall fall!" and he prayed again, hoping that his prayer would give him the skill to recharge the weapon quickly before the second janissary could counterattack. With the innate delicacy which simple, unlearned men instinctively feel more deeply than their betters, Charilaos now addressed his prayer for assistance in a double murder not to the gentle Virgin but to St. Peter, remembering that that impulsive Apostle had once with a sword struck off the ear of a man about to do a wicked thing.

Michael was cautioning the older man that in so far as it was practicable it would be wise not to stray too deeply into the vineyard. Not only had the attitude of the Greeks become more threatening, but the original orders which had established the line had not been changed. The older man was respectfully suggesting that there had also been no change in the immemorial orders which required a sentry to take reasonable precautions in the matter of concealment. Did the young archery officer wish to read an old campaigner a lesson in elementary tactics on so beautiful an evening? There was a hint of rebuke in the crusty old soldier's question, despite its respectful tone. Michael laughed and said "No, just try not to ruin these poor people's fields any more than you have to." The older man looked sharply and suspiciously at his young superior and was about to remark that some of the new generation were unnecessarily lenient toward the hereditary enemy, when suddenly Michael saw one of the vines at a little distance moving in a way that no vine ought to move. The memory of the prowler a month before flashed across his mind. Even as his eyes narrowed on the spot and saw what caused the movement, his hand flew up and fitted an arrow into his bow.

Projecting beyond the leaves was the deadly metal arc of a crossbow, drawn taut, ready to shoot. Michael could just make out the stock of the weapon against the shoulder of a man in the shadow.

It was an easy shot, not more than twenty paces away. Poised as he was, Michael aimed at the stock of the crossbow for reasons which he did not stop to analyze but which were clear in his mind: patently, this was a direct attack, or would be the instant the Greek pressed the trigger. Michael was at liberty under his orders to puncture the intruder's head; but he was accustomed to split-second shooting, and he knew that his arrow would reach the assassin before the assassin could loose his own. The impact of the arrow would ruin the man's aim, he could be captured, interned, and no serious international incident would then have occurred.

And if, Michael was also aware, the stock of the weapon happened to be metal-sheathed, as they sometimes were, the arrow would deflect and strike the man, but only in the shoulder. There would still be no incident.

He was aware of all this as a complete unworded thought, not as a series of reasoned arguments. Long before he could have explained it to himself, his arrow had shot whistling to its mark. The bowstring still sang as the arrow thumped into the stock of the Christian's crossbow. It was not metal-sheathed, but the usual wood. The arrow, sheared of its tail feathers, but otherwise undamaged, passed through it, leaving a clean round hole and burying half its shaft in the soft earth a few yards beyond. The crossbow flew out of Charilaos's hands, and Charilaos himself leaped out of the vine and fled screaming for mercy, which he did not expect, away from the janissaries.

The sentry instantly fitted an arrow to his own bow and let fly, but he missed.

"Bismillah! Commander, you jolted me!"

"If I did it was unintentional." Michael sprinted away and returned with the crossbow. "I am anxious to see this weapon," he explained. "It looks like a new one."

The sentry also examined the weapon, saying, "You missed the Greek, too."

Michael was noncommittal.

"Oh, well," continued the sentry with a faint trace of condescension, "it's not so easy to shoot a man in the twilight, Commander. You've a powerful arm! Look at that hole in the stock, two fingers of oak shot through without a splinter!" Michael had salvaged the arrow also, which the sentry silently scrutinized. Then he observed, somewhat apologetically, "I am not so young in the service that I think a man who can shoot like that could not also have hit the Greek."

"The light is bad, as you say."

The sentry wondered if the poor light had anything to do with jolting one's elbow just as one was about to kill a Gavour, but that he dared not say. Michael grinned at him, divining something of his unspoken suspicion.

"Your own aim would have been better than mine, friend; but remember, he didn't *quite* attack us, and who wants to see a poor devil of a farmer catch an arrow in the back when he's trying to run away?"

"God's name!" the old soldier expostulated, beside himself at such nonsense. "That's where the Greeks catch most of their arrows!" He bit his lip so as not to add just a bit about the softness of the new generation of commander chief archery masters.

But Michael was busy examining the weapon.

"This is much more important," he mused, and then, "Report the incident in the usual manner, sentry." The sentry, delighted at having the honor delegated to him, concluded more generously that if the new generation were soft it could also be courteous in military punctilio. Graceful unbending of this sort had often happened in Murad's time. In the reign of Murad's warlike son, it was almost unheard of.

Michael left the sentry and went to his tent to study the crossbow by lamplight. The blue tempering on the bow was still there; the Greeks had not yet polished it off to make the steel shine like silver as they usually did.

There was oil on it, another significant circumstance, since the Greeks did not habitually take care of their weapons. And there were curious little flakes of white on the steel which Michael did not understand. He rubbed one of the spots reflectively. It felt gritty to his fingertips. He touched the substance to his tongue out of sheer curiosity.

It was salt!

Suddenly a host of thoughts, dangerously charged with emotion, made Michael's head swim. The weapon obviously had just been imported—no, not imported, *smuggled* into Constantinople within the last few days. In no other conceivable way could there still be packing grease and sea salt on its steel parts.

Michael immediately presented himself and the weapon to Hassan. He asked and instantly received permission to track it to its source. He said he felt sure he knew where it came from.

"Yes," Hassan said after Michael explained his theory, "the wily old merchant is apparently still smuggling. Go to Galata at once, and this time do not warn him. This time bring him back with you. Take plenty of men. Galata is being most cooperative these days, but a city needs a show of force to keep it courteous and neutral. And, oh Michael—"

"Yes, sir?"

"I was wondering if you might not care to bring back the merchant's daughter as well?"

"To the Devil with the merchant's daughter!"

"Oh, ho! And how old a devil would you suggest? I can think of a young one who ought to have a little recreation from his archery duties. But no, I'm wrong. After your first trip you could not remember whether she was pretty as a houri or ugly as an afrit. Never mind. Forget the daughter."

Michael, despite himself, smiled. "Now that Hassan Pasha takes the trouble to remind me, I remember distinctly that she was not nearly so ugly as an afrit. It would be a pleasure, in a way, to bring her back with me."

"Well, it isn't exactly an order," Hassan said more seriously, "but it would undoubtedly speed things up if we could have the daughter present at the questioning, perhaps to be questioned a bit herself."

Michael had been smiling. It would never do to let his expression change—to betray the shudder that he felt rising deep in the pit of his stomach. Questioning meant only one thing: the cruelest kind of torture. The smile faded and froze in spite of his iron self-control; and Hassan, who knew him better than he realized, shrewdly fathomed the transformation.

Hassan shook his head. "No, Michael, don't bring the girl after all. That's a command. Leave her in Galata. She'd only complicate things damnably."

CHAPTER

26

IN the melancholy annals of the last days of the Roman Empire of the East, no date is heavier with doom than Wednesday, the 21st of June, the first day of the beautiful summer of 1452.

That was the day the Greek farmers were slaughtered.

It was also the first of three days that Michael, much against his will, spent in the city of Constantinople.

Since his curious experience in the cemetery, Michael had found himself lighter hearted than was usual for a sober, ambitious janissary, but he gave the phenomenon very little thought. He had also undergone a certain unacknowledgeable cleavage in his loyalties. He remembered how the venerable hodja, when teaching the boys religion, had once made passing reference to a pagan god of the ancient Greeks, a deity called Janus, god of a gate that faced two ways, toward the East and toward the West. He was afraid that it might be possible for a man to become like that gate. It was closed during peace. During war it was open, and during war the duplicitous orientation of Janus's faces was most apparent and most objectionable, according to the teaching of the hodja. "The ultimate annihilation of the Greeks," the hodja had taught, "will come by reason of their constitutional inability to pursue a single objective. No people that ever worshiped a creature who looks in two directions at once can withstand the powerful single-mindedness of Islam, holy Islam, which is consecrated to unity, in our polity and in our God." The logic had convinced the boys.

Now, however, Michael found his desire to see Bernardi far from unified. He tried to convince himself that he wanted to track down and eliminate a source that was supplying arms to the Christians. And, as a patriotic Turk, he did wish to do that, whatever the consequences to Bernardi. To weaken the enemy and gain recognition for a service that was certain to be commended by his superiors was a duty to his country and a legitimate exercise of his ambition.

But Michael had another idea, already half formed in his mind and growing stronger all the time. If he could, he knew that he would somehow contrive to let Bernardi, his father's friend, escape the fearful consequences of being brought back into Turkey for punishment.

Michael had departed at dawn at the head of a troop of forty men, determined to surround Bernardi's house five miles away in Galata. The guards at the gate of the city were all Italians. They welcomed the Turks with protestations of friendship, and refused, as proof of their amity and neutral position, even to look at Michael's military passport.

But when Michael rode into the courtyard of Bernardi's spacious villa, the shutters were drawn, the lawn was untended, and Bernardi's major-domo said that the merchant and Angelica had moved across the Golden Horn and taken up residence in Constantinople.

"But my master would consider his house dishonored," the old servitor said, "if I did not place it, in his name, at your disposal. Both he and his daughter have often spoken highly of you."

That doesn't make my mission any easier, Michael thought heavily.

He refused Enrico's hospitality and galloped across the bridge of boats that spanned the estuary of the Golden Horn. This bridge stretched from the Tower of Christ in Galata to the Tower of St. Eugenius in Constantinople. It was a flimsy structure, built thirty years before, after the last great Turkish siege by Murad II. With the memory of war still fresh in their minds, the Greeks had constructed it lightly, that it might be the more easily destroyed in the event of another outbreak of hostilities. No war had yet come but a generation of neglect had almost accomplished the ruin of the bridge. The janissaries laughed at the rotten planking, the waterlogged pontoons.

The friendly greeting of the Italians in Galata was by no means repeated by the suspicious Greeks that swarmed round the gate of

Constantinople. The guards were polite, almost eloquently polite; but they refused to admit the Turks.

"The commander, of course, may enter," said the Greek captain at the Tower of St. Eugenius. "But alas! The ships that usually bring us the hospitable delicacies with which to entertain our Turkish friends have not appeared lately. The fare of the city is fit only for slaves. I have positive orders to admit only one Moslem at a time."

And nothing Michael could say would make him alter his position.

"But the commander is welcome," the Greek captain repeated.

One of Michael's orderlies whispered: "They want our leaders, Commander. Do not enter the city without us!"

The sharp-eared and apparently polyglot Greek captain instantly responded: "Not at all, Commander. You, or one of your officers, or even a groom shall be equally welcome. It doesn't matter who. My orders are simply to admit only one Turk at a time."

Michael looked up at the high, wide, open gate of the ancient Greek city. For a fleeting, uncomfortable instant the double face of Janus took shape on the immemorial, bronze-sheathed timbers and grinned down at him. Michael swore softly under his breath at the impudence of mythical gods who chose to come back and favor the cause of the Gavours, or at the potency of Christian magic, or at his own fate, which, he assured himself, was written on his good Moslem forehead and which he still revered. Perhaps it was his fate that he should be given the most plausible of all opportunities not only to uncover the source of the arms smuggling but also to grant the Christian culprit a chance to escape.

He stifled a smile, as if the Janus grin had been infectious, and dismissed his men, ordering them back to Roumeli Hissar.

"I'll go in alone," he said.

Filippo Bernardi, like every Christian on the northern side of the Bosphorus, had watched the erection of Roumeli Hissar with intense misgiving. Unlike many of the Greeks, however, he beheld in the structure a sort of hourglass. "When the last stone is in place," he said to his daughter, "the sands of life of the Roman Empire of the East will have run out. And, before that happens, my daughter, you and I shall be bound for home on one of the ships I did *not* order into the 'hardware trade.' Meanwhile, I have a few more investments

222

to convert into something far more precious than gold. Which you can't get anymore anyway," he added.

He had been very busy in recent weeks, selling all the Byzantine real estate he possessed. But the market was uncertain. He hated to take a loss, yet he miscalculated the incredible speed with which Mohammed would build the castle. Every day, as the towers rose, Bernardi's prices came down, until finally he decided to dispose of his few remaining properties at rock-bottom prices, fearful lest he might have overstayed the prudent limit of safety, but bewitched by the enormous profits that his shipping activities brought him.

Bernardi had been acutely aware of his personal insecurity ever since Machmut had called at his house. He had rented an ancient, weather-beaten villa which had once been a part of the cluster of detached buildings that sprang up around the palace of the first Constantine, in the days when the Byzantine emperors made their residence between the hippodrome and the Golden Horn. It was reasonably comfortable, it afforded a view of the harbor, and it was built like a castle, thick-walled and virtually windowless. Extensive cellars and secret, forgotten tunnels, built in the early days for silent, scurrying courtiers on wily, forgotten missions, connected the villa with some known and many unknown distant points: with sewers, of course, for sanitary reasons; with one of the giant, meandering underground reservoirs, to supply the kitchens with water; with some of the neighboring buildings. A few of the subterranean burrowings ended where buildings no longer existed. Only the gibbering ghosts of six centuries of scheming Greeks, who would never act openly in daylight when they could act secretly underground, could have informed Bernardi where else the tunnels ran. However, Bernardi knew enough about them to make the villa highly desirable for himself and his daughter until he should leave the East forever and return to Venice, "where," he mused, homesick and tired, "the well known integrity of the Venetian citizenry and the high flood level of the Adriatic Sea preclude all such conceits as these useful, interesting tunnels."

When Michael rode up to the gate of Bernardi's Byzantine villa, he was met by a surly Greek steward, who barred the way and insolently told him that the Italian gentleman was not at home. It seemed to Michael that the servant spoke the words "Italian gentleman" distastefully. Michael did not like him, and wondered how deep the feeling among the Greeks of Constantinople might be against their Italian fellow Christians in the neutral suburb of Galata.

He threw the reins to the man. "Then I'll wait for him," he said shortly. He leaped down and strode past the Greek into the house, carrying Charilaos's crossbow with him. The Greek stabled the horse, because he did not know what else to do when he found the loop of a bridle in his hands. Sulkily he cursed all Moslems, all Catholics of the Latin Rite, and all high, prancing Arabian stallions that glared at honest Greek stewards with eyes like fire opals. He thought greedily of the opals in his Venetian master's collection. Bernardi had been too busy to scrutinize the references of his new Byzantine steward. He would have been astonished to learn that the Greek knew he had been buying opals lately. Bernardi, in his haste to liquidate his properties, had been accepting star sapphires and even opals, if the fire was bright. It was a time when gold, silver, diamonds, emeralds, and rubies were disappearing from the market, the treasures that dying empires bury before they bury their dead.

Michael walked directly into the great hall, where Angelica met him. Although the sun was shining brilliantly, the interior of the castlelike villa was so gloomy that wax tapers were burning in all the old sconces. Their warm, golden light shone like a sunset on the mellow old tapestries and made gold of the silver service on a dining table set for two. It glinted like a bejeweled, intimate rainbow on tall, carved goblets of Venetian glass on the table, reminding Michael of a little scar on his finger. It bathed Angelica's naked face with an aureate glow and buried itself in her luminous yellow hair. Michael impulsively wished he had let her bind up that cut.

"I am looking for your father," he said.

Angelica smiled: "You came well armed, Commander. Father isn't at home. Won't you put down some of your weapons? You are quite safe here."

Michael flushed. He was wearing only his dagger and his scimitar. He was carrying only his parade quiver of arrows, the formal, not the war quiver; and his bow, the hundred-pound bow that was shaped like the lip of a girl. Very like the lip of a girl, he now realized, though it bent less easily. Or did it? And, of course, the steel Christian crossbow, which was the cause of his hejira into the capital of the Greek empire. What did Angelica expect? Except for the crossbow, he was armed as any other officer was armed.

But as he divested himself one by one of the five units of his armament he was struck with the justice of her completely feminine remark.

"I feel perfectly safe, signorina," he said, utilizing as much of his Italian as he was able to muster under the circumstances. "Not all the weapons of this arsenal are mine. One of them I came to talk to your noble father about. The Greek at your gate says he isn't at home."

Angelica sighed and moved her white shoulders in the ghost of a shrug. "For once the steward is telling the truth. Father is down in the city on business. Selling land, I think. Everybody believes he still owns ships, but he's only selling land. Will you take a cup of coffee?"

Now Michael had a sharper, more comprehensive eye than Allah had blessed him with before he married Aeshia. Angelica did not wait for his answer. She lit a taper from one of the sconces and carried the flame over to a spirit lamp under a silver carafe on the table. To Michael the slender girl, rising to her tiptoes, reaching up to the light that set a glory shining on the corn-yellow crown of her curly head, in her gown of green, cut velvet with sleeves slashed with insets of seed pearls and lace of old gold, was a miracle to contemplate. Aeshia, if Aeshia had ever done such a thing, would have looked, Michael concluded, chunky by comparison.

Swallowing slightly, he said, "Why, yes, I'd like a cup of coffee."

Bernardi, when he returned, found them deep in conversation with each other. If he had not returned so soon, perhaps Christendom that day would have won an able champion.

But the intrusion recalled Michael to his duty. He presented the crossbow: Bernardi nodded. Michael stated his mission and confessed his treason: he counseled the merchant to flee, and take his daughter with him. Bernardi said, "Yes, of course." And Michael prepared to depart, completely miserable and completely in love, which he had begun to believe were, after all, but two words for the same thing.

But at that moment, the four mighty, brazen-sheathed gates of the city, to the north, south, east, and west, swung majestically together, and thousands of frightened men raised the heavy oaken thwarts that locked them shut.

Charilaos and the other Greek peasants had been mercilessly slaughtered in their vineyards. Emperor Constantine had decreed the instant isolation of his capital.

MICHAEL, the merchant, and Angelica had finished their dinner. Bernardi and Angelica were sipping a cordial, and the janissary was drinking Turkish coffee from a little blue porcelain teacup, fashioned without a handle by a Chinese craftsman a century before. Michael knew that he was being treated with noble hospitality.

He was on the point of departure, having exhausted every excuse for staying longer, a plausible explanation in readiness on his lips for not having arrested Bernardi—the refusal of the Greeks to allow his guard to enter Constantinople would serve—when something happened to give him an infinitely better explanation.

The first intimation that there was trouble in the city was wild shouting from a group of men that rushed past the house. Then came more shouting from a group in a different direction. It was difficult to make out individual words; some of the rabble sounded extremely drunk. Bernardi cocked a practiced ear. Drunk they were, but the overtone of the shouting was fury, not revelry. Bernardi clapped his hands to summon the steward and order the gate closed in the wall that ran along the city street in front of the villa. The steward did not answer. Bernardi impatiently pulled the tasseled cord that rang the bell in the servants' quarters, but still the steward did not respond. Only a trembling charwoman, one of his old staff of Italian servants from Galata, came up from the kitchens and peeked fearfully into the great hall, where she was never allowed except to scrub it after the gentry had retired.

She said the steward had left the house shortly after the arrival of the Turkish commander; no sir, she wasn't going to lock no gates, that she wasn't, not with people gone mad and running through the streets killing Turks! And she began to weep hysterically, trying to wipe her eyes with her apron in one hand, while with the other she made frantic signs of the cross in the direction of Michael, who had half risen from his chair. "Get him out of here!" the woman wailed, "We'll all be murdered in our beds!"

It was too late to lock the gate, but Bernardi pushed past her and barred the great front door of the villa. "Nobody knows Michael's in the house! Angelica, my dear, just take a look at the door in the servants' quarters. It's always barred, but we want to make sure." Then he lifted a taper out of one of the sconces and hurriedly mounted the winding old stone steps that led up to a small watchtower above the roof. It was from here that he had often watched the shipping in the Golden Horn. Now he turned his back to the harbor and faced the city, to ascertain the cause and extent of the disturbance.

Angelica immediately left for the rear of the house, Michael following. The charwoman, quaking in the center of the great hall, wiping her eyes and singing the cross to the four corners of the compass, wailed: "Oh, but they do know he's here! The steward told everybody!" Nobody heard her because she was alone.

From the tower Bernardi looked down into the maze of city streets already growing dim in the twilight. In every direction there were running bands of men. He could make out some of the shouting now: "Death to the Turks! Death to the murderous infidel!" Here and there some of the groups appeared to be fighting, and suddenly Bernardi recognized the ornate bronze lanterns which the imperial constabulary carried.

The mobs were fighting the police!

"Whatever started this," Bernardi muttered to the other denizens of the tower, squeaking and fluttering their furry webbed wings, alarmed at the light, "the emperor is apparently determined to preserve order in this city. Heaven bless that lone, brave man!" and he lowered the taper to light his feet down the old steps, the difficult, steep old steps that had been carved for soldiers, not middle-aged merchants.

228

Having assured himself that it was only a riot, not a war, Bernardi walked carefully and slowly, steadying himself against the wall. He wondered how he had ever been able to go up so quickly. Then he heard a commotion at the rear of the house where Angelica had gone to close the door.

"Gesù!" he swore, and tried to go faster.

Angelica had found the door unaccountably open. She had instantly closed it and whirled the iron cross blocks into place, but not before another roving band of Greeks had spied the turbaned figure beside her. They had started to pelt the door with stones, and one of them yelled drunkenly: "Deliver the dog! Hand over the Turk! We're hanging all Turks tonight, Mohammed and all the rest of them!" The door rattled with a shower of stones.

"Gesù, dear Gesù!" Bernardi murmured, cursing and praying all in one breath. He had dropped the taper in his haste and was groping his way, stumbling down in the dark.

Michael instinctively felt for his weapons, but he had left them in the great hall. He grasped Angelica by the wrist, determined to keep her by him while he went to arm himself.

But Angelica said: "Take off your turban! Quickly! You're not a Turk! Even a Greek can see you're not a Turk without that—that *thing* on!" She began to cry. Michael supposed it was nerves. He was forced to admit that a woman had a right to be nervous under the circumstances, but he hesitated to assume a disguise. Janissaries did not willingly relinquish their turbans.

Angelica saw his hesitation. With a little moan she sank suddenly to her kness, pressed her hand to her heart, and leaned heavily against the door, which at that moment was shaken by another shower of stones.

"What is it?" Michael gasped, clutching her quickly under the arms.

"My heart," she breathed, her eyes shut. "Any excitement. I've always suffered this way. Go to my bedroom, hurry, and fetch me the little green bottle of restorative in front of the mirror."

Angelica knew there was no little green bottle of restorative in front of the mirror; she also knew that there was nothing wrong with her heart, at least nothing that a restorative would cure. Unaware of the integral strength of the door, frightened by the shouting and the violence of the mob, she had simply determined to get Michael out of the way and handle the crowd alone.

Michael glanced at the door. It was heavy, honest, solid. If he knew anything about fortifications, it would take more than a few hurled cobblestones to knock it down.

"All right; but you'd better come with me."

Angelica shook her head. "I can't walk."

Michael instantly picked her up in his arms and carried her down the hall away from the door. It was the closest he had ever been to her. "Hurry!" she whispered, imagining the imminent collapse of the door. Michael did not hurry, however. He held her very gently and walked very deliberately, certain that the door would hold, and certain that his next dozen paces, from the door to the divan at the entrance of the great hall, were the full measure of time that Allah had allotted him to hold the body of Angelica so intimately close.

He laid her gently on the divan. "Rest," he commanded. Then he sprinted off to fetch the mythical medicine.

Michael's unexpected action left Angelica quite speechless, and, for some seconds, motionless. Then suddenly the door shook under the impact of a new and different attack. The Greeks had found a heavy oaken hitching post between the stables and the postern entrance of the villa. It had been set there for the accommodation of visitors who stayed so short a time that it was unnecessary to stable their horses. The post was sturdy enough above ground, but the buried portion was rotten with age and damp. Having wrenched it out of the earth, some of the men were now using it as a battering ram. The blow of the old oak beam set the villa to reverberating with a crash like the shock of thunder.

Angelica made a miraculous recovery. She ran back to the door and opened the little barred wicket and looked out. She pleaded with the mob to go away. There were no Turks in the house, she insisted.

The drunken rabble listened, not even half convinced, but willing to pause for a moment to take stock of the extraordinarily beautiful woman suddenly disclosed behind the wicket. The more sober members of the gang had also come to realize that the improvised battering ram was useless and that nothing short of a formidable army could force its way into Bernardi's villa.

In Angelica's bedroom Michael had found nothing that looked

230

like a bottle of restorative, but he found something else. Beside a little shrine, where a Christian candle burned in a votive cup of flawless blue crystal before a statue of the Gavour Mother of God, he had discovered an astonishing thing that Angelica had not meant him to see. It was a toy dagger, the blunt, little-boy weapon he had once worn and given her in the garden in Galata.

He picked it up and put it down, and picked it up again, turning it over and over in his hand. The little crosses on the hilt. It could be no other.

"God's name!"

He thrust it into the crimson girdle that marked a commander of the janissaries of Mohammed II. To have remembered him all these years! If Angelica could do that, he could afford to dispense with some of his military insignia. To please her, if nothing more.

At that moment he heard the crashing attack on the door.

He ripped off his turban, grinning wryly at the notion of passing for a Christian. He clutched a pink bottle that smelled good and might be a restorative, and started back to where, he supposed, Angelica still lay swooning on the divan.

Bernardi met him in the hall. Without a turban concealing it, Michael's close-cropped hair looked very like a Christian knight's. To the astonished merchant, Michael appeared like a reincarnation of Nicolo da Montelupo on that day, long ago, when he and Bernardi had stolen the gondolas and poled their way through the canals of Venice with the girls that their fathers would not have approved of and never found out about.

Grasping enough of the situation to cooperate, Bernardi unbuckled his cloak and cast it over Michael's shoulders. And then the resemblance left him mentally gasping: Who would have thought it! He is Da Montelupo, come back in the flesh of his youth! He is Venice! Home! But Bernardi knew better than to voice his thoughts to this young janissary. Aloud he said: "It is kind of you to consider the safety of your hosts tonight, Commander. Pray speak only Italian till we rout this rabble. I have been on the tower, and I think it is merely a riot. Shoot no one unless you have to." He stooped to rub his shins where he had barked them on the stone steps in the dark.

Michael nodded and hurried on ahead of him. Angelica was not lying on the divan. She stood at the door, the wicket open, trying to subdue the mob single-handed.

The drunken Greeks had already recovered from the momentary shock of Angelica's flaxen beauty, framed like the head of an angry icon in the golden aureole of light behind her. They were preparing another rush with their battering ram.

Hearing a noise, Angelica turned to see Michael approaching, in a European cloak, his turban gone.

"This is my brother!" she cried, as Michael, the bottle still in his hand, strode up beside her.

The Greeks shouted their derision. Yet Michael certainly did not look like a Turk. One of the men yelled, "If he is your brother, then let him kiss you!"

They all knew no Christian lady would kiss a Turk.

Michael put his arms around her and said softly, *"Carissima!"* and kissed her.

The volatile mood of the Greeks instantly reversed itself. The Greeks knew their kisses. This was no Turk, and it was certainly no brother, either. They shouted with laughter, delighted and appeased. They dispersed in search of easier quarry in less well fortified houses. There were many real Turks in the city: merchants, friends of private families, visiting dignitaries. The diplomats in the palace, of course, they dared not touch, but they hoped to capture some others and avenge their compatriots in the vineyard before Constantine's police could stop them. The emperor's quick repressive measures were already becoming known.

Filippo Bernardi, limping, cursing, and laughing, approached the kissing couple.

"They've gone," he said. "You can stop now."

And shortly they did, looking at each other in a way that made Bernardi frown.

"It was a clever ruse," Bernardi observed. "You must stay here tonight, Commander. Perhaps tomorrow, also, till the city is quieter. Then, if you must, you shall go home. Though it would please me, since it would obviously please Angelica, if you would give me permission to throw your heathen turban into the flames. Never put it on again, Michael. You have done a brave and charitable thing in counseling me to flee. This time I shall certainly do so. Come with us! The same ship that takes me and my daughter back to Venice can also take you. You are more important than you think. You have been in Europe before. Perhaps you might even find it to your advantage to return."

Observing Michael's face suddenly overcast with anger, pride, and pain, the merchant dared say no more and regretted some of what he had already said. He shrugged as only an Italian can shrug.

"Forgive me, Commander, I spoke impulsively. I misjudged your loyalty. I had hoped—well, never mind what I had hoped. Will the commander take another cup of coffee?"

That night Michael forgot his prayers. Unmindful of time, he paced the floor, looking again and again at the little toy dagger. Then, when it was nearly dawn, he reluctantly laid aside the childish weapon and made up his turban so that he could wear it again in the morning.

IN the morning a herald from the palace and a squad of crossbowmen, together with a white court eunuch, whose function was to knock at Bernardi's door and announce them with fitting formality, presented themselves at the villa and demanded the person of the Turk.

At first Bernardi protested that there was no Turk under his roof. The polite official retorted that he had positive information to the contrary. As if to prove the truth of his assertion Michael suddenly appeared dressed in his Moslem attire.

"His Imperial Majesty is taking some of the representatives of his cousin, the sultan, into protective custody," the herald announced. "Some of the people were restless last night because of a regrettable incident on the promontory of the Asomaton."

Angelica went white and clung to her father's arm. "They are taking him to prison!" The herald glanced at her and then at Bernardi, saying, "It would be foolhardy effrontery, particularly in an Italian, to presume to proffer the hospitality which the emperor himself is pleased to extend."

Michael glared at this silky-tongued threat and said: "I was under the impression that our two countries were still at peace. But I should be grieved if my presence were to prove a source of danger to my friends. Naturally, I am prepared to go wherever you wish to take me."

And as if by magic, the steward who had vanished the night before materialized from the direction of the stables leading Michael's horse.

The herald favored Michael with a low bow from the saddle. His golden chain of office clinked prettily. He lowered his ivory baton in a salute.

"You need have no fear, Commander. His Imperial Majesty has set aside some apartments in the palace for all Turkish officers and civilians of rank. The others are being housed in dry, comfortable quarters in the hippodrome. You will be released and sent home as soon as the city is quieter. The people are angry because seventeen defenseless farmers were cut down in the fields around the structure that you Turks call Roumeli Hissar. In retaliation some Turks were stoned to death here in the city last night. The emperor has decided that such rude justice must not occur again."

"Justice!" Michael snorted. "The farmers shot first. They shot at us night before last. That's why I'm here. Probably they tried a second ambush."

"That's why you're here. Indeed, Commander, indeed. That is interesting." The herald looked hard and thoughtfully at Bernardi before he again addressed Michael. Bernardi turned pale. "And now would it please the commander to mount his horse? Promptly?"

The evil-looking steward smirked. Bernardi made a mental note to crush a diamond and put the dust in the fellow's wine and bury the body in one of the tunnels, but he was not to be given the opportunity. Michael mounted his horse and the guard formed around him. The steward slunk into the center of the hollow square of crossbowmen. When they rode away in the direction of the palace, the steward was still in their midst.

Angelica stood very straight, watching the procession move away. Tears streamed down her cheeks. Bernardi tried to comfort her. "Look how they carry their crossbows, my dear. The points are down; the strings are slack. It is a guard of honor. Come, come, child. Michael will be back in Turkey in a day! Everything is going to be all right."

Angelica only shook her head wordlessly.

Just then Michael turned in his saddle and called, *"Angelica mia, thy father was mistaken. It wasn't a ruse!"*

For a moment Bernardi did not fully understand the remark,

or why Angelica blinked the tears out of her eyes and hugged him.

"Did you hear that, Father? He meant it. He meant it when he kissed me!"

"What? Oh, yes, child; yes, of course. Of course he did." But Bernardi was gloomy now. He hadn't liked the herald's look. "If I could only get my hands on that steward!"

The charwoman, trembling and ill at ease, presumed to come out of the shadow of the door and touch her master on the sleeve.

"Will they be coming for your lordship, too, because you housed the infidel?"

Bernardi frowned, indicating Angelica with a movement of his head, and put a finger to his lips.

CHAPTER
29

MICHAEL had wanted to take the little dagger with him. The years that Angelica had treasured it lent it an aura of sanctity, but when he saw the herald he slipped it out of his girdle and left it in the room he had occupied. There, he knew, Angelica would find it. He hoped she would understand that he had left it as a gift twice bestowed, bestowed now and rededicated with the deeper emotion of a mature man.

Then he went out, as he supposed, to give himself up to the reprisals of the Byzantine police. Michael was convinced that the hour of doom had struck for the Roman Empire of the East. It was his fate, apparently, to be one of the first prisoners taken by the Christians in the great war. He accepted the fate on his forehead with a bitter, unspoken rebellion, but he refused to compromise Angelica and her father. In any event, one janissary commander could not successfully fight the formidable detachment of crossbowmen that surrounded him on all sides.

He was unhappily aware that he might somehow have said the wrong thing when he candidly admitted to the herald that the attempted assassination of the sentry had been the reason for his being in Bernardi's house. He wished he had bitten off his tongue before he had uttered the words, "That's why I'm here." The herald had seemed to attach importance to the remark. Michael hoped Angelica would not suffer because of his slip. He, himself, he supposed, would soon be inspecting the inside of a Gavour dungeon, neither palatial, nor dry, nor comfortable.

To his considerable surprise, however, the guard did not demand surrender of his arms and continued in the direction of the palace. And presently Michael discovered that the herald had spoken the precise truth. The Emperor Constantine put him and every Turk found that day in Constantinople under restraint, it is true. But the luxury, the entertainment, the elaborate banquets which constituted the protective custody of Constantine on that occasion equaled and surpassed the reception which many a European monarch would have reserved for visiting royalty.

Constantine had good reasons for behaving so. There was always the chance that his appeals to the Christian rulers of the world for help would be heard. Who knew but that armies were already being massed for his aid? Since war did not break out on Thursday, nor on Friday, there was hope that it might be delayed indefinitely. Constantine deemed it wise, at that critical moment, to continue a little longer the endless temporizing that his council had always forced upon him.

He had another reason for his courteous treatment of the Turks who had been, on his order, so gently but firmly interned. If war *should* break out as a result of the skirmish around Roumeli Hissar, the emperor did not want many hundreds of Turks in his city. He could not in conscience slaughter them, and, moreover, the slaughter would be useless. Word of it would leak out; there would be terrible reprisals. Centuries of warfare with the Turks had proven the Turks' ability to out-Greek the Greeks. Whenever Greeks hanged a Turk, the Turks strangled ten Greeks. Yet if Constantine did not execute them, they would remain a perpetual source of treachery, expense, and intrigue throughout the war. The emperor had problems enough with his own divided, factious, vacillating subjects. Nearly a thousand enemy aliens would add disastrously to his troubles; they would eat up the food, corrupt the guards, and smuggle military secrets to the enemy. They would require personnel to watch them which might better be employed in fighting. And if things started going badly, they might even stage a revolt.

Therefore, on Saturday, June 24, Constantine released his prisoners and sent them to Scutari, on guilded barges, accompanied by a band of music, with every mark of respect.

On his return to Scutari, Michael heard the Turkish version of the death of Charilaos and the other Greek peasants. It appeared that the Greeks had treacherously and unexpectedly attacked the line of Turkish guards. The complaint that the Turks had first trampled down most of Charilaos's vines Michael never heard, because neither Charilaos nor any of the other desperate farmers lived to utter it.

With every one of his subjects, except his diplomats, out of the Christian capital, Mohammed was ready to unfurl the sacred green banner of the Prophet and declare war. But Mohammed, no less than the Eastern emperor, was restrained by a cautious council. The Sheik-ul-Islam said it was not necessary for the war to be jihad, a holy war. No religious principle was involved in the attack by a few Gavour farmers. The war as a war would be commendable, of course; but such a trivial precipitating incident could not be considered holy; and the stubborn, high-minded archpriest of Islam, the only man in Turkey who dared cross the sultan, remained adamant in his conviction. The imperial astrologer, also, scanning the heavens, complained that the planets were not yet quite propitious. And Khalil Pasha, the grand vizier, touching the important consideration of allies, reminded his master that the Persians might remain neutral, since they felt themselves in no danger. Neither was the attitude of Egypt wholly satisfactory, since Egypt enjoyed a profitable trade with the Christians. Furthermore, there had lately been a peculiar report that the competitive caliph in Cairo had gone into a sulk about something that had to do with a daughter of his, a girl named Aeshia, who had repeatedly married subjects of the Turkish sultan and repeatedly found herself incompatible with them.

"What subjects?" Mohammed asked.

"Imperial Majesty, one was a janissary, and one was Prince Machmut, the Beglerbey of Roum."

"I wonder what ever happened to the Beglerbey," the sultan mused. Before Khalil Pasha could suggest that it didn't much matter, the impatient sultan's mind had raced on to something more important. He tugged at his mustache and bit his lip and snorted: "Your counsels do not deter me. The only genuine difficulty is with that Hungarian in Adrianople, stinking up my gardens with his smelters, trying to cast my guns. Urban Pasha sends me word that there are flaws in the huge piece of ordnance that he said he could build and that I counted on particularly for the destruction of the walls of Constantinople."

"The walls are very high," the vizier murmured tentatively.

Mohammed scowled. "They have been called high. They have been called holy. My Christian mother sank into a faint at the rumor that her Gavour goddess had appeared on them during my father's siege of the city. Bismillah! A transparent Greek fraud! One of their shameless actresses parading herself in the moonlight in a blue robe! The walls are not holy to me, and not too high. What a Christian emperor can erect, I, the Emperor of Islam, with the help of God, bearing the staff and the name of His Apostle, can shatter to atoms!"

"With God's help, of a certainty, O Shadow of the Universe; but also with the help of Urban Pasha's mighty cannon."

"He had better hurry before I send a messenger with a bowstring!" threatened the sultan.

"Urban Pasha is said to be on the point of success. He has already proven his skill by casting hundreds of smaller cannon, agile ones, mounted on wheels and capable of maneuvering like cavalry. Why strangle the Hungarian so soon?"

"I know. I know. Not now, then; but he has delayed me. Let him bestir himself. Meanwhile—" Mohammed's fierce black eyes glittered dangerously. He ran his long sensitive forefinger reflectively against his chin, under the tough black hairs of his short bristly beard. Time, wisdom, age, and success had not yet given that beard the venerable length or the patriarchal white it would one day assume. "Meanwhile," the sultan resumed, "I will use his mobile little cannon in a preliminary venture. Let Urban Pasha send me two hundred of these wheeled cannon—no, not so many. Half that number will suffice. Keep all other ordnance in Adrianople. Route the hundred guns secretly to Gallipoli and thence in ships through the Bosphorus to Roumeli Hissar. And let it be known to *my cousin*, Constantine, that I am touched by his courteous release of my subjects. Encourage him to open the gates of his city. Tell him, by the soul of my Christian mother—nay, go not quite so far—assure him merely by the holy name of the prophet Issa, called Jesus by the Gavours, whom we both revere, that our empires never were friendlier. Make Constantine a present of a thousand pigs: Greeks eat pigs. Let them feast for now; they will be hungry soon enough. Make the Greeks long for peace.

Arrange a polo match. Arrange a parley of diplomats. Torture the Christians with hope of peace. Divide them among themselves. *And get me those guns!"*

With one minor exception the sultan had his way in all these matters. Constantine even reluctantly opened the gates from time to time as a gesture of trust that he could not feel. But there was no polo match, and no Turk, while Constantine remained alive, ever entered the city again.

While Constantine waited for Europe to come to his aid, while Mohammed waited for Urban Pasha to send him guns, the whole, anxious Christian world waited seventy days for peace. Then, on the expiration of seventy days, on a Sunday, September 3, 1452, the guns arrived.

The sultan instantly declared war.

The brazen-sheathed gates of Constantinople, immemorial capital of the Eastern Caesars, clanged shut for the last time, never to be reopened until the city should bear a new name and worship a new and angrier God.

CHAPTER
30

THE Greeks expected an immediate attack on their capital the instant the sultan declared war, but it did not come. The beginning of hostilities was marked by an unprecedented lack of activity. Some Turkish raiding parties appeared in the vicinity of the walls, but they were easily routed by determined sallies of the Christians. The Turkish sea blockade was drawn a little tighter, many ships being stopped and turned back, but no attempt was made to engage the Byzantine navy. Few men died, and most of the dead were spies that Constantine sent out to discover what was happening to some little cities that still comprised his empire: Mesembria, Bizon, Acheloum, Selembria, and a number of villages and hamlets. But the spies never returned.

Some of the Greek ministers approached the emperor and suggested that there might still be the possibility of a negotiated peace with the sultan. They said: "He is afraid of our walls. The sultan does not dare attack. Let us dispatch a delegation to him with an offer of tribute."

"Tribute!"

"We can call it a gift. When did Byzantium ever begrudge a gift to an enemy? Many of the people still wish for peace. Many influential citizens believe it possible to achieve peace by diplomatic means even now. Some of the populace agree because they can see no warlike activity. The city finds itself most uncomfortable and crowded. There are 100,000 souls in Constantinople."

"How many soldiers?"

The ministers hesitated: "Of able-bodied men, knights, nobles, officers, and soldiers, equipped with arms and willing to bear them, there are exactly 4,970, Your Majesty!"

"To man fourteen miles of walls! And we are at war. Oh, the shame!"

"The people do not want war. They suspect the sultan does not actually want war either, because there is no fighting."

But Constantine said: "How do we know there is no fighting? What has become of my spies? The sultan has captured them. The sultan is blinding me."

The sultan was. By systematically killing everybody that ventured beyond the city, he had cut all communication with other parts of the empire.

Then, when the news came, it was laden with panic. Mohammed had accomplished what he had described to his vizier as a preliminary venture. Placing himself at the head of his entire army, he had swept down upon and overwhelmed every fortified place in Constantine's empire except Constantinople itself. He had planted his hundred cannon around each town in turn, out of range of other engines of war. Mesembria, Acheloum, and Bizon fell after one volley each. Selembria capitulated almost as quickly. Not one Turk was killed. The Roman Empire of the East was now compressed within the ramparts that circumscribed the city itself.

Almost simultaneously with the arrival of intelligence of the outbreak of hostilities, the echo of Mohammed's deadly artillery was heard in Western Europe. The new weapon produced far-reaching diplomatic consequences. Nation after nation sent word to the sultan that they considered themselves neutral. To Constantine they sent letters of benevolent sympathy, detailing exhaustively their previous military commitments. Neutral like the rest, the alert French, however, quickly noting the furious efficiency of cannon, cast some cannon of their own and used them against the English, hurling the sturdy Islanders from French soil for the first time in a hundred years. Thus the cannonade that tolled the funeral knell of the Roman Empire of the East also terminated the Hundred Years' War. It did more. By teaching mankind an effective new means of destroying itself, it was soon to relegate into oblivion the immemorial institutions of feudalism. The flourishing crafts of the fletcher and the armorer were soon to become obsolete curiosities. What brought light to the Dark Ages was the incandescent blast of a gunpowder explosion, and nobody ever said it was a bad thing.

Among the sultan's janissaries, however, there was jealousy and discontent at seeing crews of grimy engineers win battles by means of a mechanical engine. Michael, leaning on his bow, which suddenly looked old-fashioned to him, watching the puffs of dusty smoke that blossomed on the battlements of Selembria when the projectiles smashed into the ramparts, complained to Hassan: "Now how can a janissary ever win a name? Wars will be won from now on by mechanics!"

Hassan said: "That's what they thought when somebody invented the catapult. Forget the mechanics, Michael. These little guns won't touch the walls of Byzantium. *They* will have to be scaled. I won my name on a tower of Ulubad. Your name and hundreds of others are waiting on the heights, where bravery has always counted and always will."

Of all the powers in Europe, only the Pope in Rome, first of the humanist pontiffs, last of the able men to occupy the Holy See for many years, scholarly, saintly Nicholas V, clearly divined the peril to Christendom. He exhorted the princes of Europe to forget their wars and fly to the aid of their Eastern religious brethren in a mighty crusade against the infidel. His exhortations fell on deaf and selfish ears. Europe was in the toils of the Renaissance, intoxicated with new thoughts, dazzled by its own brilliance, happily unaware that its too sudden emancipation from the passive ignorance of the Dark Ages was shortly to terminate in the bloody nationalism of the Reformation. Nobody listened to Nicholas V. Impotent in the face of such a world, he sighed and went back to his metrical translation of Homer and the founding of the Vatican Library. If God in His wisdom saw not fit to stir up the hearts of princes to fight for the Eastern branch of Holy Church, there was nothing for an old man to do but retire to his acres of cold marble palaces and pray.

Even the Republic of Venice at first remained neutral. She had vital interests in all the islands bordering on, some actually within sight of, the Mediterranean coasts of Turkey; many of her investments, too, were jeopardized in Trebizond, Georgia, Crimea, and far beyond Constantinople in Cherson, under the belly of the Russian bear. If any nation had an excuse to remain neutral it was

Venice, who lived by sea trade and whose lifeline to the East would instantly be severed in the event of a war with Turkey.

But a dreadful atrocity shattered all hope of peace with the sultan.

There was a Venetian ship en route to Georgia. Of course, it had to pass through the Bosphorus. And when it came to the Strangled Throat, a formidable convoy of Turkish triremes stopped her and insolently demanded an enormous tribute for the privilege of passing. The sturdy captain indignantly refused.

Thereupon an engineer in Roumeli Hissar threw off the tarpaulin from a concealed piece of ordnance. He applied his slow match to the touchhole. The piece leaped up with the violence of the discharge. A three-hundred-pound stone ball traced a graceful parabola against the incomparable blue of the Anatolian sky. Long after the event, feeble, toothless old veterans, telling stories of the war, swore by the Prophet that they had beheld an angel of Allah guiding the missile. It fell directly amidships, sundering the Venetian vessel. The ship disintegrated and sank in two minutes. A few survivors were fished out of the water. And then, though Turkey was at peace with the great Venetian Republic, all the rescued sailors were executed.

The executions were not performed in anger; they were diplomatic. With the fall of so many Greek cities, the sultan's confidence overleaped itself. All Christendom must know the stern relentlessness of his resolve; all Christendom must fear him and withhold help from Constantine. The Turkish executioners were acting under explicit orders from their sovereign.

Now no Mohammedan would decapitate another live Mohammedan. The Prophet had revealed that the hot blood of Islam was not to be shed in fratricidal conflicts. Since the Prophet had never revealed anything about cold blood, however, Moslems, when executing Moslems, always strangled them first. The Venetians, of course, being Christians, were considered unworthy of this preliminary courtesy, and their heads were summarily chopped off. As for the unfortunate captain, being deemed most culpable in the affair by reason of his commanding position, he was painfully and publicly sawed in two halves. The bodies of all the Christians were transported to Demotica, a Turkish town thirty-five miles south of Adrianople. And there, before the quaking ambassadors of a score of Christian countries, the corpses were eaten by wild animals in an amusement park.

But the Venetian ambassador reacted with unexpected disregard for practical economic considerations. He took the first ship home. The furious senators forgot their mercantile lifeline to the East. The Italian Republic went wild; Venice declared war, and what help they could give in the time that remained, they gave.

Genoa, like everyone else except Venice, remained neutral. But the Duchy of Genoa differed from the better governed Venetian republic, being traditionally a hotbed of intrigue, civil wars, family feuds among the nobility, and contending factions among the common people. The city was always full of mercenaries, caring little for whom they fought as long as their wages were regularly paid. The only stable institution in this perpetual welter of internal strife was, characteristically, the national bank. Thus, while the neutrality of Genoa as a state was a foregone conclusion, Constantine actually got more help from Genoese soldiers of fortune than from any other Christian source. One of them, rich, romantic, noble, a general named John Justiniani, entered into communication with Constantine. Justiniani would, he said, for the governorship of the island of Rhodes, ally himself with the emperor. Rhodes was historically renowned. Its governor ranked with princes and kings in the diplomatic and military hierarchy of Europe. Constantine agreed. With the connivance of the Genoese government, the blessing of the Holy Father, and the best wishes of the national bank, John Justiniani personally recruited a force of two thousand mercenaries and set sail for the relief of Constantinople, his bill for the wages of his troops in his hand, payable in advance.

No other Christian gave any help at all to the last of the Eastern Caesars.

Meanwhile Mohammed sent some additional ships through Gallipoli into the Sea of Marmara and the Bosphorus, strengthening the blockade around the city. There was no necessity for strengthening the Turkish land forces, since, for all practical purposes, the Ottoman Empire now reached within bowshot of Constantinople's walls.

Then, as was customary, Mohammed retired into winter quarters, waiting for spring, and for hunger and cold to weaken the defenders of the beleaguered city.

The only defensive measure Constantine was able to take was the destruction of the pontoon bridge between Constantinople and Galata. In its place he substituted a heavy iron chain that could stop any ship afloat. It was anchored to the twin towers of Christ and St. Eugenius, its heavy central portion upheld by ships. Behind it, in the upper waters of the Golden Horn, Constantine secured his precious navy. And prayed. And waited for a miracle. There was much talk of miracles among the Christians, and revival of many ancient, holy prophecies.

In spite of his great successes so far in the war, the sultan spent a fretful and restless winter. He amused himself with the erection of a stately palace, to which he gave the grandiose name of Jehan Numa, the Watchtower of the World; but he had no pleasure in it.

Most of the time he spent in his gardens, his wintry breath mingling with the smoke of the furnaces, alternately threatening and cajoling Urban Pasha to get on with the founding of the mighty cannon which, the sultan had publicly boasted, were to shatter Constantinople's walls to atoms.

Urban had cast and successfully tested four pieces. They were the heaviest metal weapons ever made by man. Urban could, and did, crawl into each one of them, to show his lord how huge they were.

But the imagination of the sultan was stimulated by a fifth, an experiment, which was larger still.

"With such a device Constantinople shall fall as precipitously as Bizon!" he cried exultantly. "Shoot it off, Urban Pasha, and let me hear its thunder!"

But the Hungarian slowly traced a dirty, stubby finger along a jagged, hair-fine line in the sleek bronze body of the barrel and said: "My lord, I fear it is flawed. It should be melted down and recast."

The angry monarch shouted, "There isn't time! You have delayed me already with your meltings and your remeltings and your crystallizations and your flaws. Think you that Allah can not instantly repair your bungling—if you have bungled? I can see no flaw. Such notions are cowardly and come from the Devil. Shoot the thing, man. They tell me the shot weighs a thousand pounds. Throw it into the Tunja. Let Constantine feel the shock of it in Byzantium!"

With scientific willingness to give an unlikely hypothesis a fair hearing, Urban Pasha replied: "When I was a Christian I was told that my notions came from the Christian Devil. Now that I have embraced the true faith Your Majesty tells me that my notions come from the Mohammedan Devil. When philosophers agree, who am I, an engineer, to argue with them? There may be, as Your Majesty says, something devilish in my concept of a great gun; but to me it is only a beautiful engine, beautifully obeying some unknown physical law. Does my lord command me, now, here, in his presence, to test this piece which I honestly believe to be imperfect?"

"God's name, yes! And no more talk!"

There was nothing for Urban Pasha to do but obey. With a certain excited anticipation, tempered with a liberal admixture of technical apprehension, he ordered the piece charged. Mohammed stood close by and watched the preparations. When the tedious process was completed, Urban Pasha approached the emperor and suggested, without the usual obeisance and with considerable dignity: "If my emperor will now remove his person fifty paces from the engine—"

Mohammed was not used to taking orders. His mustache bristled. "Certainly not!"

Urban Pasha shrugged and smiled queerly. Khalil Pasha, Zagan Pasha, and Baltoglu Sulemein Pasha and every other dignitary in the sultan's entourage, who had accompanied their lord to witness the testing of the great gun, instantly threw themselves on the ground at his feet. The grand admiral embraced the imperial slippers, turning slightly green in the face. No one wanted to stand three feet from the problematical, untried weapon.

"Consider your empire," Baltoglu gasped. He had prostrated himself so deeply that the pointed toes of Mohammed's slippers were actually tangled in the strands of his beard. "Let the Hungarian be flogged tomorrow for his impertinence, but do deign to heed his injunction. Think what your imperial life means to the world!"

Mohammed looked contemptuously at the admiral. "Baltoglu Sulemein Pasha," he said, "if you didn't build such fast ships I'd kick you in the face for a coward!"

Then the vizier said: "I am told that the explosion temporarily blinds those of the crew who are close to the piece. Your Majesty can better observe the effect of the projectile if you walk a little distance away."

At that the sultan complied.

Urban Pasha accepted a slow fire from one of his Hungarian aides, murmuring into his beard, with the complete theological confusion which had plagued him since his conversion to Islam. "O Allah," he prayed, "strengthen my bronze, as my Emperor says you will; Lord Jesus, have mercy on me; and thou Blessed Mary, ever Virgin, pray for us sinners now and at the hour of our death," and with that he applied the slow fire to the touchhole.

The explosion rocked the new palace. It shattered the cannon to fragments. It blew Urban Pasha and all his Turkish and Hungarian assistants out of this world—straight into the arms of the houris of Paradise, according to Turkish annals, and according to Christian annals, straight to Hell.

The bursting of the cannon wiped out the sultan's corps of manufacturing engineers, though the operational engineers still remained, of course, to work the new weapons. The accident sent Mohammed into a rage. He offered a horsetail and one of the handsomest concubines in the imperial harem to anyone who could cast a cannon of equal size, but Allah was not to see fit to inspire another genius of Urban's caliber for many generations to come. The sultan kept his horsetail and his concubine and was forced to fight the war with the four tremendous cannon that he already possessed. They were treated like costly jewels.

Thousands of slaves smoothed the road from Adrianople to Constantinople. Two hundred men gently hoisted the guns onto specially manufactured caissons that had thirty axles and sixty wheels. A hundred men on either side balanced each weapon. Soldiers guarded the workmen with orders to shoot any man who showed signs of flinching if the gun should threaten to fall from its conveyance. Rather a hundred smashed bodies, cushioning the shock of the gun, than that the gun should fall to the road and perhaps develop a flaw. Two weary months were consumed in the transport of the guns from Adrianople to the outskirts of Byzantium. Nicolo da Montelupo had traveled the same road on a mule in seven days; his son had galloped a horse over it in three; but in all the history of the world no guns of such size had ever traveled over that road or any other.

Spring, the cannon, and the armies of Mohammed II came to Constantinople at the same time. On April 6, 1453, the sultan pitched his purple and gold tent before the Gate of St. Romanus and laid siege to the city no Moslem had ever conquered.

The noose he had woven to strangle the life out of the hungry city was now completed: cannon, ships, and men. No element was lacking. It remained only to pull the noose tight, till the proud old imperial heart of the empire burst and stopped beating and died.

A T the very beginning of the siege, the sultan's careful preparations developed a totally unsuspected hitch. He had planned a quick
and decisive reduction of the city, having no patience with the
leisurely wars that sometimes took years to accomplish their results:
beleaguered cities had been known to hold out for as long as two
decades. Already his impatient mind leaped ahead for other empires
to conquer: Christian Trebizond and Georgia to the east; to the
south, Moslem Egypt, slippery, degenerate, with its competing sultan
and competing, annoying caliph; and to the west, more Greeks in
their thousand islands. And farther west still, in Mediterranean
Europe, the soaring ambition of Mohammed II dared dwell on
the prospect of invading the mainland of Italy itself. After New
Rome, Old Rome! And a reunion in Spain with his brother in Islam,
the Moorish sultan of Granada! There could be no twenty-year siege
of Byzantium.

His cannon, little and big, began to speak. The walls of Constantinople began to tremble and smoke. His ships, 480 of them,
overspread the Sea of Marmara and the Bosphorus, speckling the
blue waters with swift white sails painted with crimson crescents and
stars.

Then John Justiniani arrived with five high, heavy Genoese
galleys crammed to overflowing with two thousand reckless Italian
mercenaries.

The Turkish fleet darted at them like water bugs. The Genoese ships rammed the line of attackers and shattered them as if the lighter Turkish craft had been fabricated of glass.

Baltoglu Sulemein Pasha protested in terror, "The wind was unfavorable, my lord!"

Mohammed replied, "Your miserable sticks couldn't even slow down the ships of the Gavours! They crumpled like paper!"

"It was the adverse current, Your Majesty!"

Mohammed bit his lip and glared at the grand admiral. "Couldn't even slow them down!" he repeated, his voice heavy with menace.

Justiniani and his mercenaries reached the Golden Horn. The heavy chain was smartly lowered beneath the waves and the welcome reinforcements sailed over it into the safety of the upper harbor. The battlements of Constantinople rang with the cheers of the Christians. The chain was promptly heaved up again by toiling sailors on the supporting men-of-war until the graceful catenary curves of its massive iron links just kissed the surface of the water, effectively blocking pursuit by the sultan's ships.

Genoa's aid was substantial.

Assistance of another kind shortly arrived from Nicholas V, also by way of the sea. The Pope sent a cardinal and a suite of priests to pray for the city, but the Pope did not limit his aid to the spiritual. He sent a body of soldiers to aid with their swords the prayers of the priests who did not hesitate to hazard their lives in the besieged city. These soldiers were not mercenaries; they were the Pope's own men, all volunteers and all actuated by the highest devotion to their religion.

The Roman contingent arrived in lighter, less well fortified ships; but these, too, smashed through the Turkish blockade. The Turkish craft appeared to disintegrate at the touch of the Roman prows, and the Pope's men also reached the safe waters behind the chain. Cheers and hoots rose from the Christian fortress to sting the ears of the humiliated sultan.

Baltoglu Sulemein Pasha went into a frenzy, trembling with what might be rage, and what—as the sultan shrewdly guessed—might also be fear: "It was stupid maneuvering on the part of the Turkish captains, my lord! They cravenly tried to save themselves!"

"They knew how to die," the sultan replied. His face was pale, but the tone was thoughtful. "Not a man escaped from my smashed ships." He did not reproach the grand admiral, but he privately instituted some inquiries among the timber merchants from whom Baltoglu had bought the materials to build the ships.

Not the genius of a people but the command of a despot had brought the Turkish fleet into being. The ethos of the Turks had its genesis in desert sands and the high Mongolian steppes. No Turkish trade had ever traveled over the sea. No Turk ever willingly deserted his horse for a ship. A national navy was a new venture, without precedent and without experience. Knowing the genius and the limitations of his people, Mohammed realized how easily corruption might have crept into the building of ships.

And then, wonder of wonders, an *Egyptian* ship arrived! It rode low in the water; it was heavy with grain from the jealous Sultan of Egypt. In a way it was formidably armed, but not with armed men. The armament consisted of an imperial pronouncement from Jakmak, the Sultan of Egypt, claiming brotherly right of passage and immunity from search on the part of his cousin, Mohammed the Victorious. Islam was already greeting the Ottoman prince by his new name. To complete the armament of the Egyptian ship, a Mohammedan dignitary displayed a futwa, or ecclesiastical proclamation, from the Caliph of Cairo: it would be a sin, the futwa warned, to interrupt the voyage of this peaceful ship, which displayed its neutrality by carrying not a single soldier.

Mohammed was not deceived, but there was only one ship. He shrugged. Whatever might be in it, the contents of one ship could not alter events. He was too wise to precipitate a diplomatic crisis with Egypt, which had refused to ally herself with him and whose neutrality might be precarious. He permitted the lone Egyptian ship to pass. It immediately delivered its cargo to the hungry Byzantines: oil, grain, nuts, dates, dried fish, and salt meats.

The Egyptian ship caused the grand admiral no embarrassment.

But then help came from the Venetians: men, ships, arms, food, and even a few guns. The Venetian squadron ran the Turkish blockade as easily as the Genoese, against odds of a hundred to one.

Desperately Baltoglu Sulemein Pasha tried to throw his guilt on the Merciful Himself: "It would appear, Imperial Majesty, that Allah, who hath given dominion of earth to Your Majesty, hath given the seas to the Gavours."

But the sultan's inquiries had produced irrefutable evidence of the grand admiral's peculations. Mohammed answered: "Thou base and forsworn son of a Gavour, it would appear rather that you have built my ships of toothpicks, not of the sturdy timbers you pretended to buy. They are too light, too fragile. No wonder they row so fast! But you shall not retain the profits you have stolen at the expense of my honor and my empire!"

The unfortunate grand admiral was stripped of his titles, his estates, and even his clothes. Naked and condemned to death, he was spread-eagled on the ground in front of all the regiments of cavalry, infantry, and engineers, and even the hordes of low-born, beggarly irregulars who had joined the army in the hope of martyrdom and Paradise, having nothing in this life to live for. Four black eunuchs restrained him by his four extended limbs. Two white eunuchs whipped him savagely with whistling willow staves, which presently dripped scarlet with the admiral's blood. But the sultan, though he had decreed the admiral's death, suddenly stopped the execution. Baltoglu Sulemein Pasha was highly connected in Hungary. The Christian Hungarian ambassador was even now attending the Turkish court, smiling, friendly, collaborating, delighted in his heart of hearts that the old Greek capital would shortly fall. The sultan's unexpected clemency was a well planned, graceful gesture, designed to secure the neutrality and perhaps elicit the active support of Hungary.

But everything the grand admiral owned was sold, and Mohammed distributed the proceeds among his favorite troops, the janissaries, whose fidelity and enthusiasm he must count on in the coming final stages of the siege. Baltoglu Sulemein Pasha, now reduced to penury and the indignity of his Christian name, was dismissed in rags and disgrace, crippled and half mad with the ferocity of his flogging, and sent home to Hungary, fainting and gibbering on a mule.

Mohammed instantly appointed a new grand admiral, a man named Hamoud Pasha, whose transcendent naval genius equaled the mechanical genius of Urban, the gun founder. Hamoud conceived and executed an operation that obliterated the venal shortcomings of Baltoglu. The weakness of the Turkish ships Hamoud turned into strength. In a fantastic exercise of skill, will, and imagination, Hamoud converted the disastrous lightness of the navy into a positive asset.

Repeated penetration of the Turkish blockade had brought hope to the Christians and discouragement to the Turks. The siege had already lasted nearly a month. There was desperate danger to Islam that Christendom might learn that, although Constantinople was sealed in by overwhelming land armies, the city could still be reinforced and provisioned by sea, as had always happened in the past. The sultan's impotent navy would be the laughingstock of the world, and the siege might drag on for years. No one knew better than Mohammed that if, at little expense and without too much trouble, the nations of Europe could force him to raise the siege, they would do so. This would mean the annihilation of all his ambitious plans.

It was the brilliant scheme of the new grand admiral which put an end to Mohammed's apprehensions.

In the rear of the suburb of Galata, among the hills, between Galata and Roumeli Hissar, there was a gentle valley that sloped down to the Bosphorus. At its highest point it became level and ran through a forest of scrubby trees and dense thicket in an arc behind the suburban walls, and then it dropped down again into the extremely shallow waters of the upper estuary of the Golden Horn. The total distance from water to water was ten miles.

Hamoud reasoned: "Why not transport my predecessor's flimsy craft over this strip of land and launch them in the shallows to the rear of the Christian ships, outflanking and immobilizing them, even if we cannot successfully outfight them? If they turn on us, we can retreat, till their deep-draft ships ground themselves. Foreign vessels will not dare to join Constantine's fleet behind the chain if they know that we too are there. And best of all, Your Majesty, the maneuver will complete the encirclement of Constantinople. Up to now it has not been necessary for the Greeks to man the five miles of wall that face the Golden Horn. The Christians have been able to concentrate their men on the land side. This completion of the encirclement will stretch their thin ranks thinner still, and the effect on the morale of the Greeks will be tremendous. The mechanics of my operation are difficult, but, with sufficient manpower, eminently practicable."

The sultan beamed. "The Devil sent me Baltoglu, but Allah Himself has sent me Hamoud Pasha. Accomplish this design and I promise you that Hamoud Pasha shall be a pasha of three horsetails and governor of a province." Hamoud gasped at the magnificence of the reward. "His sons shall be born of a princess from my seraglio and his income shall rival a vizier's!"

Hamoud prostrated himself. A pashalik! Three horsetails! Touching the sultan's feet with his forehead, quickly thinking, he cautioned: "Your Majesty's benevolence touching my future sons locks love in my heart for Your Majesty; but men, not a woman just now, men by the thousands, are the object of my concern. Battalions of men to clear the thickets and construct the ramps and plant the windlasses and grease the ways to carry your ships from the Bosphorus to the Golden Horn. It should speedily be done."

Mohammed listened avidly, his quick intellect grasping every detail of the plan, his ambition afire at this scheme to turn into good fortune all the setbacks that so far had plagued his naval efforts in the war.

"Men you shall have, Hamoud Pasha. There are a hundred thousand of the *piadé*, peasants and peddlers and beggars and other riff-raff of the irregular troops that have come to win glorious deaths in my war against the Gavour. They shall do your heavy work. They are used to it. And my engineers who built Roumeli Hissar are now idle —they shall direct the laborers!"

To distract the Christians from the extensive operation behind Galata, Mohammed launched a series of attacks which kept the Byzantines massed on the land side of the city.

To make sure that no Galatan spy slipped over to Constantinople and reported what was going on in the woods, Mohammed issued a warning that if anyone were caught beyond the Galatan walls, that person would be executed and Galata itself would lose its neutral status and become subject to immediate sack. Some Galatan dignitaries, in a deputation, protested that they had no interest beyond their own walls.

Then, for six weeks, a hundred thousand men cut down the woods and cleared a strip from the Bosphorus to the Golden Horn. The engineers who had built Roumeli Hissar now built a wooden road from water to water. Massive timber cradles on rollers and skids, such as were used to launch ships, were now constructed and used to reverse the process. Windlasses, levers, and the massed weight of men dragged the Turkish ships out of the water and, during the space of a single night, propelled eighty of them through the forest over the greased roadway and launched them again in the shallows behind the Christian navy. On the advice of the Imperial Astrologer, and for practical reasons, this spectacular climax to Hamoud Pasha's

256

scheme took place in the long night hours of good visibility, between the rising of an almost full moon and dawn.

On Sunday, May 20, the starving Greeks awoke to a malevolent miracle. There, before their hollow, incredulous eyes, in the inviolable waters behind the iron chain, lay eighty of the sultan's swiftest ships.

And how they had got there nobody knew.

Gloom and despair settled over the Greeks. Constantinople had become a trap.

The Genoese mercenaries, meeting among themselves, took accurate stock of the hopeless military situation and prudently decided to sail home for Italy, where wars were not nearly so dangerous. A deputation of their leaders waited on Justiniani and the emperor and conveyed the unanimous sense of the Italian soldiery.

Constantine, haggard and worn, bowed his head for the first time in his life to a mortal. He had not put off his heavy breastplate of mail for forty-four days.

This is the hand of God, he thought wearily to himself. He was too proud, however, to allow the soldiers to witness his discouragement. The men looked to their general for an answer.

John Justiniani forgot his manners and impulsively cast his arm over Constantine's shoulder. The gesture was the measure of Justiniani's brave, impudent character. Instantly remembering himself—the person of the emperor was so sacrosanct that even his shadow could cure a disease—Justiniani withdrew his arm and winked at the men as if he knew a secret.

"My *brave* companions," he said, "you must not expect His Majesty to give you leave to mutiny; but me, I am a soldier of fortune, like yourselves. Gentlemen, you have my permission to desert. But mark you this: the strongest of you will return to the emperor and to me!"

The Italians listened, hesitated, and wondered what he meant. And that night some hundreds of them tried to escape to the Christian ships which were anchored in a line close to the protection of the chain.

The Turkish ships darted out of the shallows. A hail of arrows fell on the Christians. Their barges were overturned with grappling hooks. Scimitars flashed in the moonlight at survivors struggling in the water. A few strong swimmers made their way back to the shore and clustered under the wall, shouting and pleading for someone to heave them the rope ladders by means of which they had clambered down. It was done; and, as Justiniani had foretold, the strongest of the chastened mutineers climbed back into the city.

In the early days of the siege, the Byzantines had been able to repair the breaches in the walls with considerable speed. As the siege wore on, however, so many men died and the living were so weakened by hunger that repairs were effected with less and less rapidity.

It was Mohammed's intention to batter down the ancient walls with cannon, but in his enthusiasm for the new weapon he did not neglect the old. Fourteen separate attempts were made to undermine strategic towers on the walls. This ancient device of siegecraft, designed to weaken foundations, actually succeeded in toppling a tower or two; but in one instance the Christians countermined and met their Turkish foes underground. In the savage encounter that followed, there was a weird battle in the dark, ending with a lurid blaze of Greek fire, with which the Christians burned the Turks to death. In general, however, the soil was too rocky for significant mining operations.

Turkish battering rams were used, but they thudded harmlessly against the metal-sheathed gates. This was exactly the sort of attack the fortifications had been constructed to withstand. The gates held firm.

Turkish catapults mingled their stone missiles with the stone projectiles of the cannon. However, these traditionally effective engines were at a disadvantage, because Christian catapults from the higher elevation of the walls could vastly outrange them and had the further advantage of greater weight and permanent foundations.

And day after day the archers on both sides shot at and killed each other, mixing personal, individual death with the promiscuous death wrought by the cannon and catapults.

When Michael had been a youngster, he had once asked an instructor in siegecraft: "What happens when a soldier gets to the top of a wall? Does he have to fight his way *down* on a scaling ladder on the inside in the same manner as he fought his way up on the outside?"

There had followed the elementary lessons in city fortifications: how the wall that opposes the enemy is smooth and precipitous, but the interior is hollow and built like a castle, with protected galleries to shoot from, overhung bastions with trap doors through which to drop molten lead on the heads of the attackers, a crenelated parapet on top, and, of course, many flights of steps to the ground. Every means was employed to make access to the top of the walls easy from the inside but difficult or impossible from the outside.

While the various weapons of war on both sides were hurling death and destruction, the engineers who had built Roumeli Hissar and hauled the ships overland now constructed a tower that looked like the tower of a castle. But this tower was a stout framework of timbers sheathed with triple armor of bulls' hide. The armor was pierced with small slits through which archers, picked for their marksmanship, could shoot. And down on the ground there were great heavy wheels, for the armored tower was a mobile structure. It would be required on the last day of the siege. The Greeks observed it as it grew and took shape before their eyes. In it they saw their own death. Inside the ominous creeping structure, protected and safe from all but the heaviest missiles, the deadliest of their foes would lead the sultan's armies to a breach in the walls.

On May 21 the sultan held a council of war in his tent. He left the flap open so he could smell the acrid smell of gunpowder, an odor he had come to relish. Only the sultan sat. His ministers stood in a circle around him. Was it not, he demanded, now time for the final assault?

Zagan Pasha, Hamoud Pasha, and Khalil Pasha gravely nodded their heads. They had all seen the Christian women working feebly on the battlements. In these last days of the city the walls were repaired with marble columns from the churches and tombstones from the graveyards. Anyone who could stand helped at the winches to hoist the repair material into the crumbling walls.

But the imperial astrologer counseled delay. "It is perhaps not my province to advise a larger breach," he began.

The sultan snapped: "It is not! My ships command the sea. My cannon have rotted the walls. I can blast a breach of any size whenever I please."

The imperial astrologer was half scientist, half humbug, heir to the thousand wiles of generations of charlatan forebears; but heir also to the astonishingly accurate mathematical knowledge with which he and all the other solemn frauds of his immemorial ilk practiced their craft and imposed their authority on the credulous. A dreamy, unfortunate prince of Samarkand named Ulug Beg, shortly before being murdered by his own son, had computed some extraordinary astronomical tables. In the four short years since his death, they had run like wildfire among all the scholars and scoundrels of the East and were particularly treasured by magicians. Mohammed's imperial astrologer had his own precious copy of these tables.

He appeared to gaze into the infinite, through half-closed, otherworldly eyes. The sultan and all the military men were silent, respecting his trance, waiting for his words.

"There will come," said this man, "the Night of the Crimson Crescent, mystic, portentous; but not till then, nor thereafter for seven days, will the planets favor Your Majesty."

Mohammed scowled and shook his head impatiently. But the astrologer, still in his trance, continued:

"It will come, the Crescent red like the red of old blood. I see it soon . . . soon. Thus it hath been foretold, thus I see it, thus it shall be." And with that, the imperial astrologer opened his eyes and gazed at the council with his usual inoffensive and utterly noncommittal expression.

"Say that again," the sultan commanded. They all looked a little concerned. Everyone knew that among the hundreds of prophecies predicting the ultimate annihilation of the traditional enemy there had indeed been one which foretold that the moon would give a sign.

"Majesty, I do not know what I said."

"You said," replied the sultan, "that I could attack seven days after a phenomenon you called the Night of the Crimson Crescent. What does that mean?"

"Majesty, I do not know; but if that is what I said, that is the truth."

"If you mean the new moon, it is two weeks hence. I do not propose to wait two weeks. Moreover, new moons are silver, not crimson. The attack cannot wait on a miracle." But the sultan was troubled.

The imperial astrologer crossed his arms in the attitude of submission and lowered his head in a reverent bow. Khalil Pasha tugged nervously at his beard. Even the grand admiral looked worried, and Hamoud Pasha was not one to be frightened by the jinn and the afrits.

"Would it not be prudent," Khalil Pasha dared to suggest, "to wait at least one night to test the astrologer-pasha's prediction? He has often been right in the past."

Often been right? Behind his impassive countenance the imperial astrologer was grinning. Bismillah! Since receiving the tables of Ulug Beg he had never been wrong! The difficult thing was to synchronize the impatient sultan's rapid actions with the slow march of the planets. From the tables the imperial astrologer knew that on the following night, Tuesday, May 22, there would be an eclipse of the moon. From the dampness in the air and the pall of smoke hovering over the battle-torn perimeter of Constantinople, he reasoned that the crescent of the eclipse would appear dark red. He was not merely safely but brilliantly within his own astromagical province when, in the mumbo jumbo of his profession, he predicted the eclipse by a bewildering name.

"I will wait one day," the sultan decided.

The next night, to the everlasting honor of the imperial astrologer, the full white moon went into eclipse and shone red, like a crimson crescent.

Mohammed directed all four of his great guns against a 1,200-foot stretch of wall in front of his tent and concentrated his fire there until, four days later, the entire structure had disintegrated into a mighty heap of confused rubble beyond all hope of repair.

The planets had fought for him. As if that were not enough, the elements now fought for him. A dense fog settled over the city. Dust from the crumbling walls and smoke from the Turkish cannon fastened itself round the invisible droplets so that when the fog struck a man's face his face turned black.

The eclipse that gave heart to the Turks terrified the Christians, who saw in their black faces the mark of the beast, the stigmata of sin and disaster and death. Some said, "It is the ghosts of the sinful departed, fleeing the city." There was uncontrollable rioting and drunkenness. Panic spread in wave after shuddering wave.

Every night after the eclipse, over the dome of Santa Sophia a mysterious shaft of cold, blue flickering light appeared and shot straight up to heaven. No one had ever seen anything like it except a few of the sailors who had beheld at infrequent intervals similar lights dancing on the masts in foggy weather, but the sailors were isolated on their ships, cut off from the city. No one could be comforted by the rational explanation they might have given.

In the face of military disaster and so many sinister phenomena, Constantine, wearied, apprehensive, and ill, fell into a dead faint. He had eaten no more than the humblest of his soldiers during the entire siege and had fought as arduously as any. He regained consciousness to find Justiniani's supporting arm around his shoulders and a flagon of wine at his lips.

"Your Majesty has been starving yourself! Come, man, eat something! Me, I shall die with a full belly, like a good Genoese." With an imperious gesture he produced a furtive palace slave bearing a platter of roast chicken done up in an ecclesiastical vestment, as if the slave were about to bury the holy garment with the other sacred treasures, away from the profane hands of the imminent Turks. "Alexius, here," Justiniani said, "has been feeding me this way for a week. How can an Italian fight on an empty stomach? Nobody has dared touch Alexius since I had him wrap my meals in priestly trappings." The general laughed, delighted at his own cleverness.

Constantine accepted the wine but he pushed the food from him, looking sorrowfully at Justiniani without saying a word. The Italian appeared hurt. "Well, then, Your Majesty, I'll eat it myself. Today everybody's eating. The soldiers have broken into the stores. The people have broken into the wine shops. And, Majesty, they are drinking. Drinking themselves roaring drunk. If the Turks come now, nobody will care."

Next morning at dawn the Turks came, exactly seven days after the eclipse.

Two thousand scaling ladders went up against the walls and a hundred thousand of the *piadé* tried to climb them, but the Christians overset the ladders with long poles. The riffraff of Islam who had come to sacrifice themselves, making their humble lives at last worthy of Paradise, perished in the mud among the rotting corpses of previous assaults. The ladders were set up again, new hordes attempted the ascent again and, like the others, perished. But even as they were toppling to their deaths, Turkish archers picked off the Christian defenders on the walls with arrows. Mohammed's cannon of all caliber exploded on all sides, causing the most appalling carnage that war had ever seen. Against Christian personnel now massed on the walls, the smaller guns shot charges of little stones the size of walnuts, with devastating effect. Catapults on both sides hurled their missiles, and from the Greek engines came blazing barrels of Greek fire, tracing incandescent arcs against the sky, bursting into mushrooms of flame and smoke and scorching death among the massed ranks of the Turkish troops.

At eight o'clock in the morning of the 29th, the sultan, noting that no replacements had taken place for some time among the thinning ranks of the defenders on the walls, deemed the hour favorable for the penetration of the city.

He had promised a pashalik to the man who first scaled the walls of Byzantium. None of the *piadé* had qualified. They lay dead by the thousands in the mud under the walls, among Christians stuck full of arrows, among scorpions and snails and the bones of animals, in the vast democracy of death; but no Turk had yet set foot on Constantinople's ramparts.

A tremendous drum and a silver trumpet summoned the janissaries. The engineers set the tower in motion toward the 1,200-foot breach in the wall near the gate of St. Romanus. Mohammed's personal guards manned it. Ten thousand other janissaries advanced with it, clustering round it as though it were a standard. The mission of the men in the tower was to drop the drawbridge on the rubble that filled the breach and fight their way over the broken stones to lead the sultan's hordes into the capital.

Halfway to the breach a barrel of Greek fire struck the tower squarely, fell, and burst among the ranks that crowded around it. Greek fire was a sticky substance that coated whatever it touched and burned with an intensely hot flame which water could not extinguish. Some bags of sand had been set in a rack around the roof of the tower in the event of just such a fire as this, which, if it could not be extinguished could at least be retarded. Nothing could be done for the unfortunate victims who were covered with the stuff. They leaped into the air, trying to escape the flames, screaming.

Their clothes and presently their skins burnt off; and long after they ceased to move, their saturated turbans continued to blaze like torches.

The smoking tower halted. An engineer posted at the bags let one drop. Men on the ground threw the sand on the flames that had begun to crack the bulls' hide and lick at the corner timbers. The sand appeared to retard the fire somewhat. Then the engineer fumbled: leaning beyond the protection of the armor he was shot in the head by a handgun from the walls. Another man instantly replaced him. He too took a bullet in the neck and fell.

Hassan, who had posted himself at the drawbridge, shouted, "God's name! There's a sharpshooter over there! Get him for me, Michael, before all the engineers get themselves killed!" Michael, like all the other archers in the tower, had been shooting through a port at the enemy; but among the hundreds of Christians who had crowded to defend the breach, it was impossible to identify the sharpshooter.

"I'll try to throw down the sand instead, Hassan."

"No! You'll be killed like the engineers. I can't spare archers. Wait! I'll give the Greeks something to shoot at!"

With his dagger Hassan ripped an oversized port in the armor of the tower and set up the body of the dead engineer behind it in full view of the enemy.

"Hold him steady! Keep out of sight and draw their fire!" he shouted. "I'll go up and heave down the sand!" But Michael hadn't waited.

At that moment Hassan heard a cheer from the men on the ground. Michael had already reached the rack on the roof and begun to throw down the bags. Working the limbs of the dead man to make him look alive, Hassan drew a volley of arrows and another shot from the handgun before the howling, infuriated Christians discovered the trick. The men on the ground flung the sand at the fire and reduced it to smoldering ineffectuality. The tower began to move again, and with it advanced the whole line of janissaries, who had temporarily taken cover behind the corpses of the slain. Michael clambered back down and resumed his place at his port. As the distance to the breach lessened, he could pick out individual targets. It was easy to place his arrows in the faces of the Gavours that shone pink under their open helms. He was not close enough yet to pierce armor. When the distance was less than one hundred feet, he knew that his arrows would be able to penetrate the visors and camails that protected the heads and necks of more important targets, the officers.

Amid the smoke and the horror and the noise, Hassan found himself shouting fatuously, "I'd hate to have been down on the ground with those poor devils!" The sight of the leaping, flaming bodies of his friends was the most sickening thing Hassan had seen in war.

Michael shouted back, "We're lucky!" He knew very well, however, that of all the sultan's troops the men in the tower would be the first to be shot at when they came out from behind their armor and tried to cross over the drawbridge that would soon be lowered.

Someone at the breach with an amazingly accurate little handgun continued to pick off the Turkish engineers, especially the men delegated to work the levers that moved the wheels of the tower.

As the Turks neared the walls, the Turkish cannon elevated their fire so as not to hit their own men and rained projectiles into the streets of the city.

The drawbridge at the top of the tower was ten feet long, but twenty feet from the breach the wheels of the tower encountered the mass of rubble and stone at the foot of the demolished wall. The tower could go no farther. Hassan lowered the bridge. It was short by ten feet. Below him, crawling up the debris, he saw the janissaries of his regiment beating their captain-pasha to the goal.

"God's name!" he shouted, "the artillerymen shot too well!"

But the men in the tower pieced out the distance with a slender scaling ladder: one end rested on the bridge, the other rested on a massive tombstone that the Christians had thrown into the breach. It was an ancient memorial, ripped from a sepulcher erected in the days when Latin was still spoken in Constantinople. Few could read, and none of the janissaries paused to examine the weather-worn remnant of the legend inscribed on it: *Ora pro nobis peccatoribus nunc et in hora mortis.* . . .

Hassan led his men over the fragile, dizzy span. He leaped the last few feet, his yellow janissary shoes landing squarely on the word *mortis.* Thousands of Christian and Moslem eyes had followed the inexorable progress of the tower. Everyone saw the huge figure of Hassan of Ulubad, first of the sultan's men to stand atop Constantinople's walls. Hassan had won his pashalik and in that instant became one of the heroes of the empire. The other men followed him over the ladder. The troops on the ground, encouraged by the success of their leader, swarmed over the rubble into the breach.

The Christians let go a tremendous volley of arrows, handgun fire, and crossbow quarrels. Many janissaries fell before they could take cover among the broken blocks of masonry and return the fire.

A bullet from the first volley caught Hassan in the chest and he fell at Michael's feet. Michael dragged him into comparative shelter below the edge of the great marble slab.

In the weeks of fighting, Michael had come to recognize the face of death. He pressed his hand against Hassan's wound as if somehow he could keep his friend's blood inside his body; he felt the heart beat in spurts, warm and wet against his hand. Hassan's eyes began to glaze.

"It was that cursed Gavour writing on the stone, Michael. It means: 'Pray for us sinners now and at the hour of our death.' "

"I know. Did you see the man who shot you?"

"A knight—fat—grinning; he thinks he's safe up there—his visor's open—a silver gun in his hand."

There was only one fat, grinning Christian left in Constantinople: John Justiniani, still laughing at life, still determined, if he must die, to die with a bellyful of food. He had rallied his men to the walls on both sides of the breach. From that elevation they poured a mass of flanking fire down into the Turks who were swarming through the opening into the vitals of the city.

Michael said, "I'll get you that man." He lowered Hassan's head and wedged Hassan's body as closely as he could against the protecting stone.

"On the wall, Michael, high up on the wall. It's too long a shot. . . . *Ora pro nobis . . . mortis!*"

Some of the janissaries who had ranged themselves round their pasha to protect him with their bodies wondered briefly, as their hands flew and their bowstrings sang, how Hassan of Ulubad came to pronounce the Gavour words with so facile a tongue. No one had ever dared speculate in what country their graying commander had been born.

Michael knew that Hassan was going to die, and his whole body

267

shook with rage—all but his hands, the one that held the bow and the red, wet one that flashed up to his quiver for an arrow. But that hand must have trembled a little, too, because the arrow slipped out of it for an instant and fell to the dusty debris underfoot. The accident calmed Michael. He picked it up. The shaft was red and dirty now, fouled with some of the graveyard earth that still adhered to the tombstone. It was just. Michael fitted it to his bow and took careful aim. He saw Justiniani clearly on the wall, a round, ruddy face with a saturnine grin among the pale, frightened faces of his men. At that moment the general was extending his arm again, the deadly silver gun in his hand, taking aim at another target.

Hassan saw Michael draw. He struggled to his elbow to see what would happen. There was no pain in his face. There was, indeed, no pain in his heart, because his heart had stopped beating. He would live exactly thirty seconds more. At no time had his interest in Michael's shooting been more purely academic. Michael let fly. The arrow sped, and the gun dropped out of Justiniani's hand. The shaft pierced the steel gantlet, penetrated between the two rows of wonderfully articulated little carpel bones in Justiniani's wrist, and then traveled some inches farther, scraping the dirty wooden shaft against the flesh and the splintered bones. The wound was small, but the pain was agonizing.

"Hit him?"

"In the hand, Hassan."

"Long shot. Good shot. *Timur-Yalik!*"

Hassan nodded his head once in grave approval. He thought he nodded it again and again, but his head only sank lower and lower until his chin rested over the wound in his chest, no longer bleeding in spurts. Some few seconds of consciousness remained, though Michael drew the cloak over the open eyes of Hassan, Pasha of Ulubad.

The few seconds stretched into the long sunny hours of a summer afternoon in a Christian village that Hassan remembered well, where a boy who was not called Hassan skipped stones into a sea where the surf roared with a sound like the roar of cannon. Which was strange, because cannon had never been heard of. And then, very gently, it grew dark.

When Michael looked up, the fat man was no longer visible. John Justiniani had retired from the walls, half mad with agony. Michael shouted: "I'll follow him, Hassan! I'll get him yet!" But the shouts of the janissaries drowned out his voice: "Timur-Yalik! Timur-Yalik! *Iron Bow!*"

Hassan's last word before he died had given Michael a name.

With their general gone, the Italians deserted the walls. With the Italians gone, the Greeks lost all stomach for the fight, and the Turks swarmed into the city.

In a melee at the foot of the breach where the danger and influx were thickest, Michael observed a young knight with fair hair and a consecrated face, without a helm, with no charge on his shield, fighting wildly with a sword. A considerable force of Christians surrounded him, trying to protect him as if he were a leader of importance. Beset on all sides by the janissaries, the little group was already doomed.

Only this little island of resistance opposed the torrent of inrushing Turks. The island shrank visibly as the men fell one by one around their leader, until only a handful were left. And then the leader, whom Michael had no means of recognizing, raised his voice in an agonized shout, as desperate and bewildering as the *Eli, Eli, lama sabachthani* echoing down the ages from the lips of another Victim. Constantine cried, "Can there be found no Christian to slay me?" Perhaps in the terror and pain of his martyrdom, only seconds away, the emperor feared falling alive into the hands of Mohammed.

It was a close, easy shot. Michael could have found it in his heart to put the brave, doomed soldier out of his misery.

But Michael did not have to shoot. The man was already smothered by the final rush of his assailants. Michael lowered his bow, reflecting that he had saved another arrow for the fat man with the silver gun.

The next day some janissaries, eager for the reward which the sultan instantly offered for the person of Constantine, living or dead, went back to investigate the pile of corpses at the foot of the broken wall. After some time—there were scores of corpses—they came across the badly slashed body of a slender young man in curious hose.

On the advice of his ministers, cautious to the end, who pleaded with him not to dishearten his people by the possibility of his being killed in his crown, Constantine had fought in the harness of a simple knight; but he had refused to put off the purple buskins, embroidered with the imperial eagles of old Byzantium. And by these the Turks identified the body of Constantine Palaeologus, the last Emperor of the Roman Empire of the East.

Michael was not among the janissaries that day.

CONSTANTINOPLE had not surrendered. Constantinople was beaten and broken into. By universal custom of war, the inhabitants of a city which fought to the end could expect no mercy. And no one had ever accused the Sultan Mohammed II, from that moment, *El Fatih,* "the Conqueror," of softness of heart. Moslem military men would have applauded and Christian military men would have bewailed but condoned the slaughter of every one of Constantinople's Christian populace.

Surprisingly, however, the conqueror saved all but two thousand. Whether he did so by design or by a slip of the tongue was debatable. As a means of firing white-hot the zeal of his soldiers, Mohammed had promised even the meanest of them a rich reward: "The buildings are mine," he had said, "and everything in the city which cannot be moved; but the gold and the jewels of the Gavours, the furniture of their homes, the tapestries on their walls and the embellishments of their temples—whatever can be moved, my faithful soldiers, those things are yours. Be rich and be happy!"

Hamoud Pasha, the grand admiral, the practical engineer, who knew, if anybody did, what could be moved and what could not, had asked with the ghost of a grin: "Does Your Majesty include the population? They move."

And the Conqueror had said, "Yes."

The sack of the city was appalling. For ten hours there was no discipline in Mohammed's well disciplined army. The soldiers went wild. The churches and palaces suffered particularly, for they were full of movable riches. As the day wore on, a preposterous value became attached to peddlers' carts, masons' hods, and the ragpickers' bags, for these humble conveyances enabled a man to loot far more than he could otherwise have carried. On the other hand, wagons that were too big for a single man to handle became the cause of bloody fights among close friends. Whose is what in a common theft?

Soon only pashas and beys, whose authority was great enough to impose some order, appropriated the larger vehicles. The men who were busily filling one, if they were intelligent, shortly stole off and looked for a ragpicker's bag instead. No one wanted to add to a pasha's already great wealth. What a man could obtain for himself was his own; what a pasha might apportion him was problematical. Even the Turkish navy pulled up to the shore. The sailors deserted their ships and rushed headlong through all the gates, now open, to win what they could in the rape of the city.

But no house, unless it was barred, was destroyed. No man, unless he resisted, was killed.

Shortly another common thing came to sell among the Turks for a fabulous price: rope. In this regard the Turkish sailors, though they had come late for the pillage, profited handsomely. They had brought their own ropes with them.

There was no practical motive for killing the Christians; they were worth more as slaves. By the thousands they were shackled together in strings, exchanged, bargained for, cast lots for, and led into servitude. Each captor's mournful train of humans betrayed his character: for some were all men, who would fetch good prices as farm hands, and some were all women, notably the young, slender captives of the most elderly and dignified pashas. A few of the girls were altogether too slender to suit the taste of the graybeards, but none of the Greeks were fat on May 29, 1453.

Justiniani, because of his corpulence, had become an object of sullen hatred during the last days of the siege. When he deserted the walls with his Italians, the Greeks blamed him for the fall of the city, and, if any vestige of order had remained among the Christians, he would certainly have been killed. He and what remained of his forces fought their way from the breach to the walls that faced the Golden Horn on the opposite side of the city. Sometimes they fought bands of marauding Turkish soldiers, and sometimes they fought mobs of angry Greeks. The man who, short of the emperor himself, had been Christendom's ablest champion was reviled as a traitor by many of the embittered vanquished.

It was easy for Michael to follow the Italians across the city. The Greeks, falling on their knees, pleading for their lives, were glad to point out the direction in which Justiniani and his men had disappeared. And then the janissary with blood on his hand and murder in his face suddenly left them alone, sparing them for the whim of the next conquering Turk who came along. Michael grimly followed the trail of the hated fat man.

The hunt led to a part of the city bordering the Golden Horn. Michael reasoned that the Italians were making for the Christian ships.

Shrewd! Shrewd! Michael thought wrathfully. The murderer with the silver gun might escape him yet. From the top of a hill in a neighborhood that suddenly looked familiar, Michael saw all the eighty Turkish ships to the rear of the Christian navy pulled up on the shore under the walls. The Turks were paying no attention to the big vessels of the Gavours anchored along the iron chain. Turkish sailors were pouring through the gaping Phenar city gate. Michael supposed that the Italians would conceal themselves till the first inrush was over and then attempt to fight their way to the ships. He ran down the hill toward the open gate, to wait till the Italians showed themselves. This time his flying arrow would be lethal.

Halfway down the hill he saw some of the *piadé* battering at the street gate of a castlelike mansion. Only then did Michael suddenly realize where he was. This was the villa of the merchant, Filippo Bernardi.

His throat was suddenly constricted. Why was it necessary to beat down the gate of a trader who had sailed back to Italy before the beginning of the siege?

A cold ball of panic growing in his stomach, he forgot about the murderer of his friend. But he remembered now the level glance and the cryptic remark of the palace herald: "Indeed, Commander. So that's why you're here!"

Michael said aloud, "God's name!"

From the ineffective attack of the unmilitary *piadé* on the street gate, Michael suspected the barricade would hold for some time. He ran up to the rear of the house where he knew there was a postern

273

door. He scaled the wall and leaped into the rear courtyard. At the postern entrance of the villa he pounded furiously.

"Angelica! Signore Filippo!"

There was a bright explosion in his head, followed by an uncomfortable, dizzy period of problematical duration. When he opened his eyes, someone was trying to take Hassan's old gift, the jade and gold bow ring, off his right thumb. It was either growing dark or his eyes could not yet focus clearly.

"Four thousand apostles!" he swore, and sat up, looking full in the drunken face of Bernardi's Greek steward. There was a small cask, one of the little barrels used to contain rare liqueurs, under the fellow's arm. The steward managed to hold on to it even while he was busily trying to steal the ring.

"Oh, Blessed Lord Jesus!" the steward gasped. "I thought you were dead." More than a little unsteadily he fumbled for his dagger. Michael helped him withdraw the weapon, then dashed it out of his hand.

"Filth of a pig, say your prayers!" and he tightened his hand around the steward's throat, the powerful right hand that years of archery had caused to grow a little larger than the left.

The steward, while he could still speak, gasped, "Angelica!" and when he could no longer say a word, he shook the miniature cask, which both sloshed, as if there were liquid in it, and rattled, as if it contained pebbles, pointing at it with his other hand.

Michael instantly released the steward's throat. "What about Angelica?"

The steward rubbed his tortured windpipe.

"She's inside," he gasped, pointing through the door.

The steward was not immediately able to say another word. Fear for his life contorted his face. He nodded his head emphatically, "Yes! Inside!" He rattled and sloshed the cask. He pointed to it and then to Michael, attempting to say by pantomime that it was Michael's if Michael would only accept it. He covered his heart with his hand and tried to look inviting. He extended his arms in supplication. He fell on his knees.

"Show me!" Michael commanded fiercely.

The steward jumped up as if there were a spring in his legs, and nodded his head as if there were a spring in his neck.

Then, finding his voice, he croaked: "Did the commander think

274

I intended to murder him? When my beloved mistress has always expressed such affection for the commander?" The voice was groveling. "I wished only to quiet the commander while I advised his illustrious countrymen that there was better hunting down the street. A veritable treasure trove in one of our churches, Commander. I told them to go there and help themselves to the Mass vessels, all gold, very rich; not to besiege this empty old castle." The Greek grew confidential and bent his head close to Michael, breathing his brandy breath into Michael's face. "I wanted to save Angelica for her future pasha! After my eloquent persuasion, the Turks went away to slay the priest and rob the church. Spare me my life! Let me be your slave. My mistress should be honored at becoming a concubine in your illustrious harem. She is a luscious piece. How I envy you. She will please Your Excellency if only for a day."

"God's name, what a filth! Show me where Angelica is!" and Michael incautiously turned to precede the steward through the door. The instant his back was turned the steward raised the cask and hit him over the head again, momentarily felling and stunning him. When he opened his eyes the steward was again trying to take Hassan's bow ring off his thumb.

Michael sat up and grabbed the steward's throat and shook him like a rat.

"Bismillah! This time you shall surely die!" But Michael was still dizzy. The steward wrenched himself free and rushed for the wall, dropping the little cask. Michael heard the man fall and shriek in pain. He ran to the wall and looked down. The steward was hobbling away on his knees. No. In the gathering dusk Michael could make out that the man's knees still bent. Below the knees the leg bones had broken. He was floundering away on fractured legs. They now had an extra pair of joints. Michael drew his bow, furious at the double attempt on his life, more than a little willing to put the unfortunate human out of his agony.

Then he heard a crowd of Turks approaching, shouting *"Kiliselere!"* (To the churches!) All the invaders knew that the churches held the greatest treasures and were looting them first during this, the first night of the sack of the city.

"Oh, well. Let them claim him. Maybe somebody will patch him up for a slave." Michael lowered his bow.

After resting a brief moment, he recovered his senses. He remembered the cask to which the steward had pointed so invitingly, and kicked it through the door. It sloshed and rattled again. Then Michael went in, barring the door behind him.

He knew two rooms in Bernardi's house where Angelica would most probably be found and to these he went first, hoping not to find her. She was not in the great hall. He leaped up the stairs and entered her bedroom. There she lay on the bed, securely trussed and gagged. Her dress was disheveled and torn, as if she had struggled with someone. Michael released her.

At that moment there was a banging on the door of the villa. A band of Turkish sailors, accompanied by a few of the *piadé* had scrambled over the rear wall and attacked the postern entrance of the imposing mansion which, to judge from its great size, might afford almost as good a chance for loot as a church.

Michael had only time to whisper, "No harm shall come to you!" then, for the second time in his life, he picked her fainting body up into his arms. "But stay close to me!" Angelica was too frightened and weak to do anything else.

Michael rushed to the postern door and threw open the wicket.

At the unexpected sight of a turbaned Turkish officer with a Christian girl in his arms the attackers paused incredulously.

"Go away!" Michael commanded. "This house and everything in it are mine, by right of previous entry, according to the decree of the Conqueror. Mark the doors with the crescent. Go back to the *kiliselere!* This big house has already been stripped by its Christian owner. Now go!"

Some of the men grumbled: "Half the *kiliselere* are already looted. The rest are locked. We have to reduce them, like castles!"

Then one of the *piadé* who had fought at the breach recognized Michael.

"It it Timur-Yalik!" he shouted, "the man who shot the Gavour general and emptied the walls of the stubborn Italians! That's Iron Bow! Hassan Pasha's friend. We'd better do what he says." Everyone knew that Timur-Yalik would get a horsetail when the sultan heard of his long spectacular shot and its consequence. The Turks began to cheer him and move away; and one of them cried, "The Gavour owner didn't take *everything* out of the house! Timur-Yalik's done some stripping himself!" Angelica's torn dress was naturally supposed to be Michael's handiwork. "Good night, Iron Bow, and good

———!" The participle was short and immensely popular in every language on the face of the planet.

Angelica's Turkish was good, but that word she did not know. The meaning was clear, however, from the ribald shouts and the graphic gestures of the Turks. Her pale face flushed. Michael slammed the wicket angrily. "Timur-Yalik's in a hurry!" somebody said, laughing coarsely. "We seem to have interrupted his horsetailed lordship!"

With Angelica in his arms, Michael repaced the identical passage to the identical divan as he had on the summer day of his previous visit, when the Greek farmers were slain. As deliberately as before, as reluctant as before to let her go, he gently laid her down.

In the deserted house, alone with the janissary who still wore the turban of the conquerors of the Roman Empire, Angelica wondered wildly if she ought to expect exactly what the cheering Turks had predicted. The most, at the moment, she could hope for was that Michael would remember her with some degree of the affection that had seemed to ring in his parting shout of *"Angelica mia."* Perhaps she would spend the rest of her days in a Turkish harem. Even in the extremity of her panic, Angelica could not bring herself to think that death would be preferable to such a fate; but the flush drained out of her face, and her countenance became as pale as it had been for months with hunger, sorrow, and fear.

Hesitantly she looked up at Michael. There was anxiety, not lust, in his face.

"Are you all right, Angelica?"

She nodded, "Yes, Commander."

"Why are you alone here? Why were you bound and gagged? I thought you were back at home in Europe. Your father promised to go back!"

"Father never had the chance. It's all the fault of the Greek steward. Father was arrested by the same herald who took you to the palace. The same day. Someone told the authorities father was plotting treason with the Turks. It could only have been the steward. He was the only one who knew."

"Your father and I certainly were not plotting treason against anybody. But that doesn't matter now. What happened?"

"Father spent months in a prison down in the city. I didn't know where at the time. They nearly starved him. Then, when the war began to go against us, they treated him better and I was allowed to see him. He was transferred to another of these old villas. In the last week or so they've acted toward him almost as if he were a guest."

"What was the reason for the sudden change?"

"They began to treat him respectfully," Angelica said, "when they thought they could use him as a go-between to negotiate favorable peace terms." Michael thought that that sounded like the Greeks. "Of course, there never were any negotiations. You people simply broke in," she finished, looking away.

Michael winced a little at the "you people," but he had nothing to say in protest. "Where is he now?" he asked.

"In prison. Not far from here, in the other big villa beyond the church. I saw him today. He wanted me to stay with him. He said it was safer in prison, but he looked hungry and I came home to try to buy some provisions in the market for him. Food has been scarce," she said matter-of-factly, with great restraint, "and I had taken him most of what he had had me lay by in the cellars."

Michael looked at her sharply. He had a notion she had been starving herself to feed her father.

Angelica continued: "Yesterday, in that awful fog and bombardment, all the servants ran away except the old charwoman. She and I bought a little basket of food, and then she was killed by a cannon ball that fell in the street."

Michael remembered the terrified, faithful Venetian servant who had signed the cross at him as if he had been a devil. He had always thought of the sultan's magnificent cannon as dropping their projectiles on walls and fortifications, not on frightened old charwomen with baskets on their arms. He supposed that the Christian engineers who hurled the Greek fire that roasted his friends had felt just as impersonally about their catapults. He could only say inadequately: "War is not good, though I have been trained for it since I—joined —the janissaries."

Angelica raised her head spiritedly, and said: "Joined! You didn't join. You were inhumanly kidnaped!" She would have said more, but Michael interrupted her, changing the subject, smiling queerly: "It appears that the steward returned, however. Why? Did he harm you?"

Angelica now blushed furiously and tried to draw the torn top of her gown more modestly about her shoulders. Then, perfectly

278

candidly: "The horrible Greek did his best! But he was very drunk and he beat a quick retreat when I whacked him a few times with a poker!"

"He tied you up."

"I could still kick! And then he heard you at the door."

Michael smiled. "Good girl! He was drunk when I fought him, too. But I didn't do as well as you in my encounter. He knocked me out twice." Michael told how the steward had tried to bribe him with some liquor and then struck him with the keg. "I escaped with no honor, but I captured his weapon."

Angelica said soberly, "I am glad that God has spared you through the war, and from the treachery of the steward. Nevertheless, Commander," she said, smiling a little in her turn, "if you had known what was in the keg besides brandy, the bribe might have been harder to resist. It's father's keg, one of the things the steward came back to steal, and all the steward stole!"

"What else is in the keg?"

"Some of father's diamonds."

Michael looked at the floor unhappily. The diamonds were his, by virtue of the sultan's decree, by right of conquest. He did not want them. So was everything else in Bernardi's house, including Angelica. He did not want her either. Not by right of conquest.

Softly he swore, "Gesù!"

Angelica remarked, "That's profane, unless it's a prayer."

Michael started. Then he made a helpless gesture. "I've been told that sometimes I swear in Italian. I don't know why." His shoulders slumped wearily. "All my life I have hoped to win a name and help win a war. I thought war would be glorious, but I did not imagine a war that would end like this. Well." He straightened his shoulders again. "At least I can go claim your father. It isn't likely that much claiming has been done in the prisons. Rascals and jailbirds wouldn't sell for much."

"Claim my father? I don't understand."

Michael explained that whatever moved, including people, could be claimed for his own by the first Turkish soldier who chose to appropriate such property. "And since you and your father were so extraordinarily careless as to remain too long in this city, I will agree, for an enormous ransom, to release you both and send you back to Venice or wherever you want to go."

Angelica looked him full in the face. "For my father's freedom, you shall have your ransom, Commander. What is it?"

"Not brandy."

"There are diamonds, too, in the keg."

"Not diamonds. They don't move."

Angelica regarded him steadily. "You shall still have your ransom, Commander."

It was Michael who lowered his gaze.

"I was trying to joke, but I cannot. You have shamed me. I knew you were beautiful. I did not think a woman could be beautiful and noble and good and brave as well. Believe me, my heart is wrecked worse than the walls! In God's name, Angelica, why didn't you go back!"

"Without father?"

"I know. I know. It's all of a piece with the rest of you. So you remained, you stood by him. And now you're here, breaking my heart. What is there about you Christians! Dear Angelica, once I spied out a secret. I discovered that you had kept the Gavour dagger I gave you when I was a boy. Give it back to me. That is your ransom. And whatever made you keep it, that much of you I can treasure always. The rest is written on my forehead."

Angelica said: "For my father's sake, I will pay. I had wished a lighter ransom."

"Now I'll go get your father. That is, if there's a safe place to hide you in this house. There is a crescent chalked on every door. No Turk will disturb you. But there are still Greeks about. They might."

There was a safe place, Angelica said, but first she gave him the keys to the prison, "or any other Greek door," she explained. Then she showed him one of the tunnels under the villa, where the air smelled clean and fresh, as if it had just blown off a lake.

Michael left hurriedly. The terror of the day overwhelmed Angelica the instant he was gone. Alone, she wept a little and said aloud to the candle and the bats: "He once kissed me and called me 'his Angelica.' He doesn't feel that way any more." She felt her shoulders, thin after fifty-three days of the siege. "Am I so terribly scrawny and unattractive?" She had heard that the Turks liked plump women.

FLAMES had begun to flicker about the apse of the Christian church which Michael had to pass before he reached Bernardi's palatial prison. The church had resisted. So, apparently, had the clergy in the adjoining house where they lived.

A big man, in ecclesiastical garb, lay groaning under an immense, blazing timber from the roof of the rectory. There was no one else in sight. Michael tried with all his strength to lift the enormously heavy timber from the body of the pinioned man, but was unable to budge it. The priest stopped groaning and looked at the janissary with intense, suffering eyes.

"I'm afraid it's no use, gentle infidel. It took several of your countrymen to hold me, and rather more to lift this thing onto me."

"Try! Push up when I do!"

The priest strained. The timber did not move.

Michael looked for some means of extinguishing the fire. But fire cannot be extinguished with paving stones, and there was no water.

"Why didn't you open your temple? No one would have harmed you."

"It was full of frightened people. Everyone was afraid of being killed. I was afraid, also, to my own great sin. Most of us have already perished."

"But this! Who did this cursed thing? He shall pay for it. I am a commander. This isn't according to orders!"

The Christian smiled. "Young man, do not expect the commands of men to be obeyed when people ignore the commands of God. In justice to your countrymen, however, I will say that the timber wasn't burning nearly so fiercely when they crushed me under it. I have no doubt they thought it would soon smolder out."

On that score there was enormous doubt in Michael's mind. He remembered the Greek fire and his own friends dying.

The flames were now licking about the knees of the priest, who groaned again.

Michael snatched at his turban and began to beat at the fire with it.

"I'm afraid," said the priest through clenched teeth, sweat streaming from his forehead, "that you're only fanning the fire. Do, please, stop." Michael paused and his turban instantly burned to ashes.

He knelt close to the priest's tortured face. "Brave man," he said, "I cannot save you. Give me leave to put an arrow through your heart, in all compassion. I am skillful. For charity's sake this time, I will shoot to kill. You will not feel a thing. I cannot stand here and see you suffer. I beg you, permit me to kill you."

"There was once one Who suffered greater pain," the priest replied, but the voice was a series of gasps, and Michael could scarcely understand him. Then he said, "In my sin and my shame, I confess that your painless arrow would be welcome."

Michael drew. His hand shook. He prayed for an angel to guide the shaft true to the heart of the suffering man.

The priest observed the action. For the first time his eyes filled with horror. "Deceived, unfortunate man, *no!* You misunderstood. Put up your arrow. In the name of our Lord Jesus Christ, I forbid you to take my life!"

The fire had begun to melt the pitch out of a great knot in the wood near the priest's face. The pitch began to smoke.

Michael cried, "How can you Christians die so courageously! All Greeks are cowards. I've been taught so all my life!"

A light from the fire that was killing the priest illuminated his unblinking eyes. He spoke: "On the mountain, Jesus said, 'Ask and it shall be given you: seek, and ye shall find; knock, and it shall be opened unto you.' You need not knock, my son. The door is open now. The Turks have battered it down. You need only seek. The

282

answer is in there!" and his head moved again toward the church. The priest's eyes closed, though his lips continued to move in prayer.

"And if I ask something, sir?"

"Ask in faith," the priest replied without opening his eyes. "If you ask in faith, it shall be given you."

Michael, still kneeling, prayed: "Blessed Lord Jesus, shorten this brave man's pain. This I ask in my old faith, in the name of Your Father, in Your own name, and in the name of the Holy Ghost." In a few seconds the pitch knot belched forth heavier smoke, suffocating the priest. He choked twice, convulsively, and died.

The apse of the church, the semicylindrical wall domed with a quarter-sphere roof that stands to the eastern end of a Greek basilica covering the high altar, had now begun to buckle and crack as the conflagration took hold of the building. Light from the fire shone through the multicolored stained-glass windows, as if a high service of jubilation and thanksgiving were going on inside. The stiff, flat Byzantine saints pictured on the windows grew round and three dimensional in the wavering illumination; and after centuries of decorative, polychrome immobility, seemed suddenly restored to a life and movement of their own.

To the end of his days Michael never regarded the quick, painless death of the priest as anything but a miracle. No instructor propounding a thousand erudite volumes of theological speculations could have been half so convincing concerning the efficacy of Christian prayer as this overwhelming personal experience.

Michael entered the church—neither to seek nor to ask, but to give thanks. Without conscious recognition, he had changed. His transformation from a Moslem to a Christian had occurred naturally, fully, and inevitably, in the plenitude of soul-sure conviction, but as little heeded by himself as the burning of his turban.

In the church the whole vast area above the altar was in flames, and the altar itself had been desecrated and stripped of its precious furniture. High above it on the wall only an immense crucifix remained of the hundreds of Christian symbols which had decorated the sanctuary. This larger-than-life representation of the death of Jesus had not been molested, partly because it was out of easy reach and partly because it was only a wood carving, not even gilded. It was burning.

With the shyness of one who for years has prayed to the emptiness stretching from Anatolia to the Arabian Desert, Michael approached the intimacy of a shrine dedicated to the Virgin, and knelt and prayed.

Something like the distortion of time that had occurred at his father's grave now happened again; but whereas on that occasion time had stood still, time now seemed to race backward at a preternaturally rapid rate, stimulating his memory and mind to swift activity. The years and events of his childhood surged back with pellucid clarity. The fog of war and the smoke of cannon overspread his years as a Mohammedan: they lost shape, grew misty and cloudlike, funnelling themselves into a little compartment of his mind like the genie returning to the bottle, soon to be sealed, cast away, and forgotten.

The fire above the altar which had ignited the crucifix at length ate through the heavy timber. Michael heard a sound like a falling tree and turned to see the immense crucifix topple from its fixture and fall flaming on the ruins of the high altar. It happened to fall with the figure of Christ underneath, making Michael think of the priest who had just died.

It no longer being safe to remain in the burning building, Michael went out again into the street. To his astonishment the timber that had lain on the dead man was now reduced completely to ashes, and the body so nearly consumed as to bear no resemblance to anything that had been alive. Michael concluded that he must have been in the church more than an hour, forgetting how rapidly and fiercely rotten old wood can burn.

He touched his girdle to make sure that the keys to the Greek prison were still there. Keys to the prison, indeed! Angelica had had him wrench out the sizable bung from the keg with which the steward has twice so ignobly felled him. With her slender hand she had reached in and drawn out a handful of diamonds, dripping with brandy, momentarily yellow and wet, blazing like sapphires transfigured.

It was not so late as he had imagined. Constantinople's agony was only beginning. It takes some time to loot a dozen square miles of a densely built metropolis. The remote sections had not yet even been penetrated.

There were still Greek guards at the door of Bernardi's prison. Michael counted twelve of them, passing a bottle among themselves and talking loudly. He flattened himself against a wall, deep in the shadow cast by the climbing moon, waning, old, and misshapen, shedding its cold, liverish light over the conquered city. From his hidden vantage point Michael calculated that he could shoot perhaps half of them before the rest could run away. Despite the fact that he had shot Greek soldiers all that morning, he now found himself reluctant to shoot any more. And there was also the practical consideration that if he killed or frightened away all the guards, he would still be locked outside the prison. He knew how strong these old villas were, and did not want to waste time trying to break into this one.

On the other hand, if he strode peaceably up and attempted to bribe the guards with a gem apiece, it would be no more than natural for the Greeks to fall upon him, kill him, and rip his clothes apart to see where he had hidden the rest. How could a man have on his person exactly twelve diamonds, no more and no less?

Before shooting, Michael decided to attempt a ruse.

He drew his scimitar and ran at them shouting the battle cry that had meant death to the Greeks for fifty-three days:

"Allah! il Allah!"

The guards, stunned by the sudden attack, could not immediately distinguish whether Michael was alone or not. Their fears peopled the shadows behind him with a thousand howling savages. Some of them dropped their torches, others their swords. All but two of them took to their heels and fled round to the rear of the villa. The remaining two stanchly held to their post and their bottle. This brace of worthies was more brave, more intoxicated, and more intelligent than the others. They stood firm, convinced that death was at hand and that a wise man should meet it with dignity, gloriously, drunk.

Michael watched his adversaries melt away. He thrust all but two of the diamonds in his girdle and ran into the circle of torchlight, lowering his swordpoint.

"Good Christian men," he said, "I am an Italian. These clothes I took from a dead Turk. I must see your prisoner. I've an important message for him."

The two unsteady Greeks glared suspiciously, holding their swords ready to protect themselves from the rush of men they expected to materialize out of the darkness.

When nothing happened, one of them growled, "We don't like Italians," and the other said: "I think you're a Turk. No Italian ever shouted 'Allah' like that. We don't like Turks either. Brother, let's kill him now." They raised their swords and stepped awkwardly forward. Michael knew he could cut down both the drunkards in less than a second, but the door would still be locked. And he thought he saw a furtive head peeking round an angle of the villa.

He held out his open hand with two of the biggest diamonds the men had ever seen glittering in his palm.

"Look, gentlemen," he said, "I am whatever you choose to think I am. I haven't enough of these for all of you. My shout was intended to frighten cowards, but you two heroes shall earn these. Quick, now. Let me into this house. I must deliver my message to Filippo Bernardi."

The men hesitated. They were staring into Michael's hand as if hypnotized. One of them said: "He knows the prisoner's name. That's supposed to be a secret, isn't it, brother?" The other wrinkled his forehead and tried to remember if the name was secret or not.

Michael said, "Hurry! I think the rest are returning."

The less befuddled of the guards answered: "All right, but I still think you're a Turk." He held out his hand for the jewels.

Michael closed his fist over them. "Not so fast, my friend. First open the door. Or do you think I ought to call some of the other men? Maybe they'll be the ones to earn these diamonds."

The guard said: "Oh, no. We'll take them! Don't call."

The other bobbed his head up and down and pronounced with the grave wisdom of intoxication: "Brother, this is no Turk. This is an Italian, no doubt of it!"

They opened the door. Michael gave them the jewels, one to each man. They bowed simultaneously, magnificently, and slammed the door shut on him.

Behind the door he heard them say: "It is a pleasure to have another Italian hypocrite in our prison. Let him join his fellow traitor. They'll both be dead before morning."

Perhaps three minutes after the door slammed shut, Filippo Bernardi, cowering on his prison bed, heard fierce shouts and the clash of steel from the courtyard, then Greek voices, shrieking in pain or screaming for mercy. It was apparent that the Turks had penetrated this part of the city and were killing the guards. The merchant was convinced in his heart that he was living out the last minutes of his last hour. The Greeks would now slit his throat as an Italian traitor, and, if they spared him, the Turks would strangle him as a Christian smuggler.

Then, unexpectedly, there was a closer, more intimately threatening noise—the clang of a steel sword against the door of his room.

Bernardi rose to his feet. "Enter," he said wearily. "The door is open."

With the dignity of utter exhaustion and hopelessness, the merchant adjusted his glasses and peered to see whether his murderer would be a vengeful Greek or a conquering Turk. It was neither. Instead, a turbanless figure in the yellow shoes of a janissary strode into the focus of his spectacles; as the image grew sharp, Bernardi recognized Michael.

"Commander!"

Michael shook his head, smiling. "No. Michael da Montelupo." Very briefly he tried to explain all that had happened.

Bernardi's despair gave way to hope, and hope robbed the old man of the momentary courage with which he had risen to face death. Bernardi sat down again on the bed, pale and trembling.

"It is a miracle," he said in a low voice. "I'd almost forgotten they sometimes happen."

Michael concluded his hurried recital: "And so I came to 'claim' you, signore, though I am no longer a janissary and no longer command anything."

"Except your soul! And perhaps you'll command a great deal more than that," Bernardi answered in a tense voice. "But this is no place for talk. I must get back to my daughter."

The shouting had died down outside. Michael opened the shutter a cautious crack and glanced down into the court. The Greeks were dead. The courtyard swarmed with ragged, turbaned men.

"It is the *piadé*, Signore Filippo."

There was a grating noise and an impatient banging on the door. Someone was trying the iron keys from a dead guard's ring, one after another, in the lock.

"I may be as much of a prisoner as you," Michael said. "It will be awkward to explain to the *piadé* how a janissary came to closet himself amicably with a Gavour while the Greek guard were still alive. I cannot successfully shoot our way out against so many."

Bernardi suddenly asked, "Have you any more diamonds?"

Michael reached into his girdle and drew out the jewels that had filled Angelica's hand and somewhat more than half filled his own.

"Your daughter entrusted me with quite a number, signore."

Bernardi sighed at the sight of the gems but he thought swiftly. "Your story must be true," he said. "Today only a madman would convert to Christianity in Constantinople. God has touched your heart—or your head." Then he added vehemently: "She didn't entrust the diamonds to you! Michael, they're yours, and many, many more! If we live, I'll tell you why they are yours. Later, when there's time, but now—" Bernardi felt himself strong again as a plan for escape worked its magic on him. "Now you must darken those yellow shoes. Here!" He emptied a bottle of wine over them. "There, I've shod you in purple, like an emperor! Now, get rid of that bow. Throw it under the bed. Your arrows, too. Keep your sword—No! It's the wrong shape. Under the bed with it. Now my cloak around you—so. Dear God!" Again the uncanny resemblance to Nicolo da Montelupo struck him. "This time the soul as well as the body has come back! We shall fight our way out, Michael, but not with swords. Some day, please God, you will be old. Then you will have to fight with subtler weapons. Son of my friend, come down and let me show you how an old man fights."

With every vestige of his Turkish costume hidden under the long Venetian cloak, Michael followed Bernardi down the stairs.

"If you're thinking of bribing Turks," Michael whispered, "it won't work."

"It always works," Bernardi replied. "It's just more expensive than bribing Christians, that's all."

At the door Bernardi began to shout at the top of his voice, "Gentlemen! Gentlemen! Let us out!"

There was a momentary pause and a silence. "Save us!" Bernardi cried. "We are prisoners of the perfidious Greeks! Try the big key, gentlemen! The rusty one, shaped like a double cross. That will unlock this door!"

In other circumstances Bernardi's Turkish would have made Michael smile. The keys jangled. The proper one rattled in the lock. Bernardi whispered, "Don't say a word. Let me talk." The door swung open. The leader of the *piadé's* gang stepped over the threshold.

"They're mine," the Turk said, pointing to the Christians.

Bernardi awkwardly assumed the Oriental posture of submission. Michael, looking at the floor, followed the action in as ungainly a manner as he could contrive. He thought he had once seen the leader of the mob selling dried fish in a Brusa bazaar.

Bernardi addressed the leader. "I yield myself and my idiot son to the noble pasha-commander," he said.

The crowd began to hoot and shout with laughter: "Ali's got a horsetail from the Gavour! Hail Ali, Ali Pasha!" and some of them bowed mockingly. The leader's face darkened in anger.

Bernardi made his voice a cringing whine: "We are neutral Europeans from Galata. We never wanted to resist. The cursed Greeks locked me and my unfortunate son in this house. He was born deaf and dumb. You can see for yourself he is cross-eyed." Michael looked up. His eyes were monstrously crossed. "And for the pasha-commander," Bernardi continued, "I have a gift, because he has saved us from the Greeks." Bernardi reached out his hand. Michael saw the leader's hand make a reciprocal motion, the instinctive gesture of a street vendor. Half a dozen diamonds trickled into the open palm and sparkled there for a split second before the grimy fingers closed on them.

The man asked, "Have you more of these?"

Bernardi laughed. "Does a man carry all his wealth in his hand? Certainly I have more. My rooms upstairs are full of them!" He flung the rest of the handful of diamonds down the hall. They bounced like shining hail. The rabble rushed through the door and fell upon them, clawing each other, fighting for the fortune that every dancing sparkle represented.

One Turk did not enter the house, however. While the rest flung themselves through the open portal, he lingered, eyeing Bernardi with a sinister, appraising glance. Bernardi and Michael stepped out of the prison. The man stepped forward and met them. Bernardi held his finger up to his lips with a conspiratorial air: "And for you, Effendi," he whispered, "I have saved the best! Would you shut the door just a trifle? The others must not see this magnificent jewel!"

The man hesitated. Then, glancing cautiously over his shoulder, he turned to close the door. Bernardi plunged his dagger hilt-deep in the man's back. He knew exactly how to reach the heart from that angle. The dead man collapsed without a gasp.

"You were too intelligent," Bernardi whispered over the corpse. Then he and Michael ran for their lives.

The entire church was now burning with a roar like a whirlwind. One solid sheet of flame shot up from where the roof had been. Lead and glass melted out of the windows and dripped down the red-hot walls, like a water that could live in fire. A block beyond it they could still feel the fierce heat on the backs of their necks.

Michael supported Bernardi by the elbow and helped him run.

"The bribe worked, signore, but it wouldn't have worked if the men had been janissaries."

The merchant saved his breath for running.

CHAPTER
35

BERNARDI'S villa stood dark and inviolate, protected from sack by the crescents on the doors.

There is a limit to the strength which even the combined stimulus of fear of death and hope of life can impart to an old man's legs.

Walking now, Bernardi approached the villa door and fitted a key into the lock. Michael followed him inside. The merchant locked the door again behind them. Then he opened a shutter and flung away the key with so dreadful a curse that Michael, himself no stranger to picturesque eastern profanity, felt his spine tingle: "Blessed, white, leprous St. Lazarus, rot off my fingers and hands if ever they touch a Greek key again! Now, Michael, my daughter!"

But Michael paused to throw open all the rest of the shutters, and light the tapers in several rooms. "The house must look busy and bright," he said. "It is marked as being looted. Soldiers would not steal in the dark; they want to see what they are getting. This will gain time."

"We'll need it," Bernardi said, rubbing his tired legs with one hand and lighting two watchman's lanterns with the other.

In the tunnel Angelica heard a noise. She blew out her candle, clenched her fist and thrust it against her mouth till the white teeth left white marks upon the knuckles. Then, with a sob of relief, she recognized her father and ran and clung to him, weeping. There was another Christian behind him whom she did not know at first.

Bernardi patted her shoulder and lifted her chin tenderly. "Child,

291

I thank God you are safe!" Some of the urgency had gone out of his voice. Two heavy doors lay securely bolted behind him, the door to the tunnel itself being cunningly hidden in a cook's pan closet in one of the kitchens. A scheme for their safety which Bernardi had planned as he rubbed his tired legs made his voice vibrant with a confidence that Angelica could not share and which puzzled Michael. "Here is a man you know slightly, Angelica. A Christian and a refugee, like ourselves."

Angelica blinked her tears away. "Refugee? Christian?" Then, suddenly recognizing Michael in his Venetian cloak, "The commander!" she exclaimed.

Bernardi said, "It is Michael, the Lord of Montelupo. He has chosen a hazardous hour to return to the faith of his childhood, but he has related to me the circumstance of his conversion, and it would seem that God works His greatest miracles even while the heathen are destroying His temples. My dear, Michael saved my life." The merchant glanced slyly at his daughter. "It will please me if you are polite to him."

Polite to him! In a low voice Angelica said: "He saved me, too. From the Greek steward."

"Indeed?" her father remarked. "He didn't mention that. Is there anything to eat here, my daughter? We shall need our strength for what we have to do." When she did not answer, he went over to rummage in a storage chest. Reaching in he pulled out a loaf of bread, which he immediately began to munch. "You laid in fewer supplies than I warned you to, Angelica. This chest is all but empty." A thought struck him and he glanced at her suspiciously. "You've insisted that there was still plenty to be had in the markets, but, dear child, I think you've been stuffing me while you starved yourself. . . . You did, didn't you, child?" His voice was tender.

Angelica had gone toward Michael, both hands outstretched to clasp his. He had instantly taken her into his arms and kissed her on the mouth. They were still kissing when Bernardi, his mouth full of bread, looked up from the barren chest and the single loaf. He held up the lantern, watching them tolerantly.

"I stopped such an embrace once before," he remarked quietly, "calling it a ruse, which I thought it was. And I confess that I was pleased to have it so, greedily ambitious to handle your patrimony for a while longer, perhaps forever. Now I must stop you again, for a better reason. Are you two children aware that over our heads at this moment there are two hundred thousand Turks and a hundred thousand Greeks, any one of whom would be delighted to slaughter us all? Have a bite of this bread. We must get out of the city at once."

Bernardi offered the loaf to Angelica. He thought of the meals she had brought him in prison and felt ashamed of himself. She refused it, however. Both Angelica and Michael at that moment could honestly state that they were not hungry.

Michael said: "The only way out of the city is through the streets, and the streets are getting more dangerous for Christians every minute. The best plan is for me to put on my janissary equipment again, shackle you two, and conduct you to the gate as my slaves."

Michael looked so rueful at the prospect that Bernardi burst out laughing.

"No, Michael; the streets aren't the only way out of the city. And we are not going alone. This time you must not refuse to come home with us."

Michael said honestly: "I wanted to come before. I loved your daughter then. I conceived that my honor and religion forbade it. If she will have me now—I am penniless, however!"

The grave, interminable financial negotiations that preceded a Moslem marriage were Michael's only criterion as to how such things were arranged in Christendom.

Bernardi snapped: "Oh, nonsense. You're richer than—than— good God, I think you're actually richer than I am. On the ship I shall show you the last thing your sainted father, my best friend, the only friend who ever trusted me completely—I shall show you the document with which he made me your guardian. He thought he was giving me a power of attorney for only a few weeks while he rode to Adrianople to try to obtain your release from the janissary corps. That document became his will. I have never, never quite betrayed your father's trust in me. Though the temptation has been strong, and grown stronger as the years went by, when you appeared irrevocably Mohammedanized . . . and as the treasure grew."

This confession was difficult for Bernardi, and for a moment he lowered his head as if he were afraid to look Michael in the eye. He looked up again quickly, however, and said, "As for my daughter's 'willingness to have you,' as you put it, I am not so blind even in this gloom that I cannot see the stars in her eyes! Up, now, and to my ship!"

There were no wells in Constantinople. Without water a city will perish of thirst in a siege. Therefore, in the early centuries of the Roman Empire of the East, the Latin-speaking emperors had excavated immense reservoirs in the rocky soil under their capital and filled them with clear, pure water conveyed by a system of spendid aqueducts from hills beyond the city. These stupendous feats of building rivaled the cliff caves of the Pharaohs in magnitude and excelled them in beauty, colossal memorials to the genius of old Roman engineering. The cisterns, extensive as lakes, were built to last forever. Their thousands of marble columns constituted the fundament of vast stretches of the city, upholding mighty cathedrals as well as light, flimsily-built slum sections, city streets, and whole parks where, through the ages, giant trees had grown. Sometimes their thirsty roots smelled the moisture underground and grew long, ghostly tendrils snaking down through the undisturbed silence and gloom till they touched the placid surface. At the point of contact there grew a web of white, hair-fine tendrils to drink up the water. Few Greeks ever understood why some of the trees throve so magnificently.

The location of these vast underground caverns was repeatedly forgotten and repeatedly rediscovered, only to be forgotten again as generation after generation of Byzantines grew more and more literate but less and less practical.

In the long, harrowing night of Tuesday, May 29, 1453, with turbaned conquerors looting the marble city of the Caesars, the ancient vigor of the Romans found its ultimate counterpart in the youthful vigor of the Turks, who could erect a Roumeli Hissar in ninety-two days and drag by main force eighty ships ten miles through a forest in one night.

"But some of the reservoirs are known," Bernardi said, "at least, to one who could foresee their utility and expend some effort and money to trace them. I have known men to get rich going bankrupt: it is always prudent to plan one's retreat in an orderly manner."

They took up their lanterns, and Bernardi led them into the depths of the tunnel, which presently curved and grew narrow until they had to walk single file. The gradient became steeper as the

294

passage spiraled under the foundations of the villa through the heart of the hill on which the building stood. Around one abrupt turn Michael could see nothing but a blank wall, as if the tunnel had ended; then it appeared as if Bernardi, in the lead, were slowly sinking into a black hole in the earth.

Bernardi cautioned them, his low-pitched voice echoing eerily along the walls, "The steps are difficult. Walk carefully." He felt his way down a steep flight of steps cut spiralwise down into the rock and stone-hard earth. Michael followed; Angelica followed him. A damp wind and the smell of water blew up from the surface of the reservoir below. The flames in the lanterns fluttered and smoked. "There are some fifty steps in all," Bernardi called confidently. He seemed to know where he was going. "Do not be alarmed. There's a sound skiff at the bottom. At least," he added to himself, "there should be. . . . Are you all right, Angelica?"

"Of course, Father." But the hand in Michael's shook.

This was the retreat that Bernardi had planned as a desperate resort if war should catch him unaware, but he had not planned to be arrested and held in confinement until the final day of the siege. The confidence in his voice was half hope, half bravado. Among the hundred thousand inhabitants of the fallen city, it was almost incredible that others should not know the secrets of the reservoirs. It was possible that the skiff had already been discovered and stolen by refugees entering by other tunnels. At the bottom of the shaft, where the steps ended in a stone landing about as big as a bed, he held up his lantern and searched anxiously into the darkness. The footing was dank with moisture absorbed by the stones and slippery with vegetation that could grow in the dark, moss and white mushroomlike fungi. He nearly fainted with relief when he saw the skiff tied up where it should be, white with mildew.

"It was freshly painted two months ago," he said. He kicked the stern with his foot. The wood thudded firm, and the reassuring sound echoed back from the high vaulted roof and the myriad columns of the reservoir. "Can a janissary scull a boat, Michael? We'll have to break the sweep into a paddle otherwise. I am much too tired to exert myself now."

"I can do it," Angelica said.

Michael replied, "Janissaries aren't boatmen, but a Venetian never forgets how to handle a scull."

He knew he ought to stand up to work the sweep, but the floor boards were slippery. So he sat down in the stern to get what speed he could in that posture, while Angelica and her father cautiously settled themselves on the bare planking in the center of the little boat. Michael worked the skiff slowly away from the landing, which instantly disappeared into the darkness.

"Keep close to the wall," Bernardi advised. "It is a longer way, but the only way we shan't get lost." In the utter silence his voice instinctively sank to a whisper. The towering wall of the reservoir, formed of huge granite rocks wonderfully chiseled and fitted together, slid into the circle of light cast up from the lanterns and disappeared again to the stern, causing the curious illusion that the wall, not the boat, was moving. Out in the gloom on the other side the huge columns that supported the roof appeared to march majestically through the black, unruffled water.

As they progressed underground beyond the hilly area where Bernardi's villa stood, the roof overhead grew thinner, and from time to time, when a city street happened to be above them, they could hear muffled noises and far-away shouting.

So, it may be, the dead in their graves hear the sounds of the living, Bernardi thought; but he kept the morbid speculation to himself. "We had best darken our lights," he said aloud. "Our next port of call may be occupied." Reaching back to draw the shades around the lanterns, he saw Angelica's hand resting on something round. "Now what little keepsake did you treasure enough to bring with you, daughter?"

Angelica said, "The brandy keg, Father. I thought anything that could tempt a Greek and open a prison door and stun a janissary was worth saving."

Her father looked at her admiringly. *"Angelica mia,"* he said, "you are a miracle! For the second time this precious thing saves my life!" He pulled out the bung and swallowed a mouthful of brandy. He felt diamonds against his lips as he lifted the little keg. With a grateful sigh and a careful hand he refitted the bung and knocked it firmly into place with his knuckles. "I think I never had a more refreshing restorative. Michael, if your arms are tired I can prescribe a good Christian tonic. Also, it will quiet your splashing for a moment. There is no need for such speed."

Michael laughed. "I must relearn some Christian habits more at my leisure, signore. For the moment I dare not trust internally what did so much external damage."

Meanwhile, he was more cautious with his sweep. A vertical rectangle of black emptiness now loomed up in the surface of the wall, which continued to move past the dim light of the shaded lanterns.

"Be silent," Bernardi whispered. "It is the landing."

Michael stopped sculling and used the sweep as a rudder to steer alongside the landing. It was like the one they had left an hour before, but this one was occupied, and one of the occupants was still alive. Bernardi threw open the lantern shutters. In the sudden clear light they saw a boat bashed to pieces by hurled stones, mute witness to a frantic struggle.

"They resisted," Michael said sadly, "and the Turks went wild."

Among the dozen corpses of the men and women, mercilessly slaughtered as they had fought their way to the boat, which could only have taken them to an equally dangerous part of the city or lost them forever underground, was one of the turbaned conquerors. He was a janissary, bleeding the remnant of his life away from a dozen mortal wounds, horribly blinded by the bare, clawing fingers of the desperate victims who had preceded him in death. His arms flailed weakly before his face as if he were still defending himself, and his head jerked up and down like a fish out of water. Filaments of crimson snaked out from the stones of the landing and traced a slow pattern on the black surface of the water.

Angelica stifled an involuntary scream and ran toward the stairs. Michael held up his lantern. He and Bernardi looked at the agonized Turk and then at each other. Then the merchant asked, "Will you or must I do what is necessary?"

Michael's hand went to the dagger at his waist. "I will do it, signore. I know him."

Bernardi supported his daughter slowly up the stairs. He heard Michael say gently, "Rest thou in the Paradise of your God, comrade," and in a moment Michael rejoined them, his face white and set in the ruddy light of the lantern.

Far off on the surface of the water another lamp was burning, illuminating the marble columns so they shone like a forest of petrified trees. Their skiff had drifted away, propelled by the force of their feet as they leaped to land. For once the merchant had forgotten his diamonds.

Michael was now armed. There were arrows in his girdle; a bow was in his hand. He looked at them strangely. "I knew him," he said again.

Bernardi laid his hand gently on Michael's shoulder for a moment. Then he said: "There is a bakery shop above us not a hundred yards from the Gate Phenar. If the gate is open—"

"All the gates are open," Michael said.

"Good. We must contrive to get through the gate and walk, if we cannot steal a skiff, under the walls till we come to my warehouse on the Galata side."

Michael said, "That's a long way, signore. Perhaps we can do better."

The bridge between Galata and Constantinople had been destroyed by the Greeks as a security measure in the first days of the siege; but after Hamoud Pasha had set his ships down to the rear of the Christian navy, the Turks had built a pontoon bridge near the same place, formed of eleven hundred big wine barrels helpfully donated by neutral Galata. On this structure the sultan had planted some light cannon. Their small shot had proven effective against personnel on the walls, and the bridge itself had been used as a means of transport for troops during the final assault of the morning.

"There may be some watchmen or engineers on the bridge, signore; but if there are not too many I may be able to save us a tedious walk around the shores of the Golden Horn." He tried the strength of the bow. It was a good one.

They pushed open a trapdoor in the floor of the bakery shop between a work table and a cold furnace, where the fire had been out for days, there having been no flour to bake in Constantinople. The bodies of the shopkeeper and his family lay huddled in a corner. The shelves were empty and the hampers and bins had been broken open.

"No Turk did that," Michael said. "No Turk was hungry."

Torchlight shone through the broken shutters and the smashed door. Outside they heard running feet and men shouting in Italian.

"They are Genoese," Angelica said, catching the accent.

Bernardi listened. "It must be Justiniani and his mercenaries." The three hid in the shadow of the shop and watched perhaps fifty

298

men hurrying down the street. Their progress was hampered by their leader, who seemed scarcely able to walk. In the torchlight Michael could see that he had cast off his steel corselet, as if it were too heavy for him to carry. His undershirt was slit to give his right arm more room to swell: from the hand to the shoulder it was puffed up stiff, green, and jointless, like a gigantic cucumber. As the stumbling, gibbering man passed the door of the shop, Bernardi observed: "Somebody shot Justiniani with a poisoned arrow. Did the Turks employ poison generally, Michael?"

Michael averted his face, which had suddenly contorted into stark fury. He was praying a Christian prayer for strength not to put another arrow into the rolling eye of the fat man with the silver gun.

Some Italian refugees, looking fearfully over their shoulders, followed in the wake of the little band of soldiers who had chosen this relatively quiet moment in the early hours of the morning to make a dash for their ships. Conquered and conquerors alike moved slowly or slept exhausted just before dawn on the first morning of Constantinople's servitude.

Bernardi said: "Michael, I doubt if you'll need your Turkish bow. It would look suspicious. Let us fall in with our fellow Italians, behind the Genoese. This is a heaven-sent opportunity."

Michael broke the bow savagely in his hands. "Bismillah!" he cried, "God's name!" It was the last Moslem oath he ever uttered. He flung the pieces of the broken bow against the cold side of the bake oven. Angelica wondered at his towering anger. As surreptitiously as possible, they joined the group behind the Italians.

Justiniani was out of his wits with pain, but his lieutenants had taken command and planned the escape shrewdly. The Turkish army had momentarily disintegrated into two's and three's and individual soldiers, all heavy with sleep and burdened with loot and strings of slaves. The fifty-odd Italians fleeing for their lives still presented a compact and formidable aspect. Why fight for fifty mercenary soldiers at four o'clock in the morning when a hundred thousand rich civilians could be taken at will with less effort? Why lose one's personal captives or drop one's personal pillage when the Italians could escape only as far as Galata? The Turks who saw them laughed. The Italians were fleeing so hopefully for their ships! It was what the

Italians would see when they passed the city gate that made the Turks laugh.

Under the walls on the shores of the Golden Horn the Genoese set up a dismal wail.

In the first gray light of dawn they saw all that remained of the Christian navy under full sail.

Rumor had already outrun and exaggerated the truth. A few terror-stricken men, swimming out to the ships, pleading to be taken aboard, breathlessly related the death of both Justiniani and the emperor and described some scenes of local battles which, because they bore the stamp of eyewitness truth, were assumed to be universal. The sailors naturally imagined the indiscriminate slaughter of all Constantinople's inhabitants. The Christian captains promptly dropped the massive iron chain into the mud of the Golden Horn and hoisted sail for Europe, disaster signals atop their masts and on their lips the news of a catastrophe that would rock the world.

Slowly and dispiritedly now, the Genoese walked single file across the pontoon bridge. Some Turkish watchmen who had been set over the cannon prudently hid under the planks while the soldiers and refugees passed over, like one long, unhappy string of slaves, Justiniani fainting and delirious at their head. The Galatan doctors who treated his wound had unwittingly sealed in the infected dirt that the arrow had picked up when it laid in the dust for an instant, and they wondered, when three days later Justiniani died, how so small an injury could kill a man, and attributed his death to witchcraft or some poison unknown to Christians.

Near the rear of the column, Bernardi fretted at the slow pace.

At the gate of Galata all the refugees were reluctantly taken into protective custody by the neutral, uneasy city officials.

No one questioned three of the refugees who chose to turn off and lose themselves among the dark alleys and deserted warehouses along the Galata waterfront.

On Bernardi's sleek little caravel, moored alongside the sugar-cane warehouse, Bernardi's captain had struggled all night with his conscience, his fears, and a mutinous crew.

"It is true that the roads are open," he argued with the men. "The Turkish ships are pulled up on the shore, and nothing blocks our escape but a flimsy string of empty wine barrels. But if you idiots could read the master's instructions, you would know that the instant we tie up in Venice without him we shall all be hanged as pirates. The doge himself will be waiting. Did Filippo Bernardi ever fail to foresee every possibility?"

But the men protested that they would rather be strangled by a Christian rope than by a Turkish bowstring. Bernardi's old major-domo and the captain persuaded them, however, to wait until dawn.

And at dawn Bernardi, Angelica, and Michael appeared in the door of the sugar-cane warehouse and came aboard.

The merchant, half dead with fatigue, instantly went to bed in his cabin, attended by his faithful major-domo.

"We'd nearly given you up for lost, Signore Filippo. The men might have seized the ship."

Bernardi muttered sleepily, "She's riding a trifle high in the water. Why didn't you order the captain to put on more ballast?"

The major-domo made a sweeping, hopeless Italian gesture. "But my lord, every day until the siege became serious I expected more of those heavy chests that you sent for so long. And after that the men became restless. . . ."

For an instant Bernardi appeared wide awake again and glared at the major-domo. "Do the men know what is in the chests?"

The old retainer placed his hand on his heart: "Before God, signore, only I know that it is gold, the treasure into which your lordship has converted your Byzantine properties. The men would have risked hanging and sailed away without you if they had known."

Bernardi closed his eyes again and said, "Thou'rt a trusty old dog, Enrico. You didn't even look. The gold and jewels went home two months ago by another ship before the siege. The ballast is only silver. . . ." Bernardi went to sleep.

He roused only long enough to finish his thought when the roar of the ship's cannon disturbed his slumber, blasting a gap through the sultan's wine barrels. "Tomorrow I'll show Michael our ballast. Penniless! He's richer than I am!" He heard the men cheer as they sailed through the sundered bridge.

The sweeps strained in their locks. A strong young breeze streaked purple swathes across the waters of the Golden Horn and thrummed in the tightening stay lines. The morning sun burned the harbor clean of coiling wisps of night mist and cast an iridescent glory on the taut sails. The fleeing ship sped down the estuary and slid her sleek prow into the current that streamed west out of the Black Sea. Westward she skimmed, doubling the promontory of the fallen city —westward under the broken battlements and riven turrets of the Seven Towers. The powerful current added its speed to the speed of the wind, toward Gallipoli, the Aegean, and the vast blue reaches of the peaceful Mediterranean.

The sea lay open all the way to Europe.

EPILOGUE

IN Venice one day in 1467, a Venetian lad, being twelve years old and curious, asked, "Father, was there ever a good Genoese?"

Venetians generally disapproved of the Genoese. Michael remembered that Justiniani had been Genoese. "I suppose there are some good ones, son. I've just never happened to know any."

Michael looked out of the casements across the canals to the arsenal where his ships and the ships of his father-in-law, long equipped only for peaceful Turkish trade, were now being fitted out for the new Turkish war.

"It's time for your Turkish lesson, Nicolo. Whether we trade with the Turks or fight them. Turkish is a good language to know. Tell me, son, what is the word for ship?"

"*Gemi.*"

"And for silken stuffs?"

"*Ipek kumashlar.*"

"For cannon and gunpowder?"

"*Toplar ve barut.*"

Michael glanced slyly over his shoulder, but Angelica had laid aside her needlework and was busy in another part of the villa.

"And an old, old word meaning Iron Bow?"

Filippo Bernardi, vastly corpulent, looked up over his spectacles, thicker every year, chuckled and went back to scowling at a commercial paper on the table in front of him where he saw listed the rising costs of gunpowder nowadays.

Young Nicolo promptly answered, "Timur-Yalik." Then, "Is it wrong to be friends with a wool dyer's son, Father?"

"Not necessarily, Nicolo. Not if he's a good boy. Who is he?"

"Well—he's Genoese, too. But I like to hear him talk. He says the world is round. Is the world round, Father?"

"The old Greeks used to believe so. Long before Christ was born they used to teach that the world is round as an apple. I'm sure I don't know. You'd better ask your grandfather."

Bernardi grunted. "It's flat enough so ships don't fall off the edge of it. That's all I care about. Don't bother me. These prices!"

Michael said, "What is your friend's name?"

"Christopher."

"And his family?"

"I don't know, Father."

When the boy had gone, Bernardi looked up again and grumbled: "Christopher somebody, a wool dyer's son, *and* a Genoese! Distinguished companions you permit to associate with my grandson!" He shook his head. "Michael, you have never got rid of some extraordinarily liberal notions that the Turks taught you when you were a boy. I must say, Michael, I cannot approve of this."

THE END